USA TODAY bestselling author **Barb Han** lives in north Texas with her very own hero-worthy husband, three beautiful children, a spunky golden retriever/standard poodle mix and too many books in her to-read pile. In her downtime, she plays video games and spends much of her time on or around a basketball court. She loves interacting with readers and is grateful for their support. You can reach her at barbhan.com

Nicole Helm grew up with her nose in a book and the dream of one day becoming a writer. Luckily, after a few failed career choices, she gets to follow that dream—writing down-to-earth contemporary romance and romantic suspense. From farmers to cowboys, Midwest to the West, Nicole writes stories about people finding themselves and finding love in the process. She lives in Missouri with her husband and two sons and dreams of someday owning a barn.

D1351170

Also by Barb Han

Undercover Couple
Texas Kidnapping
Texas Target
Texas Law
Texas Baby Conspiracy
Texas Stalker
Texas Abduction
Cornered at Christmas
Ransom at Christmas
Ambushed at Christmas

Also by Nicole Helm

Summer Stalker
Shot Through the Heart
Mountainside Murder
Cowboy in the Crosshairs
Dodging Bullets in Blue Valley
South Dakota Showdown
Covert Complication
Backcountry Escape
Isolated Threat
Badlands Beware

Discover more at millsandboon.co.uk

NEWLYWED ASSIGNMENT

BARB HAN

UNDERCOVER RESCUE

NICOLE HELM

MILLS & BOON

First Published in Great Britain 2022
by Mills & Boon, an imprint of HarperCollins*Publishers* Ltd
1 London Bridge Street, London, SE1 9GF

www.harpercollins.co.uk

HarperCollins*Publishers*
1st Floor, Watermarque Building,
Ringsend Road, Dublin 4, Ireland

Newlywed Assignment © 2022 Barb Han
Undercover Rescue © 2022 Nicole Helm

ISBN: 978-0-263-30342-1

0522

MIX
Paper from
responsible sources
FSC™ C007454

This book is produced from independently certified FSC™ paper to ensure responsible forest management.

For more information visit: www.harpercollins.co.uk/green

Printed and Bound in Spain using 100% Renewable electricity at CPI Black Print, Barcelona

NEWLYWED ASSIGNMENT

BARB HAN

All my love to Brandon, Jacob and Tori,
the three great loves of my life.

To Babe, my hero, for being my best friend,
my greatest love and my place to call home.

I love you all with everything that I am.

Chapter One

Why did every backyard barbecue with Emmaline Ree Sheppard's family turn into a not-so-subtle hint that she was failing her mother? At thirty-six years old, Ree wasn't married. She had no immediate plans to have a family. And she didn't bake anything from scratch.

Sue her.

Ree did, however, have a job as an undercover agent for the ATF that she loved, a great house that she'd bought with her own money, and a fulfilling dating life. To be honest, two out of three of those things were true, but not having a man in her life wasn't a problem for her, so it shouldn't bother anyone else, either.

"Do you want to go inside and clean yourself up before the food is ready?" her mother asked. The woman was five feet two inches of pure spit and vinegar.

"I showered this morning," Ree said more than a little defensively. What now? She didn't know how to shower properly?

"You could do something with your hair," her mother continued, undaunted.

"It's fine," Ree said as the others quieted. Everyone but Mother seemed to hear the caution in those words.

"While you're inside, you can put up whatever's in that bag," Mother said, wrinkling her nose.

"Do you mean cheesecake?" Ree asked, her pulse rising faster than the Texas heat.

"Evelyn baked, so we'll save yours for later," Mother said with a flick of her wrist, referring to Ree's sister-in-law.

The way Ree saw it, she had two choices. Let her tongue rip and probably say things she would regret or march inside with her store-bought cheesecake that her mother had already insulted and cool off in the air conditioning.

Her mother opened her mouth to speak, so Ree put a hand up to stop her. "I just can't do this right now, Mother."

Frustration seethed as she stormed toward the house and into the kitchen with her brother on her heels. Hot tears threatened, but she refused to let them fall.

"I'm sorry if I wasn't the kind of girl who wore frilly dresses and big bows in my hair," Ree said to her oldest brother, Shane, with a little more heat than she'd intended. She smacked her flat palm against the kitchen counter of her mother's ranch-style house.

"She doesn't mean it like that, Ree," Shane defended. She'd gone by the nickname Ree for as long as she could remember.

"Oh, really? How am I supposed to take a comment like that?" she countered. "And what's wrong with my hair anyway?"

"Nothing. You look fine. And for the record, you would look beautiful no matter what you did with your hair. All I'm saying is that you might be taking every comment she makes to heart." He put his hands in the air, palms out in the surrender position, when Ree shot him *the look*.

"She went straight from my hair to attacking my store-bought cheesecake," she continued, holding up the box. "We all know I don't cook."

"Bake," he corrected.

Wrong move, Shane.

"Are you kidding me right now?" she asked.

"I still don't think she meant it so harshly," he said with a look of compassion.

"Fine." She circled the small room. "Tell me how I should react."

"You could crack a joke, for one," he started.

"She would love that coming from me," she countered. "Because Mom has always had one amazing sense of humor when it comes to her only daughter."

"She laughs at my jokes," he stated, sounding more than a little defensive.

"Case in point," Ree said on a sharp sigh. Her brother had no idea what it was like *not* to be their mother's favorite. He couldn't help himself. She also acknowledged he was trying to calm her down out of love.

Shane cocked his head to one side and studied her like she was part of a final exam and he was about to fail the class. "Are you sure this is about her?"

"Yes," she quickly countered. Too quickly? "Who else riles me up like our dear old mother?"

"You shouldn't refer to her like that," he said, shaking his head.

She resisted the urge to tell him that she had a pretty good handle on what she should and shouldn't do because when she dialed down her frustration, she could acknowledge he was right. Ree was all defense right now when she should probably figure out a way to calm down. She'd been on edge since her most recent undercover case ended a few days ago. Her partner, Agent Quinton Casey, aka Quint, had left quite an impression on her. They'd shared a sizzling kiss that had replayed in her dreams more than once in the past few nights. Quint was most likely onto a new case by now. One that worried her because of its connection to the death of his best friend and former partner.

"She sure knows how to push my buttons," she defended, gripping the edge of the counter so hard her knuckles turned white.

"Don't take this the wrong way, but I'm pretty sure the feeling is mutual," he said.

"Not you, too," she said.

"What?"

"Hopping on the 'Mom bandwagon' and making me feel bad for having words with her," she continued. This discussion should have been over before it started. Ree was having a moment and wasn't ready to let her frustration go. Why was that? It wasn't like her to hang on to hurt. An annoying voice in the back of her mind pointed out she was always defensive when it came to her mother. Was it true?

The creak of the screen door opening in the adjacent room broke into the moment. Ree walked over to the fridge, then shifted a couple of cartons around to make room for her store-bought cheesecake. Forget that it had been her mother's favorite and most requested at birthdays. Shane's wife had baked sourdough bread, and French macarons with raspberry-rose buttercream. Evelyn loved to bake, and Ree planned to eat both. But it needed to be okay that Ree wasn't into the same things. Wasn't variety the spice of life anyway?

Shane disappeared into the living room as she flexed and released her fingers a couple of times in an attempt to work off some of the tension. This was the reason she'd stopped coming to Sunday suppers. She didn't enjoy the stress that came from interactions with her mother, and it just became easier to stay away than to face another letdown.

As Ree took in a slow breath, she heard her ex-boyfriend's voice in the next room. Preston was Shane's best friend, so it wasn't out of the norm for him to show up at a barbecue. So why was she suddenly not all that happy at the prospect of seeing him?

"Hey," Preston said as he walked into the kitchen. He was six feet one with a runner's build. He had light blue eyes and sandy-blond hair. He had a one-inch scar on his left cheek that she used to think was sexy, and would be considered good-looking by most standards. Women lit up when he entered a room. Shouldn't she do the same?

"Hi, Preston. It's good to see you," she said, and tried to mean it.

He walked over to her, and then leaned forward for a kiss. She turned at the last moment, offering a cheek instead. He planted one on her, but it was the most awkward thing. She mumbled an apology and took a step back.

"How have you been?" she asked, pretending that didn't just happen.

"Good," he said, taking her in with his gaze. "How's work?"

"Same. Good," she parroted, realizing this shouldn't be such an awkward exchange. The two of them might have dated at one time, but those feelings were long over. She'd considered reconnecting with him for a second while on her last assignment, but she was thinking clearly now. A voice in the back of her mind said she'd needed a diversion from the out-of-place attraction she'd felt for her partner. Quint was the opposite of Preston in just about every conceivable way, but a workplace romance could be a career killer.

"I'm just going to check on the kids," Shane said, not making eye contact as he made a beeline for the back door.

Great. He was leaving her alone with Preston. *Way to go, Shane. And thanks for the support.*

"Yeah, so, maybe we should join them?" she asked as her brother practically bolted out of the kitchen.

"Or we could stay in here and talk," Preston offered.

"Okay," she said for lack of anything better. Besides, facing down her mother while Ree was still riled up probably wasn't the best move.

Preston motioned toward the small table in the eat-in kitchen. "How about iced tea or lemonade?"

"Sure. Go ahead," she said. "I think I'll have a beer." Her thoughts immediately drifted to the way she'd left things with Quint. She'd asked him to call if he ever wanted to get together for a beer. As expected, her phone had been silent. There was no way he would pass up the opportunity to chase Tessa's killer.

"This early?" His eyebrow shot up.

"Day off," she said by way of explanation, but in truth she was just trying to get through this gathering. She moved to the fridge and then grabbed a cold one. Where was her grandfather? He would definitely join her in a beer despite the fact that it was the middle of the afternoon. She was such an inexperienced drinker she'd be taking a nap in an hour. Then there'd be a headache. But it would be almost worth it to see her mother's disapproval again. At least this time she'd have a reason to be disappointed in her daughter. "You know what? Never mind. I think I'll put on a pot of coffee instead. Want a cup?"

Preston shook his head. His expression said it was unthinkable to drink coffee in this Texas summer heat.

She would have a Coke if there was any. Her mother had a couple of rules. No guns. No soda. No fun. Okay, Ree added the last part on her own.

"So, how many days off do you have?" Preston asked.

"A couple," she said. "I just got off an intense assignment so…"

She stopped right there when his nose wrinkled and his face puckered like he'd just sucked on a pickled prune.

"What?" she asked, even though she should know better at this point. Work talk was off-limits with Preston.

The back door opened and her mother walked in, saving Ree from the conversation sure to come after Preston's expression morphed to frustrated. The same old song and dance that Ree was in a dangerous job and should look for something with a desk attached to it.

"Oh, Preston, I didn't realize you were coming today," her mother said.

Really? Because Ree was 100 percent certain her mother *did* know he was invited.

"I'm here," he said, walking over and giving her mother a peck on the cheek.

"Ree, would you mind bringing out some ice?" Mother asked.

"Not at all," she said, noticing her mother never once glanced in Ree's direction. She was being silly. She was a grown woman, a successful woman, and her mother's disapproval shouldn't hurt so much. "I'll be right out."

"Thanks," Mother said before motioning toward Preston. "And make our guest feel at home."

Wow. Was she not?

"Okay, Mom. I'll make sure Preston puts his feet on the furniture and walks around in his underwear," she quipped.

Mother's disapproval was written all over her face before she seemed to shake it off and put on a forced smile. At least Ree had given the woman a reason to be upset this time.

"I'll be outside," Mother announced, nose in the air. Maybe Ree shouldn't have poked the bear. Shane probably had a point. Ree was most likely making the situation worse with her attitude. She would apologize later and do her best to smooth things over. She would also stand her ground. Just because her father was killed in the line of duty almost twenty-five years ago didn't mean the same would happen to Ree. Agencies were even more cautious now, and agents were better trained. Mistakes happened like with any other job. Those mistakes sometimes resulted in a fatality. It was a terrible reality in this line of work. Ree had no intention of becoming one of those statistics.

The sound of gravel spewing underneath tires caused her heart to skip a few beats.

"I haven't seen my grandfather in so long. I gotta go." Ree wasted no time rushing to the front door.

The truck speeding toward her didn't belong to her grandfather, that was for sure. As she stepped onto the porch, she got a good look at the driver. What was Quint Casey doing here?

QUINT HAD NO idea if he was about to be asked to turn tail and head back from where he came or if he would be welcomed with open arms. Based on the fact that Ree had come out the front door and was heading toward him, he wasn't going to have to wait long to find out.

He parked behind a slew of vehicles. Clearly, there was some kind of family gathering going on. Sunday supper? Hadn't Ree mentioned something about this being a ritual?

Seeing her again caused his chest to squeeze and a knot to form in his gut. She looked good standing there, leaning against a convertible, all long legs, red hair and emerald eyes. Their last kiss came to mind, causing his pulse to jump up a few notches. Did the vehicle belong to her? Because for one quick moment, he could see her behind the wheel on a sunny day with her hair in the wind.

Arms crossed over her chest, toe tapping, a look of curiosity stamped her features.

He exited his truck and walked toward her as a guy took two steps out the front door, stopping on the porch.

"You're about the last person I thought I'd see here," Ree said with a smirk.

"Boyfriend?" He nodded toward the guy behind her, standing far enough away not to be able to hear their conversation.

"No. Friend." Her smile faded, her gaze narrowed and her chin jutted out in a way that made him realize she was defensive on this subject.

"Is there a place we can go to talk?" He'd come all this way. He might as well go for broke.

"Why are you here?" she asked, not budging.

"To see you," he said with a wink. Stating the obvious no matter how funny he tried to be with it didn't seem to impress her much. His attempt to lighten the mood fell flat. "In all seriousness, I'd like a word if you can spare fifteen minutes of your time."

"Everything okay, Ree?" her friend asked, but his voice wasn't filled with a whole lot of confidence.

Quint gave her a look.

"His name is Preston," she said, looking annoyed.

Quint would give it to the man. He was attempting the whole knight-in-shining-armor routine. The move signaled how much the guy cared about Ree. Most folks would walk the other way when confronted with a person of Quint's size and general demeanor. He knew he didn't exactly give off a friendly vibe when he didn't need to for a case.

"Ree?" Preston said a little louder this time.

"All good," she said, sounding more frustrated than anything else. "It's work-related."

"At Sunday supper?" Preston asked with disdain in his tone.

Quint folded his arms across his chest, figuring this conversation was about to become real interesting based on the sparks in her eyes.

"Mind if we talk about this later, Preston?" she countered. "I need to speak to Quint alone."

"This the guy from your last case?" Preston didn't seem to realize this wasn't the time to dig his heels in.

"You know I don't discuss the details of my work," she said without looking back. She kept her gaze focused on Quint, almost daring him to say something.

He figured this wasn't the time to take the bait. Her shoulders were locked up and there was more tension radiating from her than gunfire at a shooting range.

"But at the ranch?" Preston didn't seem to know when to stop.

Quint wiggled his eyebrows at Ree. The move was probably not smart. And yet he couldn't seem to stop himself.

Ree's face broke into a wide smile. She mouthed the word *jerk*. Then she turned around and walked over to Preston. Whatever she said to him worked, because he touched her on the shoulder before turning around and heading inside.

When she whirled around on Quint, all the humor was gone from her face. "What do you really want?"

"You," he started, but she cut him off with a look.

"What if I'm not an option?" she asked, stopping a foot in front of him. She mimicked his body language, folding her arms across her chest as she jutted her chin out again.

"We worked well together before," he stated.

"I'm honored you would want me back, but—"

"You haven't heard the details yet," he continued.

"Don't need to," she argued. "You're going after the jerk you think is responsible for Tessa's death. Aren't you?"

"All I'm doing is following the evidence from our last case. And like it or not, we make a good team. We already have an established cover story. It's less work to—"

"Oh, so you're saying you don't really want me. You just want someone easy." She drew out the last word.

"Not what I meant at all," he countered.

"Yes it is," she said, poking him in the chest with her index finger. "It's exactly what you said."

"Okay. How about this?" he started, figuring he needed a new tactic. "I miss working with you."

Ree rolled her eyes.

"You're going to have to try harder than that," she said. "Actually, never mind. You need to dial it down a few notches."

This was exactly the fire and sass he'd missed over the past couple of days. Not that he would admit it publicly.

"You're a good agent. I need someone who can step right in and work beside me without getting in the way," he stated as honestly as he could.

"I can't do it, and we both know why," she challenged.

"Do we?" he asked. She gave away nothing in her eyes as to whether or not he was making any headway with her.

"You could just pull rank and get me assigned," she said. "Why come here and ask in person?"

"Because you're the best damn agent I've worked with in a long time. I don't want anyone else by my side on this case. And you know how to hold your own," he said. "If none of that convinces you, I'll add that I think we make a good team."

Again, he was having a difficult time reading her as she stood there. At least she hadn't delivered a hard no.

"I can't read your mind." He finally broke the silence. "Any chance you'll consider it?"

"Not a good idea, Quint" was all she said before turning to walk away.

He couldn't leave without a reason, so he followed her.

Chapter Two

"Hold on."

Ree stopped, but she didn't turn around as Quint's masculine voice traveled over her and through her. They had barely closed the books on their last case, where they'd brought down a money laundering scheme being run out of a combination restaurant and bar. They'd learned the person Quint was truly after, a guy by the name Dumitru, was farther up the chain and much harder to reach. Going undercover with Quint while he was on a witch hunt wasn't her idea of smart.

Then again, she worried about him bringing in a brand-new partner after the two of them had developed good working chemistry. Their recent undercover sting had been akin to baptism by fire, but she'd learned a great deal from the ATF's most seasoned agent. They had chemistry to burn, but that definitely fell into the "cons" column.

At six feet three inches of stacked muscle, stormy sapphire-blue eyes and strong chin with just the right amount of stubble, Quint Casey would be considered sexy by most standards. His muscled torso formed an improbable vee at the waist, and he had the kind of body most athletic recruiters would have killed for. He had the whole "chiseled jawline, strong, hawklike nose and piercing eyes" bit down pat.

"I can admit that I'm not the easiest person to get along

with at times. Is there any way you would consider taking on another undercover case with me?" he asked with eyes that locked onto hers, causing more heat and electricity to fire through her. "We have to move fast on the information we have, and I can't think of a better partner."

"Are you sure about that?" She was starting to waver despite the warning bells sounding off in her head. Their chemistry had felt special and not easy to duplicate. "Because there are other agents who would give their right arm to work with you."

"I'm one hundred percent," he said with full conviction as he studied her. "Can I ask a question?"

"Go for it," she said, figuring she might as well hear what he had to say. The least she could do was listen after he'd made the long trip to her mother's ranch. Plus, she could admit part of her would rather be out here talking shop with Quint than doing the family supper bit. It was getting harder to feel like she fit in anymore, especially since her grandfather seemed to be a no-show.

"What's *really* holding you back?" he asked.

"Are you sure you want to know?" She didn't bother to hide her shock at his question.

"I can handle whatever it is," he said. "Trust me."

Famous last words, she thought. But if he really wanted to know...

"The personal stakes are high for you, and I'm concerned mistakes could end up being made because of it." There. She'd said it. Tessa had been killed by accident while Quint was trying to bust a weapons ring that went by the name A12. Dumitru was the leader and he'd been present at the bust. He was also the only one who got away that night. The others who'd been busted ended up dead in their jail cells.

"That's understandable," he said after a thoughtful

pause. A look passed behind his eyes, nothing more than a flash, really, that said she'd struck a nerve.

"There's a reason lawyers aren't allowed to try cases for family members," she continued.

"Conflict of interest," he stated.

"As much as I hate to say it, because I do realize you're the best person we have at the agency," she continued, doing what she could to soften the blow. "But even you can't deny how tempting it would be to follow a lead when we should stay back and analyze if you feel like you're close to the person responsible for Tessa's death."

Quint nodded, his expression unreadable.

After a few uncomfortable beats of silence, he turned around and walked toward the driver's side of his truck.

"Quint," she said, but he kept walking. She ran over to him and placed her hand on his shoulder. "Talk to me."

"What's the point?" He opened the door and claimed the driver's seat.

"I don't know. This is how people work things out." She wedged her body so he couldn't close the door without hurting her. The irony that she hadn't discussed her feelings with her mother, yet she was forcing him to talk, sat heavy on her chest. Why was it so easy to dish out advice and so difficult to take it?

"Your mind is made up," he said, reaching for the handle. "There's basically no point in continuing this conversation. Don't worry, I won't request you for this assignment."

"Wait. Wait. Wait," she said. "What do you mean you won't request me? I thought it was already a done deal."

"No. That's why I came here to talk to you in person," he stated. "And the fact that you think I would go behind your back only proves I didn't know you as well as I believed."

"I just thought—"

"What? That I'd make arrangements without consulting you first?" His look of frustration was a nail in her gut. "If you'll move out of the way, I'll get going. I've taken up enough of your time." He nodded toward the backyard. "Your family is waiting. You should get back to them."

Ree stood there, dumbfounded. Words tried to form, but her mouth wouldn't move. Since she couldn't speak, she decided to act. She stepped up and slipped into the back seat.

"What are you doing?" he asked, craning his neck around.

She shrugged and put her hands up, palms out, in the surrender position.

"I'm trying to leave," he said.

"Then you'll have to take me with you." She finally found her voice. The thought of Quint tackling this assignment with a new partner, one he barely knew, wasn't something Ree was willing to allow. Granted, he was a professional and at the top of his game. Did he make mistakes? Yes. Everyone did. She'd made several that he hadn't held against her.

"Does this mean you're trying to weasel your way back into my good graces?" Quint quipped.

"We'll see about that when you hear what I have to say next," she said.

"Sounds like I should be very afraid," he stated, his tone a little lighter now. The stress wrinkle on his forehead was near-permanent.

"I need a minute to think about what you're asking before I make a decision," she started. "So that means you get to spend the day with my family if you want me to consider taking the assignment."

"It would be easier for me to call upstairs and make

the request," he said as his gaze found hers via the rear-view mirror.

"Yeah. That's true." She nodded. "But you won't do that."

"And why is that?" he asked, arching a dark brow.

"Easy," she said. "You want me to show up willingly and in a good mood. Force me and we both know I'll have an attitude."

"I have seen your temper," he agreed with a smirk. One that caused her stomach to free-fall. Her attraction to him definitely fell into the *con* column. One very solid *pro* was his experience. The idea of working with him again was growing on her. A small part of her wished he'd called for that beer instead. But dating a coworker was probably a bad idea. "Fortunately for you, I don't scare easily."

"Sounds like I'm one lucky lady." She twisted up her face as she rolled her eyes.

"That's a fair statement," he quipped.

Ree sighed. They'd used their simmering attraction to sell the newlywed routine on their previous assignment. She'd been tempted to cross a line with him more than once in the cabin they'd shared on the last bust. At least she'd be going into this case with eyes wide open.

Hold on a sec. Was she seriously considering taking the assignment?

"What do you say?" she asked. "My family is probably holding out on serving food. We'll have a small but angry mob soon if I don't get over there."

Quint stared at her for a long moment.

"I don't normally do family get-togethers, but I'll make an exception this time," he said. "Just don't think this is going to become a habit."

"As long as you remember that I haven't agreed to anything yet," she said.

Quint stepped out of the truck and then held his hand out. "You will."

"What makes you so certain?" She took the offering, ignoring the now-familiar jolt of electricity that came with contact. Her heart hoped she could take being in close quarters again with Quint.

"I'm going to charm the hell out of your family," he said. "I'll have them eating out of my hand by the time I'm through. You'll take the case just to get them off your back."

Ree laughed out loud as she dropped his hand.

"Yeah?" she asked with a raised eyebrow. "Good luck with that one."

The man had no idea what he was getting into.

QUINT HAD THIS. No problem. He could handle families despite the fact that he'd grown up the child of a single mother. How hard could it be? It wasn't like he was socially inept. He'd been to quite a few parties over the years. He'd done his fair share of socializing at department functions despite preferring a quiet night at home on his days off over spending time with a dozen people he barely knew. So why was a thin sheen of sweat forming above his eyebrows?

He'd spent the better part of the past ten years pretending to be someone else for a living. Surely he could put on the same mask and get through a couple of hours with these good people.

"Ready for this?" Ree asked before pinching the bridge of her nose and exhaling a long, slow sigh.

That was probably not a good sign.

"I've dealt with worse things than a family barbecue," he snapped. The words came out a little more heated than he'd intended. Why were his nerves getting to him?

Ree was important. He respected her work. It was natural for him to want her family to like him. Or so he tried to convince himself.

"Let the fireworks begin," she said so low he almost didn't hear her.

Ree led the way around the side of the house. A couple of kids were running around, blowing bubbles and hopping in and out of a small plastic pool filled with water from a garden hose that snaked over the edge.

The sun glared and for a half second, Quint almost doubled back to get his sunglasses. He decided against it at the last minute, figuring her family would want to look him in the eye.

There were a couple of wooden picnic tables underneath a towering oak tree. A miniature plastic table sat in between. Laughter filled the air as a slightly older woman with the same fiery red hair as Ree carried a basket to one of the tables. This whole scene was something out of a Norman Rockwell painting, and definitely out of his comfort zone. This seemed like a good time to remind himself he was doing this for Ree.

Instinct or habit had him reaching for her hand. He stopped himself midreach. They weren't playing the married couple right now, and based on the stare-down he was receiving, Preston fit into this family far better than Quint ever would.

"Hey, everyone, I'd like you to meet one of my coworkers." Ree clapped her hands together just in case no one got the message based on her booming voice—a voice that echoed across the several-acre lawn. Ree held her hand up like she was presenting an auction item. "Everyone, this is Agent Quinton Casey. Quint, this is everyone."

He suddenly felt like a bug underneath a magnifying glass on a hot summer sidewalk.

"Hey," he said, then gave an awkward wave that he was

pretty sure made him look more like Howdy Doody than a top ATF agent.

Ree's mother gave a curt nod before turning to the other table with her basket. Preston's stare-down continued. Little did the guy know that with Quint's martial arts training he wasn't the guy Preston wanted to pick a fight with. Then again, Quint wasn't here to stir up trouble.

One guy stood up and walked over to the perimeter of the manicured lawn where Quint stood.

"I'm Shane, Ree's brother." He stuck a hand out in between them. "We've talked over the phone a couple of times."

"Nice to meet you in person." Quint took the offering and received a vigorous handshake.

"I'll just leave you two to get to know each other," Ree said with a half smirk before taking off toward a cooler. She grabbed two cold ones, popped open the tops and brought one back to Quint before making a beeline for the kids' table.

Ree with kids? He didn't think she was the type to hang around with the little rug rats on purpose.

"Do you want to come over and have a seat?" Shane asked. "I'd like to introduce you to my best friend, Preston."

"We've met," Quint said quickly. A little too quickly?

"Oh," Shane said, looking at a loss for words.

"But, hey, it can't hurt to get to know each other better." Quint figured his attraction to Ree would cool down quite a few notches if he got to know the guy who had to be an ex-boyfriend.

"Great." Shane led the way over to the picnic table where Preston sat. He pointed to one of the men sitting beside Preston. "That's my brother Finn."

Finn glanced up and smiled. "Nice to meet you." He

almost immediately went back to his conversation or hostile negotiation with a little tyke with the same shock of red hair.

"That would be my son Liam who is doing all the talking." Shane practically beamed with pride.

"Cute kid," Quint said. As far as kids went, this one would pass muster. He had a round, angelic face that was dotted with freckles.

"Thanks," Shane said. "Over at the other table are Patrick and Connor."

The two perked up when they heard their names. Both glanced over and waved before returning to animated conversation. The family resemblance among the Sheppards was unmistakable.

Shane took a seat beside Preston, so Quint took a spot opposite them both.

"How long have you known Ree?" Preston asked, gripping his plastic fork so hard it might crack.

"Not long," Quint admitted. "But I do feel like we got to know each other fast."

"Really?" Preston's eyebrow went up. "That's odd."

Shane made a face at his friend before saying, "Ree can be a closed book to most people."

"Nature of the job," Quint defended. "When your life depends on selling the fact that you are newlyweds, barriers break down real fast."

Mrs. Sheppard gasped at hearing the last part. She clutched her chest with her free hand and took a step back.

"It's no big deal, Mom." Ree shot a look of apology at Quint.

He'd clearly overstepped his bounds. Duly noted.

"If you really knew Ree, you wouldn't talk about the dangers of work around her family," Preston said, low and under his breath.

Quint took in a slow, deep breath. Turned out he wasn't as good at this family thing as he'd expected.

Ree walked over to him, giving her brothers a death stare. She plopped down beside him, turning her back to the table.

"Do you want to get out of here?" she asked, and he could see her clench her back teeth.

"Is that a good idea?" He didn't want to make matters worse.

"It is as far as I'm concerned," she countered.

"You asked me to stay. It's up to you when I leave," he stated, and meant every word. Based on the chilly reception from her mother, a picture was emerging. Ree had touched on her family dynamic a little bit while they were on their last assignment, but seeing it firsthand put the reality of the situation smack in his face. He would unpack it all later. For now, he just wanted to do whatever it took to make Ree happy so she'd agree to the assignment.

"Let's get out of here," she said, pushing up to standing.

"Hey, Ree. Where are you going?" Shane asked.

"Somewhere people know how to treat a guest," she said.

With that, she marched around the side of the house. Quint followed, figuring his popularity with her family took another hit.

"I'll follow you in my car," she said.

"Where to?" he asked.

"Anywhere but here." Her voice shook with anger.

Footsteps sounded behind them. Quint turned to see Preston jogging up.

"Ree, don't leave like this," Preston said, stopping at the corner of the house.

"I have to prep for a case," she said by way of defense.

She stopped next to her convertible with her hand on the door handle but didn't turn around.

Quint headed to his truck, figuring it wasn't his place to listen.

"Really? Are you choosing work again? Because you're going to turn around in a few years and realize you're all alone." Preston's voice held far too much disdain for his own good. The man seemed to have no idea the land mine he'd just stepped on. A person like Ree needed support, not more criticism. She was clearly taking enough from her mother. The last thing she needed was to hear it from someone she was in a relationship with. But Ree didn't need Quint to step up and defend her. She'd do a fine job on her own.

In fact, as he hopped into the driver's seat, he could practically hear all of Ree's muscles tensing at once. He had no idea what her response ended up being. All he could hear was her tires searching for purchase on the dirt road before her vehicle whipped right past his.

Chapter Three

Ree pulled over to the side of the road and waved at Quint to pull beside her. She rarely lost her temper, but her last button had been pushed, and she refused to have the same argument with Preston that had ended every attempt to have a relationship. This was history repeating itself. She should have known better. Losing her temper was right up there with epic bad ideas, but she'd done it anyway. Then there was her mother to consider. Ree would have to circle back and make peace. She also made a mental note to skip Sundays at the ranch when this next case was behind her.

"My house is about a mile from here. Want to go there and have a cup of coffee?" she asked, figuring they could go over the details of the assignment there. Plus, she could pack.

"Lead the way" was all he said.

Her heart thundered at the thought of Quint in her personal space. She shook it off, focusing instead on the work ahead. Another assignment, this time even more dangerous. Not that she minded. All it made her realize was that she wanted to be that much more prepared. The recent Greenlight Restaurant and Bar sting had blown wide open faster than expected. This case might follow in its footsteps.

She wanted to be as prepared as possible. Although,

to be fair, these operations took on a life of their own in the heat of the moment. All the preparation in the world couldn't stop unknowns from coming into play.

Ree parked on the pad beside her two-bedroom bungalow. She waved for Quint to park behind her car. There was no reason for him not to hem her in, considering the next time she left would likely be with him.

Rather than wait around for him, she walked to her front door and unlocked it. Leaving it open behind her, she set down her purse and keys on the console table lining the hallway. Coffee would help clear her mind after the encounter with her family. Preston had been a jerk to Quint, but that wasn't the main reason she felt so put out. Being on bad terms with her mother always put her on edge, and it seemed like there was nothing she could do to stop the woman from worrying.

A quick knock sounded from the next room before she heard Quint's boots shuffle across the tile floor.

"I'm in the kitchen" was all she said.

Having him in her home sent a thrill of awareness skittering across her skin. Awareness of his masculine presence. Awareness of his strength. Awareness of his spicy male scent as he stepped into her small kitchen. A file folder was tucked underneath his left arm. She figured it contained the details of their next assignment.

She made quick work of fixing two cups of coffee, handing one over as steam billowed.

"Thank you," he said before taking a sip. "Can't say it's better than the beer you handed me a while ago, but it certainly keeps the mind sharper."

She smiled at his offhanded remark as he winked.

"Let's have a seat at the table." She motioned toward the adjacent room that had a round table with two chairs, realizing her furniture was meant for regular-sized people and not those with the kind of height and rippled muscles on Quint.

He made it work, figuring out a way to fit and look comfortable in the process. But that was just Quint. He could make just about anything work and look good doing it.

After setting his coffee mug down, he placed the folder on top of the table. Using his index fingers, he pushed it to her side. This folder was something that could be bought at a corner drugstore.

"This doesn't look like a work file." She took a sip of fresh brew, enjoying the burn on her throat.

"Nope. It's personal."

"Information you've put together on your own?" she asked, not liking where this conversation was headed.

"Yes and no. I have gathered some of the intel from work." He shot a look because he must realize she could turn him in.

"What exactly are you getting me into, Quint?" she asked, wondering how many lines he'd be willing to cross if it meant catching the man responsible for Tessa's death. "What if we don't catch Dumitru this time?"

Quint stared at the rim of his coffee mug for a long moment. When he looked up, he said, "I'm going the distance on this one, Ree. You can decide what you want to do at any time. You're not locked in. If it gets uncomfortable, you can walk. No harm, no foul."

"Those sure are pretty words," she said right back. "We both know I won't walk away from an assignment and leave you vulnerable. If you're supposed to walk in there with a wife, I'm not going to ditch you when it gets rough."

"Fair enough." He gave a slight nod.

There was no way he would leave her stranded in the middle of a case, and he had to know the reverse was true.

"Let's see what's inside this file." She opened it. There

was a rudimentary tree drawing with branches. Some had labels. Others didn't. At the top was Dumitru's name. At the bottom were the names she recognized from Greenlight. "So we don't know how many layers there are between Greenlight and Dumitru."

"No, we don't. All I can say for certain is this 'transportation' operation out of Houston is somehow linked to him." He used his fingers to make air quotes around the word *transportation*.

"Someone who owns a trucking company would have an easier time hauling weapons," she stated. "There's a whole lot of scrutiny on a business like that, though."

"You're not wrong," he said. "Which is why I don't believe they're as involved as it looks."

"A decoy?" she asked.

"Yes. They're owned by a shell corporation out of the Bahamas." He pointed to the name, Trux.

"I'm guessing Trux owns other businesses," she said.

"I'd like to find out if they do. We both know the challenge of tying shell corps to actual businesses," he said.

"Which is why the trucking operation is most likely real," she reasoned.

"It could lead us to greener pastures, and that's why I want to follow through with this investigation." He picked up his mug and took a sip.

"Okay, just please tell me I don't have to serve food to anyone else. I'd like to shelve my serving tray, if you know what I mean," she said on a sigh. Being a waitress at Greenlight had pushed her to the limits of good acting. Not to mention those double shifts that left her feet aching.

When he didn't speak, she mouthed the word *no* as she looked up at him.

"There's no food involved," he said with the kind of smile that probably broke a lot of hearts.

"Seriously?" she asked. "Again?"

"It's not my fault restaurants and bars are known hangouts of the kind of people we bust. If they hung out in churches, they probably wouldn't end up on our list in the first place," he defended.

"When are you going to be the one to parade around in clothes that leave far too little to the imagination?" she asked, and they both laughed.

"I could, but I doubt anyone would pay to see it." He smiled as he turned the page from the tree. "Check out the rap sheets on some of these guys."

Six pages were then turned over one by one, each with a different face and fact sheet to go along with it.

"Since those are from your files, I'm guessing they tie back to Tessa's case," she reasoned.

"You would be correct," he said. "I'm always going to be on the lookout for these men. One of whom is supposedly associated with the gunrunners."

"Houston, huh?" She shot him a look.

"We have a problem," he said.

"Okay, you already know I'm on board. There's one rule. No corny NASA jokes," she said.

"Does that mean we don't have a problem?" He laughed at his own witticism. Before she could protest, he added, "I'm just kidding. No more space humor. Scout's honor." He did a thing with his hand that was most certainly not the right gesture.

"Somehow I doubt you've ever been a Boy Scout," she muttered under her breath.

QUINT HADN'T KNOWN what the outcome would be when he'd shown up at Ree's mother's ranch. One of the last things he expected was to be at her house, discussing the case. He'd shown up on a whim, one that was paying off.

"Thank you," he said in all sincerity.

"Don't thank me now," she stated with more than a hint of mischief in her eyes. "Save it for when we put these jerks behind bars."

"What about Preston?" He would be a jerk if he didn't help her see what she might be giving up for this life. "He seems like a nice guy, Ree."

Shock stamped her features.

"I caught you off guard. Sorry about that," he said.

"No. Don't be." She blinked a couple of times, like that might somehow help her switch topics.

"I wasn't trying to ambush you, Ree. I promise," he stated.

"Do you seriously want to talk to me about my relationship with Preston?" Her cheeks flamed, making her even more beautiful. And, no, he didn't want to discuss her exboyfriend, but she needed to.

"I've been around the block a few times while working this job," he began. "If you look at our fellow agents, the divorce rate gets pretty high."

"Meaning?" She studied him.

"This job isn't easy on spouses, let alone new relationships," he continued, treading lightly. "I do realize it isn't my place to tell you one way or the other how to handle your personal life."

"You're right about one thing," she stated. "Okay, maybe two. The divorce rate is high. This job isn't easy on new relationships. But Preston and I aren't exactly new to each other, and I'm not seeing him. He's my brother's best friend, and I'm pretty certain my mom is responsible for him showing up at Sunday barbecue. I can say with one hundred percent honesty that I had nothing to do with it. So why the lecture?"

"It's not. Take away what you will from this conversation. All I'm trying to tell you is that a good person is worth slowing down for. Because if you spend all your time invested in work, that's all you'll have at the end of the day." There. He'd said his piece. He would leave it at that.

"You sound like my mother," she said. The blow struck hard in the center of his chest.

"I believe in your work and think you're a damn fine agent," he said by way of defense.

"Good. Because marriage and family aren't everything they're cracked up to be, you know," she said. "Some people don't even want children."

"Seriously?" He couldn't hide the shock in his voice.

"Not you, too." She rolled her eyes and smacked her flat palm against the table.

"I already told you that I'm not some macho jerk who believes women should be chained to the kitchen," he said. "I just thought that since you came from a big family you might like to have the same thing for yourself one of these days."

"You were just at my mother's house, right?" Her voice sounded incredulous.

"Yes," he said.

"And you were witness to how frustrating a big family is," she stated. And then she seemed to catch herself, remembering that he'd had just the opposite growing up. "Right. Sorry. I know our upbringings were very different."

"When I first walked up, the place looked like a Norman Rockwell painting," he stated.

"You do realize that's the fantasy. The 'real' involves fighting and people constantly sticking their noses in your business," she stated.

"Having people who care whether or not you live or die doesn't seem like such a hardship," he admitted. In truth, he didn't dwell on the past. There were few people he'd ever talked to about the school liaison officer Quint credited with saving his life. He'd told Ree the whole story, figuring they needed to know each other's backgrounds in order to sell the newlywed concept. And yet he'd been on similar assignments before without divulging so many details from his past. The only person who knew about his background was his best friend, Tessa Kind. And she was dead.

The tension in Ree's facial muscles softened.

"I'm sorry" was all she said. Those two words washed over him. Not because she said them but because of the compassion in her eyes and in her voice while she spoke.

"I know," he said, and meant it. There was something special about Ree that he didn't want to spend a whole lot of time analyzing. The few kisses they'd shared still haunted him as the best he'd ever experienced. Going there while on an assignment seemed like the quickest way to let everything get out of hand.

Besides, he'd gotten what he came for. She'd agreed to take the case. They would head out to Houston to continue the marriage cover story as he moved on a man named Constantin, who was another step closer to Dumitru. Quint's growing feelings for her would only help him stay sharp. And moving forward, he would need to be as much on his game as he ever had been.

"I better pack so we can get on the road," Ree said.

"Sounds like a plan," he stated. "I'll give Agent Grappell a call to get us set up for the night." Grappell was the desk agent assigned to the case. He worked with them on the Cricket Creek case as well, and would be an asset to the team in Houston.

Maybe with Ree on board he could finally find justice for Tessa.

Chapter Four

"We'll work the same cover as before," Quint said to Ree as she sat in the passenger seat with the opened file on her lap. "As a newly married couple who are very much in love."

"I'm guessing the boot comes back on, then," she said, studying the tree drawing.

"It's a good way to counter my size, but we can ditch it," he said. They needed to make him seem like less of a threat to lower a target's defenses. The trick had worked like magic in Cricket Creek, but it came with its downsides. For instance, him forgetting to put it on.

"So you'll have walked away from your moving business due to this injury that came from moving a piano," she said, reviewing the facts.

"That's right," he confirmed. "Just no boot this time. I'm healing."

"And we had our first date at the pizza place on Third Street in Austin," she continued.

"There's no better place for craft pizza," he said with a smile.

"And Ronnie always comes out to check on the table when you order the day's special," she said.

Quint nodded.

"You'll be restocking, washing glasses and keeping the bartender happy as a barback in a popular country-and-western bar this time, so no heavy trays of food to carry," he said.

"No heavy food trays to carry." She didn't mind that part so much.

"This place is supposedly frequented by guys who are associated with Dumitru. One of the girlfriends of someone high up in the operation is a bartender there. Her name is Lola, and her boyfriend's name is Constantin," Quint said. "Your job is to try to get as close to her as possible."

"Got it," she said.

"Word of warning, Constantin goes by the name Lights Out because he likes to kill people while they're sleeping." Quint's tone was all business now.

This definitely made her realize they'd moved up the crime scale a few notches. This case had the potential to be even riskier, the criminals more violent and dangerous. Then there was Quint's lack of objectivity to consider. She had to trust he would step back when necessary. And yet knowing him and how determined he was to get to Dumitru, that might be asking the impossible.

"Before we get into this, I need to know you'll listen to me if I say it's time to pull back," Ree said. He shot her a look that said he didn't appreciate the comment. She put her hands in the air in the surrender position. "I've gotten to know you pretty well recently, and I've noticed that once you get on a trail, you don't let up. The trait is great for a case when it's applied at the right time and for the right reasons."

"But?"

"I think we both know what comes next without me spelling it out," she said.

Anger radiated off him in palpable waves. To his credit, he gripped the steering wheel tighter and clamped his mouth shut. They both knew she was right. The fact that he didn't argue made her believe he might just listen to her in a sticky situation.

"Noted," he finally said. "And I give you my word."

His promise was good enough for her. Time would tell if he could stay true to his word. In the meantime, she wouldn't overthink it.

"I'm guessing since this is Houston that I'll be working a honky-tonk," she said.

"And you'd be wrong," he said with a smirk.

"What? No cowgirl boots this time?" She feigned disappointment.

"You get to wear tuxedo shorts, suspenders and a red bow tie," he said.

"Please tell me this is not a strip club," she begged.

"It's a trendy place," he said. "The barbacks have a different outfit than bartenders and waitresses. You'll have the most skin covered. But you'll have to wear black fishnet stockings every night so I'm not sure how you feel about that."

"Great," she said. "I'd rather have on those and be fully covered, thank you very much."

"You won't get an argument from me there," he said, surprising her with his honesty and protectiveness over her. It wasn't the same as she was used to from Preston and her mother. Theirs made her feel like she was incompetent at her job. Quint's concern for her came from a place of not wanting her to be forced into doing something she wasn't comfortable with, which wasn't the same thing. He believed in her and came across as proud of her for being capable in her profession. His protectiveness wasn't suffocating.

"Do you have a picture of Lola by chance?" Ree asked.

"It's grainy," he said, pulling into a downtown apartment building garage. "You'll be working at a bar in the

GreenStreet area. This place is within walking distance. It's a studio, so tight quarters, but we don't have a whole lot of belongings, and it's fully furnished."

"Corporate apartments?" she asked, figuring the ones rented by companies for business travelers were normally the ones that came set up and ready to go.

"That's right," he said. "All we need to do is unpack our clothes. I'll set up my laptop at the bar-height counter separating the kitchen from the living space."

Ree nodded. They'd spent a week in a one-room cabin on their last case and did fine. This shouldn't present a problem.

"We're on the seventh floor this time," he said. "Agent Grappell said Lola lives in the same building on nine."

"Maybe we'll run into each other in the elevator," Ree said.

Ree glanced at the number on the wall where he'd parked. Their spot was number thirteen. She hoped it wasn't an ominous sign.

"What's our apartment number?" she asked.

"Seven-three it is," he said with a smile.

At least the two of them were off to a better start than on the last case, where she'd tried to lay down the law on day one and he'd planted a kiss that still made her lips sizzle every time she thought about it.

She grabbed her bag as he disappeared into a door marked Elevators. He returned with a cart that looked like something a bellman would bring. Folks must move in and out of the building frequently if these were at the ready. It made sense when she thought about the fact that several of these apartments were used as corporate housing. Businesspeople would show up with nothing more than a couple of suitcases and whatever technology allowed them to do their jobs.

Ree waited until the cart was loaded and they were safely in apartment 73 before asking the question that had been on her mind since they'd parked. "Does Lola live here with her boyfriend?"

"From what Agent Grappell could uncover, Lights Out visits her and spends a lot of time here, but he has a house in Galveston on the bay side. His brother lives with him, and Grappell didn't have a whole lot of intel on the brother," Quint stated.

"That sounds suspect," Ree said. The only people who avoided being in the system were criminals. Big-time drug dealers were known to "borrow" vehicles or hire drivers rather than own one so the registration couldn't be traced back to them. She always knew someone was a lifetime criminal when she went back to find their picture in a high school yearbook only to discover there was none. People who intended to live a life of crime from an early age went to extremes to ensure there was no trail that could easily identify them.

"My thoughts exactly," he agreed as he stood in the middle of the room. "Home sweet home."

"Home" was an open space with a kitchen that could best be described as a kitchenette. One person could fit inside there, and it would be a stretch for someone Quint's size. The entryway was barely big enough for him to turn around in without bumping into a wall, but the room opened up nicely and the back wall was basically all glass, allowing for a ton of light. Their last place, the cabin in tiny Cricket Creek, Texas, had been much darker.

"It's very modern and clean. I'll give it that," Ree said as she stepped into the middle of the living area. Around the corner from the kitchen was a raised platform and niche that held the bed. A wall of closets was to one side. "Is there laundry?"

"In the building, just not in the apartment," he said.

The furniture was sleek and modern with clean lines. It was basically what she expected from a downtown Houston apartment.

"This place looks like something out of a magazine," she said, walking over to the closet with her suitcase. "I can't say the furniture looks especially comfortable. It's not exactly what you'd be able to sink into to watch a movie, but it does look chic."

"My thoughts exactly," Quint said. "It's like living in a museum where you'd be afraid to mess anything up."

"Everything has its place," she agreed. "The bed is decent-sized, though. And it looks comfortable for a good night of sleep."

"I can take the couch," he said.

"Not again," she countered. "This bed is big enough for both of us. You can stay to your side. We can put a row of pillows in between us. But I won't let you sacrifice sleep again." She shot him a look. "No arguing."

"I WOULDN'T WANT to fight with my wife," Quint fired back with a smirk. "You know the old saying, *happy wife, happy life.*"

Ree rolled her eyes.

"You know I can see you, right?" he said.

"That's the whole point," she said before unpacking her suitcase and offering to do the same for him.

"I got it," he said, moving next to her and taking over a third of the closet. He had a pretty basic wardrobe of jeans and black T-shirts.

"I don't know if you're trying to sell the whole 'tech worker' bit, but your wardrobe fits the lifestyle," Ree said when she examined his clothes. Quint had posed as a tech student on their last assignment as well. It was meant to be a second career after selling the moving business he'd started with a partner.

Quint laughed. "No one has ever complained about my clothing style before."

Tech workers were notorious for having a closet full of basically the same clothes—jeans and T-shirts. The idea being that the brain could only handle a certain number of decisions each day before paralysis set in. The Silicon Valley set didn't want to waste one of those on clothes. It was smart when Quint really thought about it and made him feel a whole lot less lazy about his wardrobe.

"I didn't say it looked bad on you," she said as her cheeks turned a couple shades of pink. Ree turned away from him and picked pretend lint from a dress hanging in the closet.

Rather than reply, he said, "We should probably get a feel for the building and grab supplies."

"When do I interview for the barback job?" she asked.

"Done deal. The agency has an in with the club owner. You start tomorrow, and your uniform will be ready when you check in for work. Randy Halo owns several bars. He married a supermodel a few years back. She got into some trouble. The agency got her out in exchange for information. To make a long story short, she still owes the agency, and her husband doesn't want a criminal element in his club. He runs legitimate businesses and wants to keep his licenses," Quint explained.

"Good for him," she said. "Plus, a bar owner keeping a liquor license seems pretty important to keep the doors open."

"Lucky for us, he saw it in the same way," Quint said.

"Or lucky for him. Otherwise, it doesn't sound like he'd have much of a business right now," she quipped.

"Very true," Quint agreed. "Sadly, you're going to have to stay on your feet for entire shifts again."

"Nothing a bucket of ice won't cure," she said. "Before we get too deep in the case, mind if I check on my grandfather? He was most likely running late earlier, but I'd feel better if I heard it from him. You know?"

"Knock yourself out," he said. "I'll be in the kitchen to give you some privacy."

They both laughed at his comment when they glanced around the room. The kitchen wouldn't provide much solitude, but the gesture counted for something.

Quint moved into the other room and checked the fridge. He could open the fridge and freezer without hitting anything, and he could turn around in the space. That was the extent of his ability to move. Ree was quiet in the next room, and he took it as a bad sign.

A minute later, she showed up at the counter between the kitchen and living space. She claimed a barstool and blew out a breath, setting her cell phone down in front of her.

"No answer." She motioned toward the time showing on her phone. "And it's barely eight o'clock."

"Did you leave a message?" Quint asked. He didn't hear her, but that wasn't proof. She could have spoken quietly into the phone.

She shook her head.

"I texted him instead," she said. "Our cell phones aren't compatible, so his doesn't always register when I call and vice versa."

"The last person I dated had a problem with our incompatible phones," he said. "I'm pretty certain it's the reason we broke up. She would call and I wouldn't get the notification. When I didn't return her call in a reasonable amount of time, she thought I was out playing the field."

"You wouldn't do that to someone you cared about," Ree said without hesitation.

"Tell that to Amber," he said.

"Amber's the one missing out, then," Ree said without stopping to think much about her words. How did she understand him better than someone he'd spent six months getting to know? Not that he was complaining. All good partnerships started with a fundamental knowledge of each other's personalities and ticks.

"I couldn't agree with you more," he said. "But she seems happier with Todd."

"What kind of name is Todd?" she said with a smirk.

"I know…right?" He kept the joke alive. They both knew there wasn't anything wrong with the name. It was common.

"Were you in love?" Ree asked without looking up from her screen.

"With Todd?" he balked.

Ree shot him a look that would make any high schooler sit up and take note.

"I cared about her," he said.

"Not the same thing, and we both know it," she countered.

"It's as close as I can get," he said in all honesty. Too bad his answer seemed to cause her to deflate.

A knock at the door caused them both to jump, and the tense moment happening between them passed.

Chapter Five

"Who is it?" Ree asked, checking through the peephole at her new apartment. Quint drew his weapon, flipped off the kitchen light and stood at the ready a few feet away from the door. Quint produced their wedding rings from his front pocket before handing one over.

"Angie," said a female voice. She sounded college age and not much more.

Ree opened the door.

"You just moved in, right?" Angie asked. She was five feet three inches of tiny frame and thick horse-mane blond hair.

Ree folded her arms, leaned against the doorjamb and smiled. "That's right. My husband and I are still unpacking."

It was a tiny lie.

Angie had a dotting of freckles across her nose and an enthusiastic disposition, like cheerleader perky. She was a cutie but couldn't be much more than twenty-two.

"I live next door with my boyfriend," Angie said. "We've been here for a few months but haven't really made any friends in the building yet. I've been studying for my LSAT while Brad works. My parents think my roommate is one of my best friends from college. They'd kill me if they knew I was living with Brad."

"Where does Brad work?" Ree asked, figuring it never hurt to get the lay of the land since there was a total of four apartments on this floor. Angie must have been watching them through her peephole. They'd been careful not to say anything that could blow their cover in the garage or on the way inside the apartment.

"He's a fireman." Angie's eyes lit up at every mention of her boyfriend.

"Cool job," Ree said for lack of anything better. She'd been told she could get away with saying she was still in her late twenties, so she let her shoulders round a bit and put on a bigger smile.

"Right?" Angie said. She looked Ree up and down. "Do you work out?"

"When I can," Ree admitted.

"The building has a great gym on the second floor. They bring in CrossFit classes and Zumba," Angie said. "You do Zumba, right?"

"Yes. CrossFit is a little too intense for me," Ree said, twirling a lock of hair with her index finger as she tilted her head to one side.

"Same here, but Brad is obsessed." Angie's eyes lit up again. She seemed like a sweetheart. "But he also likes weights. He says CrossFit is bad for building muscles."

"I'm more of a runner," Ree said. "If I take a class, it would probably be Pilates."

"I love Pilates." Angie clasped her hands together and bounced.

"Maybe we'll take class together sometimes," Ree said before adding, "I should get back to unpacking. I start my job tomorrow, and we have so much to do. The fridge is empty, and we haven't had dinner yet."

"Okay. It was really nice meeting you," Angie said before leaning back on the heels of her tennis shoes. She waved as she took a step back.

"Same to you. And I'm serious about Pilates," Ree said as she slowly closed the door, watching which apartment Angie headed toward. Apartment 2. Ree made a mental note that Angie and Brad lived in 72 as she closed and then locked the door.

"Looks like you made a friend," Quint said, flipping on the light before returning his weapon to his ankle holster.

"Since Lola lives in the building and she's twenty-five, I might run into her at the gym. She might take classes, and now I'll have a buddy to introduce me around. I get the impression Angie is social. She's the type who would chat up a stranger at the gym," Ree said.

Quint nodded. "I got the same impression."

"Are you hungry?" she asked.

"Starving," he confirmed.

"Me, too. Shall we go grab dinner out?"

Quint nodded, then gave Ree a once-over. "We should grab a drink while we're out."

Ree knew exactly what he had in mind.

"It wouldn't hurt to figure out what my new place of employment looks like," she said with a smile. Then she glanced down at what she had on. "Just give me a few minutes to change clothes and freshen up, and I'll be ready."

"You look perfect in my book," Quint said so low she almost didn't hear him. He crossed the room to the cabinet wall and grabbed a fresh pair of jeans and one of the few collared shirts he'd brought. It was black as pitch, and her heart skipped a few beats thinking how damn good he was going to look in it.

Fifteen minutes later, they looked like a very different couple as they exited the apartment and then the building. Despite the downtown area having plenty of lights, there were shadows cast everywhere. So many places to hide in plain sight, Ree thought as the prickly feeling of being watched crept over her.

She reached for Quint's hand and then leaned into him as she surveyed the area, pretending to take in the restaurants and bars.

"How about tacos?" Quint asked, squeezing her hand. The move shouldn't be as reassuring as it was. He realized what she was doing, and this was his way of acknowledging it. He lifted their clasped hands and pressed a tender kiss to the back of hers. The move sent a sensual shiver skittering up her arm.

The watched feeling returned.

"That's not a fair question. Always tacos," she teased, trying to force lightness she didn't feel.

Quint guided them across the street to a corner restaurant. The place was small and crowded. They got in line just inside the door to place their orders when Quint tugged her toward him and wrapped his arms around her. She turned her face to the side, to the glass door and wall of windows, and scanned the area to see if anyone had followed them. It shouldn't come as a surprise that no one seemed to have, except for the eyes-on-her feeling she'd had on the way over.

The line moved inch by inch.

"All I can say is these better be the best tacos I've ever had in my life," she warned as her stomach growled.

Quint dipped his head and pressed a kiss to her lips, and she got lost in his masculine scent for just a few seconds as she looked into those sapphire-blue eyes of his. Eyes like those should be outlawed. She could stare into them all day. *And night*, a wicked little voice in the back of her mind added. The voice was up to no good, and that was exactly what would come of her falling for this agent…no good.

Still, standing here, she couldn't help but be under his spell while his arms looped around her waist, holding her so close she could feel his heartbeat as it raced against his ribs. A little piece of her hoped she was having the same effect on him as he had on her.

Both seemed to realize touching that hot stove would set the whole house ablaze. For one moment, Ree couldn't help but think how incredible it would be to dance in the flames if only for a little while.

And then she recognized a face from Quint's file. The midtwenties male stepped inside the restaurant and moved behind a group of three people so they blocked Ree's view of him. It dawned on her that Quint had been on the bust that had killed his partner, Tessa Kind, and the two of them were currently chasing the same group down. What if Quint was recognized?

QUINT FELT THE exact moment every single one of Ree's muscles tensed up. Her body, flush with his, gave her away. She looked up at him with those emerald green eyes that made him lose his train of thought, and then subtly nodded her head toward the door.

He shifted to the left as they took another step closer to the order counter. Music thumped, giving the feeling they were already in a nightclub. This place must make amazing tacos to have a constant line at nine thirty on a Sunday night.

Ree moved to the beat. With her body against his, concentrating on anything else took effort. He took another step backward at her urging. They were getting close enough for him to turn around and check out the menu that was above the pair of order takers. As he turned, the profile of a male from the past came into view.

Quint pressed his hand against Ree's back, tapping his

fingers and giving a slight nod as he turned, turning his back to the male. Quint couldn't put a name to the familiar face. It had to be in his files back at the apartment, locked in the tackle box that was still in the back seat of the truck that had been assigned to the case.

This was going to bother him until he got back to the files. Was Mystery Guy associated with Constantin? Could Quint somehow get a picture to jar his memory later? As it was, the guy's profile was familiar, but Quint could be reaching. Ree had locked onto the Mystery Guy first. Had he followed them into the taco joint? Did he recognize Quint from the bust?

Ree cleared her throat and pressed a hand to Quint's chest.

"Honey," she said, urging him to move another step toward the order counter. They'd decided on their last assignment that "honey" was acceptable but "babe" was fingernails on a chalkboard to them both. They'd detailed out the rules of engagement. They'd shared information about each other, like the fact that her favorite color was blue and her second-favorite color was green. They'd decided to call each other by their rightful first names in public and he'd had documents made up with the last name Matthews. He just realized he'd forgotten to give her wallet to her. His had the credit cards and his driver's license, but hers was a different story.

Quint's turn to order would be next, so he spent a minute studying the menu before deciding on two number threes. Ree went with two brisket tacos. They ordered a pair of beers before being handed a buzzer and told to step aside. This whole scenario was a lot like ordering at Starbucks, minus the pager. He didn't take it as a good sign they needed one in the first place.

Taking the couple of steps, he glanced over his shoulder. He located the trio but not Mystery Guy. Quint's gaze flew to the glass door as it was closing behind a male figure leaving the line.

He bit back a curse and the urge to follow. Instead, he tugged his "wife" against him, her back to his chest, and whispered, "He's leaving."

She reached for his hand and then squeezed. The implication that this guy got what he wanted—confirmation he'd found Quint—loomed in the air.

The pager went off. They made their way to the pickup counter. Ree took the pager and then set it in the basket with others as a smiling kid who couldn't be a day over eighteen handed them a tray.

Ree thanked him as Quint grabbed their dinner tray, then followed her to a table outside and on the side of the restaurant in a space sectioned off for restaurant guests. It was warm out but not unbearably hot for a change. Quint set the tray down. Ree pulled their taco baskets off the tray and set them up with their beers before Quint took the tray to its return spot on top of the garbage can next to the exit. He used this as an opportunity to skim the area for Mystery Guy.

He was nowhere in sight.

"Damn," Quint said, returning to the table.

Ree gave a slight nod before picking up a taco. She cleared her basket in a matter of minutes and stopped talking in the process.

"You really must have been starving," he said to her.

"I wasn't kidding earlier." She wiggled her eyebrows at him as she wiped her mouth clean. He probably shouldn't let his gaze linger on those kissable lips of hers. Frustration at the missed opportunity to get a good look at Mystery Guy had Quint tied up in knots.

If his cover was blown on the first day, he couldn't let

Ree walk into that bar alone tomorrow night. Mystery Guy had no doubt seen the two of them together. If this guy was related to the case, life just got a whole lot messier for Quint and Ree.

"I feel like I might have seen Mystery Guy before in your files," Ree said.

"We can check when we get home," Quint offered.

Ree nodded.

"Ready?" he asked as she finished the last sip of her beer.

"Sure am," she said, pushing up to standing and gathering her trash. Disposal was easy. Their table was taken almost immediately.

"Did you like your dinner?" she asked, leaning into him as he put an arm around her shoulder.

"No taco has the right to taste as good as those," he quipped with a forced smile, in an attempt to lighten the mood.

Ree laughed, and the sound was almost musical.

Quint needed to shake off the gloom-and-doom feeling before it took hold. A strong mindset was the most important asset he could bring to an undercover operation. Mystery Guy might have been a random person who'd decided against waiting too long for tacos no matter how good they were. It wasn't a crime to leave a line he'd barely been in. If the same guy turned up at the bar, Quint would grab Ree and explain the situation. As it was, checking him against the photos in the file could wait.

Besides, she'd already picked up on the guy and would be watching out for him. She'd realized something could have been up with the man.

The Houstonian NightClub, HNC, was a five-minute walk from the taco restaurant, so roughly eight minutes from home. Driving Ree to and from work would leave them less exposed, but it was too close and would cast suspicion if anyone was paying attention.

Music could be heard thumping from halfway down the block. HNC took up two levels. A staircase to the left and above the bar was made of some kind of material that looked a lot like glass. A couple of guys sat strategically at the bar below, occasionally glancing up to check out the ladies in short skirts who were on the stairs. Sexist jerks.

Quint was more than a little relieved for Ree that she wouldn't be subjected to another uniform like the one at Greenlight on their last case. He did note, however, that the waitresses were attractive. The bartenders were drop-dead gorgeous and seemed to be the attraction. There was a mix of men and women behind the bar, mostly the latter. Waitresses wore less clothing than barbacks. They had on the same tuxedo shorts, but theirs fell higher on their legs, and the unbuttoned tuxedo shirt barely covered their breasts. There must have been a workout requirement to be a waitress, because they all had abs most would kill for. They also had tiny waists and larger-than-normal breasts. Some were blondes and others varying shades of brown, but HNC definitely had a type for their personnel.

A bar covered an entire wall to the left. There were tables and sofas almost like he'd seen in five-star hotels. To the right was a dance floor with an extensive lighting system that would rival any concert he'd ever been to. Guys were dressed in every variety of black shirt possible, and the women were glammed up, full makeup and hair, and looking like they'd just walked off a runway or red carpet. The median age for the women was thirty. Meanwhile, the men averaged higher. There was a mix of distinguished gray-haired men with women who looked like supermodels on their arms and youngish, newer-money men. New money always wore the most bling. The best way to tell

how much money an older guy had was by how expensive
his watch was. This place could be a showroom for Rolex.
The women looked like they were in one of those reality
shows about who could marry a millionaire.

And at the far end of the bar… Mystery Guy.

Chapter Six

Ree must've seen Mystery Guy from the taco stand at the same time as Quint, based on how much his muscles involuntarily tensed. She navigated them to an open table on the opposite side of the bar before scanning for Lola. As it turned out, all Ree had to do was follow Mystery Guy's lead. He was ordering a drink from someone who matched Lola's description.

In fact, there was a run on drinks at Lola's end of the bar, considering the number of single men who seemed uninterested in any of the women in the area. This area of the bar was lit in sea-blue lighting, which made it a little easier to see. Lola had black hair that ran halfway down her back. Even from Ree's position across the room, it was easy to see Lola was beautiful. She had a look that was difficult to pinpoint. European? Latin American?

This whole situation would be so much easier if Ree could just walk into the bar, flash a badge and start interviewing people. Of course, she also knew that would be the death of a sting operation. These cases took a whole lot more finesse. Was that part of the thrill?

Constantin was nowhere to be found. Apparently, Mystery Guy wasn't ordering a drink, because he nodded at Lola, smiled and then headed toward the door. Was he leaving?

The move caught Ree off guard and she didn't want

to be seen by him twice in one night, so she immediately hopped on Quint's lap and wrapped her arms around him, shielding much of her face. To hide the rest, she whispered, "Sorry." And then she planted a kiss on Quint's lips that sent her own pulse racing.

He deepened the kiss, causing her stomach to free-fall. This didn't seem like the time to compare this kiss to their last back in Cricket Creek, but this one easily blew the other one away. And that was saying something. There was a hunger and urgency in their movements as their tongues collided, searching and teasing. Beer had never tasted so good on someone else's lips before.

Had it really been less than a week since their case ended? Because this felt like a lovers' reunion kiss after being separated for months.

Ree forced herself not to read too much into it as she pulled away enough to ensure Mystery Guy was walking out the door. He was, and he never looked back. Ree exhaled, trying to slow her erratic heartbeat. She couldn't help but smile as she leaned in to his ear and whispered, "He's gone."

Quint brought his hands around to cup her face before laying a tender kiss on her lips. Then he pulled back and pressed his forehead against hers. "What are you drinking?"

"Whatever the most popular drink is," she said, figuring there was some type of signature cocktail at a place like this. There weren't a whole lot of beers in hand when she'd scanned the room after walking in. This was a mixed-drink crowd.

He hesitated with her still on his lap, so she scooted off and claimed the other chair at the table. He shook his head, and she was almost certain she heard him say the word *damn*.

Having an effect on the legendary Agent Quinton Casey probably shouldn't be such a source of pride. Except there was something about this man that rattled her to the core. This wasn't the time or the place to dig into finding out what that was. While he moved to the bar, she checked her phone. Still no word from her grandfather.

Everything had to be okay, though. Her family knew better than to interrupt her while she was in deep undercover. If anything had happened to her grandfather, someone would have reached out to her by now. He'd most likely just let his phone run out of battery and forgot to charge it. He wasn't nearly as tied to his cell as Ree was. The thought of being without hers caused her chest to squeeze with anxiety. Had she become too dependent on it? Probably.

And yet it proved useful time and time again on investigations. She needed to grab her assigned cell phone and lock her personal one in the tackle box. Could she touch base with home one more time before she did?

During her last assignment, she'd kept her personal cell phone on her. It had been a mistake when Shane had called and upset her. Since the risks on this case went up considerably, she wouldn't take any chances her personal information or contacts could be jeopardized no matter how much she wanted an update on her grandfather.

Ree tucked her cell back inside her handbag as Quint made his way over with cocktails in hand. His came in a highball glass whereas hers looked like a beach-blue martini. It required skill to make it through the crowd, which was thickening by the second, without spilling.

He set both drinks on the wooden tabletop with a grin as a few heads turned after he'd walked past. Jealousy wasn't something Ree normally could be accused of. Quint brought out a different side to her. She chalked it up to being protective over her new partner who was supposed to be her husband.

"You have many talents I had no idea about," Ree said as he reclaimed his seat opposite her.

"The drinks cost almost as much as my first car," he said with a laugh. Despite the jokes he'd been making tonight, the concern lines etching his forehead told a different story. He was worried about this one no matter how much he tried to hide it. She doubted anyone else could tell, but she'd gotten very good at reading him on the last case.

"Our building isn't cheap," she said, referring to the fact that Lola lived on the ninth floor. Ree had automatically assumed Constantin paid for the apartment, and that might very well be true, but Lola might be able to finance the place on her own with the kinds of tips she should be making in a place like this.

"That it is not," Quint said, holding out his arm. "I need a new watch."

"You have the exact kind of watch a student should wear," she said. On their last assignment, his cover was that he left the moving business he owned to go to school for a day job working on computers. "Besides, we'll be living off a percentage of the tips bartenders make for at least the next year while you finish your certification."

"Maybe I should stay with what I know," he quipped.

"We talked about this, honey," she said, putting on a show of frustration in case anyone was paying attention.

Glancing over at Lola, Ree wondered if she could pop over and introduce herself. Tell the bartender that Ree was a new hire and would start work tomorrow. Lola seemed to be the busiest bartender in the whole place.

After a few minutes passed, she thought better of interrupting Lola while she seemed to be jamming.

"You're right. Stick to the plan," he conceded. "By the

time this ankle fully heals, I'll be working a corporate nine-to-five."

"That's the idea," she said. "And I'll be a 'kept' woman." She made air quotes over the word *kept*. It was good practice for them to get into character in a loud bar where music thumped. It would also make listening in on Lola's conversations trickier, Ree figured.

"Let me know whenever you're ready to go finish unpacking," Quint said before downing his drink.

She'd been sipping on hers. A quick glance around, and the rubber plant next to her got a splash of vodka and whatever made the drink blue. It tasted good, but she wasn't a big drinker and could still feel the beer from dinner.

She made a show of setting her glass down on the wooden tabletop. "I'm ready whenever you are."

Quint stood up at the same time she did, putting them toe-to-toe. She glanced up at him, locking eyes, in a near-fatal mistake when they stood this close. He cracked a smile that was worth more than a thousand words, dipped his head and kissed her. This time, he didn't deepen the kiss.

He very well could have for the effect it had on her.

"Nice" was all she said as she took a step back, thinking she didn't need to get too used to this. Because she could really go there with a person like Quint.

QUINT REACHED FOR Ree's hand and then linked their fingers. The pace of the eight-minute walk home was a fast one. He scanned both sides of the street, searching for Mystery Guy. There was no sign of him on either sidewalk. The thought that he could live in one of the buildings around here disturbed Quint. The guy could be watching them right now. He instinctively tugged Ree a little closer at the thought. He could protect her better if she was right next to him.

"I need to grab the tackle box out of the truck before we head up," Quint whispered to Ree.

She nodded, looking a little defeated. Her new cell phone would be inside, and she would have to hand her personal phone in.

"You haven't heard anything about your grandfather yet," he said.

"No, I haven't," she confirmed.

"I'm sorry, Ree. I know how important he is to you," Quint said, giving her hand a squeeze.

"I have to believe he's fine," she said. "And he probably is. If something had happened, my family would have contacted me by now, so I'm taking it as a positive sign they haven't."

"That's a good attitude as long as it feels right to take that approach," he said.

"It does," she stated with a little less enthusiasm. She was struggling, and there wasn't anything he could do about it. Unless…

"I could call your brother for you," he said. "Shane would recognize the number of my burner phone. I'd have a good chance he would pick up."

"No, but thank you," she said. "It's a sweet offer. Maybe I could send a text to apologize after blowing out of there. Let them know I'll be over after the case wraps to say I'm sorry in person."

"I'm sure they would appreciate the gesture," he said. "And in case you're worried about me calling him again, I deleted his number and all traces of it have been erased from the phone." Shane had given Ree bad advice on day one of the last operation and had convinced the agency to give him Quint's number. The move had caught Ree off guard, and Quint vowed never to go behind her back again when it came to her family. He should have told her right away when it happened but didn't, thinking he was protecting her relationship with her brother. It had had the opposite effect.

"I appreciate it, Quint," she said, taking the phone he held out to her. She sent the text, and a response came back almost immediately.

"Shane said he was very happy to hear from me," she stated with a broad smile.

They detoured to the garage, where he picked up the tackle box and a blanket she'd forgotten earlier. There was a throw pillow underneath that she grabbed to take upstairs and personalize the apartment a little, or so she'd said when she'd thrown it in the back seat.

Once back in the apartment, he spread photos out across the counter, searching for the familiar face from earlier.

"Do you see him?" Quint asked. All he knew was that Mystery Guy's hair was black and long enough to curl up at the collar. Quint wished he'd seen more than a flash of the guy. Flipping through the small stack of pictures, Quint couldn't find anyone with this guy's profile.

"Not yet," she said.

He sat on the stool and thumbed through the photos again, slowly this time. Shook his head when she didn't pinpoint anyone. "I could have sworn I recognized him from your file," she said.

"Maybe you got your wires crossed," he said. It happened. For now, Mystery Guy was just that…a mystery.

"It's late, and it's been a long day," Ree said with a small nod and smile. "I should probably get ready for bed."

She turned toward the bathroom, took a few steps, then paused at the doorway. "It means a lot coming from you, by the way."

"Anytime," he said. "And I mean it."

Quint thumbed through the photos once more, studying each even more carefully. Something niggled at the back of his mind, but he couldn't place it, and putting too much emphasis on it wouldn't help. He tucked the photos inside the folder before replacing them inside the tackle box. There wasn't much more that could be done until morning, so he locked the box, then put it inside the coat closet to the right of the door, figuring most wives wouldn't want a tackle box in the same cabinet where they kept their clothing.

Clearly, this one hadn't seen a boat, dock or fishing hole, but anyone who busted into the apartment wouldn't know that. Maintaining an image was important. Doing what was expected was necessary. If anything stood out as unusual, their cover would be in jeopardy.

Quint started making a mental checklist of everything that needed to be done in the morning. Groceries. Supplies, like a laundry basket and detergent. He could gather everything easily enough.

Ree emerged from the bathroom wearing a pair of cotton pajamas that hugged her curves a little too well. Quint cleared his throat.

"You're up in the bathroom," Ree said, her voice a little too sexy.

"Yep," he stated. "Your new cell phone is on the counter. I'll be out in a few minutes."

She walked over to the flyer on the counter.

"Pilates at nine o'clock tomorrow morning. I have a feeling my new buddy, Angie, will be there," she said.

"I'll hit the weights while you take the class," he said.

Angie seemed like the nosy-neighbor type. Could they get information from her about the building's other residents—residents like Lola?

Chapter Seven

Ree stretched her arms as she opened her eyes to the sunlight filling the apartment. The clock on the nightstand said it was already eight o'clock. Pilates was in an hour, which gave her time to grab coffee… Hold on. There was no coffee in the place. The kitchen was empty, and they hadn't gone out for supplies last night.

There was also no one sleeping beside her. Quint had been an early riser in the cabin, too. She'd conked out before he'd made it out of the bathroom last night. Did the man ever sleep? She hadn't heard him leave, either. But then, she'd always been a heavy sleeper. Came with being a Sheppard, if she could believe her older brother Shane. But then, he'd also said he hadn't slept since his three-year-old son had been born. With a new baby in the house, she wasn't sure how he did it.

Throwing the covers off, Ree slipped out of the comfortable bed in the quiet nook of the apartment. It only took a few steps for the rest of the apartment to be in full view, which she saw as a good sign.

Quint was hunkered over his laptop at the breakfast counter. He glanced over at her. "Good morning."

"It would be a better morning if I'd stopped off at the store for coffee grinds last night," she said, half teasing as she made her way to the bathroom. After freshening up and changing into yoga pants and a sports bra with a loose shirt over it, she stepped out almost ready to face the world.

Quint held up a mug.

"What is that?" she asked.

"Maybe you should check for yourself," he said with a smirk.

Ree wasted no time racing over to him. "Coffee? How?"

"I got up early and didn't want to disturb you, so I ran to the store," he said before going back to studying his laptop like he wasn't a hero. "Made a pot and figured you would want a cup when you got up."

"You are seriously amazing. You know that, right?" she said.

"If you think that's impressive, I stopped off for bagels, too." He wiggled his eyebrows at her, which made her laugh. This man was one of the best agents she would ever hope to work with, and he had serious food skills. He'd kept her caffeinated and well fed on the last undercover operation, and here he was doing it again.

She moved around to the other side of the counter. The bag was sitting next to a stainless-steel toaster. What the place lacked in space, it made up for in style. All the appliances were top-of-the-line. In some ways, this kitchen was perfect, because she could literally reach every cabinet in any direction by taking a step to her left or to her right. She would never be accused of being chef material, but if she had to cook, this kitchen would make it easy.

"I never want to have to work with another partner again," she said as she popped a bagel in the toaster. "Did you eat?"

"All done here," he said.

"What time did you get up?" She glanced at the sink and saw no dirty dishes.

"Five…give or take," he admitted, taking a sip of coffee. "I couldn't sleep."

"Was it because of Mystery Guy?" she asked, blowing on her fresh brew before taking a sip, and enjoying the burn on her throat.

"Partially," he admitted. "I'm also trying to figure out how to get myself a job where I can be close to you at the bar."

"I highly doubt we'll get lucky enough for you to get access to the computers like in the last case, despite our cover," she said.

"I had the same thought. Except most people aren't great with computers, so maybe we can find an in for me with someone at the bar," he said. "There has to be a way."

"If anyone mentions needing help, you know I'll mention you," she said. "I have a feeling that I'm going to be busy all night, though. Did you see how hopping the place was on a Sunday night?"

He nodded.

"Imagine what the weekends must be like," she said.

"You're starting on a Monday. Maybe that will give you a chance to get your bearings," he pointed out.

"What about Randy? Does he have cameras in the place?" she asked.

"He only places them in the back office," Quint stated.

"Can't he give you a job?" she asked.

"It'll be suspicious if a husband-and-wife team show up and suddenly both work for him," Quint said.

"That's a good point," she admitted. "Plus, it isn't like he's involved. He's fully cooperating."

Quint nodded.

Ree scarfed down the bagel almost the minute it popped up. The warm bread was exactly what she needed to power through a Pilates class with Angie. She polished off her coffee and rinsed out the mug. "Do you think I need to take my own towel?"

"They have some down at the gym," he informed. "I already checked it out for you."

"Nice. Thank you," she said, then realized she didn't have a yoga mat. "Do they, by chance, have mats downstairs?"

"Yours is rolled up by the door," he said. "I thought you might need one, so I picked one up while I was out. It's amazing what you can buy at the corner store in downtown Houston when you're out at a ridiculous time of the morning."

She laughed.

"I owe you one," she said. "Make that two considering you bought bagels and three when you consider the coffee... Hold on a minute. Are you trying to butter me up?" She folded her arms across her chest in a playful move. The case was dangerous and she took her work seriously, but these moments of brevity broke up the tension and allowed for breathing room, which was much needed considering cases extended days and sometimes weeks.

"Consider it a thank-you for taking the case," he said. The look he gave her said he meant it, too. "I wouldn't want anyone else having my back right now."

"You're welcome," she said, thinking how nice it was to work together. Could they be partners? Or would his past always keep him at arm's length?

Her answer came a few seconds later when she felt a wall come up between them. He shifted in his seat and redirected his focus to his laptop, and there was nothing she could do to bring him back. He'd experienced a level of hell she could only imagine in blaming himself for the death of his pregnant partner and best friend. Quint had been set to become the baby's godfather.

Quint had let his partner talk him into holding off on telling their boss about the pregnancy. Apparently, she'd asked for time so she could deliver the news on her own terms. The baby's father exited the picture after learning about the kid on the way. Then, during a bust with multiple agencies involved, Tessa was killed by friendly fire. Quint couldn't stop beating himself up. It was clear that he blamed himself, because he'd said Tessa and her baby would be alive right now if he'd stood his ground. Department policy would have had Tessa assigned to desk duty, and Quint would have gone into the bust alone. That was all true. But the part he was missing was that he couldn't accept the reality that he wasn't responsible for other people's choices. Lack of communication between agencies was responsible for Tessa's death. It was a harsh reality and serious risk when working with other agencies. Mistakes happened when busts were rushed.

Ree glanced at the time. Eight forty-five. Time to head downstairs to Pilates with Angie.

"I'm going down," she said to Quint. "Are you coming?"

"I'll be there in a bit," he said without looking up from his screen.

Ree grabbed the yoga mat and her key before heading downstairs. She figured getting there early would give her a chance to socialize with others in the building. She pressed the elevator button and waited. It came up quickly and by the time the ding sounded, a door opened behind Ree.

"Hey." Angie's perky voice shouldn't have surprised Ree.

She turned and greeted her neighbor.

"Looks like you're heading to class," Angie said, holding up her mat. "Same."

Angie stepped inside the elevator behind Ree and pulled

the rubber band from her wrist before using it to tie her hair back. Had she heard Ree's door close? Had she been listening for it? Angie was either that nosy or that lonely. Firefighter hours could be to blame, considering they worked several days on and a couple of days off. It was probably great for studying but also most likely made for many dinners for one.

The good news was that Angie could end up being a useful source of information. She seemed about as pure as the driven snow, so Ree didn't worry about Angie being involved in criminal activity. She might, however, have the scoop on the building.

"How's studying going?" Ree asked.

Angie exhaled in dramatic fashion. "Hard. It's hard. I took a practice test last night and got nowhere near the score I need."

"That's tough, but at least you have a baseline. Did you at least figure out what you needed to focus on?" Ree asked.

"I did, but this is going to be harder than I thought," Angie said. She held up her yoga mat. "I've taken enough of these classes to become a certified teacher." She laughed. "If the whole 'law school' thing doesn't work out I could have a real career doing this."

Angie rolled her eyes and Ree laughed. She was going to like taking class together.

The elevator dinged and the doors opened to the second floor.

"Wow." Ree glanced around, taking in the massive glass-enclosed space. "Does the gym take up the whole floor?"

"Yes. It's great, isn't it?" Angie said.

"I'm impressed." Ree walked the circle around the elevator bank, noticing a certain black-haired bartender stretching in one corner.

"Follow me," Angie said. "We're early. I'll take you on the tour."

"You know, I'm feeling a little stiff after sitting in a truck yesterday during the move. Mind if we tour after class?" Ree asked. "I should probably stretch now."

QUINT PULLED OUT the tackle box and checked the photos again. There was still no sign of Mystery Guy. Whatever niggled at the back of Quint's mind frustrated him to no end, since the information was so close but just out of reach. Was it a piece of valuable intel? Was it unrelated and something from a past bust? Was it something that could mean the difference between life and death in this case?

He wasn't so worried about himself, but Ree's safety came to mind. What if Quint had knowledge that could end up getting her shot but couldn't access it until it was too late?

After logging in to the agency database, Quint had spent the morning checking through his old case files and came up short. His mind had always been sharp and his memory had been good as gold. The only explanation for the lapse was stress. So he needed to calm the hell down and get a grip or risk putting them both in more danger. Since that was unacceptable, he opened files from two years ago.

Forty-five minutes later, he realized he was going to miss his workout window if he didn't get changed and downstairs in five minutes. Ree had left the apartment early, but her class was in full swing by now. He'd heard the neighbor's door close and voices in the hallway. Angie must have been listening for Ree this morning. The woman was persistent. He would give her that much. Or bored. The second was likely considering the fact that her live-in boy-friend was a firefighter. Their schedules were demanding.

Quint figured Ree already realized how much of an asset Angie could be in learning who was who in the building. A smart, bored young person was a good bridge to the goings-on in the building but, damn, Quint was beginning to feel old. His body definitely screamed at him for being over forty and trying to keep the same muscle-punishing workouts. What could he say? It was hard to dial it down when he was used to breaking a good sweat and lifting a certain number when it came to weights.

He changed into something more suitable for the gym, figuring he could get away with an arms-only workout this morning. The injured ankle excuse would keep him from running in public, which had always been his go-to when he needed to clear his mind for a case. Then there was Tessa. His thoughts could go down a dark path there, especially when images of Tessa in his arms, taking her last breaths, assaulted him. She'd said she was sorry, but he didn't deserve the apology. In fact, it should have been the reverse. Tessa would be alive today if not for him.

Those thoughts got him moving toward the elevator to check on Ree. She was fully capable of doing her job, an equal in every way that counted. And yet he had to confirm she was okay with his own eyes.

The elevator doors opened almost immediately after he pushed the button. Had someone come to the floor while he was getting dressed? No doors had closed to his knowledge. He noted that he had to be close to the kitchen to hear activity in the hallway.

The ride down stopped at almost every floor and the elevator was jammed full by the time he reached number two.

"Excuse me," he said, navigating his way as people stepped aside and out to allow him to exit. He thanked them before surveying the area. The glass walls and doors made seeing into the gym easy enough.

He took a few steps and froze. Ree was on what looked like a midclass water break standing to the side of the room with Angie and Lola. Lola made eye contact and he did his best to hide his momentary shock. Did she catch him?

Chapter Eight

Ree saw Quint almost the second he entered the second
floor. There was just something about his physical presence that made people stop and stare, herself included.

"Looks like your husband made it after all," Angie said.

"He's a keeper," Lola said, making eyes at Ree. "And
he looks as good in workout clothes as he does in jeans."

"He sure is and he certainly does," Ree said. She didn't
have to fake her appreciation for Quint's good looks. What
could she say? The man was easy on the eyes.

"What happened to his foot, if you don't mind my asking?" Angie said.

"He owned a moving business and dropped a piano on
his ankle," Ree said as the others winced. "It hurt like hell,
but I think it's going to be good for us. Now he's working
on certification in computer science and starting a new
chapter in life."

"You must be set with insurance," Lola said, and Ree
was beginning to see a practical nature come out.

"His business partner let insurance lapse without saying a word," Ree said. "We sold our half of the business,
which sets us up for a few months and helps with medical
bills, but that's why I'll be working at HNC."

"You should have stopped by and said hello last night,"
Lola stated.

"You seemed busy, and I figured we would meet tonight during my shift anyway," Ree said.

Lola smiled. It was a shame she was linked with Constantin.

"It'll be nice to know someone at work. We moved here for a fresh start," Ree said, playing the "new kid in town" card to her advantage.

"Of course. I remember when Esteban and I came to the States two years ago from Argentina. We didn't know anyone at first. But then I got the job at the bar and he found work. Life got better," Lola said.

"Is Esteban your husband?" Angie asked as her gaze dropped to Lola's ring finger. Having Angie around was so helpful. It kept Ree from having to ask a lot of intrusive questions. Leave it to a bored person who happened to be a social butterfly to do the work of ten investigators.

"No. No. Nothing like that." Lola shook her head for emphasis. "Esteban is my brother."

"Ohhhhh," Angie said. "That's really brave to leave your country and start over."

"I wasn't here long before I met my boyfriend, so it turned out fine." Lola's gaze dropped, and Ree saw there was a story there.

"It's good. It all worked out," Lola said, but there was a wistful quality to her voice that Ree didn't need to be good at her job to pick up on.

Rather than let Angie continue digging, Ree decided to rescue the conversation. "The bar looked pretty busy last night. Is it always that crowded on a Sunday?"

Lola shot a thankful look at Ree, and she realized she'd just won major points.

"It is. The money is so good on the weekends," Lola said. "When do you start?"

"Tonight," Ree said with a tentative smile.

"You'll do great," Lola reassured. "Mondays are the slowest, so that'll give you a chance to figure things out before the Thursday night crowd hits. Thursdays through Sundays are our busiest. Believe me, you'll need to be ready for those." Lola turned to Angie. "You should come by. Take a break from studying."

"Maybe I will." Angie perked up. "My boyfriend is working tonight, and I don't think I can look at another screen for at least two days."

Lola's forehead wrinkled as questions formed behind her eyes.

"Angie's boyfriend is a fireman. And she's studying for the LSAT."

Angie practically beamed. She was one of the purest souls Ree had ever encountered. Good for her. Working at the agency had tainted Ree more than she cared to admit. It became obvious when she met a sweet soul like Angie just how much Ree had moved away from being a doe-eyed kid herself. Seeing the worst in society did that to a person. Of course, locking up the bad guys went a long way toward restoring her faith in humanity. Focusing on the good guys out there made it all worth it.

"Did you say your husband knows what to do with computers?" Lola asked, a slightly desperate quality in her eyes.

"He's good with them," Ree said.

"Mine has been turning off for no reason," Lola said. "Esteban has no idea what to do to fix it. Any chance your husband would be willing to take a look?"

"No promises, but it can't hurt for him to try," Ree said, stunned it was so easy to get Quint an in so quickly. "We can ask him after class."

The instructor had taken her place at the front of the room and was slowly stretching on her mat while turning the music up. Clearly, a hint to set down water bottles and rejoin her.

"Will he still be here?" Lola asked, motioning toward Quint.

"He should be. He's been all about chest and arms since the accident that injured his ankle," Ree said. "Living with him wasn't easy while he was in recovery and couldn't work out."

"I can't imagine," Lola said, and her horrified expression made Ree smile.

"Sounds rough," Angie agreed as they each took their mats with her in between. Buddying up to Angie had paid off big-time.

The back half of the class almost kicked Ree's behind. She was a runner and had taken the occasional hot yoga class. Pilates with weights had been harder than she'd expected. Then again, she'd been out of a workout routine for a couple of months now aside from going for the occasional run.

The instructor ended class with an inspirational quote and a deep bow. Ree was in serious need of a shower. She grabbed a towel and met Angie and Lola at the "hydration station" wondering why they couldn't just call it what it was…a water fountain. Then again, she figured the building owners could charge more in rent if everything sounded fancier than it was.

"Let me know when you're ready to meet my husband," Ree said to Lola.

"I don't want to disturb his workout," Lola said with a little headshake.

"He won't mind," Ree said. "But you could always come over later and bring your laptop with you. We're in apartment seven-three."

"I'm on the ninth floor, same apartment number," Lola said. "If you don't mind. I'd love to come by before work."

"How's three o'clock sound?" Ree asked.

"Perfect to me," Lola responded. She was genuinely likable, so the thought that she lived a double life with a man who went by the name Lights Out was surprising. But then, Ree had seen just about everything in her line of work. Nothing should surprise her anymore.

"Do you guys want to head out for breakfast?" Angie asked.

Something behind Angie caught Lola's eye.

"Excuse me," she said.

Ree turned in time to see Mystery Guy from last night standing at the gym's door. There was no way he was Constantin, so why was he here?

"How about you?" Angie asked, focusing on Ree.

"Sorry. I ate before I came down," she said. "I better let my husband know we're having company later. You're welcome to stop by if you'd like."

Ree had made the offer out of courtesy, not expecting Angie to take her up on it.

"Sure. Three o'clock is great," Angie said.

"See you then," Ree said, deciding this would keep things lighter and more social.

"Should I bring anything?" Angie asked.

"Just yourself," Ree said before walking over to talk to her "husband."

"Hey, beautiful," Quint said, before leaning forward and pressing a tender kiss on Ree's lips after she joined him in the weight room. The move was for show, and he'd done his best to be convincing. His body's reaction wasn't part of the plan. It wanted to haul her against his chest and do a whole lot more.

The cover was necessary so Quint wasn't busted staring at Mystery Guy, who seemed to be escorting Lola to the elevator.

"We're having company at three o'clock," Ree said, her emerald eyes sparkling a little more than usual. He blamed it on the lighting.

"Angie?" he asked.

"And Lola," she stated with more than a hint of pride in her voice.

"I'd rather have you to myself, honey." He kissed her again. He threw out the line in case anyone was listening. There was a sprinkling of guys at the gym, all doing their own things with weights. One was in front of mirrors, grunting while powerlifting. Another was off to the other side on a machine. Give Quint a dumbbell set and a weight bench and he'd be good to go.

Mystery Guy and Lola took the elevator and disappeared from view a few moments later.

"You'll have to share me for a little while," she said, leaning into him. "But after work, I'm all yours."

"Promise?" he teased, trying to lighten the mood. The comment stirred emotions deep in his chest.

She leaned in and whispered, "Did you see him?"

"That sounds right up my alley," he said in a cryptic answer.

"Are they gone?" Her lips were so close to his ear he could feel her warm breath. It caused the hairs on his neck to stand at attention and blood to flow south.

"I'd definitely say yes to doing that later," he said, continuing the ruse in case they were being overheard or watched. As it was, they had Mystery Guy in the building and connected to their current case, and Lola was coming over at three o'clock. Good progress was being made already. His cell buzzed. He fished it out of his pocket.

There was a message from Lynn Bjorn, their boss. Call in fifteen minutes.

"Looks like my workout is over," Quint said, showing her the screen.

"I'll grab two waters before we head up," Ree said with a smile before turning around and heading toward the small glass-door fridge.

Quint forced his gaze from her sweet backside, thinking he'd much rather do something else in fifteen minutes. A call from the boss at this stage of the investigation never signaled good news.

He toweled off and then wiped down the weights out of courtesy before following Ree to the elevator. The water was cold and refreshing going down his throat.

"I might not have been there long, but I managed to work up a decent sweat," he said.

"You're welcome to the shower first if you want," Ree said. "I can take mine after the call with your mother." Those last three words were for the couple's benefit who'd jumped in the elevator before the doors closed.

The guy was tall and somewhere in between Quint's and Ree's ages. He would guess closer to Ree's. The guy's— Quint performed a quick check for wedding bands and saw a matching set—wife was definitely closer to Ree's. The pair was opposite in pretty much every way. He was tall and she was short. He had sandy-blond hair whereas hers was a dark brown. His eyes were blue; hers were brown.

It wasn't until the pair got off the elevator on the fifth floor that Quint realized what was bothering him about the couple. He stifled a few choice words, waiting until they got inside their apartment before walking to the bedroom area to let a few rip.

"I saw it, too." Ree joined him, perching on the edge of the bed after grabbing a towel from the bathroom and folding it to presumably protect the bedspread from her sweat. "The haircut. The subtle way he walked with his right arm extended a little bit farther from his hip like he was used to a gun being there. What is other law enforcement doing in the building?"

"That has to be what the call with Bjorn is about," he said, flexing and releasing his fingers a few times to work off some of the tension that had been building since the text. "They might be unrelated to this case."

Ree shot him a look. "What are the odds of that happening?"

He put up a hand in surrender. This development sent his blood pressure soaring. Then there was the frustration this morning of not being able to place Mystery Guy from last night. Speaking of whom… "Did Lola say why Mystery Guy was in the building?"

"We didn't talk about him," she said. "I didn't even realize he was standing at the elevators until she walked away."

"I saw him when he came out of the elevator a few seconds before she turned around, but that was about it," he said.

"He must have known when her class would end," Ree pointed out as the cell phone in Quint's hand buzzed.

"Guess we're about to find out what the deal is with the other couple," he said before answering.

"I have news," Bjorn said. The fact that their boss was all business was another bad sign.

"I'm putting the call on speaker," Quint informed her before tapping the screen. "Ree is here with me."

"Good," Bjorn said. The sound of her issuing a sharp sigh came over the line. "I know this isn't going to go over very well, so I'll get straight to the point. The DEA is involved in the case, and we have agreed to cooperate."

Quint's blood pressure spiked again.

"Why is that?" he asked, clenching his back teeth to hold back from what he really wanted to say.

"We both know why the DEA would be involved," Bjorn said matter-of-factly. "Drugs."

"This complicates things," Quint said after a long, thoughtful pause.

"I know," Bjorn said.

Did she, though? Or had he become so good at hiding the truth that even his boss was blind to him?

Chapter Nine

Ree tucked a loose tendril of hair behind her ear as she studied the phone. Looking directly at Quint right now would only make matters worse. She heard the struggle in his tone of voice and knew exactly what this news would do to him. An investigation including multiple agencies would send him back to that place a little more than half a year ago where his partner was killed. Quint might ultimately blame himself for not forcing her to go to Bjorn, but the mistake came from multiple agencies rushing to a bust.

"Speak up, Agent Casey," their boss said.

"I'm here," he responded. "Just processing how to make this work."

Ree did glance up at that comment and saw the anguish in his eyes that belied the calmness in his tone. She reached out and touched him on the forearm, taking it as a bad sign that he immediately pulled his arm back like he'd just bumped into a lit burner. She took a second to consider her next move carefully. The option to request to be removed from the case would get her home to check on her grandfather. It would also leave Quint stranded. They could come up with an excuse, and he could continue with the investigation. But she was the one with the job at the bar. Ree was already making inroads with Lola. It was only a matter of time before they figured out who Mystery Guy was now that Ree had an in with the bartender.

On the flip side, Quint was a talented agent. There was a reason he was considered the best to the point of having legendary status at work. He'd taken a big hit in losing his partner and best friend. The situation was sad from every angle. Was he over the loss? Probably not. Was he determined to find Dumitru and make him pay? Absolutely. This being personal for Quint raised the stakes of an already-dangerous assignment.

Still, she couldn't walk out on her partner. She knew it the minute she glanced over at him and they locked gazes. The slight nod she gave told him the answer he seemed to be searching for. His sigh of relief shouldn't make her want to walk over and loop her arms around his neck. And yet the kisses they'd shared sizzled like none other in her past, probably in her present and most definitely ever would in her future.

"Who is going to be our contact on the DEA side?" Ree asked, breaking the silence.

"That will be Nicholas Primer," Bjorn supplied. "We've worked with him before, and his team is top-notch."

"Sounds good." Ree grasped the sales job their boss was doing to soften the blow. Bjorn must realize how bad this was for Quint. He stood at the window, absently rubbing the stubble on his chin while engaged in what looked like deep thought.

"The details and contact information are uploaded to the case file," Bjorn said. The phone went quiet for a few long seconds. "Agent Casey."

"I'm here," he said after clearing his throat. He didn't turn away from the window, and Ree took that as a bad sign.

"You're good, right?" Bjorn asked.

"You saw my file. I've been cleared to work for months," he countered. "I passed all the psych evals you requested. Why would you be concerned about me now?"

"Good. That's what I wanted to hear." Bjorn sounded relieved. She wouldn't be if she was standing in the room. The tension thickened as Quint seemed to get lost inside his head.

"I'll check the file ASAP," Quint promised before lifting his elbow up against the window as he pinched the bridge of his nose like he was staving off a headache.

"Let me know if you have any questions or difficulties with any of Agent Primer's team," Bjorn said. She was lingering on the call like she was waiting for a definitive sign Quint was on board.

"We will," Ree finally spoke up. "Thanks for the information. We look forward to working with Agent Primer and his team."

Quint sucked in a breath but seemed able to hold his tongue as Ree ended the call.

"The couple from the elevator," he said through what sounded like clenched teeth. "Let me guess... Agent Primer."

"We'll know when we open the file and see his picture. But, yes, I'm assuming the same thing," she said. When one of her brothers got in a mood like this, they were best left alone. A couple of days would pass and whatever they'd been angry about would blow over. Partnerships didn't work like that. She had to figure out a way to get Quint to speak to her.

He grunted as he stood there, staring.

"I know this probably brings back bad memories—"

"You don't know hell about what happened," he said, raising his voice. "And you don't know hell about what it cost me."

"No, Quint. I don't. But I will if you sit down and talk to me," she said evenly. "I can throw on a pot of coffee and we can move to the living room where we can talk like civilized adults."

Her words must've pushed the wrong buttons, because when she glanced over at him, his entire face was red.

"If you want a civilized adult, go talk to Agent Primer," he said, and his voice seethed.

"That's not fair and you know it," Ree countered, her own temperature rising to a level barely below boiling point. A few calming breaths brought her heat level down a couple of notches.

Quint, on the other hand, looked like a teakettle that was about to burst.

"Hey," she started, taking a softer tact. "You're right about one thing. I don't know." She paused to give those words a minute to sink in. "I don't know anything about what you went through or how it must have felt." Again, she paused. "All I can say is that I wish you'd talk to me and help me understand."

"It wouldn't bring her back," he said with so much anger the walls practically shook. "There's no use in dredging up bad memories."

Having grown up with four brothers, Ree knew a thing or two about when she'd lost a fight. This was one of those times. She pushed up to standing and grabbed the towel she'd been seated on.

"I'm going to take a shower, put on a pot of coffee and then open the file. Your choice as to whether or not you want to join me for two of those three things." With that, she made a beeline to the bathroom. She closed the door a little louder than she'd intended, and then turned on the spigot. Ten minutes later, she was clean and ready to face the other room.

Ree had no idea if Quint would even be there, let alone still in a sour mood, but time wasn't a luxury they had much of. Ree wanted to prep for the three o'clock with Lola. Then there was her shift tonight she had to mentally prepare for.

She walked out of the bathroom. At least Quint had left the spot at the window. He was probably gone, and that might be for the best. Let him cool off before they took another go at being civil with each other. Besides, seeing the pain in his eyes was a dagger to the heart and not something she was eager to get back to.

The smell of a fresh pot of coffee hit her the minute she turned left to head into the main living space. It was a welcome scent. Quint stood in the small kitchen with the light out. It was tucked inside the apartment near the door and fairly enclosed so as not to allow a lot of the natural light from the wall of windows inside.

"I made a cup and opened the file." He motioned toward the sofa, where the laptop sat on the coffee table, looking ready to go.

"I'll make one and join you," she said, but he shook his head. He filled a cup and handed it through the pass-through counter. "Thank you, Quint."

He didn't respond. Instead, he grunted and then walked over to the sofa.

QUINT SAT DOWN in front of the laptop. Ree joined him a few seconds later, sitting close enough for their outer thighs to touch as he opened the case file.

"Figures," she said, and then took a sip of coffee. Primer's face filled the left-hand side of the screen.

"Knew it," Quint said with a little more frustration than intended. Then again, the emotion seemed to be playing on repeat today.

"I'm guessing the female who was with him is also an agent," Ree said.

Quint clicked a couple of keys and brought up her picture next. "Chelle Mickelberg."

Ree sat back and scooted away from Quint. "Lola mentioned having a brother named Esteban. Do you think it's possible he's Mystery Guy?"

"It would make sense," Quint reasoned. "Her brother might know her schedule and need something from her."

"That would explain why he showed up after class today," she said. "They could be roommates, too."

"True," Quint agreed. "I'm not sure why the agency didn't tell us about a brother's possible involvement in her life."

"She mentioned that the two of them came to America together," Ree supplied. "It's possible he's living under the radar, possibly illegally."

"Grappell should be able to dig around and get an answer for us." Quint pulled up his email and then fired off a quick note to Agent Grappell. He was one of the best and having him on this case provided consistency, which went a long way in Quint's book. He would take all the wins he could get.

"What else?" Ree asked.

"Study the file on Primer," Quint said. "Looks like he's been decorated more than most professional athletes."

"A rising star at the DEA?" she asked, but the question was rhetorical, so Quint answered by way of another grunt.

They both realized what a pain a guy like that could be to have around. He sounded like the type who would want all the glory and most likely take credit for other people's work. Guys like that cared more about building a thick file of accolades and were usually all show and no substance.

"I should probably be the designated go-between on our side," Ree said.

"Are you afraid I can't keep my cool when I need to?" He twisted up his face.

To her credit, Ree maintained a calm but distant disposition. "Do I need to be?"

"No," he said dismissively.

"Good. Your answer doesn't change anything. I'll be the point person," she said. "Are you okay with that?"

He pulled up Primer's file and then turned the screen for her to see it. "His contact information is right there, but we should probably both have it just in case we aren't together when contact needs to be made."

"That's fair." She retrieved her cell phone and entered the information into her contacts. "Looks like he's going by the name Nick Driver."

"People pick whatever name is easiest to remember. Driver is close enough to Primer," Quint reasoned.

"He also kept his first name like we did," she added as she studied the screen. "Did you see this?" She pointed toward a line that indicated the agent would be working in the office of the bar as a new events and marketing manager.

"As long as he cooperates when necessary and stays out of our way when not, I don't care if he buys the place," Quint bit out. This complicated his infiltrating the office to be the computer guy. Randy, the owner, was on the up-and-up, but doing computer work would have given Quint a reason to hang around the bar more.

"If you can believe his file, he's one of the best at what he does," Ree said. She must have made the same assumptions about the agent based on her tone. "I'll reach out to him in a few minutes."

"The female agent, Chelle, is going by Shelly Driver," Quint pointed out.

"What does she do for a living according to her file?" Quint scrolled down.

"Turns out, she's a yoga instructor," he said.

"Please tell me she doesn't work in the same building," Ree said on a sigh.

"It's bad enough they live here," he stated. "They could have moved into one of the other buildings on this block. But, no, she won't be working in the building. The studio where she's employed is on the same street as the bar."

"It must be close, then," she reasoned.

"That's probably a safe bet." He entered the studio address into Google Maps. "It's two doors down."

"Figures," she said. "You'll still be able to come to the bar for a nightcap. I can sell it as you going to school during the day while I sleep in after a long night of work."

"As long as it won't cast suspicion on you," he said.

"Lola remembered us from last night," Ree said, and he picked up something different in her tone.

"Speaking of her, we probably should have introduced ourselves at the bar. But it's fine. Right now, we should probably make lunch and get ready for her to drop by," he said.

"You're right about introducing ourselves that first night. I had the same thought but decided not to interrupt her. No going back to change it now," she said on a shrug. Little mistakes were expected on a case. They couldn't get too inside their heads about what they couldn't go back and fix. "I'll join you in a second. I want to order a few things to personalize the apartment."

"Suit yourself." Quint pushed up to standing. He still hadn't showered after working out, so he did that first.

By the time he finished and hit the kitchen, Ree was done with her online shopping.

"It's wild that I literally just placed an order and the items will be delivered in—" she checked the time "—less than four hours."

"The benefits of city life," he said.

"I've lived my whole life in a small town," she said. "I travel all around the state for work now and have seen the benefits of urban living." She paused for a thoughtful moment. "At the end of the day, I don't need a lot to be happy. A cold drink, a little space between me and my neighbors, and a good book is all I need to be happy."

"No companionship?" he asked, wondering if she intended to spend the rest of her life alone.

"That's what the book is for," she said.

"Fair enough," he responded.

"How about you?" she asked, taking a seat on the barstool at the pass-through counter leading to the kitchen.

"What about me?" he asked, noting she'd turned the tables.

"What makes you happy?" she asked.

He resisted the temptation to say her, so he waved her off instead.

Chapter Ten

The DEA's involvement in the case could undermine the
work Ree and Quint were putting in. Ree didn't like it one
bit. The fact that it seemed to be a trigger for Quint wasn't
helping matters. His body language had changed the second he heard the news. And if she was blind to that, anger
practically radiated off him.

While he pulled together lunch, she reached out to Nick.

"No answer?" Quint's eyebrow came up in disapproval.

She left a message for Nick that was cryptic enough in
the event it was intercepted and then nodded toward Quint.
"I'm sure he'll get back to me when he can."

There were all kinds of reasons Nick might not have his
phone with him in the apartment. But it could be a power
play. His way of letting her know she wasn't a priority. In
which case, he was a class A jerk, and working together
was going to be real "fun."

A quick lunch of grocery store–prepared chicken salad
on a lettuce leaf was enough to keep her stomach from
growling. Before she knew it, there was a knock at the
door.

Ree hopped up and checked the peephole. She opened
the door and welcomed Angie inside. "What is that?"

"I made a little bowl of trail mix. I hope it's okay," Angie
said. "It didn't seem right to show up empty-handed."

"Of course, it's great," Ree said, taking the large bowl. "Warm?"

"I like to pop mine in the oven and pour it into a warm bowl." Angie blushed. And then Ree realized why. Quint stepped into the entryway.

"You must be Angie," he said, sticking out his hand. "My name is Quint."

"I, um." Angie cleared her throat before continuing. She shook his hand, and her cheeks turned several shades darker. "Saw you down at the gym today. Nice to meet you."

"Any friend of my wife's is always welcome," he said, seemingly unaware of the effect he had on the opposite sex. Or maybe he was just so used to it that it no longer registered.

A twinge of jealousy pinched in the center of Ree's chest.

"I'll put this on the counter," she said.

"Thanks," Angie said, following Ree as Quint took his spot in the kitchen.

"Did you get any studying in today?" Ree asked.

Before Angie could answer, there was another knock at the door. Ree excused herself, checked the peephole, and then froze. What was Nick Driver doing standing on the other side of the door when he should have called first or returned her text?

Ree took a step back so she'd be in Quint's view, and then shook her head. The face she made should hopefully clue him in to the fact that this scenario was about to go downhill quick.

"Hey, honey, I asked a neighbor to borrow a couple of eggs," Quint said, maintaining a straight face while in full view of Angie, who'd taken a seat across from him.

A shot of adrenaline caused Ree's heart to pound. She

cracked the door open and made a face that she hoped would tell Nick just how unwelcome he was at the moment.

The agent started to speak, but she shushed him, praying Angie couldn't hear. The young woman was a busybody. Quint started whistling, providing some background noise as cover.

"Thank you for the eggs," she said to the agent.

His eyebrows drew together before it seemed to dawn on him this wasn't a good time.

"Anytime," he said with a salute.

She mouthed the word *go.*

"Tell your husband to stop by when he has a chance," Nick said a little louder this time.

"Anything important I should pass along?" Ree asked.

"No. Just swinging by to say hello," the agent said with a scowl.

"Will do, then," Ree said before saying goodbye and closing the door. She could only hope Angie hadn't caught on to the fact nothing had been handed over and Nick had no idea about the eggs.

Angie rounded the corner after Ree fisted her hands and before she made the "handoff" to Quint. The wall should have blocked their real activity from her view. Quint opened and closed the fridge.

"Who was that?" Angie asked.

"This new guy I met at the gym. His name is…" Quint pretended to draw a blank, which was smart when Ree thought about it, because now it could be anyone in the building.

"Is he on seven?" Angie asked. "Because I know everyone on our floor and some from others."

Before Quint could respond, another knock interrupted them.

"I'll get it," Ree said. She turned around and checked

the peephole before opening the door again. "Lola, come on in. Angie just arrived as well."

Lola smiled as she entered the apartment. She had a laptop tucked under one arm and a bottle of wine in her free hand. She leaned in cheek to cheek and made a kissing noise as she greeted Ree warmly.

"I brought this for you and your husband." Lola held up the wine. "Welcome to the building and to Houstonian NightClub."

"You didn't have to bring us anything," Ree said, taking the bottle and stepping aside so Lola could greet Angie with the same warm acknowledgment.

"Please, it's nothing," Lola said with a small headshake. "A small gift."

Quint joined them, and another twinge of jealousy hit when Lola gave him the same treatment.

"I see you brought the offending piece of technology," Quint said.

Lola smiled. She seemed less affected by his looks, but she was probably hit on dozens of times a night by wealthy, good-looking men. Then there was Constantin, her boyfriend. A guy with the nickname Lights Out probably didn't like his girlfriend flirting with anyone else. She would have learned very quickly to hide any reactions she had to other men.

"Yes," she said. "I hope you can fix it. My boyfriend keeps telling me to buy a new one, but then it has to be set up again and I have all my pictures stored on this. I'm used to it and I know how it works."

"I'll give it a look and see what I can do," he said as she handed over the device.

"And I'll open this." Ree held up the bottle. "Four glasses?"

"I'm in," Angie said with a bounce.

Lola nodded.

"Honey?" Ree asked Quint. He moved to her and planted a tender kiss on her lips.

"If you're pouring, I'm drinking," he said with a wink. "Why don't you ladies take the living room and I'll work over here at the counter?"

Angie and Lola moved to the living room and took seats on the sofa while Ree located a corkscrew and then handed it and the bottle to Quint. She was fully capable of opening the bottle herself but had learned a long time ago the best way to get cooperation from others and disarm them was to show weakness in their presence.

Quint opened the bottle as Ree pulled out four glasses.

"Lucky us, they all match," she quipped, trying to shake off the heaviness of their earlier conversation and the near-miss of Nick showing up moments before Lola. As it was, Ree couldn't be 100 percent certain the two of them hadn't walked right past each other as she left the elevator and he got on. At least Lola hadn't seen him at Ree's door or questioned them about the agent.

Ree filled four glasses as Quint retrieved his laptop from the living room and set it next to Lola's on the counter.

"In case I need to look something up," he said.

"He's so good with those things," Ree said, setting a glass in front of him using the pass-through. She balanced two glasses in one arm and held the third in her free hand. Walking into the living room without spilling was a true testament to her ability to save every drop of a good wine.

"Password?" Quint asked over his shoulder. Lola shouted out something that sounded a lot like her birthday.

Ree sat on the plush rug opposite the bowl of treats and hoped Quint could get something from Lola's computer.

"This is great, thanks," Quint said to Lola. Shock struck like a stray bullet when her wallpaper filled the screen. A kid who was the spitting image of Lola and looked to be about two and a half to three years old was the background for a cluttered desktop.

First things first, Quint organized her desktop. He moved icons into a new folder he created and marked *Stuff*.

"I need to run a diagnostic tool," he said aloud, but he doubted anyone heard him over Angie's laughter and the buzz of conversation. Ree's opening the bottle of wine was a brilliant move. There was plenty of time for the drink to wear off before her shift, and it might loosen up Lola and Angie.

Quint grabbed the flash drive he'd set out in case he got the chance to use it and plugged it in. Thankfully, she didn't have an Apple product since they did away with regular USB ports a while ago, and that would have made this job a whole lot more difficult.

As he copied her hard drive, he poked around on her device. There wasn't much more than an endless number of pictures of her kid, and Constantin. The ones with Constantin only went back a year or so, giving Quint the impression the kid didn't belong to him. She seemed to mainly use her PC for surfing the web and shopping. She kept way too many tabs open, so he closed all of those. Her battery was low.

"I'm guessing the power cord is at your place," Quint said.

"Yes," Lola said, turning to look at him. "Do you need me to go get it?" She started to get up, but he waved her off.

"I have enough power to get by, but you should think about replacing the battery if you want to keep this laptop around. Keep it charged between ten and ninety percent for optimal life," he stated, figuring he needed to throw out a few facts for credibility's sake. He was also doing his best to distract himself from the fact that Nick had shown up after Ree called and left a message. It was exactly the kind of thing that could make a case go haywire, and he planned on having a few choice words with the DEA agent when the time was right. The incident was also going in Quint's report. Normally, he would cover for anyone and have a fellow agent's back. If this guy was as great as his file would have everyone believe, he should have known better than to pay a surprise visit.

When the files were finished copying over to the flash drive, Quint pulled it out and set it to the side.

"I noticed you have virus protection software installed," Quint said to Lola.

"Isn't that a good thing?" she asked.

"No. No." He shook his head. "It's the first place hackers look."

"I thought it was the opposite. It has a shield," she said.

"The software keeps a back door on your system for any experienced computer nerd to walk through. I'm removing it now," he said.

"Won't that leave the front door open?" she asked. Good analogy.

"I'll build a custom firewall," he said. "It'll be the best way to protect what's inside."

She nodded and said, "Ahhh, okay. That sounds much smarter."

Quint was finished uninstalling her so-called virus protection software and the firewall was up in less than fifteen minutes. "Normally, when a computer just shuts down by itself it's overheating, it has battery problems, the heat sink fan is being temperamental or there's a virus."

"It sounds like I've been holding the door open for a virus," she said. "Maybe that's what is happening?"

"It's possible. It might take a few minutes to check." He downloaded virus-scanning software before adding, "The most likely culprit for something like this would be bad RAM. It's swappable, but let's hope it's a battery issue. That's easier to replace."

"Do batteries just do this?" she asked, leaning in his direction.

"If the battery can't give consistent voltage due to it being old or having something like water damage, then the laptop will shut off," he informed.

"Water damage is possible. I sometimes have it open in the kitchen when I'm using it for a recipe," she said. "My kitchen is the same size as yours."

"That might explain it," he surmised. "I'll order a new battery and have it delivered to your place."

"I'm in nine-three, same as you. The only difference is the floor," she said with a proud smile. Looking at her now, he realized she reminded him of the famous actress Penélope Cruz. He would mention it to Ree later.

He ordered a new battery for Lola to be delivered to her place. The convenience of online ordering would provide her with a brand-new battery tomorrow. He had to give it to Houston, it had the online ordering and delivery operation down pat. He also thought about Constantin and his truck business. How easy would it be to slip trucks in and out of the city along with all the home deliveries going on? Pretty damn easy.

Glancing over at Lola, seeing her quiet strength, he wondered how she'd ended up in a relationship with someone like Constantin. Looks could be deceiving, Quint knew firsthand, and yet she didn't seem the type to be involved with the criminal element.

The round, angelic face beaming at him from the computer might explain why she worked at the bar. She could work nights while the kid slept. She must have someone to help with mornings considering the fact that she was at Pilates this morning. There was no kid in sight now. Did she have a live-in babysitter?

The computer dinged, indicating it was finished with the scan, as Quint took a sip of the wine. He checked the screen. There were two suspicious apps he could uninstall, and one he figured he should leave in. But how did he tell her someone had installed spyware on her laptop?

Chapter Eleven

Ree glanced over at Quint. From his profile, she could see that he'd found something he didn't like on Lola's computer.

"Who needs a refill?" Ree asked, draining her glass of wine. It gave her a good reason to get up.

"Yes, please," Angie said, hoisting her glass.

"I'll take one as well," Lola stated with a smile. She had a warmth to her that made it so difficult to believe she would be involved with criminals. It was a real shock to think she was in a relationship with someone like Constantin.

"I'll be right back." Ree set her glass down on the coffee table, figuring it would be best to bring the bottle to the conversation. Angie was a good conversationalist and kept Lola engaged while Ree retrieved the bottle from the kitchen. There was enough inside to cover three of them. Ree had only half filled the glasses earlier since it was before dinnertime and most people objected to a heavy first-round pour. Get one glass in them, and they usually lightened up on the refill.

Ree palmed the bottle, wishing she could ask Quint what was going on. He turned toward her when his back was to the others and shot a look that confirmed she saw what she thought she did. There'd been a discovery.

Heading back into the living room, she also saw the intensity in his eyes. She'd seen it for the first time in Cricket Creek during much of the investigation there. He'd finally started letting his guard down by the end of the investigation. Bringing another agency into the case caused a few more walls to come up between them.

"So, Lola, who was the hottie at the elevator today?" Angie finally asked. The younger woman's cheeks were a darker shade of pink, indicating she was probably a little tipsy.

"No one important." Lola shook off the comment. "Plus, where is your fireman today?"

"We have yet to meet him," Ree added. Lola shot a look that said she appreciated the distraction.

"At work," Angie said. "Y'all, the man is always at work." This was the most Southern Angie had been since they'd met. Ree cracked a smile at the slip. Apparently, a little afternoon wine brought out the South in Angie.

"Probably makes it easier to hide him from your parents," Ree pointed out.

"They would kill me if they knew," Angie said before taking another sip and smiling like a kid who'd just gotten away with eating the last cookie from the jar and no one knew who did it.

"Why not just sit them down and have a talk? You're…" Ree drew her eyebrows together. "How old did you say?"

"Twenty-two," Angie announced. "The problem is that they're paying for my apartment."

"What about Mr. Fireman?" Lola asked.

"He moved in with me because I refused to live with him. He was in a house with four other guys and the place smelled like stale beer and pizza," she said, wrinkling her nose.

"Do you really want to spend the rest of your life with a slob?" Lola asked with a look of sheer disgust.

It made Ree laugh.

"Sorry," she said to Lola, "but your face just cracked me up."

"Y'all, my guy is clean. It's half the reason he was ready to move out, but he's still in a lease until the end of October, so he pays for the other place and we live here," Angie said. "It bothers him to no end that my family doesn't know he lives here. He's been threatening to tell them the next time he sees them. Says we're living a lie."

"He sounds like a really stand-up guy to me," Ree said with compassion and a whole new respect for the fireman.

"If you don't hurry up and marry that guy, I will," Lola teased. A ringtone sounded and she immediately reached into her handbag. "Excuse me." She practically jumped up as she pulled out her cell. After checking the screen, she immediately moved toward the door.

"Hello," she answered as she headed into the hallway. The rest of the conversation was out of earshot.

Angie locked gazes with Ree and made a face. Ree shrugged.

"She sure hightailed it out of here quick," Angie said.

"I hope everything's okay," Ree commented. She checked the clock before polishing off her glass of wine. "I have to be at work in an hour and a half."

"At your new job?" Angie's lips compressed like she was struggling to hold back a laugh.

"I know. It's probably bad form, but I'll just eat some more of this amazing trail mix to soak up the alcohol and I'll be fine." Ree shifted the lighthearted conversation with Angie.

A minute later, Lola came back inside. Her shoulders

were rounded, and it looked like someone had deflated the air in her chest. All confidence was gone.

"Everything okay?" Ree asked as she and Angie turned their attention to Lola.

She held up her phone and apologized. "I forgot about a meeting that I have with a friend. It's stupid of me."

"I'll have your laptop ready in a few seconds," Quint said. He turned to look at her when she didn't immediately respond. "Is that okay? Because I can stop the scanning process right now and hand it over if you need to go."

"Five minutes is probably enough time, right?" she asked.

"I can make that work," he said. "It's just doing its thing right now, searching for any additional problems." He hesitated like he was engaged in an internal debate. Then he leaned toward Lola and quietly said, "There is something I should probably show you on here."

"Oh?" Her voice rose a couple of octaves, and she seemed to realize this wasn't going to be good news.

"See this." He pointed to the screen, but Ree couldn't see what he was referring to from her spot on the living room floor.

She tucked her feet underneath her bottom and grabbed another handful of the snack. "This is so amazing. What all is in here?"

Angie had been staring at Lola. The younger woman cleared her throat and started listing off the ingredients. While she did, she stared at the bowl.

"This is called spyware," Quint explained so low Ree had to strain to hear him.

"What's that exactly?" Lola asked, sounding a little put off.

"It's probably what you think it is. It's a way for someone to access your computer remotely," he explained quietly.

"Like, they don't have to be in the room?" she asked.

"They don't even have to be in the building," he stated. "This program will allow the person on the other end to read your emails and see what websites you're on."

Lola exhaled a slow breath.

"Thank you for telling me," she said.

"I didn't touch it. Whoever installed this would know if I blocked access," he said.

"I see." Lola's shoulders straightened and her back was now ramrod straight. Chin up, she said, "I appreciate knowing what is happening."

"I just thought you should be aware," he said with a whole lot of compassion and sympathy.

She nodded, and even from the adjacent room it was easy to see she was trying to hold back tears.

"And pretzels," Angie said proudly.

"Without them, it wouldn't be this addictive." Ree rejoined the conversation. Was Lola really so naive that she didn't think her criminal boyfriend would keep tabs on her? Based on her reaction to the news, the answer was yes. Was it possible Lola had no idea Constantin was a criminal?

More questions joined those when Ree saw the sweet, angelic face fill the screen as Quint closed down the program scanning for more viruses. Turned out, the real cancer was Constantin. In Lola's life? On Lola's computer? On society.

Worse yet, was he the father of her child?

"I better go. Thank you for everything," Lola said to Quint.

He'd debated keeping the information to himself, but her reaction told him a whole lot about the state of her relationship with Constantin. He closed out the window running the scan when it was finished, and then handed over her laptop. "You have a beautiful kid there."

"Thank you," Lola said with a smile that would warm the room in a freeze. "Lili is my life."

There was something about the way she said those last few words mixed with the wistful look on her face that made him realize she would do anything for that kid. Possibly even stay in a relationship that was no good for her.

Angie said her goodbyes as she followed Lola out the door after Quint handed over the laptop. Lola thanked him more times than necessary for his help. She turned to Ree.

"I'll see you later tonight," Lola said.

"See you soon," Ree stated.

Ree cleaned up the dishes in the living room before setting the half-empty trail mix bowl in front of him. Neither spoke until they heard Angie's door close and the elevator ding.

"I'm just going to check," Ree whispered as she walked over to the peephole. Her silence had him curious as to what was going down in the hall. It took a solid minute for the elevator to ding again, and then Ree came around the corner. "She stood in front of our door like she was contemplating knocking."

"I wasn't sure if it was a good idea to tell her about the spyware or not," he admitted. "She might have wanted to come back to ask questions."

"She needed to know," she said. "But I did see how shocked she was when you told her."

"It was the last thing she expected to hear," he agreed.

"Do you think it's possible she doesn't know what line of work Constantin is in?" Ree took the seat next to him. She seemed careful to keep her leg to her side, ensuring there was no incidental physical contact.

"It's hard to say," he stated.

"Maybe she'll start questioning her relationships more," Ree surmised.

He nodded as he inserted the flash drive into his laptop. "We got lucky that she doesn't have a MacBook."

"I'm guilty of the same thing," Ree said. Her expression was all business now when it came to him. It was probably for the best this way. Keep everything professional and not blur the lines, because it was quicksand—easy to step into and impossible to get out.

He pulled up the picture of Lola's child. "What do you think the chances are Constantin is this kid's father?"

"How old would you say this kid is?" Ree asked, studying the photo.

"Two and a half to three years," he said.

"Okay," she said, nodding. "Lola has only been in the country for two years. A pregnancy lasts nine months, so that means she would have known the guy three to four years ago when she was still in Argentina."

"Constantin is Romanian, so the odds he would have been in Argentina seem slim," Quint reasoned. "I'll send Grappell another email to ask how far back our intel goes to see if there's a chance he was in South America. He did just send an address for a warehouse not too far from here associated with the company All Transport. Said we might want to check it out."

"Okay. Duly noted." Something else caused her stance to shift, soften.

"I know we're supposed to follow the facts and not let personal beliefs or intuition cloud our judgment, but I really don't want Lola to be like one of those jerks."

"There's a quality to her that makes it feel impossible to me, too," he said.

"It would be hard to fool both of us," she reasoned.

"All we can do is keep ourselves open to both possibilities," he finally said.

"Agreed," she said before glancing at the time. "Holy hell, I have to get ready for work."

"While you do that, I'll see what I can find on the flash drive," he said.

"You didn't install spyware on her system, did you?" Ree asked as she stood up and then pushed the chair in.

"No. Whoever installed the spyware in the first place knows enough about computers to make it dangerous for me to take that route. I just copied everything," he said.

"Right. That's smart," she said.

"Thank you," he responded, figuring he'd take all the compliments he could get at this point. As it was, he felt like a jerk for his reactions earlier. There was no reason to take out his frustration about working with another agency on Ree.

He needed to remind himself of the fact every chance he got, because he'd picked up on the distrust in her eyes since the phone call with Bjorn.

Quint clicked on the mail icon. It was password-protected. He figured Lola would use the same one as before, the one that unlocked her computer and felt like a birthday. He tapped his fingers on the counter as he tried to recall the numbers. They came to him after a few seconds. He entered the numbers *0424*.

The mail opened and filled his screen. Could he get the answers they sought there?

Chapter Twelve

Ree applied light makeup and fixed her auburn hair, slicking it to one side in a low side pony. Her uniform would be waiting at work, so she dressed in her interview outfit from the Cricket Creek job that was still packed in her overnight bag. She'd washed it and then thrown it back inside the bag with the rest of her clothes from the trip. The suitcase had never made it back into the closet, and the clothes never made it back into drawers. Turned out to be handy when this case popped up out of nowhere.

Not exactly out of nowhere. She'd half expected a call at some point asking if she'd like to join Quint. What she hadn't anticipated was him showing up at her mother's door. That had taken guts. It had shown his determination to work with her again on this case since he was willing to put himself in a situation where he wouldn't be welcomed.

She buttoned her white blouse, thinking the high but fashionable collar might be a mistake in this heat. She'd try not to end up soaked with sweat before she walked inside the bar. The high-waisted forest green pants fit well enough to show off the long legs she'd worked hard to tone at the gym. The cuffs struck just above her ankles, and black spiked heels added a couple of inches to her decent height. No one would accuse her of towering over anyone, but with good heels she could almost look someone who was six feet tall square in the eyes.

"Ready or not, here I come," she said as she joined Quint at the counter. He was in the exact spot where she last saw him, studying the screen.

He leaned back and turned to look at her. His eyes widened when he said, "Damn."

"What?" She could feel the red blush crawling up her neck again at the way he looked at her with appreciation in his eyes.

"You look beautiful" was all he said.

"This is the same outfit I wore at the cabin that first day," she reminded him.

"Then I was a jerk for not saying it when we first met," he said.

"I think you were busy defending yourself from the demands I was placing on you," she said with a half smile. She'd gone in like gangbusters on that first day.

Quint smirked. "Standing up for yourself is sexy."

Well, now Ree really didn't know what to say.

"I have to go. Did you find anything on there?" She motioned toward his laptop, needing to change the subject. His compliment didn't change the fact that a wall had come up between them or the challenges they faced working with the other agents.

"She's squeaky-clean so far," he said. "But then, most criminals are good about hiding their activities."

Quint closed the laptop and stood up. "I did get her daughter's birthday, though. April twenty-fourth."

"That helps," Ree said. "Ready?"

"Always," he said.

"Will you be coming in for a drink later?" she asked as they walked toward the door.

"I'll skip it tonight since it's your first shift," he said.

"Okay." She hid her disappointment. "I'll text you when I know what time I should be done."

Quint opened the door, and then held it for her as she walked past. She thanked him as she headed toward the elevator bank. There was something nice about chivalry not being dead. She pushed the elevator button and led the way toward HNC. The heat practically melted her, but at least her hair was off her neck. The collar turned out to be a bad idea even though Quint reassured her that she still looked beautiful as he turned her in at the door.

For show, he kissed her until her toes curled. A growing part of her wished those kisses meant something besides work. The logical side of her brain kicked in, reminding her that office romances had about as much of a chance of working out as spring flowers did of budding in December.

"See you back here when your shift is over," he said, leaning his forehead against hers like he needed a minute to gather his thoughts after the kiss. A self-satisfied smirk upturned the corners of her lips. Thank the heavens she wasn't the only one affected every time their lips touched.

"You two should be more careful or your agency might think something is really going on between you." Nick Driver's voice cut into the moment and his tone struck a nerve.

Quint pulled back and they both glanced around to make certain no one else heard the snide comment. Ree half expected Quint to speak up, but his jaw muscle clenched instead.

"Uncool," Quint said low and under his breath. Nick kept walking, unfazed.

"Later it is," she said to Quint, trying to pull his attention back to her before turning and walking in the door. She glanced back in time to see him standing there, arms folded.

Ree checked in with the shift manager, Julian, before getting her locker assignment and uniform. She changed in the back room and tucked her clothes and purse into the locker before securing it closed. The lock had one of those dials on it like a safe. She memorized her combination but was reassured the shift manager had a master key in the event Ree blanked out on what she'd been told.

Randy, the owner, had arranged for Ree to be Lola's barback. She walked over to the bar where Lola was bent down and arranging something on a shelf behind the bar. Ree brought over a tray of clean glasses and cleared her throat on the approach so as not to surprise Lola.

"I'm not ready," Lola said, her voice cracked.

"Okay, I'll come back," Ree said, turning with the heavy tray hoisted on her shoulder.

"Ree?" Lola glanced over but didn't stand up. Her eyes were red and puffy, and it looked like she'd been crying. She squatted down and grabbed a roll of paper towels, pulling off one and blotting her eyes with it. "Don't leave. I didn't realize it was you."

"I can give you a few minutes," Ree said, hating that Lola was upset but secretly hoping this might be the in Ree needed to get the bartender to open up about her personal life. It was good for the investigation, but Ree also wanted to know if she could still trust her own instincts.

"No. No. Don't be silly. That tray must weigh a hundred pounds." Lola waved Ree in.

Ree set the tray down on the countertop. It was filled with highball glasses, and the tray of expensive crystal probably cost more than a month of Ree's salary. "Where do these go?"

"Right here." Lola pointed toward a shelf just under the lip of the bar and within easy reach.

"Are you okay?" Ree asked, scooting the tray down as she moved closer to Lola.

"Yes, but please don't let Julian see me like this," Lola pleaded, blotting her eyes again. "He doesn't like anyone to bring drama to work."

"Okay." Ree was almost finished putting away the last of the glasses when Julian turned and headed toward them. She smiled and said out of the side of her mouth, "He's coming over here."

"That's no good. He'll fire me, and I need this job." Lola said a couple of words in Spanish that Ree was pretty certain most sailors would understand.

"Julian, I have a question about something in my locker." Ree artfully moved herself out from behind the bar and toward the back room. All she could do was buy Lola a little more time to pull herself together.

Julian took the bait, looking like he genuinely wanted to help. Of course, it probably didn't hurt matters that Randy had personally hired her. Julian had to know he was out of his league with her. The fact that he seemed eager to help when he scowled at quite a few of the other employees told her that he treated Randy hires more nicely.

"I really couldn't figure out if I'd closed and locked this correctly," she said, feigning helplessness while stuffing down the frustration that she hadn't been able to come up with anything better off the top of her head and on short notice.

Julian tried the metal handle that shifted up like her old high school locker. The one she never used because she went to a large high school that had A/B days, rendering the locker useless.

"It didn't open, so looks like you're good," he said with what looked like a forced smile.

"Good. Thank you," she said, figuring she needed to

come up with another question or two in order to stall him. "How many people will we have on the floor tonight?"

"It's Monday, so we can expect half the crowd we normally get. I scale down the number of employees accordingly so we don't waste money," Julian said. He seemed especially proud of his answer as his chest puffed out just a little bit when he spoke. It signaled that he took pride in his work, which was always a good thing. How would he react if he knew the girlfriend of one of the biggest area weapons runners worked behind his bar?

Would he care as long as she showed up for work and kept customers happy?

"That's really smart," she said, trying to play up to his ego.

It worked. He practically beamed. He also probably figured she'd be reporting back to Randy.

"Do I get another uniform or should I plan on washing this one every night?" she asked.

"You'll get two," he said.

"Okay, great." An heir and a spare, she thought.

"Your size is popular, so the reason you have only one is because the other is on back order," he said. "Let me know if you need a day off in between shifts in order to have time to do a wash."

"I can take care of that easily," she said before shifting her weight to one side. "I just want to say that I can't thank you enough for this job. It means a lot to my family."

Julian swatted empty air.

"You'll be an asset to the company," he said.

She highly doubted most barbacks were treated this well.

"As soon as an opening for waitress comes up, I want you to know I'll be looking to you to possibly fill it," he said. Now he really was laying it on thick.

"I don't want to skip the line if someone else deserves it," she quickly said.

"No trouble at all. It'll go to the person best suited for the job," he explained as someone yelled his name. He spun around. "I better go see what that's about."

"Of course," she said, hoping she'd bought Lola enough time to dry her eyes and throw on a little makeup to cover the redness. She returned to her station to find Lola on her feet, wiping down the bar and whistling as she worked. If Ree didn't know better, she would have no idea that Lola had been crouching behind the bar crying ten minutes ago.

"Thank you," Lola said as Ree took her place, finishing putting away the last of the glasses.

"Anytime," Ree said, and really meant it.

QUINT'S SPANISH WAS a little too rusty to decipher all of Lola's emails, so he uploaded the contents of her hard drive to the case file on the database. There were linguistic specialists who could take it from there. Using Google's translator, he was able to get the gist of anything that drew his eye. So far, Lola came out clean. There was also a computer specialist who would dissect everything else. It had taken Quint the better part of the night, but Ree's text that the bar was about to close came just before midnight. She'd said it would take only fifteen minutes to finish breaking down since the night had been slow and everyone had pitched in to make closing go as smoothly as possible.

Nick Driver was still on Quint's mind. He needed to be made aware of just how uncool the stunt he'd pulled was and how little a repeat would be tolerated. At the very least, it was unprofessional not to respond to Ree's text and then show up at the door. Then there was the snide comment in front of the bar. Quint's hands were tied on how to get the message across. He couldn't confront the guy or shoot a note to Bjorn to complain. She was already on high alert when it came to Quint working in cooperation with another agency.

Quint would sit on it for a while and see if any ideas turned up. He also didn't want to undermine Ree, who had agreed to be the go-between. By the time he exited his building and made the walk to HNC, Ree was standing out front with Lola.

"Hi, honey," Ree said, walking over to him and rising up to give him a kiss. He dipped his head and met her halfway. The kiss caused his pulse to skyrocket. It was strange, because he was usually used to kissing a fellow agent by the time they worked together on a second assignment. This shouldn't be any different. Driver's earlier comment sat heavy on Quint.

"Hey," he said, hearing the gravelly quality to his own voice. At least his reaction to her made the whole newlywed cover seem far more credible. He would leave it at that.

"We started to head home but decided to wait for you here in case you came from a different direction," Ree said. She glanced over at Lola. "Thank you for sticking around with me."

"No problem," Lola said, checking her phone. "It's what we do for each other, right?"

Ree's smile could light a city block during a blackout.

A Lamborghini roared up on the road next to them. Lola caught Ree's gaze. "Looks like my ride finally showed."

"See you tomorrow?" Ree asked.

"Tuesday's my night off," Lola said, rushing toward the vehicle like her life depended on it. She climbed in the passenger seat and shot a quick smile at Ree, who waved.

"I'm worried about her," Ree said as Quint linked their fingers. There was something right about holding Ree's hand. It made him feel like his demons might stay at bay for a while.

"How was your first night?" He needed to redirect the conversation to something a newlywed would ask as he turned them toward their building and started the walk back.

"It was good. I didn't make a lot of money, but it wasn't busy. Lola trained me throughout the night and we fell into a good rhythm. Julian sent most everyone home early. He let me stay since I'm new," she said.

"Makes sense," he said as they fell in step together.

"Everything was wiped down half an hour before closing," she said, leaning into him. The move was for show, but a small piece of him hoped it meant she'd forgiven him for how he'd acted toward her after the call with Bjorn.

"Sounds like it was a good way to get your feet wet before the weekend crowd hits," he said.

"That's why I don't get a day off this week," she said. "Julian thinks I'll be better off learning over the next few days before business picks up."

"I can't imagine what a Friday or Saturday night looks like when Sunday was as crowded as it was," he said as they reached the building.

"Apparently, the crowds start on Thursdays," she said.

"Doesn't anybody have to wake up early the next morning for work?" he mused.

"I guess not," she said as they entered the glass elevators. Almost the minute she stepped inside the apartment, the shoes came off. She kicked them beside the door with a groan. "Heels are definitely harder on the feet than boots."

"How do you wear those all night?" he asked.

"Practice, but that doesn't mean it feels good," she said, heading over to the sofa and plopping down in her work clothes. Her gaze flew to the boxes stacked neatly on the opposite side of the sofa. "My order came?"

"As promised," he said.

"I'm way too tired to open those boxes tonight. It'll give me something to do first thing in the morning," she said.

"Do you want Coke or something stronger?" he asked.

"Stronger," she said. "Definitely stronger."

Quint poured her a glass of wine and opened a beer for himself. One drink wouldn't hurt either one of them and after learning the DEA was on the case, Quint could use something to help him relax. He almost laughed out loud at the thought. A twelve-pack wouldn't make a dent in how frustrated and stressed he was and had been all day. Having a drink with Ree was the best part of his night so far.

Chapter Thirteen

"When I got to work, Lola was behind the bar crying," Ree informed Quint as she took the glass of wine from him. Their fingers brushed, and she was comforted by the familiar jolt of electricity.

"Did she say why?" he asked as the sofa dipped underneath his weight.

She tucked her feet underneath her bottom as she turned toward him. "She told me that she got in a fight with Lili's father."

"Mystery Guy?" he asked.

"He now has a name, too," she confirmed with a nod. "Matias Gimenez."

"Does he live here in the States?" he asked.

"He followed her and is demanding custody of Lili," Ree said.

"That wouldn't fly over here, but it could happen in Argentina," Quint stated. And then it seemed to dawn on him. "That's the reason she came here two years ago, isn't it?"

"We didn't get that far in our conversation with Julian around, but that's my guess as well," she confirmed.

"I need to send Grappell the name and get a background check on Gimenez," Quint said before retrieving his laptop. He sent the note while she enjoyed the click-click-clack of the keyboard and the wine.

"There," he said before closing the laptop.

"Lola seems like a decent person. I'm not sure why she would let herself get mixed up with someone like Constantin. Matias doesn't exactly give me good vibes, either," she said.

"Women are attracted to powerful men. It's biology," he said.

"I'd like to think we've evolved from the caveman days," she said with a grunt of disapproval.

"No doubt we have. But biology takes a while to catch up," he said before taking a sip of beer. "What about Nick Driver?" Quint's jaw muscle ticked when he mentioned the DEA agent's name.

"No one mentioned him and, after our exchange, I didn't ask about him," she said. "He's supposed to work in the office, so I'm guessing that means only during the day." She drew her eyebrows together and frowned. "Right?"

"I believe so, unless there's an event at night. You'll have to attempt contact again if you want to find out. Hopefully, he'll start to upload his notes to the file we are supposed to make important case notes in," he said. "So far, it's empty in there."

"I'm not giving him my information on Lola," she argued.

"No one in this room would ask you to," Quint said without hesitation. His response came so fast she didn't have a ready comeback. "Meetings with him are too risky with a nosy neighbor and these paper-thin walls."

"I agree." Ree sent a text to Driver, asking if he found out anything he'd like to share, and waited for a response. None came.

"Should I be surprised by this at this point?" she asked, holding up the cell.

"Probably not, but we have to keep trying if only to appease Bjorn," Quint stated. "I'm not sure where she got her intel about him, but he doesn't strike me as cooperative so far."

"What about the laptop?" she asked after agreeing.

"I didn't find anything we can use. She seems on the straight and narrow," he said.

"Which makes even less sense why she would get herself involved with Constantin," she repeated. "I sound like a broken record, don't I?"

"You're just reasoning through it. I agree with you, by the way," he said. "Especially after peeking into her laptop. It was nothing but check-ins with her mother from what Google Translate could tell. I really should have paid more attention in high school Spanish class."

"Same." Ree broke into a smile. "I did find out why Matias was at the taco place last night. Lola asked him to stop by there on his way to the bar and bring her a couple of number twos. She said her boyfriend hadn't left the bar yet and she didn't want a scene. The delay tactic almost didn't work since he bolted."

"Constantin knows Matias is in town?" Quint asked.

"It surprised me, too, but Lola's worlds were colliding so she asked Constantin to give her a chance to work things out with Matias about Lili," Ree said.

"Did she say how long Matias has been in town?" Quint asked.

Ree shook her head. And then it dawned on her why he would ask in the first place. "That's the reason Constantin installed spyware on her computer, isn't it?"

"Jealousy can make a man do stupid things," Quint said. "Someone like Constantin wouldn't know what it is to trust another person's word."

Ree nodded agreement there. Boundaries and trust weren't exactly in the vernacular of most criminals. Those who'd made it to the top built their empires on power, greed and fear, using fear to breed loyalty.

"You already heard Lola is off tomorrow," Ree said.

"Are you guys planning to meet up for Pilates class in the morning?" he asked.

"No. I don't want to seem too eager to hang out," she said. "Angie has been great for forging a relationship with Lola. But classes every morning might make me seem too available. Plus, I need to personalize the apartment if we're going to have guests over again."

"And we are newlyweds. We wouldn't want to be away from each other too often," he pointed out.

"Exactly," she said as she looked around. "I have to say, we've moved up compared to the cabin."

"I would agree with you there," he said.

"Which also reminds me of Zoey," she said. "I wonder how she's doing in Austin."

"Better than she was in Cricket Creek, no doubt," he said. "I can ask Grappell to check up on her while we're undercover if it would make you feel better."

"That would be great," she said.

"He can check on your grandfather as well," he continued.

"If he digs around in my personal life, he might not be well received," she reasoned. "As much as I want to confirm my grandfather is fine, I have to trust someone would have gotten word to me if anything had happened."

She also didn't need the distraction of thinking of home while on a case. Why the same logic didn't apply to Zoey was a puzzle, but it didn't, and Ree wanted to know how the young woman from their last case was doing. Ree had convinced the eighteen-year-old to go to a battered women's shelter when her no-good boyfriend was arrested. Zoey was a sweet young woman who needed a hand up to thrive. At least, Ree prayed Zoey hadn't checked herself out and gotten into trouble again. She really was a good person who'd landed in a bad situation.

Ree thought about the puppy she'd planned to foster to give Zoey something to look forward to when she was able to stand on her own two feet again.

"Everything okay?" Quint asked. She looked up at him only to realize he'd been studying her.

"Yes," she responded, shaking off her reaction to his concern. "Of course. It's just thinking about a sweet young person being manipulated by a boyfriend, or anyone for that matter, makes me sad."

"Thanks to you, Zoey is getting the help she needs," Quint said, and there was so much compassion in his voice.

She blinked a few times trying to stem hot tears that were threatening to flow, and focused on the rim of her wineglass.

"You should be smiling and celebrating," he said comfortingly, bringing his hand up to her chin before lifting it until her eyes met his. "Without you, that young woman would be out on the streets right now. I doubt she would have listened to reason. The fact that you cared about her showed her there are good people in the world who want the best for her. I seriously doubt she's ever experienced that kind of unconditional care in her life."

If she didn't want to cry before, she really had to work not to now. "Thank you, Quint. Thank you for saying those sweet words. They mean more to me than you could possibly know."

This time, she leaned forward and kissed him. Not for show. Not to sell the cover story. Not to convince someone the two of them were in love. But because she wanted to.

QUINT PULLED BACK from the kiss first, pressing his forehead to Ree's, thinking how easy it would be to get caught up in the moment, lost in her, and then what? Ruin a great working relationship? There hadn't been anyone since Tessa he wanted to be alone in a room with, let alone trusted enough to work beside.

His feelings for Ree were inconvenient. And they had to stop. She was emotional, seeking comfort. That was the only reason for the kiss. Period. His heart tried to mount a defense, but he couldn't lead with something he didn't trust. His heart had kept him from pushing Tessa to tell Bjorn about the pregnancy. Tessa had done such a great job of pleading and convincing him to go against his better judgment.

"It's her, isn't it?" Ree asked quietly. "You're thinking about her right now, aren't you?"

"How could you tell?" He truly wanted to know. He'd been a master at hiding his true feelings and making everyone believe he was all right. Not much got past Ree. She seemed to catch on every time he fell into the sinkhole that was thinking about Tessa and her baby.

"The way you get quiet. It's like someone sucked all the air from the room and you have to slow down so you can breathe again," she said. "Are you sure the two of you never dated?"

The question was the equivalent of a knife in the chest. It took a long moment for him to catch his breath and respond.

"If we had, I would have told you up front," he said, and he could hear the coldness creeping into his own voice. "I barely knew you before and had no reason to lie."

"It's just that you get so intense when you're thinking about her," she said quietly. "It stands to reason that your feelings might have gone deeper than you are willing to admit."

He shook his head.

"I know exactly where I stand on my and Tessa's friendship. We couldn't have been closer if we'd been blood related. Others in the department couldn't believe we weren't a couple, but I thought maybe you knew me a little better than that by now," he said, stopping before he blurted out what he really wanted to tell Ree. The truth was that he never felt toward Tessa the way he felt every time he was around Ree. How was that for messed up?

Ree pulled away from him and took a sip of her wine. The air was cold where she'd been a few seconds ago. He followed her lead and took a swig of beer, sitting back, rubbing the scruff on his chin.

"We need to come up with a plan to meet Constantin," he said, redirecting the conversation. They'd talked about him enough for one night. He knew where this was coming from. The past had been dredged up ever since the phone call with Bjorn. Hell, he'd been dealing with his frustration all day as a result.

Ree was observant, insightful. She would have read him earlier and known exactly why he hated the idea of cooperating with another agency. She deserved a lot of credit for not calling him out on it or requesting he remove himself from the case.

"I have an idea about that," Ree said. "But I'm guessing Lola will be in Galveston tomorrow with him, and I'll be at work tomorrow night. Plus, she's met both of us, so if we turn up in Galveston unexpectedly it'll raise a red flag."

"Not a good idea, especially this early in the case," he said.

"Which is why I think we should set the alarm, grab a couple hours of sleep and check up on his warehouse operation. It would probably be best to follow up under the cover of night when it's too dark to recognize anyone," she said.

"True, but you have to get through a shift tomorrow night. Won't that be hard to do without enough sleep?" He didn't want to be the one to push her past a breaking point. As for Quint, he could get by on forty-five-minute naps throughout the day just fine. Most people weren't in the same boat.

"Since I'm not going downstairs to work out in the morning, I can sleep in," she said. "Didn't Agent Grappell give us an address nearby for the warehouse?"

"It's not too far, on the outskirts of the south side of the city," he said. "I can show you on the map if you'd like." He'd already mapped out the route from the docks in Galveston to the warehouses.

"I'll see it for myself in a few short hours." She shook her head. "I should probably get ready for bed and try to grab as much sleep as possible before we head out."

"What time should I set the alarm for?" he asked.

"How about four a.m.? That should give me time to brush my teeth and throw on a jogging suit," she said.

"Just shy of three hours away," he said, taking a sip of beer and settling into the sofa.

"This should help." Ree pushed up to standing and then drained her glass. She returned it to the kitchen before disappearing into the bathroom.

Quint grabbed the laptop and pulled up Google Maps. He plotted the most direct course to the warehouse. There would be no weapons out in the open. Constantin was smarter than that. The legitimate shipping business had to operate as a front for his criminal activity. Who would really notice if a shipment disappeared off the books every once in a while? In a big shipping operation like this one, paperwork could "disappear," giving Constantin the opportunity to load up the occasional semi. A vehicle that large could carry an unimaginable amount of firepower. A shipment every few weeks or months could slip under the radar. The other possibility, of course, was breaking up a large shipment of weapons into smaller ones and loading them onto multiple trucks either with a false bottom or using a cargo net to hold cases underneath the trailer. In these cases, the required pit stops to check weight might be just a little off the manifest. Since scales weren't exact, a lot of illegal cargo and drugs made it across the US border using this method.

While he was online, he checked the case file to see if Driver had uploaded a report. There was nothing. So far, all he and Ree had been told about the other team was they were DEA, which meant drugs were involved. A shipping operation could move drugs in the ways Quint had already considered. The twist with narcotics of any kind was finding a way to throw off drug-sniffing dogs, difficult but not impossible. Getting away with illegal activity meant always staying one step ahead of law enforcement.

There were two facts that when put together didn't give the impression Driver was going to play fair on this case. First, the unannounced visit that could have put the whole investigation in jeopardy. Second, the lack of an update.

Quint's hands involuntarily fisted. He took in a couple of deep breaths in an attempt to calm down. As it was, he had an urge to find Driver and tell him what he thought about his secrecy and sterling record.

Driver wasn't the only reason Quint was frustrated tonight. He'd blown an opportunity to tell Ree how he really felt about her, to let her know how special she was to him. Little did she realize his friendship with Tessa was no threat to how he felt about Ree. He and Tessa had been more brother and sister than anything else, and that was exactly how they'd kept it. The kicker with Tessa came in the form of not being able to protect her, and in not being able to keep her baby safe.

Both *should* be alive. Tessa had been due last month. Tessa had been afraid she wouldn't get the "mom" gene. She'd feared the baby would grow up and hate her. Quint had calmly reassured Tessa none of those fears were going to come to fruition because she had him to help keep her on track as a parent. She wasn't alone in this. And the fact that she was this concerned before the baby was even born meant she was most likely going to be an amazing parent.

As far as Ree was concerned, he also realized anything beyond a working relationship would be out of the question. The quickest way to kill a good partnership was to date.

No matter how strong his feelings were or how much they seemed to grow as he got to know her, it was probably for the best for him to leave the topic alone. Muddying the waters in their work relationship was the surest way to lose her. He couldn't take another hit like that.

"Your turn," Ree said as she exited the bathroom.

"I'm good," he responded.

"Okay, you'll wake me up in a couple of hours, then?" She stood at the doorway to the bathroom, looking like she was resisting the urge to speak up about whatever was on her mind. The way she looked at him convinced him the questionable subject was him.

"With a bucket of ice water," he said, smiling, trying to break up some of the sudden tension in the room.

"This seems like a good time to remind you that I sleep with my gun next to the bed," she teased back.

"Gentle shaking it is," he reassured. "And make sure the safety is on on that weapon."

"Always," she shot back before crossing over to the bed.

He refocused on the screen, ignoring the urge to join her.

Chapter Fourteen

Quint's whiskey-over-ice voice drew Ree out of a deep sleep.

"Time to wake up," he repeated quietly. There was nothing quiet about the reaction her body was having to him
standing so close, whispering next to her.

She blinked her eyes open to a dimly lit room that cast
shadows over his carved-from-granite jawline. The day-old
stubble on his chin gave him an even more rugged look.
Sexier. Ree sat straight up, pulling the covers to her chin.

"I'm good," she said, needing to put a little space between her and his unique spicy male scent. As she breathed
in, he filled her senses. Her pulse kicked up a couple of
notches, making caffeine a little less necessary. Turned
out, all she needed was Quint standing next to her to wake
her up.

"Coffee?" he asked.

"Are you actually an angel?" she teased, needing to
redirect her thoughts to something lighter and less sexy
than Quint Casey.

"On it," he said, walking away with a knowing smile.

Ree took in a deep breath and threw the covers off. She
headed straight for the bathroom and splashed cold water
on her face. After brushing her teeth, she pulled her hair
off her face in a ponytail and dressed in an all-black jogging suit that should help her blend into the darkness.

She joined Quint in the kitchen.

"Here you go," he said, handing over a fresh brew.

"You are definitely an angel," she said with a smile.

"No one has ever accused me of being that before," he lobbed back. It was nice to see him in a lighter mood. After the phone call with Bjorn yesterday she was more than a little concerned he'd gone to a dark place that he wouldn't be able to return from.

She wiggled her eyebrows and took a sip of coffee after blowing on it. "How do you make the perfect pot every time?"

"I'd tell you, but I'd have to kill you." This time, he pretended to cut his own throat with his finger as a knife, and what should have looked corny turned out sexy instead. "Ready?"

"As much as I'll ever be," she said in response, noticing that he'd changed into a black T-shirt and jeans. Even his running shoes were a dark gray that would easily disappear in the darkness.

She secured her weapon in her bellyband holster and made sure her zip-up covered it. There shouldn't be any activity in the building at this late or early hour—depending on how one looked at it.

Quint opened the door for her, then followed her to the elevator. They made it down to the truck without running into a soul, as expected. The drive to the warehouse district took roughly forty minutes. The roads were narrow two-lane jobs. The streetlamps were few and far between. There was an abundance of fields on both sides of the road and weeds tall enough to touch Ree's backside if she got out of the truck here.

Remote locations were always eerie. There were generally only a couple of ways in or out. The moon was full, though, and that provided extra lighting. It was gorgeous, too.

"Everything okay over there?" Quint finally broke the silence.

"Ever just sit outside and look at the moon?" she asked, thinking it was probably an odd question for a person like Quint. He didn't strike her as the type to sit outside and marvel at nature.

"Would it surprise you to know that I have?" he asked.

"As a matter of fact, yes," she admitted.

"Why is that?" he continued.

"I just don't see you sitting around a campfire while looking up at the stars," she said.

"Not at my age, no," he said. "When my mother died, I was so angry that I didn't know what to do with myself or all that pent-up frustration. I took off running and didn't stop until my chest felt like it might burst. I realized I'd stopped at this huge lake. Eyes wet, chest heaving, I dropped down and lay on my back next to the water. When I looked up, the cloudless sky was an incredible shade of deep blue. There were so many stars it would take five lifetimes to count them all. The sky was like a crystal canopy over the earth. The full moon dialed up the brilliance. Ever since then, I make sure to get outside once a week and look up at the sky. Full moons like this one are my favorites."

"That's a beautiful story, Quint." Ree was without words as to how much it meant to her that he'd shared it.

"Let's hope the full moon tonight is our good-luck charm." He pulled the truck into the first lot.

"Where is All Transport?" she asked, looking at warehouses and lots that extended as far as the eye could see. There was very little lighting in each parking lot.

"Halfway down, there should be a street. All Transport

should be three warehouses to the right," he informed her as he checked his cell phone.

"But you have a better idea than driving up or around the building, don't you?" she asked.

He nodded.

"I figured we could walk back here by the wire fencing and then cut a left through the buildings," he said. "Make our way over on foot. It'll be the quietest way to get over there and easier to get the lay of the land."

"Agreed."

"You're welcome to stay back here as an anchor or come with me." He held up an earpiece they could use to communicate back and forth with through a cell phone. "Or we can both go." His next option came with two earpieces and communication devices. "Your decision."

"Easy one," she said. "I'm coming."

"Okay. Then take the spare key in case we get separated or one of us needs to hightail it out of here," he said.

She pulled up their location on her cell phone. "The four-way stop we went through a couple of blocks ago is our rendezvous point." It would be their meetup if all hell broke loose, which happened in these scenarios. Ree had noticed it happened less often when she had a solid plan in place.

"Four-way stop it is," he said before checking the time. "It's almost five a.m., so, say, six fifteen?"

"Sounds good to me," she said. Should the situation get ugly, they needed to give the area time to settle down before trying to meet again. An hour should be plenty of time, but this was the worst-case-scenario plan. They were wired with comms devices and could literally stay in each other's ears as they split up.

Ree secured her comms device and earpiece. She tucked her cell phone underneath the seat and pocketed the key in

a zipper pocket before exiting the truck. The current plan
was to stick as close together as possible as Quint met her
around the back of the vehicle. She let him take the lead
since he'd been the one to study the area while she'd slept.
She'd seen enough to get her bearings, marking notable
landmarks as they made their way down the back alley-
way near the fence.

The tall metal fence would almost certainly be wired.
Three rows of barbed wire at the top gave this area a prison
yard feel. The dome lights at the back of each warehouse
provided a weirdly uniform look.

Three warehouses, then a left turn. There was enough
space in between each building to maneuver a semi even
though the bay doors were in front. Each building had one
bay in back large enough to accommodate a semi. There
was a metal door underneath the dome light. And a concrete block leading to the door. There were a few parking
spots cordoned off with yellow stripes. The uniformity of
it all gave more credibility to the prison look.

The concrete below her, on the other hand, was cracked
and had potholes the size of her foot. She had to navigate
carefully so as not to roll an ankle. An injury at this point
would get in the way.

There was a dotting of vehicles parked behind the buildings. They had to stay close enough to a building and stay
flat against it, should someone walk out of the building
for a smoke break, but far enough away not to be picked
up by the cameras. Those were predictable, too. Most of
them pointed directly at the bay doors, which made the
most sense. The biggest threat would be robbers.

Quint's hand came up, fisted. Ree froze.

QUINT HEARD A door open in the direction they were
headed. He flattened his back against the wall, and Ree

followed suit. A pair of male voices followed. He strained to hear the gist of their conversation.

"Mack is on his way for the drop-off. You can't be here," one of the men said. Based on his voice, it was impossible to get a sense of his size and weight.

"You keep talking about how great his stuff is, man," the second guy stated. "It's time you introduced me to this Mack person."

"No can do," guy one said. "Go the hell back inside before he gets here."

There was a long pause.

"All right. All right. Don't get your panties in a wad," the second male acquiesced.

The problem was, the sound of guy number one's footsteps meant he was coming around the side of the building in about three…two…one…

Quint reacted instinctively, reaching out for the guy and spinning him around until his back was against Quint's chest and Quint's right hand was over the guy's mouth, his left arm wrapped around the guy's thick torso. Thick Guy tried to bite Quint's hand as he threw an elbow backward, connecting with Quint's rib cage. Quint grunted as air expelled from his lungs. Thick Guy left Quint no choice.

He dropped his left hand, putting Thick Guy into a choke hold. The guy tried to shout, but couldn't get enough air in his lungs to make it happen. He tried to wriggle his way out of Quint's death grip. Also not going to happen. Not on Quint's watch.

Thick Guy tensed and jerked until the fight was drained from him. Then he went limp in Quint's arms before dropping onto the concrete.

"Help me position him," Quint whispered to Ree, a little winded himself after the altercation.

Ree came around and situated Thick Guy into an up-

right sitting position. She put his hands in his lap, his head
to one side, and then crossed his legs before the two of
them sprinted toward the target warehouses.

"We don't have a whole lot of time before the guy back
there comes to," Quint said to Ree. She'd linked their fingers as they ran, pushing the pace.

"I know," she responded. "Let's just get eyes on the location and drop off one of the devices you brought to see
who comes by here and if we can ascertain whether or not
this is where weapons are coming through."

He hadn't told her about the camera that was the size of
a pin or the listening device that was the size of his thumbnail. He wouldn't need to for her to realize he'd brought
them. The law said the devices couldn't be placed on private property. Public land was a whole different story,
though. Sidewalks were fair game. The listening device
had decent range. The sound could be amplified. But it
needed to be within reasonable reach of the building to be
able to pick anything up. Its success depended on whether
or not there were any devices that might block it. If there
were, Quint could be certain illegal activity occurred at
this site. Gathering evidence in a defensible way in court
was the issue.

Ree squeezed his hand as the buildings came into view.
There was activity on this side of the warehouse district.
Trucks moving in low gear and dimmed lights. He counted
three from this distance. Two heading toward their target and one moving away. The low hum of the engine cut
through the quiet night.

A vehicle with a loud motor roared from a short distance behind them. The drug dealer?

It took less than a minute for the sound of tires peeling
rubber to split the air.

"Hey," a male voice called out.

Ree hit the deck, pulling Quint down with her. He practically landed on top of her and didn't bother to shift his weight off her so as to provide cover. He balanced on his hands and feet, hovering over her instead of crushing her.

"Abort," he whispered, but she shook her head.

"Let's give it a minute," she said so low he could barely hear her.

"Bad idea," he said, unable to keep the dark-cloud feeling at bay.

Ree stayed silent as the commotion from behind them died down. It was far enough away that it didn't seem to rattle any cages over here. Maybe Ree was right and they could make a fast drop before hightailing it out of there. Quint had never been one to question his own decisions, and yet his instinct to abandon the mission had been wrong. He'd snapped to judgment when he should have stayed calm instead and analyzed the situation.

Not good, Casey.

He'd never questioned his ability to do his job effectively before now. Quint needed to have a sit-down with his partner when they got back to the apartment.

"Looks clear," she finally said. "Ready?"

He shook his head before rolling away from her. "You go."

Quint looked up at the full moon and the blanket of stars against a cobalt blue sky.

"Are you sure?" she asked, sounding a little confused.

"Positive." He rolled onto his stomach. "I'll stay here and keep watch, provide cover if needed. You're smaller. It might be easier for you to get in and out."

"Okay," she said, not wasting a second or maybe just not giving him a minute to rethink the offer. Either way, she was off to the races. Quint pulled his gun from his holster and palmed it, ready to fire if need be. His thumb hovered over the safety mechanism, and his trigger finger was ready to tap should the need to protect Ree arise.

He watched her dark silhouette as she kept a low profile, moving across the parking lot with ease. She zigzagged back and forth to trees before crouching low, he guessed to drop a device. After moving to a second location in much the same manner, she made her way back. Trusting her had been the right move.

After holstering his weapon, he hopped up in one fluid motion and led them back toward the truck. Instead of going to the back fence, they made a wide circle, coming at the truck from the opposite side of the street. The second they cleared the last building and the truck came into view, Quint froze.

There were two guys circling his truck.

Chapter Fifteen

Ree tugged Quint's hand until he moved back a couple of steps. The doors of the truck were locked. The registration would trace back to a made-up name and address in North Texas. Her cell phone was tucked underneath the passenger seat, out of view. They hadn't left anything in plain sight that could tie them to law enforcement. The tackle box wasn't even inside the truck. There was nothing to panic about.

Except her heart raced and her pulse thumped at the base of her throat. The pair of idiots wore ripped sleeves. Nothing out of the ordinary for a warehouse district. In fact, they looked like truck drivers, but they could be dockworkers with those thick arms. It would also explain the lack of sleeves. No doubt these were friends of the guy who'd been stepping outside to meet his dealer.

From this distance, she couldn't hear their voices to know if one of the guys had tried to follow his coworker outside. She didn't want to be any closer to them as they studied the truck. One took his cell phone out of his front pocket and snapped a couple of pictures. One of the license plate. Even if this guy had a way to track the plate, which she highly doubted, it would lead to a dead end.

Metal glinted in the second guy's right hand. Ree realized what he was up to a moment before he bent down and sliced a tire. Well, that was going to be a headache to replace. Once the guys grew bored, she would retrieve her cell phone and any incidental items that could identify them, and they could abandon the truck.

The jerk with the knife tried to break the driver's-side window by slamming the butt of the knife into it. All he accomplished was drawing his hand back as the knife went flying. He moved toward it and shook his head before bending down and picking up the blade. Then he palmed the handle and jabbed the tip into all four tires.

Headlights cut through the darkness, sending the two jerks running back toward the warehouse where she and Quint had encountered the guy who'd been trying to score drugs. The semi drove on by as Quint leaned against the building. He exhaled. Slowly. He pinched the bridge of his nose like he was trying to stem a headache.

On a sigh, he said, "Ready?"

"As much as I'll ever be," she said.

They reached the vehicle and retrieved her cell and a backpack. Quint emptied the insurance papers from the dash, stuffing them inside the bag. He grabbed the license plates next. Those, too, went inside. He pocketed his burner phone as they emptied their communication devices along with earpieces in with the plates.

Quint zipped and shouldered the backpack before they headed back the way they'd come. On foot this time. Ree checked for bars and, thankfully, got a couple.

"We should be good to go as soon as we're clear of this place," she informed him.

He grunted in response.

By the time the sun came up, they'd walked within range to get an Uber. Quint made the call to Bjorn to arrange to have the truck towed and provide a replacement vehicle. It was long past breakfast when the Uber driver pulled up a block from their building, where they'd asked to be let out.

Ree could only imagine what they must look like. Hell? Or was that too kind a word? Her thighs burned from the morning's walk coupled with last night's shift. Her stomach growled because they'd both decided to go straight home rather than ask the driver to stop at a drive-through. But it was the humiliation burning her the most. How had they allowed those jerks to get to their vehicle?

"Are you ready for a light run?" Quint asked, clearly thinking the same thing she was. They could jog back to the building.

"Not really, but let's do it anyway," she said.

Quint laughed, and it was the first break in tension in what had turned into a monster of a morning. The quick trip to plant comms devices and maybe gather a little intel was successful in that they'd accomplished their mission. Having to abandon their vehicle and request a replacement was the worst.

Ree picked up the pace, jogging past Quint. Being competitive, he blew past with a laugh. He might be pretending not to be tired, but she heard the heavy breathing as he went by. Saving her energy, she was close enough to home to be able to pull off one last burst of energy as they rounded the corner to their building. Seeing the front doors, Ree turned up the gas. She pushed her legs and pumped her arms, barely passing Quint in time to smack her hand on the glass.

"I won," she said before pushing the door open and bolting toward the elevator.

The next thing she knew, he sprinted past her, reaching the elevator button a few seconds before she did.

"Who won now?" he quipped.

"Guess the first one to the apartment breaks the tie," she

said, throwing a playful elbow into his ribs as she pushed past him into the elevator.

He gave a lot of side-eye when he joined her, but the corners of his lips upturned into a grin. As they neared the seventh floor, Ree realized he would be ready for her tricks this time. So she positioned herself in front of him to face him, grabbed two fistfuls of his black T-shirt and hauled him toward her. Pushing up to her tiptoes, she planted a steamy kiss on Quint's mouth.

For a moment, she got lost. The faint ding of the elevator registered, bringing her thoughts back to the present. She pulled on all her strength and shoved off, using his chest as leverage. He took a step backward, looking a little dazed as she pivoted and then raced to their door. Her flat palm smacked against it, and her body soon followed. Her left shoulder stopped the momentum, landing hard against the surface.

It caught her off guard that Quint didn't soon follow. She looked in time to see him launch himself toward the opening as the doors closed. Ree laughed. She couldn't help herself. The indestructible Agent Quinton Casey at a loss?

Pride filled her chest that she could knock him off balance at least half as much as he did her. She pulled the door key from her pocket and bolted inside as the elevator doors opened again and he shot toward her like a bullet.

"I win," she shrieked, unable to stop laughing.

"Because you cheated," he said, closing and locking the door behind him.

"Winning is winning," she said. "Besides, I didn't tell you to stand there once those doors opened. That was your choice."

He mumbled something she couldn't quite make out and probably didn't want to anyway. It couldn't have been good considering his tone. But then they both broke out laughing.

"You took this round, Sheppard. But the game is not over yet," he said.

"Really? Because I'm pretty sure the game ended when I tagged the front door first," she shot back.

"We'll see about that," he said as he walked right past her. He sat down at the counter and opened his laptop. His expression turned serious. "I'm pretty certain we're about to get dressed down by Bjorn for losing the truck."

"These things happen," she said, taking the chair next to him. "Plus, we took all the necessary precautions. We couldn't have anticipated a drug deal at nearly five o'clock in the morning."

"Murphy's Law," he agreed.

"It could have been worse. We're both still here," she said without thinking. Damn. Damn. Damn. If she could reel those words back in, she would. "Sorry, Quint." She reached over and touched his arm. His muscles tensed with contact. She apologized again and withdrew her hands.

"Promise me something," Quint said, and his voice became serious enough to make the hairs on the back of her neck prick.

"No can do until I hear what you're asking," she said, sitting up a little straighter and folding her arms across her chest.

"Give me your word you won't go behind my back to Bjorn at any time during this investigation." He didn't look up or over when he said the words that were equivalent to daggers in the heart.

"I can't make that promise, and you never should have asked," Ree stated flat out. This apartment suddenly felt too small. With nowhere else to go to get a little breathing room from Quint, she marched into the bathroom, making it just in time for the first tear to spring from her eyes.

An email update came in from Agent Grappell. It was about Zoey. Quint read it and immediately jumped up from the stool. He made a beeline for the bathroom door. His first thought was how relieved Ree would be when she heard the news. He raised his fist to knock, then froze midreach.

In his estimation, he was the last person she wanted to see, let alone speak to. Damn. He needed to get outside and get some air. Ree's cell phone buzzed as he walked by it on the counter. He kept going until he was out of the apartment, out of the elevator and out of the building.

Maybe he could walk off his frustration at the very least.

Forty minutes later, and Quint was no closer to an answer as to why he'd felt the need to ask Ree not to go to Bjorn. She balked because he'd been a jerk. An apology didn't seem nearly enough to undo the damage. She had every right to be frustrated with him. Hell, he was angry with himself.

A few more blocks and he'd turn back. The least he could do while he was out here was refocus on the case. There could be another update from Agent Grappell by now. Quint had blown out of the apartment in such a hurry he'd left his cell phone behind. But he never went anywhere without a weapon. His was secured in the ankle holster strapped underneath his pants leg.

By now, Ree should be out of the bathroom. She deserved to know what was going on with Zoey, so he started the trek back, picking up speed the closer he got to the building. As he rounded the corner, he almost slammed into a guy. Quint sidestepped in the nick of time, but a voice in the back of his mind told him to halt. The guy he'd almost slammed into was Nick Driver.

Quint spun around. "Hold on there."

Driver stopped but didn't turn, so Quint walked directly over to the man. "You live in my building, don't you?" Quint said, staring him in the face.

Driver nodded, looking a little less than comfortable around Quint. Good. Driver *should* be cautious.

"Then maybe you've heard about me by now?" Quint continued, undaunted.

"I have," Driver stated, his lips compressed like he was holding his tongue. *Good.*

"This case will go a whole lot easier if we both make an attempt to get along. Don't you agree?" Quint said, holding back as much of his frustration as he could.

"I was just about to suggest the same," Driver said, trying a little too hard to mask the fear in his voice by coming off overly confident.

"Then from here on out we work together, right?" Quint asked.

Grudgingly, Driver nodded again. A muscle in his jaw ticked, but he didn't seem stupid enough to challenge Quint. Since there was no use in standing there in the morning heat, he said goodbye and walked past Driver.

Quint passed Angie on the street as he headed toward the front doors. He hoped she hadn't heard what had just gone down.

"Morning," she practically chirped.

"How's the studying going today?" he asked with a courtesy smile.

"About to get started." She held up a thick workbook. "Heading out to a coffee shop so I won't get distracted by cleaning the apartment."

"If you don't pass the test, you could always use that

thing as a weapon," he quipped, motioning toward her workbook, trying to keep the mood light.

Angie laughed.

"I guess it could do some damage if needed." She shook the book. "Yep. Definitely."

"Keep it close by," he continued. "Just in case."

"Did you go for a run?" she asked.

"Guilty," he said. "But I wouldn't call it much of a run."

"Take it easy," she said. "Or Ree will kick your rear end."

"She does all the time," he joked before exchanging goodbyes.

The elevator seemed to be taking its sweet time once he got inside. He made it up to seven, selfishly hoping Ree would still be awake. In case she'd dozed off, he slipped inside quietly.

"I'm home," he whispered, not wanting to surprise someone who carried a weapon at all times.

"I'm awake," she said. The reassurance was appreciated. "Where did you take off to?"

"Went for a walk while you showered," he said. "Tried to clear my head."

"Did it work?" she asked. The tension in her voice said he'd lost ground with her.

"Probably not." He joined her at the counter. "When did you get out of the bathroom?"

"A minute ago," she said.

"Good. I wanted to be the first to tell you that we received an update on Zoey while you were in there," he said. "She's still at the women's shelter in Austin and, according to one of her counselors, is making real progress."

Ree exhaled, and her chest deflated. A look of pure relief washed over her features.

"That's the best thing I've heard all day," she said with a lightness in her tone that had been missing earlier.

"I should probably let you know that I ran into Driver on my way back to the building," he stated.

"Oh?" she asked as an eyebrow arched. "How did that go?"

"Good. I think," he said. "He seems clear on where I stand with him. That's always a good thing, right?"

"Depends," she said on a sigh. "On whether that makes him easier or harder for me to work with now."

"I'm going out on a limb here, but I'll say easier," he said.

The small shift in her caused his chest to puff out, and all he could think about was the steamy kiss in the elevator earlier.

He walked away before he did anything to rekindle that fire.

Chapter Sixteen

The news about Zoey perked up Ree's spirits. "What about the truck?"

"Bjorn responded to my email. She's handling it," Quint stated with a frown.

"That doesn't sound good," Ree said. "What did she say?"

"Probably not words I should repeat," he said. "Something about hell freezing over before we get a new vehicle. She's having the truck towed and new tires put on. She said the fastest she can get it back to us is tomorrow and that we'd just have to walk until then if we needed to get somewhere."

"Ouch." She stretched, thinking she should probably rest a little while before her shift tonight. At least it was Tuesday and wouldn't be crowded at the bar. "It's probably too early to pick up anything on surveillance. I dropped the camera in a good spot. Not sure I was able to get close enough for the listening device."

"You did what you could considering how everything went down," he said.

"If we keep the same truck, it'll be hard to go back to the warehouses," she reasoned.

Quint nodded.

"Too bad Lola isn't working tonight." Ree figured she'd

made inroads with Lola and wanted to capitalize on the progress. "Any word about Esteban or Matias?"

"Hold on, I'll check." Quint refocused his attention on the laptop, turning the screen so they both could see. He checked his email first. There was nothing there from Grappell.

His cell buzzed before he could check the case file. He located it and checked the screen, sucking in a breath when he saw the number. "Hello."

There was a moment of silence. Followed by him asking if he could put the call on speaker. The answer must've come quick because he glanced at Ree and gave a small headshake before standing up and moving back to the window he'd stared out during the last call with their boss. Ree had seen the number and knew exactly who was calling.

"I didn't…" He paused. "No." Another beat passed. "If he hadn't have…then I wouldn't have needed to."

From the sounds of it, Quint was being dressed down by the boss.

He said a few "Yes, ma'ams" into the receiver before ending the call.

"I'm betting that call had to do with your run-in with Driver a little while ago," she said, venturing a guess.

Quint issued another sharp sigh. "Apparently she got a call from Richard Magee."

"Because you had words with Nick Driver?" Communication from the head of the DEA seemed like overkill. "Didn't you say that happened less than half an hour ago?"

He nodded. His lips thinned, and his gaze narrowed. Anger came off him in palpable waves.

"Hold on a second," she said. "This can't be right. Why would Magee get involved in a case this low down the line?"

"Turns out Driver and Magee are in-laws," he informed. "Driver married the guy's daughter."

"Nepotism?" she asked, but the question was rhetorical. "No wonder the man has so many accolades in his employment jacket."

"No one wants to upset the head honcho," Quint said with disgust. "There's probably some truth to his abilities in the field."

"I'm still good with taking communication lead with the other team. This doesn't change anything for me," she admitted. Her record might not have as many honors in it but she was confident in her abilities and her job as a top-notch agent.

"You might want to rethink being associated with me," he said, but she could see that he was just frustrated. An agent of Quint's caliber would take nepotism about as well as a sucker punch. In a fair fight, Quint would come out on top. Pull strings and he could end up in trouble. Any one of them could. One thing was certain. Their instincts about the DEA agent being trouble seemed spot-on.

"I'm good, Quint," she reassured.

He caught her gaze and held it for a long moment before giving an almost imperceptible nod. "Let's get on with the case, then."

"Good. Where were we?" She picked up on a hint of appreciation and respect in his voice that made her swell with pride. Quint was a well-respected agent, and his opinion of her mattered. His respect was important to her, and his confidence in her gave her a boost.

Ree's cell buzzed. She picked it up and checked the screen.

"Looks like our counterparts are calling now," she said.

"What can I do for you?" she asked after exchanging pleasantries.

"I'm working with Agent Driver on the DEA side of

the case, and I just wanted to call to apologize if my partner came across in the wrong way before," the agent said.

"Thank you, Agent—"

"Please, call me Shelly."

"Thanks for reaching out, Shelly. I believe our partners spoke earlier and cleared up any confusion between us," Ree stated.

"I'll do what I can on my end. My partner leans on his family ties a little too closely for my liking," the agent continued. "I hope this conversation stays between us."

"I have no reason to share," Ree said. The frustration in Shelly's tone sounded very real, and she was certainly saying all the right things. What legitimate agent would want to work with someone who was aided based on a family connection?

"I can share that we were brought on to this case as part of a bigger investigation into Matias Gimenez," the agent said.

"Gimenez is a drug runner?" Ree asked.

"Afraid so," Shelly confirmed. "We've been following him in Argentina, but he keeps coming back to the States. We didn't know he was heading to Houston until very recently."

"Because of his daughter, Lili," Ree said.

"That's correct. Gimenez works for a high-value target in Latin America," the agent continued.

"So he's powerful," Ree stated, thinking that if he got Lili back to Argentina, he had a chance of keeping her there and away from Lola.

"Very," Shelly said, then came, "Hold on."

The call became very quiet for a few long seconds.

"My partner is coming back and he isn't up-to-date on this call," Shelly said. "I have to go now, but I hope we can all work together."

"Wouldn't have it any other way," Ree stated.

The call ended.

Ree turned to Quint. "Well, that was an interesting conversation."

"I PIECED TOGETHER that Matias is the reason the DEA is involved," Quint stated, figuring the betrayal might have been the best thing that could have happened if it gave them an in with Shelly.

"He's powerful, Quint. If he takes Lili back to South America, Lola might never see her daughter again." Ree exhaled, and her shoulders rounded forward.

"We have to figure out a way to protect Lola and her daughter," he said without much internal debate. From what he could tell so far, Lola was a decent person who'd gotten wrapped up in a bad situation. He'd noted the phenomenon of intelligent women allowing men who were bad for them to slip past their radars. It happened more than it should, and he reasoned the men were usually charming, a common personality trait among narcissists. They could slide right in and break past normally guarded walls. He'd watched it firsthand with Tessa, who didn't put up with a whole lot of nonsense. Her baby's father had slithered around her carefully constructed walls, and Tessa had beaten herself up over allowing it.

"I'd like that very much," Ree stated. She paused a moment before shifting gears back to the agent and her phone call. "She didn't give me the impression she was thrilled to be working with Driver. I didn't have to read between the lines to pick up on it."

Quint nodded. "It hadn't occurred to me how awful it must be to get stuck on an assignment with him."

"It seems to be part of the reason she reached out to me," Ree said.

"When the call ended, I noticed you didn't say goodbye. In fact, your forehead wrinkled like it does when you're confused about something." He probably shouldn't have just admitted how well he knew her habits, but there it was.

A hint of pink colored her cheeks as she nodded. "She had to go because he was coming back. She didn't say from where, and she ended the call abruptly."

"You think we can trust her." It wasn't a question.

"Yes," Ree said, answering anyway.

"I agree," he said. "Reaching out to you put her at risk. She took all the chance in that exchange. She also gave you information we didn't have before and isn't showing up in the report."

"I'm guessing that was her way of extending an olive branch," Ree stated. "I just hope she's given due credit when this is all said and done. I have a feeling she'll be the one who deserves it between the two of them."

Quint nodded.

"Did Bjorn come down pretty hard on you?" she asked, wincing a little bit.

"Nothing I can't handle," he said, which was true. He didn't know how it might affect the case, and that bothered him. Could he have handed the DEA a reason to keep their cards close to their chests? Driver was already.

Quint's cell dinged. It was the sound attached to email notifications.

"Let's hope for some more good news," he said, moving to his laptop. The news about Matias sat in the back of Quint's mind as he powered up the device and then opened his email. Ree joined him.

"What does it say?" she asked, her back toward the kitchen.

"There's no record of Esteban entering this country legally, according to Agent Grappell," he informed.

"Which doesn't necessarily mean he's doing something illegal or came here to commit a crime," she pointed out.

"No, it doesn't. He could be here to support his sister," Quint reasoned. He'd been an only child, but Ree, on the other hand, came from a large family. As much as she'd talked about her brothers smothering her at times growing up, she'd also made it clear any one of them would walk through fire to save another. Was it the reason Esteban was in the country? To protect his sister in some way? Or his niece? The last thought resonated with Quint. Even though he'd never met Tessa's baby, he would have gone to any length to protect her after learning about the pregnancy. He'd felt an instant bond with the child, born out of his brotherly love for the baby's mother.

"Esteban is most likely here because of Lola and Lili," he said. "I can't prove it. Yet. But I'd bet my life savings on it."

Ree sat for a long moment before finally nodding in agreement.

"It makes sense when I really think about it," she said. "If I was a single mother, my brothers would want to protect me."

"Doesn't rule out criminal activity, though," Quint continued. "We don't know how he makes his living while he's in the States. Whatever he's doing, he must be getting paid under the table, because there's no IRS record of a salary."

"The IRS is the first place Grappell would look for employment records," Ree agreed.

"There's no Social Security record, either," he said before looking at her. "See if you can find out from Lola why they relocated to the US a few years ago."

"I can already tell you it coincides with having the baby," she said.

"Interesting," he noted.

"Isn't it?" she responded. Then added, "I haven't gotten Lola to talk about what brought her here, or met her brother, but I'm guessing it has to do with having the baby and not wanting her brought up in Argentina."

"Have you been there?" he asked.

"No." She shook her head. "Why?"

"Beautiful country in many respects. Beautiful people, too," he said. "Still a little too machismo for my taste, if you know what I mean."

"I can't imagine Constantin would be thrilled to know Lola's ex was in the country," Ree pointed out.

"I can't imagine it would go down well between the two of them," he agreed.

"Matias would get custody even if he wasn't tied to a powerful person." She caught on fast. Her sharp mind was one of her many incredible qualities.

"Unless she had connections, which I'm doubting in this situation," he said.

"Is there any chance Matias is the one who put the spyware on her computer?" Ree asked.

"Good question." He stopped to think about it. Would Lola ever allow Matias to be alone in the room with any of her personal items? He highly doubted it. "My first thought is no. Maybe you can get close enough to her to find out."

"She is still a puzzle to me," Ree said on a sigh. "I just keep going back to the fact that she doesn't give me any vibe that she would be involved in criminal activity."

"And yet it seems to be all around her," he pointed out. "We already mentioned the whole *birds of a feather flock together* saying. There's a certain amount of corruption in every country, and South America is no exception. She's either part of it or running from it."

"That's what I keep coming back to," Ree stated. "If

she wasn't part of it, why does she seem to be surrounded by it all the time?"

Quint compressed his lips in a frown. *Birds of a feather?*

Chapter Seventeen

Ree had tried to rest after her conversation with Quint in order to be ready for her shift. Her mind kept churning over the new information instead. She dressed, ate a quick dinner salad with Quint, and was out the door and to work fifteen minutes early for her shift.

Lola was correct. Tuesdays were slow. There wasn't a whole lot to learn about being a barback. She worked for Annie, who was a popular bartender, but one who kept to herself on breaks. Glasses needed to be clean and at the ready at all times for the bar area Ree was responsible for. Garnishes needed to be chopped and ready to go. Basically, it was her job to make sure her bartenders had everything they needed, when they needed it. HNC didn't like its selective clientele standing around waiting for a drink a second longer than necessary.

Not having a whole lot to keep her busy made time tick by at the slowest possible pace. Midnight couldn't get there fast enough. Not five minutes after, Ree walked out the front door to a waiting partner.

"How was it?" he asked when he got a good look at her face.

"Don't ask," she responded, linking their arms as they walked the couple of blocks back to the apartment.

"Hungry?" he asked after they got through the door.

"Very." She toed off her shoes and loosened her bow tie. "Just let me change into something more comfortable."

He nodded before ducking into the kitchen as she made a beeline for the bathroom. Her robe hung on the back of the door, so she slipped out of her clothes and into the thick terry cloth. She secured the tie around her waist before joining him at the counter. "What is this amazing smell?"

"The best Tex-Mex restaurant in Houston if you can believe a 'rate my food' app." He nudged a plate of the best-looking enchiladas toward her.

"Sour cream chicken?" she asked, taking a deep breath and inhaling the scent of great food.

"For you," he said, "and a beef chimichanga for me."

Ree wasted no time eating her food. "I can't imagine better Tex-Mex than that."

"I forgot to get the drinks," he said.

"Who could care about drinks with food this amazing?" she teased.

He brought over a Coke for her and black coffee for himself.

"Excellent choices," she said.

"I aim to please," he said before asking if she learned anything tonight.

"Nothing new and very little in the way of tips. Note to self, ask off Tuesdays," she said with a snort. "Did we get anything from our surveillance equipment?"

"The sound is terrible," he said, referring to last night's adventure. "We won't get anything useful from the listening device."

"Not a complete surprise," she said. "I couldn't really get close enough."

"The lab might be able to do more with it," he said. "Maybe not a total loss there."

"And the camera?" she asked, hoping the truck tires

weren't slashed for no reason. The whole incident did get them in hot water with Bjorn.

"That one is better." His fingers flew across the keyboard as he pulled up footage. "The agents in Analysis will watch round the clock so we don't have to, but I did manage to record suspicious activity."

A pair of men walked to the opposite side of the truck in the middle of the day, making seeing what they were exchanging impossible. But they were trading something.

"Drugs?" she asked, figuring the warehouse district was a good place for narcotic sales. It was on the outskirts of town, and most of the business running out of there seemed legit.

"Could be," he said. "But watch as this guy walks around." The camera homed in on a face.

"Esteban?" she asked.

"Looks like Lola, doesn't he?" he asked.

"It's a little grainy when it's blown up, but I can see the resemblance," she said. "Does that mean he works for Constantin?"

"It could explain being paid under the table," he stated.

She nodded. A piece of her wished Lola weren't involved with sketchy people, but signs pointed elsewhere.

"I can't get over the fact that someone like Lola would attach herself to a guy dealing drugs in her homeland and then come here and get mixed up with someone who ran weapons," Ree said, thinking out loud.

"You like her, don't you?" he asked.

"Yes," she admitted. "But how could both of our intuitions about her be wrong? Gut instinct accounts for some, but we have training and experience to back it up."

"Have you ever been wrong? Misjudged someone?" he asked. "Because I have."

"You're right," she reasoned, trying to quash the niggling feeling struggling to convince her otherwise. "I've made a few mistakes."

"The really good ones can trick even a seasoned agent," he said. "Not a whole lot gets past my radar, and that used to make me cocky."

"What happened to change your mind?" she asked. He was right. She'd learned never to trust her instincts and to follow the evidence, but there was something about Lola— an innocence?—that had Ree second-guessing herself. The evidence so far pointed to Lola knowing exactly what she was getting into.

"There was a case in Dallas where I was one hundred percent certain a kid was innocent. He played the victim role with an abusive stepdad. His mother was a drunk and used to pass out at like eight o'clock every night on the couch. The stepdad was a class A jerk, doing everything from laundering money to running bootleg," he said. "Looking back, evidence pointed to the kid being involved. But I made excuses for that kid every step of the way. I bought the story that he was seventeen and stuck in a bad situation. Turned out he just looked young. He wasn't related to the woman passing out on the couch every night. Her son lived with his father in Oklahoma. This guy altered the kid's ID and was living on-site helping run the small-time business."

Ree wrinkled her nose. "Stinks to be wrong."

"Stinks to high heaven," he retorted. "The thing is, I kept catching him in lies but chalked it up to the abuse. There were no physical altercations. The guy was getting into bar fights and coming back cut up. The so-called stepdad had no idea this guy was telling on him, and I swore to my boss this kid wasn't involved and needed counseling services and a safe place to live."

"Why do you think he fooled you?" she asked.

"He came up with a story that had a few parallels to my own background. I guess I saw myself in that kid." He shrugged. "Some people are just evil manipulators."

"How did you figure it all out?" Ree asked, figuring every agent had a story about being snowed when they should know better.

"The real kid showed up to check on his mother when she didn't respond to his texts for a couple of days. He got worried and had his real father drive him down from Oklahoma to see if she was okay," he said. "We got her to sober up for a bit, and she cried pretty much nonstop. She was clueless about what was going on under her own roof because they plied her with alcohol every night and made sure she was passed out by a certain time. She had no idea one of the people under her roof was using her son's identity."

"Those are terrible people, taking advantage of someone with a disease like that," she said with disdain.

"There has to be a special place in hell for folks like them," he stated with enough heat to melt an ice cube in the dead of winter in Siberia.

"Agreed. And in our line of work, we get to be the ones to make sure they're locked up until they get there," she said. It was the main perk and something she needed to remind herself of almost daily, especially during a case. It could be a little too easy to focus on the bad side of their line of work and lose sight of the whole reason they did it.

Quint nodded.

"Did you ever follow up to find out what happened with the mom and son?" she asked.

"She got clean and stayed sober," he said. "Last I checked, which was almost a decade ago, she'd moved to Oklahoma to be closer to her son."

"That's a sweet ending," she said as warmth filled her.

She also noted that the mistake he brought up was from more than a decade ago. "Quick question."

"Shoot," he said.

"Are you telling me you haven't pegged someone wrong in more than ten years?" she asked, figuring there was no way.

"A hair more than fourteen to be exact," he said. "But Lola could prove me wrong on that point at any time."

Ree hoped she wouldn't.

QUINT CLEANED UP the dishes, figuring Ree needed to get sleep after last night and then working a shift. "Speaking of Lola, does she work Wednesdays?"

"I think so," Ree said. "I'm pretty sure I saw her name on the schedule."

"Good. I should probably figure out the vehicle situation so I can head down to Galveston tomorrow night while you're working and see what I can dig up on Constantin and his brother. There's a restaurant down the street from their place that I hope to dig around in," he said.

"Wish I could be there with you instead of at the bar," Ree said, sounding like a kid who'd just been told the candy ran out.

"You'll be busy with Lola, getting information," he said.

"That's the hope," she stated, rubbing the soles of her feet. He shifted his gaze away from the terry cloth robe and how it parted just above her knee, revealing the silky skin of her thigh. She pushed up to standing. "I'll grab a shower and hit the sheets."

He didn't want to think about how nice it would feel to be in bed beside her, or how easy it would be to get used to waking up next to her.

"I'll clean up in here and upload a report to the shared folder. The other couple in the building needs to know we've already been to Constantin's warehouse and that we've dropped comms devices. The analysts will share any data relevant to their case," he said, deciding he needed to refocus on something besides bed and Ree.

"Thank you," she said, "for taking care of all these details and, again, for keeping the good food rolling. I don't ever want to be on an assignment with anyone else but you. I'm used to fast-food tacos and burgers with maybe an occasional shake thrown in. You keep me fed with the most amazing food and even remembered my favorite drink is Coke."

"Don't worry about it," he said. "Besides, I'd throw on that uniform in a heartbeat and work as a barback if I could."

Ree laughed out loud, and it was the most musical sound. She really seemed to have no idea the effect she had on men, or more specifically on him. The last part was for the best, because there was no way a relationship between the two of them could go anywhere, he thought as she disappeared into the bathroom. He wasn't thinking right if he was even considering the consequences the two of them dating might have.

On a sharp sigh, he loaded the dishwasher and uploaded the info to the shared folder before closing down his laptop. Both of them could use a good night of sleep. He'd mapped out his Galveston trip earlier while Ree was at work, so there wasn't much more that could be done tonight anyway. It was a shame that she couldn't go with him, but the two of them together would be more easily recognizable now that Constantin had seen them when he'd picked Lola up from work. Going alone, Quint could throw on a ball cap and keep most of his face hidden.

By the time he shut everything down, Ree was out of the bathroom. He expected her to be asleep when he finished his turn. Instead, she was sitting on the bed under the covers, staring.

"Everything okay?" he asked as he climbed in bed.

"Yes, I'm just taking a few minutes to process," she said, patting her side of the bed.

He met her in the middle and she leaned into him, resting her head on his shoulder after he looped his arm around her shoulders.

"Do you ever think about leaving all this behind and having a family someday?" she asked. The question came out of left field.

"To be honest, not before Tessa was killed. I thought having a family was the worst thing a parent could do to a kid," he said.

"You do realize what you just said there," she said.

"I'm mostly referring to my father," he pointed out. "I've already told you my mother should have been nominated for sainthood."

"I don't even have time for a puppy," she said in a sleepy voice that tugged at his heartstrings.

"No. Not with a job like ours," he said.

"Have you ever considered how awful that is?" she asked.

"Not really," he admitted, thinking she was sleep-deprived and probably barely awake at this point. "I wouldn't mind getting a dog someday, but now is definitely not the right time."

"I don't even have time to foster a puppy for Zoey," she said, and now her words were a little slurred. She was definitely only barely awake.

"Not right now, you don't," he said. "But things could change."

"What things?" she asked. "Did you know that I'm thirty-six years old and still not married?"

"You don't look your age, and I mean that as a compliment," he stated before she could get defensive.

Ree yawned.

"I should have a puppy someday," she said.

"Yes, you should," he agreed, figuring she wouldn't remember this conversation in the morning.

"Do you want to have a puppy together?" she asked. "We could take turns taking care of it."

"That would make it hard to work on cases together, wouldn't it?" he asked, thinking how much he would hate to lose her as a partner even if that meant raising a puppy together.

"You would make beautiful puppies," she said through another yawn.

Quint couldn't help but laugh at that one.

"What did I say?" she asked.

"Nothing you'll remember in the morning," he said.

"We would have beautiful children," she said, curling up against his side.

Quint froze. For a split second, he could envision their child. He'd want a little girl who looked exactly like her mother. Fatherhood? He shook off the reverie, thinking he would never be that cruel to a kid.

Chapter Eighteen

"I don't think I've slept so deeply in my entire life." Ree sat up and stretched her arms out with a yawn. The smell of fresh-brewed coffee wafted across the room, but there was no sign of Quint. "Hello?"

Panic settled over her for reasons she couldn't explain. He should be here. She threw off the covers and shuffled into the kitchen. Quint was gone. The bathroom door was open when she walked by, so she already knew he wasn't in there. She searched around for a note before locating her cell phone. There was no text or phone call.

Just as she was about to hit DEFCON 3, a key slipped inside the lock and the door handle jiggled. She moved to the door as it opened.

"Where did you go?" she asked, examining him for signs of injury. None were visible. He did, however, have a bagful of bagels from the café down the road. The fact that she'd overreacted caused her cheeks to flush.

"Bjorn arranged for a new truck to arrive overnight, so I inspected it. Looks almost as good as new," he said with a look of surprise stamping his features. He held up the bag. "While I was out, I decided to pick up breakfast."

Ree issued a sharp sigh.

"All good?" he asked with a raised eyebrow as he moved into the kitchen and set the bag on the counter.

"Yes. Sure. I guess." She walked around to the stool on the other side of the counter and sat down. "I'm confused about why I just had a massive reaction to my partner being gone in the morning on a bagel run." She put her head in her hands. "I slept so deeply and then woke in a panic when I realized you were gone."

"I'm here," he reassured her in that whiskey-over-ice voice of his. She reminded herself not to get too used to it. This case would end, and they would go back to their respective lives. There was no guarantee they would ever work together again.

"The odd thing is that we're nowhere close to wrapping up this case. Why would I panic if you weren't here?" If she couldn't figure it out, there was no way he would.

"It's probably just stress-related," he said. "No big deal."

"You're probably right," she said, hoping it was true.

"It'll pass," he said. "But I'm honored you would worry so much about my safety."

"You're important to me, Quint. Of course I'd be concerned about what happens to you," she stated as he passed a cup of coffee over.

"This should help," he said.

"You know what it is?" she asked after thanking him and taking the offering. "I have a bad feeling about you going to Galveston alone tonight."

That had to be the problem. It was the only thing that made sense.

"I'll be careful," he reassured.

"I know," she said. "Just take a few extra precautions if you don't mind."

Women's intuition could be a powerful thing, and hers was issuing a warning. She figured it had to do with Quint.

"Should we let Shelly know about your trip tonight?" she asked.

"Nah, I'm only going to gather intel," he stated. "There's nothing to report yet."

She nodded, taking a sip of fresh brew, desperately needing the caffeine boost.

"You asked if I wanted to share a puppy last night," he said, handing over a plate of bagels and cream cheese.

"Oh, really?" she asked. "Was I awake?"

"You sounded out of it," he said. "How'd you sleep?"

"Great. Better than ever actually," she admitted. The feeling came back, but she ignored it. Quint was probably right. It was probably stress-related. She'd gone from one case to the next without enough time off in between, and then there was her grandfather. He was probably fine, too. She was on edge, blowing this whole morning out of proportion. "Normally, after a night of sleep like the one I just had, I'm refreshed in the morning."

"Maybe you need a few more nights of sleep to fully recover," he said.

"I guess so," she said. "It's odd."

"We're all off our game every once in a while," he said, holding a bagel plate of his own along with a fresh cup of coffee. "Should we log on and see if there are any updates this morning?"

"Why not?" she asked on a sigh, resigned to her strange mood. This wasn't good. Ree was never off her game while on a case. "I don't have to be at work for hours anyway."

Before Quint logged on, he retrieved her personal phone from the tackle box and held it out. "You'll feel a whole lot better if you check on your grandfather."

Ree took the offering with a smile.

"Thank you," she said before texting her brother Shane. The response came back almost immediately.

He's good. Tired. But good.

Relief washed over her as she showed the screen to Quint.

"Looks like I was worried for nothing," she said.

"It shows how much you care and that's never for nothing," he countered before returning her cell to the tackle box, locking up and sitting next to her.

"Oh, look at this. We have an update from the other team." He clicked on a folder in the joint case file after logging on.

"Anything good in there?" she asked.

He skimmed the contents.

"Nothing we don't already know," he stated.

"Let me guess, Wonder Boy gave the update," she said.

"Looks like it," he confirmed.

"Well then, it has no chance of actually being useful," she said.

Quint laughed.

"You're in a mood this morning," he noted.

"Yes. Sorry. I don't know what's wrong with me," she admitted.

"Take it easy today, then," he said. "Rome wasn't built in a day, and this case won't live or die based on whether or not you take the morning off."

She polished off her bagel.

"I'm climbing back in bed, then," she said after brushing her teeth. She retrieved her coffee mug. "You can join me if you want." She quickly added, "To drink coffee and possibly go back to sleep."

"Shame," he said, low and under his breath, as he brought his laptop over. When he spoke again, he turned up the volume. "We can check the footage together."

"Or we could talk about something besides work for a change," she said, then realized how that sounded. "I mean, get to know each other a little better. We are supposed to be married, and although we did already work a case together, I think it was solved in record time."

"You want to talk?" he asked, but it was a rhetorical question. "We'll talk. Fair warning, though. I'm not all that good with words."

"I'll be the judge of that," she said with a smile. She was still puzzled by her reaction this morning and wanted nothing more than to put that behind her and start the day all over again.

On the bed with a topped-off cup of coffee, she positioned her pillows as a backrest. Quint moved beside her, sitting on top of the covers.

"Are you comfortable?" she asked.

He nodded and mumbled that he was as he opened the laptop. "How about you?"

"How about me what?" she asked, feeling the moment the air in the room shifted, charging with electricity.

"Comfortable?" he asked, and his voice had a sexy, husky quality to it.

"Yes" was all she could manage in response. The word came out as more of a croak than anything else. As it was, her throat dried up and her tongue felt like she'd licked a glue stick. She swallowed to ease the dryness, to no avail. She coughed to clear her throat. "Anything on the footage?"

He was pulling it up as she asked. "We'll know in a few minutes."

As he scrolled, she felt the warmth of his body against hers and the desire that flowered inside her. The kisses they'd shared suddenly took center stage in her thoughts as warmth flooded her. She couldn't help but wonder if Quint felt any of these same sensations, because she was suddenly the Fourth of July inside.

He shifted positions and studied the screen like it was

a bomb about to detonate and the only way to stop it was with eye contact.

"Ree," he finally said.

"Yes," she answered.

"I'd very much like to kiss you right now," he said.

"What's stopping you?" she asked as a dozen butterflies released in her chest. Her stomach free-fell at the prospect of their mouths fusing again.

"This time, it would have nothing to do with work," he said. "And it's a line that probably shouldn't be crossed."

"You're right about the first part," she said. "The second thing you said is debatable."

"Are you saying you want me to kiss you as Quint, not your 'husband'?" he asked.

Rather than answer with words, Ree turned toward him and pressed her lips to his. The heat in her body sparked, and a flame burned low in her belly as she parted her lips for him, and he drove his tongue inside her mouth.

Her heart raced and her breath quickened as she bit down on his lower lip. The taste of dark roast coffee was so much better on Quint.

QUINT REPOSITIONED THE laptop onto the nightstand next to the bed, breaking apart from kissing Ree for a few seconds. In those moments, he hoped logic would kick in and tell them not to ruin what had the potential to be a great professional partnership. It didn't. In fact, logic seemed to have walked right out the door and left the building. Kissing Ree again was an all-consuming need.

Matters weren't helped when she climbed on his lap after he reclaimed his spot on the bed. In the heat of the moment, all he could concentrate on was the feel of her soft lips against his and the sexy little moan of pleasure he swallowed that jacked his pulse up a few more notches.

He was consumed by her incredibly silky skin and how it would feel underneath his hands, a ridiculously thin piece of cotton the only thing separating her body from skin-to-skin contact.

"I'd like permission to touch you," he said, his mouth moving against her lips.

She took one of his hands in hers and repositioned it to her full breast. Her nipple beaded with contact, and all blood flew south. Ree brought her hands up to his chest, her fingernails digging into his shoulders as the kisses deepened, and she started rocking back and forth. He dropped his hands to her sweet, round hips as they sped up, and desire flooded him.

In the next moment, she shrugged out of her pajama shirt and tossed it onto the floor. He cupped her incredibly perfect bare breasts in his hands as she released another one of those sexy moans. His T-shirt came off next before he chucked it on top of the pile.

When her gaze met his and locked on, something stirred deep in his chest. There was a second of hesitation on his part because he realized in that moment if this went further there'd be more than a professional partnership on the line. The only question remaining was whether or not his heart could take it. Because making love to Ree would be a game changer. One he wasn't certain he could come back from and just be friends again.

"Are we good?" she asked, her emerald eyes sparkling with need.

Consequences be damned, he said, "Never better."

And then he shifted his weight to remove his jeans and boxers to free his straining erection. In the next couple of seconds, Ree slipped off her pajama bottoms and straddled him. She started to lower her body, but he stopped her.

"What's wrong?" she asked.

"Nothing. I just want to slow down and look at you," he said.

A red blush crawled up her milky skin, concentrating on her cheeks. Blushing made her even more beautiful, if that was possible.

"You are gorgeous," he said, and he could hear the huskiness in his own voice. Being here in this moment with Ree felt like the most natural thing in the world. He had every intention of enjoying each inch of her incredible body.

"I'm not," she said in almost a whisper.

"Then you don't see what I do," he said, smoothing his hands along her hips, moving up and over her stomach until reaching her breasts. Her breaths came in bursts as he touched her, really touched her.

Her back arched as she moaned with pleasure when he dropped his hand to the apex of her thighs. Using the pad of his thumb, he massaged and teased until her eyes were wild with need and he could sense her body ached as much as his.

"Now," she managed to say. "I need you inside me now, Quint."

The sound of his name rolling off her tongue spurred him on. "Hold on a sec."

He retrieved a condom, ripped the package open using his teeth, and then she helped him sheath his stiff length. Once again, she climbed on top of him, straddling him, her sweet heat within inches of absolute ecstasy.

Both hands on her hips, he eased her body down until he was able to dip his tip inside her.

"Quint," she whispered, "more."

He didn't respond. Couldn't respond. All he could do was slow down as much as possible so this whole thing wasn't over before it began. It had been a long time since he'd been with someone who sparked this level of need in him…maybe never. He was both fascinated by it and concerned.

To hell with concern. Right here, right now, he wanted to bury himself inside Ree. She slowly rocked her hips as he kissed her, letting her take the lead. His hands roamed her warm, silky skin.

Game changer all right.

That was the last rational thought he had before giving in to the need scorching his skin and threatening to consume him like a raging wildfire. He surrendered to the feeling, to Ree, and hoped like hell the fire didn't devour them both.

Chapter Nineteen

Ree opened her eyes to a quiet apartment. She felt around for Quint, searching for his warm body. He wasn't there. She heard a noise coming from the living room area, the click-click-clack of fingers on a keyboard. Did this man never sleep?

She lost count of how many rounds of sex they'd had as she stretched out her arms, feeling more relaxed than she had in too long. Waking up after multiple rounds of sex with her work partner should make her feel different…right? Nervous to be around him? Unsure of what this did to their partnership, maybe? Instead, all she could think about was seeing his gorgeous face again. And coffee. Definitely coffee. She'd already let two cups get cold today and, despite not being able to erase the silly smile from her face, needed a caffeine boost.

"Hey," she said after throwing on her robe and walking past him on her way to the kitchen.

"I'd say good morning, but it's a little late for that," he said, shifting the laptop onto the sofa and joining her in the kitchen. He wasted no time kissing her, and a little sense of relief washed over her that he wasn't going to pretend like the last few hours hadn't happened.

"Good afternoon or whatever," she said, looping her arms around his neck as he deepened the kiss and need

welled up inside her. How? She'd already had more or-
gasms today than she could count. How on earth could
her body rally, asking for more?

Quint's flat palm splayed against the small of her back
caused her stomach to free-fall again. What could she say?
The man did things to her body she never knew were possible.

He pulled away first and took a step back, leaning his
slender hip against the counter. His shirtless chest was
temptation on a stick, but she stopped her fingers from
reaching out to him. She had enough time for coffee and
an update before she needed to get ready for her shift.

"We got some interesting news," he said as he waited
for her to pour her coffee and then take the first sip.

"Oh, yeah?" She gave a little mewl of pleasure that
seemed to spark Quint's interest.

"The person Esteban was meeting with has been iden-
tified as Constantin's brother Baptiste," he stated.

"It would make sense that Esteban might be running illegal operations, since he's under the government's radar,"
Ree reasoned.

"Same with Constantin's brother. He isn't listed on any
of the company paperwork and flies back and forth to Eu-
rope rotating names. He's also been John and Ian," he said.

"Isn't Ian the same thing as John in other countries?"
she asked.

Quint rocked his head.

"Let me guess, his nickname is John the Baptist," she
said.

"You would be correct. Turns out he likes to dump bodies in rivers," he informed.

Ree shivered. Yes, her job was dangerous, but a lot of
times she was busting gunrunners who moved a lot of
merchandise at gun shows pretending to be "collectors,"

which fell under special rules in Texas and didn't require a license, and not this level of evil.

"And he was the one meeting with Esteban?" she asked, already sensing the answer.

"Yes," he confirmed.

"This casts Lola in a whole new light, doesn't it?" she asked.

"If you follow the evidence and take out personal opinion, then yes," he said. "But you know what? Something has been bothering me, and I finally figured out what it is."

She took a sip of coffee, very interested in his revelation. Quint wasn't just a legend at the agency, he was a damn good agent.

"Criminals are usually suspicious of everyone around them," he pointed out. "Right?"

"Seems to come with the territory," she agreed.

"Why wouldn't she have suspected spyware on her laptop?" he asked.

"She was genuinely surprised by the news and looked a little panicked," she admitted.

"Not exactly the actions of an experienced criminal," he stated.

"No, they are not." She took another sip and contemplated the new perspective. "Maybe she'll open up to me a little bit more tonight. I wish I could get her out of the bar for a girls' night out but I'm guessing Constantin keeps a pretty tight grip on her outside of work."

Quint nodded.

"Do you have a picture of Baptiste to show me in case he comes into the bar?" She wanted to know who she was dealing with and be able to monitor who interacted with Lola.

Quint exited the small kitchen, returning a few moments later with the laptop. "The picture is grainy, but here you go."

She memorized his features, which was easy considering he looked like a slightly younger, slightly darker-haired version of his big brother. "I do see the family resemblance."

Quint nodded.

"It's unmistakable," he said.

She took a step closer and pressed a tender kiss to his lips. "Be careful tonight going to Galveston without me." What she really meant to say was "without backup," but figured he probably knew what she was trying to say.

"Always am," he said with a spark in his eyes. "But you can keep kissing me all you want until I fully comprehend the message."

"I keep kissing you and I'll never make it to my shift on time," she stated, and she wasn't kidding. She could stand there and kiss Quint all day long. Since that wasn't an option, she chugged her coffee instead. "In fact, I should probably get ready."

"Killjoy," he said, tugging at her arm as she walked past and he balanced the laptop with his free hand.

"You have no idea how difficult it is for me to go to work today," she said with a smile.

"Same." He dipped his head down and kissed her. It was tender with a hint of so much more. She'd had "so much more" earlier today and had to say that she wouldn't mind a few more rounds.

"We should probably think about getting serious," she said after he pulled back and they both took in a deep breath.

"It may be too late for that," he practically mumbled.

She reminded herself not to ask for clarification as to whether or not he was still talking about work.

Ree dressed in her uniform and returned to the kitchen half an hour later.

"There's a salad in the fridge if you're hungry. I'd volunteer to bring you dinner at work, but I doubt I'll be around," he said. Those words sat a little heavy on her chest. This seemed like a good time to remind herself just how stellar an agent Quint was and how capable he was of taking care of himself in potentially dangerous situations.

"I'm still not thrilled that you'll be going to Galveston without backup," she admitted, pulling a Caesar salad from the fridge.

"It's just me getting the lay of the land. Nothing more. There won't be any engagement," he reassured.

So why was she still stressed about him leaving? Galveston was only a forty-five-minute drive without traffic. He could be there and back before her shift was over. Whatever was bothering her, Ree needed to shake it off.

"ARE YOU READY?" Ree stood in the hallway looking a little too good.

"Let's do this." Quint would be ready to go to Galveston the minute after he returned from walking Ree to the bar. "And don't worry about me. I'll be careful."

"I know you will. You're important to me," she said by way of explanation, giving him a kiss before they headed out the door.

Partners relied on each other in life-and-death situations. Was their personal relationship clouding their objectivity?

Quint didn't want to put a whole lot of stock into the thought as they stepped inside the waiting elevator. Instead, he reached for her hand and entwined their fingers. The move had become habit in a short time, and the link more reassuring than it probably should be.

Neither spoke or seemed to feel the need to fill the air with words. Instead, she squeezed his hand like it was a life raft.

"I could hold off on making the trip if it—"

"No. Go ahead," she reassured him as they hit the lobby floor. "You'll be fine without me."

"You're pretty amazing," he said to her, and meant every word.

"I know." She smirked. The playfulness was back in full force as they walked outside into the Texas heat.

He shook his head and smiled.

Ree nudged him and gave an almost imperceptible nod to the right. He glanced over and, out of the corner of his eye, saw Baptiste holding a little dark-haired girl's hand and walking toward the building. The kid was unmistakable... Lili. She had a small ice-cream cone in her other hand.

He squeezed Ree's hand to acknowledge he saw them. Baptiste the babysitter? This whole scenario didn't sit well.

"Interesting" was all Ree said.

"Isn't it?"

There was no use trying to talk about it here in the open. It did make Quint wonder if he should stick around here rather than head down to Galveston. Then again, this might be exactly the time to make the trip. If Baptiste was here, then Constantin might be as well. Quint could nose around at their home base without too much concern for being caught.

Ree stopped short of the front door of the bar.

"It sure is hot outside today," she said.

"I do feel the temperature heating up," he agreed. There'd been no sign of Matias, so Quint would check to see if Grappell had any intel on his movements.

"Drive safe." She gave him a quick kiss and then a look that stirred something deep in the center of his chest.

"See you at the end of your shift," he promised.

"I'm holding you to that," she said before turning around and walking inside the glass doors.

He saw Lola waving Ree over and figured she was ready to dig into conversation. Again, Lola didn't seem the drug-running, weapons-trading type. Was she that good at fooling people? At tricking him? It had been a long time since anyone had snowed him to that degree. There'd been questionable folks in the past he could put on either side of the equation and not think twice if he'd put them in the wrong bucket.

Maybe Ree could get information from Lola and they could get a break in the case. There were a lot of random dots that needed connecting. The most disturbing piece of information was Baptiste with Lola's daughter.

Quint hoofed it back to the building, truck key in hand. True to Bjorn's word, the vehicle had arrived with new tires this morning. She'd threatened to personally charge him for the expensive set after hearing from the DEA director.

He hopped in the truck and made the drive to Galveston in record time, noting the Fish Shack at the entrance to Constantin's neighborhood. Constantin's home was on the bay side. It was painted a teal blue and looked like something he'd expect to see in Key West, complete with a mounted sailfish hanging on one of the outside walls.

There were no vehicles parked underneath or on the parking pad, which didn't mean no one had eyes on the place. In fact, from where he stood at the house next door, he'd already noted two cameras. Did Constantin live here? This was his address of record. It was possible he had another place in Houston closer to his business that might be rented under someone else's name. His brother's? There could also be a cash-only deal going on without a paper trail. Criminals had plenty of tools at their disposal to help them stay under the radar. A large part of law enforcement was trying to stay one step ahead. Or at the very least not falling too far behind.

There was a light on in the kitchen of Constantin's house and light flickering as though a TV was on. Someone could be there to watch the place. On second thought, the person would most likely have transportation. A housekeeper might make sense. Someone to cook and clean for Constantin and his brother, and basically look after the place while they were gone.

Not much seemed to be going on here, but he pitched a listening device toward the place, nailing a pillar. He moved toward the water, checking for a boat. The main reason to live bayside was to have a place with direct water access. A boat was secured, so nothing to report there. The thought occurred to him to hop into the water and swim over, dropping a listening device and tracker onto the boat. Another set of cameras would make going undetected next to impossible.

Constantin and his brother must stay here at least part of the time. Lola had mentioned going to Galveston on her day off.

Since this trip was turning out to be a dud, he hopped back inside his truck and visited the nearest restaurant. If Constantin wanted to go somewhere for a meeting, the Fish Shack would be the perfect place. It had a dive-bar feel with dim lights and lots of privacy in the booths. The bar took up one side of the place, running along the right wall. A few folks dotted the long counter.

"Table for one?" the twenty-ish hostess asked. "Or will you be sitting at the bar tonight?"

Quint patted down his pockets. "You know what? I

just realized that I left my wallet in my truck. I'll be right back."

"Okay." The hostess practically beamed.

Quint walked out, hopped in his truck and got back on the highway running toward the city. There was no use spending much more time in Galveston. This seemed like Constantin's private residence, where he took Lola and Lili, and not where he did business. Good to know. If anything was going on worth knowing here, the listening device should help find it.

The drive home went by fast as Quint turned the radio to a country-and-western station. Randy Travis was on, so Quint rolled down the windows and turned up the sound. As he got closer to his building, he rolled the windows back up, turned off the radio. There was something about a warm late-summer night and the sound of Randy Travis's voice that gave Quint the feeling everything was right in the world.

Or was the feeling coming from the thought that Ree would be off work soon? He parked in their spot and then headed up to the seventh floor. Her shift didn't end for another couple of hours, so he opened the laptop and grabbed a power bar to tide him over while he fiddled around.

Esteban's connection to Constantin and Baptiste wasn't a stretch. After all, Lola and Constantin were in a serious relationship. Matias's being in Houston shouldn't surprise anyone considering he was Lili's father. Quint made a note in the case file asking if Matias had been involved with Lili her entire life or if he'd recently found out about his daughter. He wished he could just ask Lola outright, but getting too personal would look suspicious. He'd won some trust by telling her about the spyware. There was no need to blow it now.

Quint requested as much DEA information about Matias as they were willing to give. Somehow, he doubted Driver would pony up information, but Shelly might see the question. She'd made it clear she wanted to cooperate and didn't share her partner's views. In fact, she was the one person who seemed more put off by having to work with Driver than they were. Rightfully so. As much as Driver annoyed Quint, at least they weren't partners. He couldn't imagine working side by side with Wonder Boy.

That being said, Quint figured he could ask Ree to reach out to Shelly now that her number was on Ree's cell phone. The numbers were phantom if anyone tried to trace them from the outside. They would link to a made-up identity.

Quint took a power nap before freshening up and heading out to the bar. Once there, he stood, arms crossed, leaning against a barricade blocking vehicles from driving in front of the pedestrian area and glanced around. Constantin sat in his Lamborghini, the engine idling. Either the transport business was incredibly lucrative, or crime paid. His money was on the latter.

Lola stepped out with Ree, who smiled at him the second she spotted him. There was something extra special about her smile tonight. A piece of him wanted it to be about what had happened earlier between them. Instinct said she got information from Lola. Then again, maybe it was both. He could only hope that was true. Either way, he was about to find out.

Chapter Twenty

The minute Ree made eye contact with Quint, her chest squeezed, and she was filled with warmth.

"Bye," she said to Lola, who waved before getting into the bright yellow sports car. Seriously? If Ree had the kind of money to spend on a vehicle like that she most certainly wouldn't buy one that was highlighter yellow. Constantin might have good taste in girlfriends, but that was where it ended.

Quint hauled her against his chest and kissed her. Properly. Thoroughly.

"The first kiss was for me," he whispered, his lips so close to her ear she could feel his warm breath. A sensitized skitter ran the length of her neck.

He linked their fingers and held tight as they made the trek back to the apartment. Once inside, he went straight to the fridge while she changed into something more comfortable.

"How did it go in Galveston?" she asked.

He gave a quick rundown.

"Did you find out anything new at work?"

"It was far too busy to talk," Ree said with disappointment in her voice.

Quint muttered a curse.

"I need to do laundry tomorrow before work," she said

as a knock sounded at the door. Her heart galloped as she walked over to the door and then checked the peephole. She opened the door to Angie. "Hey. Everything okay?"

"It's late, I know," Angie started, balancing two glasses of wine in her hands. "Can I come in? I brought alcohol."

"Um, yeah, sure. Why not," Ree said, stumbling a little bit. She took a step back. "Come on in."

"I can run down and throw in a load of laundry while the two of you talk," Quint said.

"You'd do my laundry?" Ree asked, not bothering to mask her shock. And then she realized that might sound funny coming from a married woman.

Angie must have been in her own world, because she walked on in and plopped down on the sofa, setting the wineglasses down on the coffee table. Ree shot a look toward Quint, and he smiled.

He mouthed the words *no worries*. "I'll heat up your plate of leftovers and bring it into the living room. Looks like Angie needs to talk."

"Thank you, honey," she said before walking over and planting a sweet kiss on his lips.

"Save more of that for later," he said with a wink that brought on a serious smile. The man was gorgeous and funny. He was smart and could handle himself in pretty much any situation. Her heart needed Bubble Wrap for the damage a person like that could do given direct access. Was it too late?

"What happened?" Ree asked as she turned to face Angie and headed into the living room.

"I heard your door open, so I knew you'd be up. I hope this is okay," Angie said. Her face twisted in distress.

"Totally fine," Ree said, taking a seat. "It would have been totally unacceptable without the wine, though."

Angie laughed. Quint brought over a warm plate of food

and set it on the coffee table before excusing himself. All hope there would be a sexual repeat of this afternoon died as Angie settled in.

"What's wrong?" Ree asked.

"This test is going to be the death of me," Angie whined. "It's so stressful and my parents will kill me if I don't get a decent score. Do you know how proud of me they sounded when I told them I was going to apply to law school?"

"I'm sure they'll understand," Ree pointed out. "You've been studying your behind off."

Angie kicked into her version of life with her parents and their expectations as Quint slipped out the door with a bag of laundry in his hands.

Quint had one of those eyes-on-him feelings as he exited the elevator and then opened the door to the laundry room. He'd turned around twice only to find an empty hallway. He was either becoming paranoid or starting to second-guess himself. Neither was good for his line of work. His backup weapon was tucked neatly inside his ankle holster and within easy reach, he thought as the hairs on the back of his neck pricked.

He loaded up the washer, bought soap from the vending machine and turned around to find Baptiste standing in the doorway. There was no chance this was a coincidence. And Quint realized it because Baptiste wasn't carrying any laundry. The fact that the man leered at Quint was another clue. There were no weapons in Baptiste's hands, so that was probably a good sign he didn't intend to take Quint out of this room in a body bag.

"Need to borrow any soap?" Quint asked, sizing his opponent up. Baptiste was considerably smaller in stature, but Quint would put money on the younger man being surprisingly strong. There was something about his wiry build that said he was scrappy. His nose had been broken at least twice. There was a sizable scar above his left cheek.

"No." The one-word answer revealed a thick accent.

"Mind if I continue, then?" Quint asked, using the stall tactic to size up his opponent. As it was, he was going to have to walk in front of Baptiste to get to the washer on the other side of the room.

Baptiste shrugged. "Don't mind me."

Quint took in a breath and crossed the room. He dug his thumbnail into the packet of laundry soap, creating a sizable hole that he kept plugged with said thumb.

As predicted, Baptiste threw a punch and bum-rushed Quint all at once. Quint unplugged the soap and flung it into Baptiste's eyes. He yelled a few choice words as he threw a shoulder into Quint, driving him into a stacked dryer unit. He came up with an elbow to the face and heard a snap when he made contact. Another broken nose? This guy was about to get even uglier. Up close, he already had the marks of a professional boxer.

Baptiste drew up his knee but Quint hopped out of the way just in time, having anticipated the move. As Baptiste blinked what must be blurry, burning eyes, Quint emptied the rest of the soap there.

The move caused Baptiste to scream out in pain and throw a flurry of punches. One of them connected to Quint's jaw, another to his nose.

"What's your problem exactly?" Quint asked, countering with a punch to Baptiste's rib cage.

The man doubled over and dropped down to his knees. Quint kicked him with the toe of his boot before walking away and buying another packet of laundry detergent as Baptiste regrouped.

"Don't you ever look at the little girl I was with earlier again," he finally spit out.

"Or what?" Quint asked as he walked past the man and then loaded his soap into the machine. "You'll do what to me?"

"Not just me… My brother will make certain you never walk again." Baptiste rubbed red eyes as he nodded toward Quint's ankles.

"Yeah? Tell your brother that his threats don't scare me and I'll look at anyone I damn well please," Quint said through clenched teeth. He'd taken a punch that was going to hurt later once the adrenaline wore off. Frustration burned through him. "But for the record, I don't give a rat's… Let's just say little girls don't do anything for me."

"Tell that bitch of a wife of yours to watch it," Baptiste said as he backpedaled toward the door. "She's poking around where she doesn't belong."

"How about this instead? Mind your own damn business. My wife can speak to whomever she wants, whenever she wants. She's a grown woman who can think for herself." Quint felt the trickle of blood from his own nose and figured there'd be some explaining to do when he got home. "And if anything happens to this laundry, I'll know exactly where to look."

Baptiste hesitated at the door. He'd underestimated Quint. It wouldn't happen again. Next time, if there was one, Baptiste would be more prepared.

"Hear what I said" was all Baptiste said before turning to walk away.

Quint made his way back to the apartment, needing to stem the nosebleed. He walked into the apartment after unlocking the door and went straight into the kitchen, hoping the distraction in the next room would stop Ree from figuring out what had just happened. She'd had a bad feeling earlier today, and he didn't want to worry her.

But make no mistake about it, Quint considered himself warned by Constantin.

His first thought was that Constantin knew about the trip to Galveston, but Baptiste hadn't mentioned anything about it. He'd been concerned about the little girl. As much as Quint wanted to give the guy a medal for his "genuine" concern, he recognized a threat when he received one.

"Hey, honey," Ree said in a subtle tone that said she needed to be rescued.

"I'll be right there," he said, wadding up a few paper towels before pressing them to his nose. He blotted the towel and realized there was a small cut on the side of his nose. He made a move to go to the bathroom but got caught halfway there.

"Honey?" Ree said.

"Bathroom" was all he said. "It's a nosebleed. The weather must be changing."

"I get those, too," Angie said, clearly having had some wine. "It's how I know the seasons are about to turn."

Quint didn't look over, and to Ree that would be suspicious as hell. Angie kept prattling on about living a lie and how hard it was not being honest with her parents, how she was about to fail the LSAT, and how they'd blame her boyfriend if they ever found out about the living arrangement, which clearly they would at some point. She seemed certain of it.

"If they love you, they'll understand if you get a bad score," Ree reassured her, but she was drowning.

"I don't know," Angie said. "They're so judgmental and have such high expectations of me. I feel like I disappoint them all the time."

"I bet they're proud of you," Ree said, but there was no conviction in her voice. Was she reminded of her own family's disapproval of her job? Of her mother's disappointment in having a daughter who didn't turn out to be the person she'd hoped?

"Maybe," Angie said.

"And you know what? Who cares if they aren't?" Ree finally said, and he had to fight the urge to go into the next room and cheer. Ree was an intelligent, kind, funny and beautiful woman inside and out. How any mother wouldn't burst with pride at having Ree as her daughter was beyond him.

He grabbed his first aid kit out of the cabinet and checked the mirror. The cut wasn't bad. Thankfully, the cut wasn't on top of his head. Those could make a person think they needed a trip to the ER for how much blood came out of the tiniest nick.

After cleaning himself up, he figured hopping in the shower might give Angie the hint to leave. Fifteen minutes later, he joined Ree and their company in the living room.

"I'll grab the laundry," he said as Angie stood up. Her wineglass was empty, as was Ree's, and the tension in Angie's face was gone.

"I should go," Angie said, picking up both glasses.

"I'll walk you out," Quint offered.

At the door, Ree touched his forearm. Her gaze lingered on the cut on his nose. He gave a slight nod.

"I'll come to the laundry with you," Ree offered. "Meet you at the elevator?"

"Sounds like a plan." He realized instantly that she'd caught on and was going for her weapon.

Angie split, heading into her apartment. Quint held off on pushing the elevator button. At this time of night, it wouldn't be difficult to get one. Ree joined him a minute later. She hid her waist holster well, but he knew what to look for.

After linking their fingers, he retrieved the elevator. A

car waited on their floor, so the bell dinged immediately. It was the same car he'd used a short while ago, and probably a good sign there hadn't been any activity since. He'd feel even better if this was the only elevator.

The walk down the hallway had him tightening his grip on Ree's hand. A few steps before the laundry room door, he filled her in on what had happened before he let go of her fingers so they'd be ready to pull a weapon in a heartbeat should the need arise. Quint figured being ready for Baptiste had given him all the advantage he'd needed to dispatch the threat. Being caught off guard always put someone at a disadvantage. His ribs were feeling the pain from a few of those jabs. His face hurt. But he was alive and kicking, and nothing had happened that a good night of sleep and an ibuprofen couldn't cure.

"Washer's done," he said as they entered the quiet room. Ree went right and he went left as though they'd practiced this routine a hundred times. When her side of the room was cleared, she gave the hand signal. He did the same before they reunited at the washer with her clothes inside. She was quiet as she worked and he could tell she was processing the information about him being attacked.

Together, they moved the load into the dryer, checking each piece for signs a listening device had been planted. He doubted it and, based on her expression, so did she. It was important to consider every possibility.

They sat in silence while the dryer spun the clothes around, keeping an eye toward the door just in case. He used a washer as a backrest as she leaned against him. He looped his arms around her, clasping his hands. She stood, back to his chest. Quint could stand like this forever.

The dryer stopped, so they emptied it, draping clothes over their arms so they wouldn't wrinkle.

Once back inside the apartment, Ree immediately said,

"I'll take care of these." She shooed him away. "Now, tell me everything that happened with Baptiste in the laundry room."

He sat on the edge of the bed.

"Nothing too terrible happened. He didn't like the fact that I saw him with Lili earlier in the day," he said. "Then he warned me about you getting too close to Lola."

"I've been wanting to tell you something all night but Angie was here," Ree stated. "Constantin takes Lola to Galveston on her days off like we assumed. Constantin has his own place near here, though. It's a house, and he's been pressuring Lola to move in with him. She's been holding off, says she isn't certain he's 'the one,' but I can tell it's something else. There's something about her disposition that changes when she talks about him."

"She did just find out he was most likely spying on her via her laptop," he pointed out.

"That's true," she said. "And a very good observation. It might be the stress of realizing her boyfriend doesn't trust her that causes tension in her face muscles now when she talks about him. I have nothing to compare her reactions to since the subject didn't come up before she learned the news."

Quint nodded.

"Learning your boyfriend is spying doesn't exactly help if there are any trust issues in the first place," he added.

"True again," she agreed.

"What about Esteban?" he asked. "Were you able to get information about him?"

"Only that he does work for Constantin sometimes, and that information didn't come directly from Lola, by the way. He stopped by the bar and seemed to be frustrated about something. I overheard that Esteban is basically being blackmailed into running these 'special errands' as he called them," she informed him.

"He wants nothing to do with Constantin's business?" he asked.

"Absolutely not," she confirmed. "He said he wasn't sure how long he could keep doing it.

"Her response came immediately," she said. "She told him there was no choice."

"Sounds like Constantin is holding Esteban's illegal status over his head," Quint reasoned. He'd seen it before in past cases. Some folks were just born bad, ready to embrace the wrong side of the law. Others were brought to it by environment, growing up in a rough family situation, neighborhood or both. Then there were those who came to it by circumstance, a quick need for money and the feeling there was no other alternative, or, like in Esteban's case, blackmail.

"My mind went there, too," she admitted as she hung up her work blouse. "And that could be another reason why there's tension in her relationship with Constantin. She might not have known what she was getting into with him when they first started dating. Now, though, she's figuring out the real him, and it's not looking good."

"Knowing Constantin's business also makes it more difficult to leave him, and she would realize that he wouldn't want any loose ends running around. Also, the fact that Matias is in town complicates life for Lola and possibly Esteban," Quint noted. "I'd like to find out from the other team when he arrived in Houston, how frequently he shows up here and if they have a sense of when he might leave.

"Can you reach out to Shelly and find out everything she knows about Matias? There's not enough in the file to go on or give us any real insight into the man," Quint said.

"Lola doesn't like talking about him," Ree said.

"I've never met a person who enjoyed bringing up their past mistakes," he stated.

Ree nodded. "I'll shoot a text to Shelly while we're thinking about it." She hung up the last of the clothes and retrieved her phone. She sent the text and then set her phone on the nightstand, giving him a look that said things were about to get interesting between them. "Maybe we'll hear back by morning."

Quint shrugged out of his T-shirt as Ree climbed onto the bed, toward him.

Her cell phone picked that moment to interrupt them.

Chapter Twenty-One

On a sharp sigh, Ree backpedaled and grabbed her cell from the nightstand. Shelly. "That was fast."

"What did she say?" Quint asked.

"Word is that Matias is planning to duck out of the country. He's acting nervous and jumpy, and they want to move on him soon," she said.

"Wait. Hold on a minute. If they move on Matias, our investigation is done." Quint grabbed his shirt and his phone. "We can't allow that to happen."

"The department heads will work together—"

"No, the DEA will walk all over Bjorn, and I can't risk losing this trail toward Dumitru," Quint countered.

"No one is losing anything yet." Ree tried to inject some calm into a situation that had gone from DEFCON level five to one in two seconds. She read the rest of the text. "Arresting him once he leaves the country is that much more difficult, so Nick is pushing to act as soon as possible. Word of warning, he will move in the second he gets clearance."

Ree texted back asking how soon that might be. The response came almost immediately.

"Okay, so, it's looking like it could literally be any moment. We should probably be hearing from Bjorn soon and the DEA is 'promising' to give us as much warning as they can." Ree formed actual air quotes with her fingers when she said the word *promising*.

"We all know how this goes down. They won't give us a heads-up until they're on their way to the bust, seconds before making it, or done. All our work up to this point goes up in smoke." Quint fisted his left hand, and she figured he didn't even realize he was doing it. He white-knuckled his cell phone.

"Hold on. Shelly is typing again," Ree said. The message came through. "She doesn't think it'll go down before tomorrow night, if that helps at all."

"It does," Quint stated through clenched teeth. "We have less than twenty-four hours to figure out our case or get preempted by Wonder Boy over there."

Ree thanked Shelly for the information and the heads-up.

Ree said to Quint, "At least we know.

"What are the chances we can stay in place after the drug bust?" she asked, knowing it was too risky because everyone around Lola would be scrutinized. Since Ree's employment at the bar coincided with the bust, there was no way she wouldn't be suspect. At the very least, she would be scrutinized. It wouldn't be good for her or the case they were building against Constantin. Something dawned on her. "We must be getting close ourselves."

"How so?" Quint's eyebrow arched.

"What happened in the laundry room earlier. There's no way we would be sent a warning if Constantin and his brother were comfortable. Right?" she asked, snapping her fingers together. "We struck a nerve by me getting close to Lola."

"There's no way Baptiste saw me gawking at Lili, since I wasn't," he said. "I barely looked in their direction."

"Constantin is getting overly protective because…"

"I doubt they picked me up on their cameras in Galveston, because that was one of my first thoughts," he said, brainstorming out loud.

"If they did, it sure was fast," she said.

"There were a whole lot of cameras around the actual residence in Galveston. It didn't occur to me they could be on the neighborhood entrance as well," he reasoned.

"Baptiste didn't bring it up, though. He focused on Lili and Lola," she said.

"He might not have wanted to show his hand on the Galveston residence," he admitted. "There's a chance he might not have wanted me to know they saw the truck."

"I'm sure Constantin is keeping tabs on the building," she said. "We're new tenants. I work with Lola."

"All true," he said. "You have a few things going for you in that you let Angie take the lead of creating a friendship."

"That's probably why Lola doesn't suspect me of anything," she admitted. "But Constantin and his brother would pick up on those other things.

"Lola jumped at the chance to bring her laptop to you," Ree said. "Did that mean she was looking for a friend or a way out?"

"Too bad we can't march up to the ninth floor and ask," Quint stated.

"Wait a minute. That's a really good idea actually," Ree said.

"It's too risky. I've already been told to keep you away from Lola," Quint warned.

"Not me." Ree pointed next door. "Angie has a habit of showing up at people's doors, sometimes with wineglasses in hand."

"Or possibly coffee," he said. "Then again, Angie was headed to a coffee shop yesterday morning to study. Maybe she could get Lola out of the building. We could talk to her outside of here if Angie can get Lola out of the building without a tail. Maybe get a better feel for where Lola's head is in all this. Her brother wants a way out. The two seem close."

"Think we can get a message to Esteban?" she asked.

"I doubt it, and it would be too risky. We don't exactly know what his involvement is in all this," he said. "He might not want to work for Constantin, but that doesn't mean the guy is in the clear in my book."

"Right." Ree's cell buzzed again, indicating another text had come through. She grabbed her phone and checked the screen. "You've got to be kidding me."

"What?" Quint patted the bed in the spot next to him.

Ree moved beside him. "Shelly just warned us to keep an eye on our tires if we want to go anywhere tomorrow."

Quint was up and off that bed in the space of a heartbeat. Ree quickly followed, jumping in between him and the path to the door just in case he got any ideas. Instead, he started pacing. "That son of a bi—"

Ree put both hands up in the surrender position. "I know, but we need to be smart about how we handle this information."

"It was a so-called drug deal at the warehouse," Quint continued. "The 'dealer' had to be connected somehow to Wonder Boy as maybe an informant."

"That makes the most sense," she reasoned as anger heated the blood in her veins to the boiling point. Still, she managed to keep it together long enough to thank Shelly. "She is taking a big risk in telling us this."

"I know" was all Quint said.

"Lola gave me her phone number at the bar tonight," Ree said. "I forgot to mention that earlier."

"That could be what prompted the laundry room visit," he reasoned.

"True," she agreed. "Shelly could get into a whole lot of trouble sharing this with us, so please don't go storming up to Nick and give him a black eye even though he deserves it."

"I'm angry, not stupid. There's no way I'm giving him the satisfaction of taking my badge, even if it's just for a suspension, because of his actions," Quint said.

"Agreed." Ree circled the opposite way as she paced. Twice they almost collided, stopping for a second before sidestepping and moving on.

"The only question in my mind is, what are we going to do about it?" Quint said.

ALL QUINT COULD see was red. It was a hue that colored everything in the room, including Ree as she passed by. On her, however, it looked good. Hell, everything looked good on Ree.

"You're right about one thing, though," he said.

"Which is?" she asked as they looped past, making another round.

"I really want to punch the smug bastard," he said.

"He got us over a barrel with Bjorn," Ree stated.

"Damn right he did." More of that anger threatened to break through. He'd been managing it so far, but that didn't mean the teakettle wasn't about to boil over. "He put us exactly in the position he wanted, and now our hands are tied as to standing down while he takes over his side of the bust."

Ree stopped him midpace. She checked the time, which confused him.

"Is there anything that can be done about this in the next fifteen to twenty minutes?" she asked.

"Other than come up with a plan as to how we're going to take that bastard down and still protect our case?" he asked.

"All I see is red and I can't think clearly." She smoothed her flat palm over his chest. "But I can think of a great way to burn off some of this energy so we can."

That was pretty much all the encouragement Quint needed. In the next few seconds, hands roamed and at some point clothes ended up in a pile on the floor. Their bodies ended up a tangle in the sheets. And his heart ended up taking a huge hit.

After an incredible round of making love, she fell asleep in his arms. Quint followed soon after.

He had no idea how many hours had passed by the time he opened his eyes again.

"I'll make coffee this time," Ree said, peeling off the covers.

He wrapped his arm tighter around her. "Or we could just stay here. It'll only take a few seconds for me to be ready for another round."

Ree laughed. "At this rate, we'll never get out of bed."

"Sounds like a good plan to me," he said.

"But coffee first," she said, pushing against her restraints—his arms. "And then I promise you can have your way with me as much as you like."

"I'll make sure you keep your promise," he said.

"Oh, did I just hear Quint Casey make something that sounded like a commitment?" she said, clearly teasing, and yet the words struck like a physical blow. Was that what was happening here? And why did those words make him want to run in the opposite direction? Being with her in bed felt like the most natural thing in the world. Why did a few words hit him like a pole to the chest at a hundred miles an hour?

He mumbled something as he let go of her and then grabbed his clothes out of the pile. She sat on the edge of the bed for a long moment, silent. This was probably where he should say something to her that would explain the situation or how he truly felt about her. Except no words came. The only thing he knew for certain was that he cared about her more than he had anyone in a very long time. Maybe ever. But what did that mean for their partnership?

Relationships could come and go. Finding the perfect partner was a whole lot rarer. Quint sighed as he slipped on his T-shirt, boxers and then jeans, one leg at a time.

"We have to get Lola alone" was all he said as he crossed the room with his laptop. "Let's see. I haven't checked this in a while, so…"

He booted up the system after setting the device on the counter.

"Send her an email," Ree suggested, her tone clipped. Her back was to him as she made coffee.

Could he explain himself? Smooth things over with her? The last thing he wanted to do was make the situation worse.

"Think we could get to Lili?" he asked.

"It's possible," she said.

And then it dawned on him. "Why didn't I think about this earlier? Matias is about to leave, and suddenly Lili is at Baptiste's side. I'd bet money he and Constantin are protecting her because they realize Matias is about to bolt."

"That would explain Lola's nerves at the bar all night and possibly her discussion with her brother," she said. "Now that I really think about it, I think she told him to hang on a little while longer."

"She could be the key to all this," he stated. "She would do anything to keep her daughter safe."

"Are you suggesting we blackmail her into testifying?" Ree asked.

"It wouldn't be the first time a government agency used a kid to get someone to testify, but no," he said. "I'm proposing we get her alone and offer her protection if she's willing to go to court for us as a witness."

"Esteban has seen the inner workings of Constantin's business," she said with a nod. The coffee maker finished doing its job, so she turned her back to him and poured two cups of black coffee. When she turned around, her face was unreadable. "Here you go."

"Thank you," he said, taking the offering.

"Based on the conversation with Lola, Esteban wants to be free of running errands for Constantin," Ree said.

"Which doesn't necessarily mean he's not a criminal," Quint said. "But his sister and niece could be incentive to take the offering of a fresh start."

"You said Lola exchanges emails with her mother," Ree said. "How would that work exactly? Lola is all about her family, based on what I've seen so far."

"There's no father in the picture," he said. "I could take a request to Bjorn for the mother to be relocated along with Lola, her daughter and brother."

"You think our boss would go for it?" she asked.

"We won't know if we don't try." He opened the case file, and there it was. The report that said the DEA was about to close their case. Quint bit back a curse.

"What is it?" Ree asked.

"It's official." He turned the screen around to her so she could read it for herself. "The file was uploaded half an hour ago."

"At least Shelly gave us a heads-up it was coming," she said.

"And the knowledge that her partner was not to be trusted on any level," he stated.

"Do you think Bjorn would go to bat for us? Ask for a little more time?" Ree asked.

"Not after the truck incident. She's already angry with

me," he said. Quint exhaled slowly. "Not unless we can give her a damn good reason without throwing Shelly under the bus."

Ree took a sip of coffee.

"I might have an angle," she said.

"I'm all ears." Quint hoped the idea had teeth to it. He wanted to bring down Constantin and his brother more than ever, and before the DEA could make their move.

Chapter Twenty-Two

"Do you think we could get Agent Grappell to rush a warrant?" Ree asked, stuffing down the hurt from their earlier conversation in order to focus on the case again. "All we need is access to the warehouse. You could go in as a distraction."

"Constantin could lie. Say he had no knowledge of what was going in and out of that warehouse. It doesn't directly tie him to any crime," Quint pointed out.

"It would be enough to arrest him. While he's detained, I'd have time to work on Lola to see if I can convince her to testify," Ree stated.

"Are you suggesting we go behind Bjorn's back?" he asked.

"Not so much behind her back as doing our jobs without telling her first. We do that all the time," Ree said. "You know how these investigations go. Sometimes things have to move quickly."

"What about the DEA? Matias will get spooked if we go for an arrest with Constantin and Baptiste," Quint said.

"All I can do is ask Shelly to give us a heads-up moments before the arrest goes down," she said. "I trust her."

"We'd have to in order to pull this off. A simultaneous arrest?" he asked. "There could be a lot of moving parts."

"However, what are the chances Matias is going to be in the same location as Constantin?" she asked.

"Good point there," he said. "Okay, I'll see what Grappell thinks."

Quint grabbed his cell phone and made the call. Phone calls like this happened on cases from time to time when judges had to be awakened for warrants. Time was of the essence in this case. The thought of wrapping it up and moving on from Quint to let him chase Dumitru crossed Ree's mind. Was she getting in too deep on a personal level with Quint? These things happened, too. The intensity of an investigation coupled with the fact that two people were relying on each other in life-and-death situations caused people to sometimes confuse that with true intimacy. Those in-the-heat-of-the-moment relationships always fizzled out, leaving the partnership all kinds of awkward. Agents sometimes asked to be reassigned to work with different partners, and the gossip mill usually figured out the reason. It always came back to a romantic relationship.

How could Ree have been so naive?

She wasn't, a little voice in the back of her mind pointed out. She was falling in love. Two totally different things. Once the partnership was over, the couple would be, too.

Quint ended the call and gave a thumbs-up signal. "Grappell will text when he has the warrant secured."

"Good." It was the only word that came to mind despite feeling the exact opposite. "Do you think this can all go down while I'm at work tonight? It's Thursday, so the shift will be busy, but I should still be able to pull Lola aside, especially if I get there early."

"You've made good progress with her in a short time-frame," he said.

"I think she sees me as a friend," Ree said. "I just hope we're turning her world upside down for good reason."

"Putting a dangerous criminal behind bars is always a good reason," Quint pointed out.

Ree nodded. In theory, she knew it was true. But Lola had come to this country presumably to build a better life for her daughter. Her brother came along, too. Again, her mind snapped to him wanting a better life.

Quint was busy typing up the request to have someone at the ready in Argentina at Lola's mother's house to grab her for witness protection. Knowing her mother was secure and coming to America might sweeten the pot for Lola. Why a woman like her would have gotten mixed up with a jerk like Constantin was beyond Ree. And then the reason dawned on her.

"This is just a guess, but hear me out," Ree started.

He stopped typing and glanced up. The second he saw the seriousness in her eyes, his expression morphed and he sat a little straighter.

"Something we said earlier resonates with me," she began. "Lola would do anything for Lili, right?"

"I believe so," he stated. "From everything we've seen and heard she's a caring mother who is doing her best to protect the little girl from her father..."

Quint's eyes sparked as Ree held up her index finger.

"What you're saying is Lola's relationship with Constantin was always a business transaction for her," he said.

"A way to keep her daughter safe from a guy like Matias, who could potentially grab Lili and take her back to Argentina," Ree reasoned.

"So, Lola meets a bigger criminal and, being beautiful, easily brings him into her life as her boyfriend. He's serious about her, but she's the one holding out because she doesn't love him," Quint stated.

"And never did," Ree added.

"But she's stuck now because Matias is always looming," he continued. "And always a threat."

"Constantin even brings her brother into the 'family' business as a show of trust," Ree said.

"It makes perfect sense to me," Quint stated.

"This is truly my first hope she'll listen to me and go into WITSEC. We can give her and Esteban a new identity," Ree said.

"In my experience, people from other countries living here illegally don't exactly trust American law enforcement," Quint said.

"That's a barrier we'll have to overcome with her," she said. "I strongly believe that if we convince Lola to take the deal in exchange for her and Esteban's testimony, she can convince her brother to go along with the plan. He wants out anyway. Even if he lies low for a couple of years, he'll be able to go anywhere he wants and do anything once he has permanent citizenship."

"She might have a difficult time turning on Constantin. We have no idea how loyal she is. He's been protecting her and Lili for at least a couple of years now," Quint pointed out. "She might not be able to bring herself to turn against him."

"That's the risk we take," Ree said. "But I don't see a whole lot of options if you want to bring this bastard down."

"This is the equivalent of a Hail Mary touchdown," he mumbled.

"Bigger miracles have happened," she responded.

He looked like he was about to open his mouth to speak as the air in the room changed. Since she wasn't ready to talk about "them" and she feared he'd spring the whole "it's not you, it's me" bit on her, she figured she'd save him the time.

"I think we've talked enough for one night, don't you?" she asked as his mouth clamped shut.

"Okay," he said.

"So let's just go to our respective corners and take a little time to figure out what we need to do to wrap this case in a big bow," she continued.

"Okay," he said.

"Fine," she commented. "And don't say *okay* again."

His lips compressed into a thin line. His expression said he was holding back what he really wanted to say. His face told her the news wouldn't be good for her. There was no reason to take that bullet while they needed to plan the next few hours.

QUINT SAT AT the counter while Ree took the sofa. There was so much he needed to say to her, but she was right about one thing. Now wasn't the time.

He spent the rest of the night mapping out a plan and lining up resources with Grappell. A couple of agents mobilized, planning to meet up at the warehouse ten minutes after Ree's shift started at four o'clock. As for Matias, Quint couldn't care less what happened on that side of the bust. Ree was right. The two wouldn't cross over because the likelihood Matias and Constantin would be in the same room was almost zero. Unless, of course, Quint factored in the bar.

Speaking of which, he intended to follow Constantin after he dropped off Lola, because he wanted to personally make that arrest. Baptiste would be under surveillance as well. He would most likely be at the Galveston house or Houston home. Quint's money was on the place closest to here while Matias was in town. In fact, it wouldn't surprise Quint if Matias stayed in Lola's apartment while she worked. It made the most sense when he really thought about it. Baptiste seemed to have an eye for movement in the building and was in charge of keeping watch over Lili at least part of the time.

His cell started dinging over the next few hours as assets moved into place. There would be four agents at the warehouse to make arrests and confiscate equipment. Quint had every intention of being the one to put cuffs on Constantin. Bonus if he got to arrest Baptiste as well. An agent was assigned to work with Quint.

It wasn't lost on him that Ree would be tucked safely away at the bar while the arrests went down. In order to be able to hold on to Constantin, they needed Lola's agreement to testify. In many respects, Ree's job was going to be the linchpin in their whole operation.

Out of courtesy, he intended to send Shelly a text before everything went down. Bjorn might be involved on the back end, so the notice might be too little, too late on his part. But he planned to do it anyway out of courtesy for Shelly giving them a heads-up. Arrests would be timed in the order of Constantin and Baptiste, then the warehouse. Any other order and Constantin and Baptiste would likely disappear. The warehouse had to be timed last.

The day was long and the apartment was quiet save for the click-click-clack of the keyboard or the occasional cell phone buzz, indicating a message had come through. Meals came and went. Information was exchanged. And then it was time to walk Ree to work.

"When this is over, I'd like a few minutes of your time," he said to Ree before they walked out the door.

"I think we've said enough to each other, don't you?" she asked. "And don't worry, I know this case is a stepping-stone to what you really want, which is Dumitru. You don't have to show up to my mother's ranch to convince me to sign on. Just give me a couple of days to get my head on straight so I can get some distance and think clearly again."

"Are you sure that's what you want?" he asked, wishing for a different answer but resigned.

"Never been more certain of anything in my life," she said. "I've been thinking a lot about what you said before. People in this job can end up jaded and lonely if they don't make time for a personal life. When this is all over, I plan to prioritize finding that."

Before he could say a word, she grabbed the door handle and walked into the hallway. Angie popped her head out.

"Hey. How are my favorite neighbors today?" She practically beamed.

"That's one big smile you have on your face," Ree said, artfully dodging the subject of the two of them.

"I took your advice and told my parents about my fireman," Angie said.

"Yeah? I'm guessing by the smile on your face they took it well," Ree stated.

"Oh, not at first. But then they came to the realization that I'm a grown adult and in love." She flashed her left hand, and there was a sparkling rock on a certain finger.

"You got engaged?" Ree asked. When she turned, a tear ran down her cheek. It seemed to catch her off guard. She quickly thumbed it away and brought Angie into an embrace. "I'm so happy for you."

"LSAT be damned. My fireman said a score on a test wouldn't make him love me any more or less. I knew right then he was the one." Angie's smile could light the building in a blackout.

Quint offered his congratulations along with a brief hug. "The fireman is one lucky guy."

"You two have to come to my wedding," Angie said

with more energy than a Chihuahua after licking a bowl of espresso.

"We'd love to," Ree said, thumbing away another tear.

He'd seen it before. This job, the isolation, the lack of a "normal" life. It could get to a person after a while. Had it gotten to Ree?

"I better get to work," Ree said, "but I'm expecting an invite later."

"How about a glass of wine tonight to celebrate?" Angie asked.

"Rain check?" Ree asked.

"You bet." A little bit of Angie's bubble burst. She really was a good kid who deserved everything in life. Quint reminded himself that people like her were the reason he did this job in the first place. It had sounded corny when he spoke the words out loud in the past, but that didn't make them any less true.

"I'll see you later," Ree promised. She paused after taking a couple of steps toward the elevator. "Do me a favor tonight?"

"Sure. Anything," Angie responded.

"Stay inside your apartment. Binge-watch Netflix. Just tonight," Ree said.

"Okayyy." Angie had no idea why she was agreeing based on the look on her face, but she was a person of her word.

"I want to hear all about what you watched tomorrow at breakfast," Ree said, knowing full well she and Quint would be long gone by then. He doubted they would even come back to this apartment after the bust. One of the other agents would come in and clean up for them, sweeping the place and packing up their stuff, which would "magically" show up at the office tomorrow morning.

After this, Quint intended to take a few days off to

regroup and catch his breath before the next case. And there would be a next case. He didn't know how long it would take to get an in with the next rung on the ladder, but it would happen. It was a shame his certainty about life ended there and not with Ree.

Chapter Twenty-Three

Lola was already at work by the time Quint dropped Ree off at the bar. Agent Miguel Brown had been assigned to work the arrest with Quint. Brown was a solid agent and a lucky draw. The two had worked together a few times and had a good rapport.

Brown followed Constantin back to his Houston house. There was one hiccup. He had both his brother and Lili with him, which meant the two of them must know Matias was about to flee the country again. It also stood to reason that Matias wanted to take his daughter with him. Thus, the double protection.

The other complication was the fact that Wonder Boy might be staking out Constantin's house, since it seemed likely Matias would show there. None of this fell into the category of *warm and fuzzy* for Quint except for the fact that Ree would be twenty minutes away at the bar working on Lola.

Quint jogged back to his truck and then hopped into the driver's seat after checking all four tires. Thankfully, they had air. Otherwise, he'd planned to put a real hurt on Wonder Boy. He met Brown a couple of blocks from the residence.

Brown was six feet two inches of football-worthy build.

His black hair was cut military short. He didn't say a whole lot, which was fine with Quint.

Quint liked working with Agent Brown, or Brownie, as he'd been nicknamed.

"Hey, Brownie. Are you ready to do this?" Quint asked.

"I've been waiting for you," Brownie quipped as he stood at the driver's-side door of Quint's vehicle.

"I'm guessing you've been watching the place," Quint said.

"The floor plan is a three-bedroom. It's a two-story, and there are cameras. I found the weak spot, though. A bathroom window on the ground floor. Fair warning, it's tiny," Brownie said.

"Why is it always the bathroom window?" Quint groaned.

"They just don't expect us to be able to squeeze through, I guess." Brownie smiled. For a man of his size, Quint heard he could morph his body to fit the smallest places.

"Let's do this." Quint exited his vehicle after firing off a text to Shelly to give her a heads-up. Weapons at the ready and no darkness to shield them, he and Brownie trucked on past a few houses until they'd weaved their way to the bathroom window in question.

"You first," Brownie whispered. "I'll cover out here."

Quint forced the window open. Bathroom window locks in old houses weren't the hardest to get through. He used Brownie's thigh as leverage to hoist himself up and in. Quint waited for his partner to climb through and join him. They listened at the door of the hall bath to the voices coming from the next room.

"Any chance you speak Romanian?" Quint asked in barely a whisper.

Brownie compressed his lips into a frown as he shook his head.

They could go in guns blazing and risk a bullet with

Lili, which seemed like a horrible idea. There was no way Quint could do that to the little girl or her mother. No. They needed a distraction.

The wait seemed like an eternity. But the break came when someone knocked on the front door. A few seconds later, an argument broke out. Baptiste came running down the hall with Lili.

Quint jumped in front of Baptiste, and then threw a knockout punch that dazed the guy, grabbing the little girl before she fell to the floor. Capitalizing on the moment, Brownie made his move. A choke hold that Quint didn't wish on anybody. His respect level for Brownie went up a few more notches, though. The little girl was winding up to belt out a cry. Quint covered her mouth with his hand and tried to get her to make eye contact. No use. She was too young to understand any of this, so he made a funny face at her as Brownie took the man to the ground in a few moves that would make any high school wrestler proud.

When Baptiste was facedown and in cuffs, Quint handed over Lili and went for the living room.

Matias and Constantin were midfight. The door was open, and Wonder Boy rushed in about the same time as Quint. Great.

"Try not to get in my way," Quint shouted to the DEA agent. Shelly was nowhere to be seen, but then, Wonder Boy probably told her to wait in the car so he could take all the credit.

"What are you doing here?" Nick asked.

Quint had no time for small talk. As it was, Constantin had come up with a gun that was presently pointed at Matias's chest. Quint dived at them both and wrestled the gun out of Constantin's hand. The weapon went flying.

"Secure it" was all Quint managed to get out. The

DEA agent didn't seem capable of rolling up his sleeves and helping.

Two on one, Quint struggled for control of the fight. He took a couple of punches to the stomach and a kick to the shin that was going to leave a mark. It wasn't until Shelly arrived that he started to get the upper hand. She jumped into the fray as Wonder Boy stood near the door with his phone in hand, texting.

This guy needed to be slapped.

"You got him?" Quint asked Shelly as she rolled on top of Matias, practically crushing his arms, forcing them against his torso.

"I got this," she confirmed through gasps. Sure enough, she wrangled a pair of handcuffs onto Matias and then sat him on his backside.

By then, Quint had Constantin in cuffs.

"Do you plan on actually getting your hands dirty, Wonder Boy?" Quint probably shouldn't goad Nick, but he couldn't help himself. People like him made the job even more dangerous.

"What did you say?" Nick asked, looking ready to pick a fight now that all the heavy lifting was done. "I'm involving local police if you must know."

"This one belongs to us," Quint reassured.

A scared little girl cried in the background. All Quint could think was that he needed to get her to her mother.

Brownie poked his head in, looking like he didn't know what to do with the screaming kid in his arms.

"Grab the car seat out of the Lambo parked out back. I need to get this baby to her mother," Quint said as he took the little girl from Brownie's arms. "We're going to take you to your momma."

The little angel with big puffy red eyes said, "Momma?"

"That's right. Momma," Quint said. Before he could

check his phone to see where Ree was, she came bolting through the door.

The little girl hiccupped as she stuck her thumb in her mouth.

"I got here as fast as I could." Ree turned around and said, "It's done. It's safe. You can come take Lili now."

Ree gave a knowing look to Quint, and he realized Lola must have agreed to testify. She came running into the house as soon as Ree gave the green light, as did Esteban.

"My mother," Lola said as she took her daughter in her arms and started gently bouncing. "She will join us. No? That is the deal. No?"

"Your mother is being picked up by our agents as we speak." Quint double-checked his phone. "In fact, she's boarding a helicopter that will take her to an airport. She'll be here in the States by morning."

"Thank you," Lola said, hugging her daughter tighter to her chest. "It's been a nightmare ever since I realized what kind of person Matias was. I didn't know, and then I got pregnant. I don't regret my daughter, but I'm so tired of this life."

"And your brother?" Quint asked.

Lola nodded. "Is waiting in the car. He never wanted any part of this. He's a good person. He did what he had to in order to protect Lili."

"You're safe now," Quint reassured. "Let's get you out of here."

Lola nodded.

"You can't leave my scene," Nick stated.

"Don't worry," Shelly said to Quint. "I'll corroborate your side of the story."

"So will I," Brownie confirmed.

"Nick, it's time you took a desk job," Shelly said. "You won't get away with this one."

Quint gave her a quick salute before ushering his witness out the door. Ree followed, staying silent until they made it to the truck. Esteban joined them along the way, and it didn't take twenty minutes for a US marshal to pick up the family.

"Best of luck to you, Lola," Ree said, and in a surprise move gave Lola a hug.

"Thank you. Because of you, she'll have a life," Lola said. "Bless you and your family."

"I don't have a family of my own," Ree corrected.

"Someday, you will. And it will be beautiful," Lola said before walking away with the marshal.

Ree turned to Quint and said, "I guess our work is done."

"I'm not so sure about that," he said. "We'll be in paperwork up to our ears sorting this mess out."

"I'll leave most of that to you," she said. "I'm tired, and I need to sleep in my own bed tonight."

She turned to walk away, but he couldn't let her leave things like that. Not with so much left unsaid.

"Ree," he started.

She stopped.

"What if I'm not ready to be done?" he asked.

"I'm listening," she said.

"How big is your bed?" he asked, hope filling his chest.

"Give me a couple of days and come measure for yourself," she said as she kept walking in the opposite direction.

"I will," he said, and he fully meant it.

* * * * *

UNDERCOVER RESCUE

NICOLE HELM

For everyone who waited so patiently
for Shay's story.

Chapter One

Veronica Shay—or Veronica Vianni, depending on what legal document a person went by—had grown up knowing how to lie. She'd had a natural aptitude for it, much to her parents' dismay. She'd courted the wrong side of the law until they'd disowned her.

She hadn't cared much at the time. After all, she'd found her own family. A place she belonged.

Or so it had seemed.

It hadn't been a happily-ever-after, and for years she'd blamed everyone else for the horror she'd gotten herself into. It had only been when she'd started to take responsibility for her own actions that things had started to change.

She packed her bag *now*, trying not to think too deeply about *then*. The way her life had changed. So much for the better. She'd turned herself into someone who did the right thing. Who took down the bad guys rather than glittered on their arm.

Shay, the head of the North Star Group, a secretive collection of skilled operatives who'd worked together to take down the vicious Sons of the Badlands gang, and then thwarted a dangerous death machine supplying military grade weapons to all the wrong people, wasn't remotely recognizable to the eighteen-year-old Veronica Shay who'd married Frankie Vianni fifteen years ago.

Frankie Vianni who was supposed to be dead, but clearly *wasn't*. And thus was a threat to every member of North Star. Because there was no way he'd forgiven and forgotten the way she'd gotten out of the Vianni Mafia family—by getting a fat lot of them killed or jailed.

Shay hadn't expected to escape unscathed. Even when Granger Macmillan had taken her under his wing and brought her in on the ground floor of starting the North Star Group, she'd been waiting for Frankie to appear.

Two years ago, he or the ghost of him had nearly killed Granger, and because of pure luck or skill it was only *nearly*.

But someone had been irrevocably hurt, and it hadn't been her. The cause for it all. It had a member of her North Star family.

She wouldn't let that happen again. No matter what she had to do. Frankie had made it clear he was making his move. So, Shay would move right back. She would act. Bullet wound or no bullet wound.

She'd finally gotten rid of Betty, one of her closest friends and North Star's doctor. Sent her off to Montana to start her new life, and thus be out of Shay's hair. Sabrina and Connor were still around, two of her lead field agents, but she'd put them in charge of a mission that had gotten a few other regulars out of North Star headquarters.

She'd hired a pilot who wouldn't ask questions, asked him to meet her at an off-grid air strip, and was prepared to deal with her past, rather than wait for it to deal with her.

Because even if the past few weeks had been calm as

she'd healed, she knew it wasn't over. Frankie was just trying to make her sweat.

He didn't know the woman she'd become.

Shay slung her bag over her shoulder and winced. In an ideal world, she wouldn't be this hurt or in this much pain, but she'd made her choice to leave ideal behind a long time ago.

She left her room. She didn't *sneak*—sneaking would make someone pay too much attention, if someone did in fact see her. Which she had planned around.

She'd created this North Star headquarters. After their old one had burned down, thanks in part to Frankie's family, and Granger had put her in charge, she'd moved them from South Dakota to Wyoming. She'd designed this compound on an old deserted ranch, and worked hard to lead North Star as they took down people doing bad in the world.

This year had been successful and yet, important pieces of her team had left North Star for a real life. Marriage and babies and futures somewhere else. *Not* risking their lives. *Not* constantly fighting the bad in the world.

Once upon a time, Shay wouldn't have understood it. She would have scoffed at it, in fact. But her life had changed since that explosion over two years ago. Was it an age thing? Was it the fact that the man most hurt in the explosion was her one and only tie to her past?

She didn't know. So much so, she wasn't fully sure who she was anymore. She didn't even know what she wanted.

Except to be free of her youthful mistakes without them touching anyone else she cared about.

Shay walked with all the authority she could muster

as she moved through the maze of hallways and then out the front door.

Easy as you please. She slid her sunglasses on her face against the blinding sun bouncing off the snow. The vehicle would be a bit trickier. Since it was North Star property, any of their tech people could have it tracked.

She still hadn't figured out this part yet. Her best bet was to take a car and ditch it somewhere. Probably in the opposite direction of the airstrip.

No one was going to let her disappear. She'd tried that already. But Vianni's men had been on her tail so she hadn't had a chance to get everything in order first. And North Star had stepped in and stopped Vianni's men.

But Frankie hadn't been there. Likely, he'd sent a group of volunteers just to see if they could breech North Star. He wouldn't risk his own life until it was a sure thing.

Shay wasn't about to let it be a sure thing. She wasn't about to let her friends, or more accurately *found family* in North Star, step in and get hurt in the process. This wasn't North Star business. This was *Veronica Shay* business—an identity no one in her current life knew existed.

Except Granger Macmillan and Nina Wyatt. Nina wouldn't tell. In the year Nina had known about Shay's past, she'd never told her husband, which meant she'd snitch to no one.

Granger… Well, he was a bit more of a wild card these days but since his past connected to hers, she doubted he was in a hurry to let anyone in on it.

So, she got in her North Star vehicle and drove into Wanayi, a small town where Shay often went to buy groceries or other necessities. She studied the vehicles in the gas station parking lot. Any would be easy enough to steal, but none of them looked like they belonged to people who'd have an easy time replacing them.

She sat in her car, parked in the far corner of the lot, keeping out of sight, watching the comings and goings trying to figure out how to accomplish her goal. After about thirty minutes of this, a cab drove into the parking lot.

As far as signs went, Shay was willing to take this one. She watched the driver gas up, head inside. While he was paying, she quickly moved across the lot and slid into the back seat.

Even cabbies didn't lock up out here.

When he returned, he eyed her through the window before getting in. If he was surprised to find someone sitting in his cab, he didn't act it. But when he slid into the driver's side, he didn't close the door. He kept it open and one leg out.

"I'm off duty. No money on me," the man said in a smoker's rasp.

Shay held two twenties over the seats. "I've got cash. Half now. Half at the drop-off point. All you have to do is drive and not ask any questions and you can pocket that cash."

The man eyed the money, then his phone sitting in the middle console. Shay figured he was considering calling the cops. She couldn't blame him. She'd even let him—once she got the hell out of Dodge.

Eventually he took the bills and slid them into his pocket. He pulled his leg into the car and asked for an address. Shay gave him one in the general direction of where she was going.

He drove, eyeing her in the rearview every so often.

She kept herself looking relaxed, her bag far enough out of reach that he didn't think she'd grab it and try something shady.

When he got close enough to the airfield she thought she could walk without hurting her injuries too much, she leaned slowly forward. "This'll do."

The cabbie slowed to a stop, eyeing her suspiciously. "This ain't nowhere."

"Exactly." Shay handed him a hundred-dollar bill, didn't hurt to sweeten the pot. "Not a soul needs to know. Got it?"

He studied the bill, then her, and shrugged. "Fine."

She didn't know if it'd be enough. Especially if someone questioned him, but it would give her a head start anyway.

Shay got out of the cab, looked around. The snow would slow her down, but it was sunny day which would keep the bitter cold at bay. She didn't look back at the cab driver. Instead, she just got to work.

She walked away from the highway. Best not to be spotted if any car passed by. She knew the area well enough, because she'd studied it when she'd chosen North Star. Before they'd gotten their own little airstrip, they'd used this one.

It was about a mile. Not long, but she was dragging. Too damn tired for a little hike. This gunshot wound was a real pain.

Finally, she reached the private airstrip. Just a long strip of earth in the middle of nowhere. A plane was parked by the tiny office building.

She didn't head for the building. If she could avoid that, and just get to the pilot, she'd be better off. She frowned at the plane as she got closer. There was something vaguely familiar about it. Then again, all planes looked the same to her. Especially these small single engine ones that looked more like they belonged in an old WWII movie.

She didn't see any evidence of a pilot, so she moved for the plane. As she got closer, she could make out a pair of boots next to the opposite wheel. So someone was standing on the other side of the plane, most likely refueling or something.

Still, Shay surreptitiously put her hand close to the gun she had concealed at her back.

When the body stepped around, she braced herself for a fight. A nasty surprise.

The man's face was a surprise, but not quite the one she was expecting.

Tall, broad and all too familiar, even if she hadn't seen that reckless smile of his in too many years to name. Not because he'd been such a stranger, but because he hadn't smiled much since his injuries two years ago.

"Where to?" he asked.

Shay looked at him and knew she had three options.

She went with the dumb one, simply because it would feel good. She threw a punch.

"I'LL GIVE YOU that one for free," Granger Macmillan said, forcing himself to smile though he didn't feel it. Not because the blow had been painful, but because it hadn't been. He'd trained Shay himself. She was usually a better punch. Which meant her wound was really slowing her down.

"You don't give anyone anything for free, Granger," she grumbled.

He might have argued with her, but since she was the

only one he made allowances for these days, it felt a little too close to a truth he didn't want to parse.

"You look ridiculous in that hat," she said distastefully. "You're no cowboy."

"I don't know." He adjusted the hat on his head. "I think the cowboy life is growing on me."

She rolled her eyes.

"But I'd never give up flying." He patted the plane's glossy wing. "So, why don't you hop in and we can head off? Time's a wasting."

"So strange I don't recall inviting you."

He kept his voice as even as hers, without the casually cutting edge to it. "Well, good thing I don't need an invitation then."

She blew out a breath, clearly trying to get a hold of her temper. The problem she was going to run into was that he knew her better than anyone—including Betty or Nina or anyone else she considered her closest friends.

Because Granger had known her *before*. Had been the hand held out to save her from the Vianni family, and he knew for a fact not one person in their current lives knew what she'd been through or what she'd done before she'd turned herself into Shay, North Star operative and eventual leader.

He knew what people had thought back when he'd been in charge of North Star and given Shay more freedom and leeway than he'd given any of his other agents. That there'd been more going on between them than met the eye.

It had bothered him, but he'd always figured the best way to fight that rumor was to keep his hands to himself and his focus on the only thing North Star had been about back then: bringing down the Sons of the Badlands.

The gang had been instrumental in the murder of his wife, but only because the Vianni family had let them be.

"This has nothing to do with you," Shay said.

His attempt at keeping his cool faded. Maybe it was the memory of Anna's death, or maybe he was just tired of constantly being haunted by a past he couldn't seem to escape no matter how hard he tried. "The hell it doesn't."

"They were after me. They shot *me*." She didn't look him in the eye when she said either of those things, so she had to know.

"I heard they were asking about me too."

Her gaze whipped up to meet his. A storm in those blue depths. Not unusual—Shay had always been something of a storm. But this one wasn't controlled the way it needed to be if they were going to beat Vianni.

"It was a distraction," she said firmly.

If he was someone else, he might have even believed her. "How do you know?"

"Why would Frankie care about you, Granger?"

"I was married to his sister. I'm not the unconnected piece you want to make me."

"Anna's dead."

Yes, she was. It had taken him a long time—too long—to really accept that. To finally grieve and let go. Maybe it was only now that he was even getting there, but if he could count himself truly healed that meant every mention of her couldn't put his back up. "Yes, Anna's dead. How does he know you're not? *We're* not?"

"I don't know. I intend to find out."

"You need a pilot." He pointed at himself.

"Yeah, one who'll drop me off and let me do what

I need to do. Not play babysitter and try to make this about him and his dead wife."

A barb she knew would land, and God help him, he couldn't quite fight it off. "Get in the plane, Shay. Before I make you."

She raised an eyebrow at him.

"You aren't yourself. You're injured and still recovering. You need help. Now, you can pretend like you don't, but it's only going to get you killed before you even land." He held up a hand. "And before you argue with me, understand that punch didn't even hurt. I damn well wish it had, but it didn't. You hiked, what, a mile? And could barely catch your breath. I've been where you are, Shay. I know how much it weakens you. You need someone. If it's not going to be me, pick your poison. But someone."

She stood there, utterly still. Granger did the same, and he worked hard to keep his shoulders relaxed, to breathe instead of hold his breath. Why wouldn't she choose someone else? That Lindstrom guy she'd brought into North Star a few months ago could fly well enough, and was big and capable of handling whatever Shay waded into.

But this was about Vianni. It was about all they'd escaped ten years ago. It was about *their* pasts.

"What about your dogs?" she asked.

"I took them out to Reece's place."

She eventually let the bag slide off her shoulder and land with a thump on the ground. "I'm not going to Chicago," she said, strain evident in her voice.

"I didn't say you were." He grabbed her bag and tossed it in the plane. "You're going to the Vianni compound in Idaho. The one you've been researching for two years, and just found the exact coordinates to…what was it? Thursday?"

She didn't look surprised that he knew it. Just resigned. *Tired.*

"I'll let you fly me there, but you'll stay back. Let me handle this my way. I'll call in backup if I need it, but—"

"No," Granger said firmly, warring with his own temper and impatience. "We do this together."

"I get that you think because of Anna you have some connection to all this. But this is about me and Frankie. You're a pawn, maybe. Just like Anna was in the end. Don't fall for it twice, Granger."

"We do this together," he repeated. "That's the beginning and end of it. You can be pissy about it, bring Anna up as much as you want, but it doesn't change a damn thing. Vianni knows who and what we are and have been, and we need to stop whoever is left of that family before anyone else we care about is put in danger. Nothing else matters. Not your pride. Not your fears. That's what got you shot."

She quirked a brow. "Oh, is that what got me shot?"

"Yeah, it is. I know. I've been there. Remember? You're lucky they didn't get those explosives off like they did when they tried to take me out. You'd be dead."

"You weren't."

"Close enough." In more ways than one. "Get in the plane, Shay. And on the way, get used to the fact that we're partners now. Full stop."

Chapter Two

Shay got in the plane because she was tired. She got in the plane because it was there and once she got to Idaho, she'd ditch Granger.

She kept insisting in her own brain she'd leave him in the dust. Kept trying to convince herself she would and could.

But somewhere high in the clouds with the white of a Wyoming winter stretching out below them in this tiny old plane, Shay accepted the fact that in this *one* moment, Granger was right.

They had to be in this together. That was the fate she'd handcuffed herself to when she'd allowed him to give her a way out of her life and inevitable death in the Vianni family.

Maybe she'd known that all along. Maybe that was why she'd been so bound and determined to do it herself.

Allowing Granger into anything always made her life ten times more complicated. But life *was* complicated. Especially when you had a well of mistakes to atone for.

So, she worked on accepting her fate. In the cold and the loud rumble of the engine vibrating her from the inside out. They would work together. Put the Vianni ghosts to bed and then…

She closed her eyes against the wave of emotion that threatened. That had been threatening for months now.

She'd held on for two years, leading North Star through taking out the rest of the Sons of the Badlands. Finding new missions. Keeping everyone together and whole and working for *good*.

But Reece Montgomery, her lead field agent and most senior agent, had left this summer. Hard and cold Reece had fallen in *love*. And something about that had fractured…everything.

Seeing him with his pregnant wife, his stepson and lately the new baby, Shay had begun to realize that all these years she'd been trying to *do* something good, she'd mostly been running away from all the bad she'd done. And all the things she didn't know about herself. And sometimes even what she did know.

Like she didn't like being head of North Star. She didn't want to be an administrator or puppeteer or whatever it was she was supposed to have been. And worse, so much worse, she didn't want to be a field agent anymore. She didn't want to go back to the grind, the deception, the fighting. Once, that had been her entire life, but she felt creaky and old now.

Veronica Shay wanted to rest. She wanted some kind of…life. Like all the people who'd become her family were finding and building.

She didn't deserve it, but God she wanted it.

Sighing, she studied the man in the pilot's seat in front of her.

She'd known him, or at least of him, since she was seventeen. Frankie had put *Veronica* on his arm for all his fancy parties, showed her off like the decoration that she didn't realize she was and pointed out Granger Macmillan to her.

That man is the enemy, Veronica. Never forget, he wants us and our kind dead.

She'd asked him why they didn't just kill him then. She'd meant it. Frankie was the grandson of a group of dirty cops who'd been exposed and arrested, but the rest of the family had come together to build Vianni part two. They didn't even pretend to be law enforcement this time around. They were a mob family. Plain and simple.

They could have taken out some lowly DEA agent, Veronica had been sure of it. Had been intrigued by the power Frankie so often claimed to have.

Frankie had given her a cold smile and told her it was complicated.

Boy, had it been complicated.

Still was, though in different ways than it had been. And now, as Granger began their descent, Shay accepted that they were going to do this together. Because he was right, even if Frankie wasn't after Granger, they both had Vianni ghosts that needed to be laid to rest.

And Shay was not at her normal fighting shape. It would be smart to lean on Granger. Who knew…who understood.

She just wished it was *anyone else*.

He landed on another isolated strip of land. With a similar setup to the last one. Small building and hangar. This one wasn't as deserted though. A short rotund man exited the office as they touched ground.

Granger got out, then helped her out of the plane. She was beyond irritated she needed the help.

"Russ," Granger said, nodding to the man staring at them.

"Mac. Gas her up?"

Granger nodded. "I'll be back in a day or two, but feel free to bill me for the week."

"Got it."

Granger ushered her away from the office and toward a small parking lot that had a few cars and trucks parked in it. Granger pulled keys out of his pocket and the small nondescript sedan's lights flashed. "That's mine."

Shay nodded and didn't ask questions about how he had a car here already, if only because she knew he expected her to. She might be working with him on this, but that didn't mean she had to give him what he expected. She was too tired to play mental gymnastics with him, and she hurt all over.

She needed a nap, a meal and her pain meds.

They got into the car and Granger began to drive like he knew exactly where he was headed. Shay had no doubt he did. That's what this man did. Made plans. Plotted. Accomplished.

That was who he was at his core. So in control. She'd once had an uncomfortable hero worship toward him. He'd saved her, given her a purpose. He'd plotted and planned and taken down the group that had killed his wife, the group that had partnered with the Vianni family to do more widespread damage.

She'd felt betrayed when his need for revenge had somewhat overshadowed the good they were doing with North Star. She'd grown disillusioned enough to bend his rules, to stand up to him. But she'd never left. She'd never fully killed that part of her that felt like she owed him.

Then everything had blown up—literally and figuratively. And she still hadn't forgiven him for leaving

North Star the way he had. Something she hadn't fully admitted to herself until this moment.

She'd called him in on a few missions lately because he'd been physically recovered. Because he was always in the wings. But their relationship had changed. Soured. There was an antagonism that had grown, not leveled out, since the explosion.

She'd convinced herself it was power plays and Granger not being able to see her as a leader even though he'd put her in that position, but part of it was that she was just…so angry with him for abandoning them, for not accepting any help. For clearly being *bothered* that someone else had saved him rather than himself doing the saving.

Shay blew out a breath. Maybe she'd figure out how to let that go, maybe she wouldn't. The important thing right now was to focus on the plan. God knew he had one.

"I have the beginnings of a plan," he said, as if he could hear her thoughts. "But I figured you'd want a say in them, so they're nebulous as of yet."

She tried to hide her surprise. Granger was not one for *sharing* plans, or listening to other people's *say*. He was used to being in charge. To barking out orders.

"But first, we need a place to stay. I imagine you have meds to take or bandages to change or something, and then we can plot out how we think we're getting into a supposedly dead mobster's Idaho off-the-grid commune."

"There's one thing I know for sure," she said. "No matter how off the grid this compound is, *Frankie* isn't." A man who wanted to pull strings didn't remove himself from that power source. He simply moved the power source.

"Well, look at that, Shay. We agree on something."

GRANGER PULLED UP to the small rustic cabin in the middle of absolutely nowhere. Though he didn't have a specific plan for how this was going to go from here on out, he'd definitely been making some plans for how to get to this point.

When he'd realized Shay was going to make a move, and alone, he'd made sure his options were in place and ready.

He unlocked the door and let her inside. Shay said nothing as she looked around the place. She hadn't even asked any questions about where the car had come from, where they were going, how he knew to stay here.

She was keeping her questions to herself. He didn't know why that rubbed him the wrong way, so he tried very hard to act unbothered.

"This should give us a day or two to figure out how we want to move forward. It's far enough away from the compound they won't be looking for us here, and isolated enough North Star won't be able to suss out our location either."

Still, she said nothing, just stood in the entry of the cabin, clutching her bag and looking around like she was taking everything in.

When she finally glanced at him, there were no questions. No demands. No excitement to move forward in making plans. There was only hurt in her gaze.

"You knew before I did, didn't you?" Shay asked. There was something like betrayal in her tone and Granger tried to pretend he didn't hear it. *Feel* it.

"Knew what?"

"That Frankie was in Idaho. Alive. Plotting." She let her bag drop to the ground. "You knew for a lot longer than I did."

He had no reason to feel guilt over that. After he'd been shot and nearly died in the explosion that had destroyed North Star's headquarters, he'd begun to question who exactly the Vianni family consisted of these days.

Sure, a mob family could hold a grudge, but most of the ones left had no love lost for Frankie. Anna had told him a small faction of the family wanted to find a way to oust Frankie. So, they should have been glad when everything Granger had been a part of back in Chicago had taken him down.

Not found a way to come after him, even if it was in connection to something else. The only explanation in his mind had been... Frankie. Mobsters had faked their deaths before. Why not him?

"How long have you known he's alive?" she asked with no inflection in her tone.

"Shay, come on. Why does it—"

"How long?" she repeated, but this time there was more heat to it. A little fire in her eyes which eased some of the guilt. If she could be mad, things might be okay.

"I don't know. I've lost track."

"Over a year?"

Granger blew out a breath. "Yeah."

"Two?"

He shook his head. "I started looking into it a few months after the explosion. I'm not sure how long it took me to find proof."

"Proof," she echoed. "So you had the *thought* he was alive and hiding out even before that?"

Granger flung up his hands, and then realized he was letting her get to him when he'd promised he wouldn't. He wouldn't let weird emotional tangles interfere with what had to be done. How was he losing that battle already? "What do you want me to say?"

She laughed. Bitterly. "I don't know. I don't know what I expected. You have never, ever, not once trusted me."

"Not *trusted* you? You've always been my right hand. I bent rules for you. I let you *question* me. I *gave* you North Star—"

She scoffed, an actual unladylike snort. "You didn't trust me to lead North Star. You couldn't just back off and let me lead. You always had to be there and—"

"You think that's the reason I couldn't let go?" He bit off a curse.

North Star had been his *everything*. After Anna's murder, he had put all that was left of him into a group that would take down the men that had been responsible for that murder. And so many others. It had been revenge, sure, but it had also been about doing something…since he hadn't been able to do something when it had counted.

North Star had been his creation. Where he'd slowly come back to life again. Where he'd first felt like maybe he could survive, and maybe if he did enough good, the loss of his wife wouldn't weigh quite so heavy.

Shay had been there for that, and could still think his inability to let go was about *trust*? "You don't know me at all, Shay." Which was fine. What did it matter?

Maybe no one else had been in his life this long, maybe no one else…

It didn't *matter*. "All that matters is making sure Frankie can't hurt you again. So, are we going to get to work figuring out how to do that or do you want me to flay myself open with apologies I don't mean?"

"You knew he was alive and you didn't tell me," she said, and there was no emotion. Just a blank sort of intensity. "Which meant you left me more vulnerable than I needed to be."

"You didn't exactly rush to tell me once you figured it out, did you?"

"Because Frankie punished you already. He made sure you knew he was instrumental in letting the Sons get close enough to Anna to kill her. As far as he's concerned, I'm the one who escaped unscathed. This is about *me*."

"I need a drink," he muttered and moved off to the kitchen. Because if he didn't, he'd say something they'd both regret.

And there were already enough of those.

Chapter Three

Shay didn't follow him at first. She was too…hurt. She didn't want to be. So he knew Frankie was still alive before her and hadn't told her? She knew he would have brought it up if she'd been in immediate danger.

But this was the problem with Granger. He was solitary. He did things in his own mind, his own way and only ever let you in when the deed was already mostly done.

That had been fine and dandy when he'd been leading North Star and she'd been a field agent, working to break down the Sons. She hadn't needed to know each individual mission's goal. Instead, she'd followed orders because they were all leading to the main purpose.

Then he'd expected her to step in and lead. Without any warning, help or guidance. And she'd tried her damnedest to do her best. Sometimes she failed, but she had never buckled under the heavy weight of pressure and guilt.

Granger should have seen that. He should have told her the moment he suspected her *husband* was alive. Shay rubbed at her chest, where it ached with a million emotions she couldn't all parse.

Maybe trust wasn't the right word. Maybe he'd trusted

her. She didn't know. But he'd never let her in. Never treated her like an equal.

If they were going to do this—actually beat Frankie once and for all—he was going to have to.

She marched after him to tell him just that. To make it clear. To lay out how this was going to go—in other words, not like it used to. They weren't boss and subordinate any longer. Savior and saved. This might be *about* the past, but it wasn't the past.

But when she entered the kitchen, he was bent over, hands gripping the counter. The bottle of beer sat next to his hand, unopened.

She had seen him angry. She had seen him…devastated, after Anna had died. She'd seen him wrap all that up and pour it into North Star. And then let it all die out when he'd been trying to recover from his gunshot wound and had just…seemingly given up.

He'd shut them out, but he'd always been at the fringes. Like a disapproving parent.

But she had never seen him look…whatever this was. Frustrated? Unsure? Maybe even just the slightest bit guilty—even if he was irritated with himself for being so.

"I did what I thought was right. I've always done what I thought was right," he said, a slight gravel to his voice that spoke of an emotion Shay didn't know what to do with.

"Must be nice." Because she couldn't be kind when he made her feel soft. She had to fight back.

He shot her a look. "Doing what you think is right isn't always doing right, Shay. Sometimes you learn too late it was all wrong."

That she understood. So well she wanted to cry. But

she hadn't cried in front of him since that night he'd gotten her out of Chicago, and she'd promised herself a long time ago she never would again.

When she trusted herself to speak, she kept her voice even and firm. Like she did with subordinates. "There's a lot of baggage here. A lot of past issues clouding the current issue. We need to set it aside for now. The task at hand is to stop Frankie. For good. It's not about keeping me safe, because he wants me to suffer not die. Or at least suffer *before* I die. So this is about protecting the people he might hurt in my name. And it's about putting the past to rest once and for all."

Granger studied her for the longest time. There'd been a time when she'd let herself get a little too invested in the ever-changing colors in his hazel eyes. When she'd been a little too curious about the small scar that marred his lower lip.

She found old habits died hard when it was just the two of them.

"All right," he said, slowly. Then he released his grip on the counter and stood up straight. "You do whatever you need to do to take care of your wound and I'll get my computer and bring up the map."

She gave a short nod and retraced her steps to her bag. Finding a bathroom, she set about changing her bandages and taking a few aspirin. Afterward, she washed her face to try to wake herself up a little. And then she returned to the kitchen.

Granger had a computer on the kitchen table and was sitting there, frowning at it and writing notes down on a little pad of paper. She stopped short because he was wearing…glasses.

He slid them off his face once he realized she was there and shrugged. "Getting old."

She found her voice, not sure why that had shocked her so much. "Aren't we all?" She moved to the table, keeping a careful distance between them as she peered at the map on his laptop screen.

She slid another look at him. He'd put the glasses back in their case and moved it somewhere she couldn't see it. Like he was embarrassed. Like needing corrective eyewear was a weakness.

She'd once thought him a kind of god. Incapable of getting old or making mistakes. She'd attempted to build herself into the same.

But people were not perfect or godlike. They were continually fallible, no matter how good they tried to be.

Granger had always tried to be good, and clearly in his own mind that meant having no weakness. Or *showing* no weakness. Now that she'd tried to live her life that way she understood how impossible it was.

She blew out a breath and focused on the computer. She didn't need to understand Granger, or feel sorry for him or worst of all, forgive him for the ways he'd abandoned her.

But she had a bad feeling that by the end of this she was going to end up doing all three.

"VIANNI'S COMPOUND IS HERE. We're here. I figure once we have a plan, we fly closer. I've got places I can land here, and here." Granger pointed at the general area on the screen. "I haven't been able to tap into how many men they've got. That's the main challenge we're up against."

He slid her a look, because they both knew who could

get them that information, but it brought in people she'd purposefully cut out of this mission.

Granger had found Elsie Rogers himself. Their current head tech, Elsie, was a genius when it came to computers. She was one of his few North Star hires who didn't have any connection to the Sons of the Badlands, and Elsie had proven herself time and time again until she'd vaulted up the ranks in his tech department.

But Elsie was also…a sweet girl, all in all. And she loved Shay like a sister. She wouldn't do what they asked and keep the rest of North Star out of it. Nor would any of her team.

Granger thought about the people he knew outside of North Star, but the past two years he'd done a hell of a job pulling back from his contacts. Of isolating himself on the old dilapidated ranch he'd bought.

"What about Cody?" Shay asked.

"Wyatt, again?" Granger grumbled. Cody Wyatt had once been one of his better field agents. A sharp mind, a great background—including tech, and a personal need to take down the Sons of the Badlands. But he'd told people about North Star, and once a person did that, they couldn't stay on as an agent.

At least when Granger had been in charge.

Granger figured Cody hadn't wanted to anyway. He'd found out he had a daughter and wanted to build a life. And he'd done it. So, Granger had been done with Cody.

Until Elsie had brought Wyatt into the last mission when Shay had been stupid enough to try and handle everything on her own.

"Cody's almost as good as Elsie with computers," Shay continued. "And he won't alert the entirety of North Star. Especially if I ask Nina to make sure he doesn't."

"I'll never understand how you're friends with his wife." Which was something he should have kept to himself. It was none of his business. Shay's relationships now...or then.

"Why wouldn't I be friends with her?" she replied, squinting at the computer screen.

Granger decided to stop being an idiot and keep his mouth shut. He should change the subject, but he found his mind was inconveniently blank.

Eventually Shay looked over at him, pale eyebrows raising. "You think Cody and I hooked up?" She laughed, not bitterly exactly. But she was hardly amused. "You are something else, Granger."

"You went on a lot of missions together," he grumbled. He'd *put* them on a lot of missions together. Until it didn't bother him to do so. Because Cody and Shay had always clicked. And that had been fine. Dandy.

"Yeah, it's impossible for a man and woman to work a *mission*, life or death usually, without jumping into bed together?" She raised an eyebrow at him. "Are you really that childish?"

"Don't pretend like there wasn't something between you two. I was there."

Shay shook her head, silky blond hair swaying with the movement. "We were friends. It was never more than that. He was hung up on Nina his whole life."

"Ah."

Her eyes narrowed. "What is that 'ah' supposed to mean?"

Granger shrugged. "He was hung up on someone else."

This time when she laughed it *was* bitter. "You're unbelievable. I was your best damn field agent for years, and you have to boil it down to having the hots for my partner?"

"I'm not boiling anything down, and you were the best damn agent I had. So, I don't know why you're getting pissed off."

She looked at him like he'd grown a second head. "You really just…don't know how to talk to people, do you? You were wrapped up in your revenge for so long, you've just plain old forgotten how to be a person?"

"Why do you think I didn't come back? Why I bought that ranch? Why I was out there by myself for the majority of two damn years? You think I don't understand that I'd lost touch with everything? It was pretty clear."

Well, that shut her up. She frowned and looked back at the computer.

"Look. Contact Wyatt if you want. If you think he can get us the info we need without putting his family in danger."

"He wouldn't."

Granger nodded. "You've got a way to contact him securely?"

"No. Do you?"

He could lie and say he didn't and keep Wyatt out of this, but that didn't get them the information they needed. And it reeked of a personal issue that he most certainly didn't have.

Maybe Shay was telling the truth. Maybe she wasn't. It had nothing to do with *now*, and the fact that it bothered him even a little was a sure sign he needed to get over himself and his need for control.

Because he hadn't been kidding. When he'd been shot and then the building he was in had exploded, he'd thought he was dead. That he'd worked so hard, been consumed by revenge, only to fail in the last moments.

To die, while the Sons and the Vianni family still were out there hurting people.

But it hadn't been Anna's death that had haunted him. It had been Shay telling him he'd started caring more about revenge than about who he was putting in harm's way.

For months as he'd recovered, that had been the thing that tormented him, weighed on him, made him wonder if he even wanted to get back in physical shape or go back to North Star.

If he couldn't trust himself to do the right thing, how did he deserve to go back to the life he'd built?

He handed Shay his phone that couldn't be hacked or tracked. No matter how little he'd believed he'd deserved it, he hadn't been able to stay away from his old life. From figuring out Frankie was alive.

From doing this.

Shay wanted to put the past to rest. Granger felt like maybe he was still trying to make up for his.

If they accomplished this, maybe they could both be free of that. He slid Shay a look as she dialed Wyatt's number.

What would either of them do with that kind of freedom?

He wasn't sure he wanted to know.

When she got off the phone, she turned to study him. Her blue eyes were cool—a clear sign she was still mad about him insinuating she'd had a thing for Wyatt.

"He should have the information we need in a few hours."

Granger nodded. "Then we'll fly out in the morning."

Chapter Four

They ate dinner in near silence, occasionally talking about the area the Vianni compound was located in. Shay mostly didn't speak because she was still irritated about their conversation about Cody.

Still, she couldn't deny that adding Cody to this mission, no matter how tangentially, was complicated. All because, once again, of that mission two years ago.

Granger had used Tucker Wyatt, Cody's brother, to help take down some Vianni and Sons members in the mission that had ended with Granger's nearly fatal gunshot wound. But some of the background had been a lie.

Vianni had been entwined with the Sons of the Badlands for much longer than Granger had let on to the Wyatts. A lie that had protected Granger's and Shay's past from coming to light.

But the past didn't stay buried. Hell, even her husband hadn't stay buried.

They went to separate rooms to sleep, setting separate alarms to get up before dawn and head out to the airfield. Granger made coffee in the morning, but he went and drank his outside while she drank hers in between rebandaging her wound and taking her meds.

Her gunshot wound was healing. She definitely felt

stronger, but it was a severe handicap in all she'd want to do if given the chance to come face-to-face with Frankie.

She still vividly remembered the first time he'd hit her. The dress she'd been wearing. The look in his eyes. The shocking, searing pain of a backhand to the face.

Because he was Frankie Vianni. He didn't need to hide the fact he knocked his wife around. It made him look strong to the people who mattered to him.

She'd like to return the favor, now that she knew how to backhand. Now that she knew how to fend for herself. Now that she understood, wholly, the difference between right and wrong. What doing *right* could feel like and accomplish.

She stepped out of the bedroom, her bag slung over her shoulder. Granger was waiting by the front door, looking down at his phone. Brooding.

It didn't matter how long she'd known him now. That she knew just how he'd loved his wife, mourned her probably even now. And rightfully so. Anna Vianni-Macmillan had been a strange blip of good and sweet in that viper pit. Shay had never wondered why Granger had loved her as fiercely as he had.

It didn't matter that all the hero worship she'd had for him in those early years had tarnished in the past two.

He was still too damn attractive for her own good.

Had a thing for Cody? She'd *wished*. Shay had desperately tried to cultivate one so she'd stop pining for a man she knew was so far off limits they didn't even exist in the same universe.

You do now.

She almost laughed out loud at the thought. No, there was far too much baggage between them, even if they were far closer to equals than they'd ever been.

He said nothing when he looked up to see her staring at him. Instead, he just nodded toward the door, and she jerked her head in assent.

They drove, in that same complete silence, back to the airfield they'd used yesterday. The office was empty this early, but that didn't stop Granger. He expertly opened the small hangar, taxied his plane out to the runway.

He threw his bag in the back, then hers.

"Do you think I'm still legally married to him?" Shay mused aloud. Maybe in part because she wanted to remind Granger she was no innocent bystander here. Maybe she'd been young and dumb, but she'd gotten herself into her own mess. He'd saved her once, but he didn't need to save her again.

"Well, Veronica Vianni is legally dead. We made sure of that. Frankie Vianni is too, so I kind of doubt it." He motioned toward the plane. "Hop in."

She blew out a breath and tried not to pull a face. She wasn't afraid of flying, even in these tiny old planes Granger loved so much. But her gunshot wound made the cramped, jarring ride more than a little uncomfortable.

Still, some things had to be done. She climbed in, trying not to wince or groan as she settled herself into the back seat and Granger into the front. He started the engine in quick, efficient moves.

"You couldn't get a plane that was built in this century?"

He looked over his shoulder at her with a grin—she had not seen him do that in so long, and now it was twice in two days. Had Granger found some level of peace in his solitary ways these past two years?

"Why mess with perfection?" He ran his big scarred

hand lovingly over the dashboard and Shay looked away, into the bright blue sky they'd be flying through soon enough.

He began to taxi down the grass field, and the vibrations of the plane went down into her bones. She really didn't understand why Granger enjoyed this so much.

Until they took off. Up above the trees and into the sky. It was hard not to understand the appeal of being above the world, above your problems. Untethered.

They flew for a while, and her mind wandered. She didn't let it go backward into the past. Only forward into how they would approach Frankie's men.

Cody's computer skills had hacked into a security system at the Vianni compound. The place had security access to eight people. There could be more of course—service people who weren't granted that kind of entry, family members who never came and went.

But the main people they needed to worry about were the people of enough importance to get clearance.

The plane shuddering brought her out of her thoughts. She frowned at the back of Granger's head. They usually didn't hit too much turbulence this low.

He was messing with dials. She couldn't see his face to examine his expression.

The plane shuddered again, harder this time, with the addition of the engine making a slightly different sound.

Shay leaned forward around Granger's headrest. "Granger?"

He didn't look back at her. "The plane's been tampered with," he said. "I've lost all my fuel."

Tampered with? Vianni? How did they know... "How. Damn it, Granger. *How?*"

Granger swore, flipping dials and gripping whatever

parts of the plane steered the dang thing. He didn't answer her question, and she understood why. The plane was making terrible grinding noises, and he was doing everything to stop them.

Shay didn't demand anything else. She didn't even watch him work—she knew nothing about planes. Instead, she did something she hadn't done since she was a little girl, and maybe once when she'd pulled Granger's lifeless body out of that burning building two years ago.

She prayed, quietly to herself as things coughed and screeched and jangled. A cacophony of noises that had her stomach twisting in terrible, terrified knots.

But what came next was so much worse.

Silence. Nothing but absolute silence.

THERE WAS NOTHING he could do from here to get the plane restarted. That he knew without even trying. But training demanded that the first step of any kind of failure was to do the most important thing: keep flying the plane. Everything else could come later, but getting the plane into a decent glide without losing too much altitude was imperative.

His guess was the fuel line had been given a slow leak so they could get up and in the air. Get closer to Vianni territory, so that Vianni could deal with the wreckage. If they knew he was the one flying, they knew that he might be able to land the plane without any injuries.

They wouldn't leave it to chance.

Besides, if they really wanted him and Shay dead, there were far easier ways to murder them. This wasn't about death.

It was about *payback*.

But he couldn't worry about any of that if he didn't land this plane.

The engine had been tampered with too based on the sounds, and he was struggling to turn the plane. Control mechanisms. Whatever they'd done, it was brilliant, because none of it had malfunctioned until they'd been in the air awhile. Some kind of timer, maybe?

Again, something to worry about later. Right now, the mountains were going to make it one hell of a challenge. He needed more room to get the plane into a safe glide, and he needed somewhere safe to land. He needed better control of the plane, and that just wasn't happening.

Whoever had done this to them had timed it perfectly. Because ten or fifteen minutes ago, there were visible fields he could have attempted to set the plane down in. With better controls, he could turn around and glide easily back to those landing spots.

He needed flat land, not the jagged peaks that surrounded them. Still, he worked to keep the plane in a steady glide as he searched the horizon.

He didn't look back at Shay. Didn't think about her. *Couldn't.* His only focus was on landing without inflicting injury on either of them. Not what she was doing or thinking or worrying about back there.

The snow would make any landing difficult—not just because of possible ice and slick conditions, but because it could hide treacherous rocks and rougher terrain than he could safely land on.

He wished he knew these mountains better. But he'd grown up in the Midwest, spent years in South Dakota. The jagged peaks of the Tetons were still new landscapes to him. He didn't know all their secrets.

He spotted what looked like a flat area that gave him

the space to glide into a landing pattern. He studied it as they flew over. From this distance, it looked flat and pristine. It could be snow cover on a lake, but that wouldn't be the worst thing.

The worst thing would be rocks.

He circled it, fighting with the controls to get the plane to turn with no engine to propel him. It took longer than he wanted, and he lost some of his altitude, but he was still in a decent glide. He could still make this work. "Okay, we're going to land here in this patch of flat terrain." *Please let it be flat.* "You're going to want to brace yourself. It might be a little bumpy."

"Shouldn't you radio for help?" Shay asked from behind him, still yelling as if the engine was on, even though there was nothing but the wind up here.

He'd thought about the radio, but in the end, it gave away too much. Especially since the Viannis were clearly already aware of his plane, where they were going, and likely had a plan once he landed.

"The call would go out to the hangar where the plane was tampered with. Better to keep on the down low and then try to contact someone we trust with my phone when we're on the ground."

"Granger—"

"It's fine," he said, reminding himself not to grip the controls so tightly. "Sit back. Hold on." Then he tuned her out and focused on what had to be done to get them on the ground in one piece. If she spoke, he wouldn't know. His entire being was focused on bringing the plane down smoothly and safely.

It was hard. To keep the glide he needed to be able to move up and down, but he couldn't lose too much altitude too fast or the landing wouldn't be where he wanted it. Everything had to go perfectly.

He managed to turn, though it was a fight with the controls. He managed to slow and narrow in on the field of land.

Everything was going right.

Until it went all wrong.

Chapter Five

The entire plane jerked, and then Shay felt herself flying forward into the seat in front of her. It jarred her wound and she couldn't bite back the cry of pain. But then she was falling to the side, the entire plane...flipping.

Shay reached out and grabbed something—anything—to try to keep herself from getting banged around. She braced herself with her arm as the plane jerked and tumbled. It was rough, but slow enough she could keep herself braced and not suffer anything more than knocking an elbow or knee against the small back seat.

She had her eyes screwed shut, her arms out straight to keep her from falling. She was breathing heavily, but slowly came to the realization that the plane had stopped moving. They were on the ground. In one piece. Well, she was *mostly* in one piece. A little bumped and bruised, but certainly not dead.

Shay opened her eyes and peered out the window. The plane was on its side, but aside from that wing that had to be broken, it was in one piece too.

"Granger?"

There was no response and a thump of fear went

through her as she scrambled to get into a position where she'd be able to see into the cockpit.

He was slumped over the control panel and crumpled into the corner. Ignoring the pain in her side, she climbed over the seat divider into the front. It was too cramped for two people, so she was half on top of him, but she had to make sure...

She swallowed at the horrified lump in her throat. Reaching over, she pulled him up off the dash. His head hung limply to the side and his eyes were closed. His head was bleeding profusely, in rivulets down his face. But his breathing was strong. She could feel the breath puff out of his mouth, feel the rise and fall of his chest.

Shay let out a shaky breath. *Alive.* They were alive. She needed to clean him up, but she'd never be able to do it in this tiny tin can.

She managed to reach over him and kick open the door, but it only flew back shut—a combination of wind and gravity.

Shay swore, searching the plane for an easier way out. The front window was cracked. Maybe she could shatter it completely and they could escape through it—but it seemed like too much work when there was a working door right there.

She'd just have to climb over him to keep the door open and then...pull him out somehow. It didn't matter how. Just *some*how.

She rearranged him so his head was gently leaning against the seat cushion. Then she awkwardly moved over him until she could push the door open with her hands. She poked the top half of her body out and looked around.

The plane had landed on the snow, seemingly smoothly,

but then had hit a big rock. She assumed that's what had caused the plane to flip.

Didn't matter the cause, she realized, *because she smelled fuel.* That was *not* good, particularly since they'd supposedly lost all their fuel. They had to get out of here.

Trying not to panic, she rearranged herself every which way she could think of to pull Granger out of the door. But it just wasn't possible. He was too big and too heavy and her leverage wasn't strong enough. She'd have to get behind him and push him out, maybe.

Shay crawled back in, muttering things to him about what she was doing while she pulled him up and managed to edge her body behind his.

She grunted at the exertion and pain in her side. Granger mumbled something too but still didn't move, so she pushed him again, this time managing to get his body in the right direction.

"The hell you're doing?" he managed to say.

She didn't know if his eyes were open or if he was conscious, so she kept pushing. "Can you get yourself out of the door?"

"I can…" He moved a little on his own, but it was sluggish. "I'm bleeding."

"Yeah, pretty badly too. Let's get out of this plane so we can clean you up. Can you move?"

This time his movements were a little bit stronger and he managed to pull himself toward the door. It took some time and she had to give him a boost, but he finally managed get himself out.

Shay followed, grabbing him at the last second before he fell off the side of the plane into the rocky snow below. She let out a long, colorful swear as pain lanced her side. But she didn't loosen her hold on him.

"I got it," he said, sounding a little more with it. "I can get down okay. Really. Let me go."

"Don't be stupid and try to stand again. You're going to be dizzy. You were out cold."

"No. I wasn't. Just a little fuzzy." He slid off the side onto the ground. He swayed, but managed to stay upright.

Shay pulled herself out of the plane. "Out. Cold," she repeated, looking at how she was going to slide off the side. "Speaking of…it's freezing out here." She looked back into the plane. Was it safe to get their bags?

He reached out and tried to pull her off the plane, but couldn't quite reach. "Don't even think about it. That thing could explode. We have to get out of the way."

"We're sitting ducks without more clothes and our guns."

"Shay."

"How about this? If you can stop me, I won't do it." She slid back into the plane. Her bag had a first aid kit, and his likely did too. Plus guns, layers of clothes, and maybe even some snacks that would get them through.

Shay heard him swearing from outside as she twisted and turned to get to the back. She managed to get the bags out. It was a slow process, but in her mind it had to be done. If the plane blew up with her in it… Well, it was a better way to go than freezing to death when the sun went down.

She tossed the bags into the front, then crawled over after them. She hoped she was imagining the smell of fuel getting more pungent.

Shay could hear Granger yelling at her, and cursing himself as he likely couldn't climb back up the plane.

"Better watch out," she called, hurling the first bag out. Then the second.

She followed, though she was still uncertain of her path off the plane. She could slide down, but she needed to control the slide and…

Her thoughts trailed off when she heard an odd high-pitched sound coming from the plane. "What's that?"

Granger's eyes widened, then he grabbed her leg and pulled her into a slide. *"Run!"* he yelled when she hit the ground.

THE EXPLOSION KNOCKED him off his feet and reminded him far too much of two years ago when he'd also been injured and trapped in a burning building that had just exploded.

Except he wasn't in a building. Or the plane, thank God. He was in the open. He only had to get back up and run away from the flames.

Shay.

He managed to get to his hands and knees, but his eyes weren't focusing. He had to blink a few times to see right, and by that time he heard her voice.

"Didn't make that head wound worse, did you?"

He managed to get to his feet. The world seemed to tilt, but Shay was next to him and he realized she was holding him up. *Hell.*

He looked down at her and she was clutching both bags she'd *insisted* on going back into the plane and getting.

"Give me one of those."

"Work on getting your own feet under you first." He realized she was pulling him along a few minutes later.

Grunting, he looked back at the wreckage of the plane, then at her.

"Your face is bleeding." Not significantly. Just a few cuts and scratches marring her otherwise smooth skin. Her blond hair had fallen mostly out of its braid and snow was melting in it.

And she laughed. Actually *laughed.* "Honey, whatever is going on with my face isn't half as bad as yours."

They kept walking, her hefting those bags and him barely being able to keep himself upright. It wasn't that he felt so terrible, it was just his center of gravity was off and something kept dripping in his eyes. Snow melt?

"You think this is far enough away?"

Granger looked back at the flaming wreckage of his plane. A little pang went through him. Sure, he had a couple planes, but he loved them all. That one had flown him to Chicago for his father's funeral four years ago.

He'd told no one. Why hadn't he *told* anyone?

"Granger? You hear me?"

"Yeah. Yeah, it's good."

She pushed him—a surprise to him since he was half leaning on her—but he landed on his butt on a flat rock.

"Don't move," she ordered.

Shay dropped the packs onto the ground. The snow was deep but hard. The air was…cold. If he thought about it, *he* was cold. And his head hurt pretty badly too.

Better not to think about it.

She pulled a first aid box out of her pack and opened it, setting it next to him on the rock. Then she frowned at the contents.

"All right," she muttered. She came to stand in front of him, now grimacing at his face instead of the first aid kit. "I can already tell you need stitches."

"It'll keep. You're not stitching me up."

"I'm good enough at it."

"Good enough doesn't fill me with confidence, Shay. Just patch it up. I can let you try to kill me when we're somewhere warmer."

"You were unconscious," she said gravely, not letting him stand to move forward. "Out cold for a few minutes. That's serious."

"I've been through worse."

She sucked in a breath at that. "Fair enough," she muttered. Reaching out, she gingerly touched his hair, slowly and carefully pulling it back from his forehead.

Their eyes met. Held. He couldn't read her expression. Sometimes, he thought he knew her better than anyone else in the world, and sometimes she confused him beyond reason. That searching look was on the baffling side.

He hadn't seen it much lately. It surprised him to realize he'd missed her looking at him like that. But then she focused on his forehead, holding his hair back and wiping the gash with a disinfectant wipe.

In quick, efficient moves, not once moving her eyes back to his, she cleaned the wound and then bandaged it. She wiped the rest of his face down.

"You lost a lot of blood."

"Head wounds. Look worse than they are."

Her frown deepened into a scowl. "Don't try to BS me, Granger." She shook her head. "I don't understand going through all this to kill us."

"I think if they wanted us dead there were other ways to do it."

She collected the wrappers and bloody wipes, containing them in a bag and then putting it into her pack. "This wasn't enough? Tampered planes and explosions?"

"Why not have the bomb go off while we were in the middle of the air? Or even at takeoff if they wanted us dead?" he asked.

"Why have it go off when we've either crash landed or safely landed?"

He didn't answer her. She was smart enough and experienced enough to answer that question herself.

She swore. "They're going to come for me."

"*Us*, Shay. They're going to come for *us*. They waited until we were together. Separate from North Star. Vulnerable, but together."

She looked around them—craggy peaks, spindly pines, a seemingly arctic world. It was still morning, but the daylight had that faded, winter cast to it. And the cold... The cold was going to be a problem.

Of course, not as big of a problem as Vianni surrounding them, and then likely torturing them. For as long as Frankie Vianni wanted to.

"I know you know what we have to do," Granger said, studying Shay as she still looked at the world around them. "Because if Frankie gets us..."

"Yeah, it won't just be death. It'll be a long, painful, torturous death."

"For both of us," he said, making sure she understood there was no *I* in this particular problem. They were in it together.

She nodded, but still didn't turn to face him. "For both of us," she agreed.

"So we have to call North Star. We have to."

She stood there, so still, like a statue if her hair hadn't

been blowing in the breeze. If her nose wasn't pink at the tip from all this cold.

"Shay."

She finally turned, giving him a small smile with a nod this time. "Yeah. Call in reinforcements."

He didn't know why, but her easy agreement made him uneasy. But clearly she just understood it was the only choice.

Clearly.

Chapter Six

Shay convinced Granger that if they called in North Star they shouldn't move very far. They walked a little to find a place to camp and set up a defensive position if Vianni did get there before nightfall.

He leaned on her, and that caused a ball of dread to settle deep in her chest. She knew he was trying *not* to lean on her and couldn't manage.

That nasty cut on his forehead needed stitches so he could stop losing blood. He insisted his vision was okay, but she had her doubts it was *clear*. Which would make his usual prowess with a gun and aim a detriment rather than an asset. Granger wasn't strong enough to hike for very long. He'd be useless at hand-to-hand combat in his current state. He *needed* North Star.

But she didn't.

Frankie Vianni was after her, because of a mistake she'd made. Sure, she'd been young, but that didn't mean she was about to let North Star—*her family*—put themselves in harm's way because of her.

She did most of the work building up fortifications in the little alcove of rocks they'd found. She wouldn't leave him defenseless, and he'd already called North Star to let them in on what was going on. They'd be here in a few hours tops. Shay just had to time it all right.

Because she had to leave them all behind, that was for sure.

"We need to get some rest. Even if they know exactly where we went down, it's going to take some time to mobilize and get here."

Granger looked at the makeshift alcove they'd made. There wasn't really anywhere to lie down, but there was a rock formation that would work as a kind of couch that they'd covered with some of their extra clothes.

Even though he was steadier than he'd been, he clearly was ready to get off his feet. He sat down first and she settled down next to him, trying to keep her body relaxed so he didn't suspect she was up to something.

They sat hip to hip, the extra clothes that had been in their packs now being used as blankets. Each of them held a gun. She wasn't sure how she was going to get him to fall asleep, and knew it was risky since he likely had a concussion.

But help was on the way, and she needed to make her move.

"I know I've taken a lot of risks in my life, but getting blown up is one of my least favorite things."

She studied him from her peripheral vision. They'd never spoken of the day of the explosion at headquarters. And she'd always wondered…

"What do you remember about the day of the explosion?"

"As little as possible," he replied grimly.

Shay nodded. It had been a bad day in and of itself, figuring out Vianni was there. Realizing the Vianni goons weren't even there for her, but for Duke Knight, who'd been one of the cops to take down Frankie's grandfather back in the day.

Shay had been torn between a fear of the past and a loyalty to everything she'd made herself into. Torn between what she knew was right, and the way Granger had been going full steam ahead into plans that didn't keep innocent people, like Rachel Knight, safe.

So, it was best to let it go. Pretend she'd never asked. Pretend it never happened.

"I was in the interrogation room with Rachel Knight," Granger said, as if he couldn't help but relive it now that she'd brought it up. "She married Tucker Wyatt, didn't she?"

Shay nodded. She'd been at their wedding. Where all the rough and tumble Wyatt men, born to the leader of the Sons of the Badlands, had been enjoying their wives and families, having eradicated that ugly past.

It had felt like so much hope, she'd wanted to get the hell out of there. The only reason she'd stayed through the reception was because Nina had asked her to.

"We were in the interrogation room with the guy who had Vianni ties, but I didn't know it yet and she did. She used Morse code to warn me against the guy we were in the room with. I knew I had to get her out of there. That we had to work together. But he shot me. Then everything exploded. After that... Well... I don't remember anything until a few days later."

Shay knew she should keep her mouth shut, but she had to know for sure. "No one ever told you how you got out?"

"I never asked. I didn't want to know." He looked down at her, because even though they were both sitting and she was tall herself, he still had quite a few inches on her. "You're asking because you know."

Shay shrugged. "Not really important."

There was a long, fraught silence. She could feel his eyes on her so she kept hers looking straight ahead. At the peaks of the craggy mountains. At the snow. The ever falling sun.

"It was you," he said, as if he'd just found out she was some kind of murderer, not the woman who'd saved him from burning alive.

"I was in there looking for Rachel, so it was hardly a rescue mission. Looked for Rachel, saw you, dragged you out."

"You're telling me you saved my life."

"I just happened to be the one who pulled you out, Granger." She frowned at the peaks in front of her. Why were they talking about this? She had to figure out a way to get him to fall asleep she could slip away with a decent enough head start. Rehashing ancient history wasn't going to allow that to happen.

She could still feel him watching her, though he said nothing. She shrugged again, shifting in her cold seat and trying to ignore the fact that the side of her body pressed to his was warm enough. "Why's it matter? You probably saved my life a time or two. We're North Star, Granger. We don't keep track." She steeled herself to look at him, to lift her chin and meet that hazel gaze of his without flinching. "That was one of your rules."

She felt some measure of triumph when he was the one that broke his gaze first. He looked down at his hands, eyebrows furrowed as he seemed to try to work through this new information.

"You were pretty pissed at me that day," he said at last, his voice rough.

Shay wanted to stand up and pace. Because she wanted nothing to do with his complicated emotions. Or the way his voice often held all the emotion he wouldn't show anywhere else.

But she held her ground, though she too looked at her hands. "Yeah, I've been pissed at you lots of days. I'd still pull you out of a burning building if I happened upon you bleeding out on the floor. Just like I'd do for any North Star operative."

"Any *other*," he repeated, in a way that had her heart jittering in her chest.

She didn't look up. Didn't dare address any of the complicated, tangled emotions filling her up. They couldn't matter.

She had to get him to fall asleep, and then she had to get out of here. To face Frankie on her own.

Just like she deserved.

GRANGER BLINKED HIS eyes open with some confusion. He hadn't remembered falling asleep, and he awoke cold and with his head throbbing as though it had been split in two.

Still, it only took him about fifteen seconds from opening his eyes till he realized he'd made a grave tactical error.

She was gone.

He got to his feet—too fast, so his vision wavered. His head felt like it might fall off his shoulders, and his legs weren't so sturdy under him either. He took a deep breath, focused and then allowed himself the moment to swear.

The world around him was pitch-black except for the riot of stars above. A dizzying array that he didn't have time to appreciate. He pawed around the space until he found his pack and felt the cold metal of his flashlight on top of the pack without having to unzip it.

She'd left it out for him. Why that infuriated him he wasn't sure. Except…how could she be this damn stupid?

He flipped on the light and used it to study the world around their little camp. *His* camp, because she'd left him.

Alone. Defenseless. *Asleep.*

It shocked him down to his bones she'd deserted him this way. And then he realized he must have been out for a significant period of time, because there were carefully constructed booby traps made of sticks and rocks and whatnot that would have alerted him to anyone stumbling upon him.

But more, she thought she was going to stumble upon Vianni before they stumbled upon him.

Purposefully. Alone.

It was infuriating. He wanted to pound something to dust. Yell into the eerie quiet rustling of night around him. But all he could do was stand there. Impotent. Alone.

Stupid, a voice whispered. *Washed up.*

He shook those self-doubts away. Maybe he'd made a mistake, but Shay had made a bigger one, and he wasn't about to let her get herself killed in the process.

When he finally calmed himself, through the heavy breathing, the raging heart, the throbbing pain that seemed to echo in his head like a drum… But no, that was *tapping.*

A signal.

A North Star signal.

He shone his flashlight beam straight up, then right, left, down. A signal, and hopefully enough to give them an idea where he was.

It was a few minutes of squinting into the dark as he turned in slow circles before he saw the little beam of light. He started moving toward it as it moved toward him.

When Granger finally recognized the man approaching him, he didn't feel any kind of relief. Just a weird twist of disappointment as he came face-to-face with Cody Wyatt.

"Wyatt."

"Macmillan."

They studied each other for a long, quiet moment. Granger had recruited Cody out of a CIA internship. Some of his contacts had told him Cody had a sharp mind and a willingness to bend the rules.

Exactly what Granger had needed at the time. He'd even given some thought to grooming Cody to take over North Star. But the more Cody and Shay had worked together, well, the less Granger had felt that interest or pride in the man.

When Cody had been forced to quit North Star, Granger had used it as an excuse. He'd told himself he'd had the feeling all along that Cody couldn't stick it out. That it had nothing to do with *feelings* and everything to do with *instinct* that he'd pulled away from Wyatt.

He'd been an asshole, plain and simple.

"Rest of the team is this way," Cody said at last. "Follow me."

Granger nodded and followed Cody through the uneven, snowy terrain. He bit back a groan at how badly his head hurt, at how cold he was. He tried to keep his breathing even as he followed Wyatt at a speed that felt close to breakneck.

"Getting old on us, Macmillan?" Cody asked, sounding friendly enough.

Granger grunted. "The head wound doesn't help."

Cody looked back at him. "Yeah, you're going to need that looked at. You could have mentioned it."

"I was afraid someone would bring Betty."

Cody laughed. "You should have realized we were bringing a whole lot more than Betty."

They crested a hill and Granger stopped cold. A little camp was set up, fire going, at least ten people surrounded it along with some pack animals.

"What the hell is this?" he muttered.

Elsie Rogers stepped forward as they approached. Their head tech agent, she had no business being here in the harsh winter night. "Elsie, you shouldn't be here."

She waved a hand, which shocked the hell out of him. Elsie had never *waved* him off. He made her nervous. Even when he wasn't the boss, she'd always scurried to do what he asked.

"But I am here," she said firmly. "You have your phone, I'm assuming, since you called. I sent you a roster. I wasn't sure how much experience you had with everyone, so I figured I'd cover my bases."

He pulled out his phone, found the file she'd sent him, and opened it.

Mission Break Free Roster

Cody Wyatt: former field operative, computer and tactical expert

Tucker Wyatt: former field operative, investigation and tracking

Jamison Wyatt: cop, investigation and tracking

Connor Lindstrom: former Navy SEAL, current operative, pilot, S&R expert with dog

Holden Parker: former field operative, explosives expert, with dog

Vera Parker: former spy, computers expert

Nate Averly: former Navy SEAL, weapons expert

Reece Montgomery: former head field operative, good at everything

Gabriel Saunders: current field operative, weapons and explosives expert

Mallory Trevino: current field operative, weapons and hand-to-hand expert

Zeke Daniels: current field operative, tactical plans, knows landscape well

He'd worked with a lot of the people on the list. Even the ones he hadn't, he'd had *some* interaction with over the past few months when he'd been dragged into a few missions as help.

He looked up at Elsie, who had a tablet in her hands. Behind her was every single person she'd put on that "roster." People he'd recruited. Trained. Some people he didn't know at all. But they were all here, because they'd all worked with Shay.

"We can bring in more people if we have to," Elsie was saying. "But these are the people we trust implicitly. We've got Betty in the nearby town, getting a little medical center set up because I doubt we're getting out of this unscathed."

She stood there, so sure of herself, and she'd always been comfortable with computers, but this was something new.

"Are you auditioning for leader, Els?"

She looked up at him, startled for a second, then shook it away. "No. That job is not for me. But this is for Shay, which means we're all going to use our strengths to get her back and safe. For good."

Granger inhaled. She was right. There was only one important mission today, and all emotions and injuries had to be set aside. "All right, let's put together a plan."

Chapter Seven

Shay was exhausted and hungry, but she didn't dare stop. She needed space between her and Granger and North Star, and she needed to find Vianni. She'd been able to orient herself enough to go in the right direction.

She'd had to bet on the fact they'd come from the general direction of where she'd figured out the Vianni compound was, rather than circle around. If they circled around instead, well Granger and North Star would be there to fend them off.

She tried not to think about that possibility. She understood the Viannis and how they worked, and if North Star hadn't interfered last month, she could have handled them then.

You would have wound up dead.

She scowled at the voice in her head that sounded far too much like Granger. Because, maybe she would have. But maybe it would have all been over. She was willing to die for that.

The sun rose, a pearly pink that softened the harsh silver of moonlight on the snow.

God, it was cold. Why had she needed to make this stand in the middle of a nasty Wyoming winter?

She kept walking, wrapping her arms around herself

as she trudged forward. Toward Vianni. *Toward Vianni.*
Toward Vianni. It became a chant. A count. An impetus.

When she smelled smoke, she stopped and paused
and looked around. No sign of it, but there was the hint
of fire in the air. Campfire.

She pulled her gun out of its holster and kept even
closer watch as she edged forward, following the smell of
the smoke as best she could. Eventually the faint sound
of voices and movement could be heard and she followed that.

She slowed her pace, creeping behind rocks that were
big enough to hide her from whatever she was getting
close to. Boulder to boulder, peeking around each and
trying to get nearer to the smells and sounds.

Eventually, she found the source of both. A campsite. She kept her head low as she endeavored to figure
out how many men were in the camp and if this was
the only one.

She positioned herself behind the rock, gun ready.
She scanned the area behind her before she set her focus
on the camp when she was sure no one else was in the
vicinity.

Shay heard voices but didn't see anyone. Still, she
could tell they were coming from the general area, so
she kept her eyes on the campfire. Her eyes ready. One
man finally appeared, and then another. They each took
a seat around the fire.

She watched and waited. They seemed to be making
coffee, and when no other men appeared, she decided
this was it.

Likely, there were more men close by, but not right
here. If she could pick off these guys, she could get the

rest of the men's attention on her, and then either fight them off and demand one take her to Frankie…or—

Well, she wouldn't think about the *or*s. She'd focus on her plan and see it through.

She studied the men. They were roughly the same size, so she focused on the one she could get a better shot off on. She adjusted, breathed, counted and then shot.

The first one went down immediately as the other spun around, already pointing his gun in her general direction.

She ducked back behind the rock, counted to five, then lifted her head again. He was charging her area and she aimed, but he returned fire before she could and she had to duck behind the rock again.

She stood and aimed, but he zigzagged at the last moment as he kept running closer. And closer. Rocks were in *her* way now. And trees. She'd lost his progress and she swore, keeping the rock to her back as a kind of protection.

She watched, and listened, keeping her breath even and her heartbeat slow so she could hear the slightest. rustle in the world around her.

Then she heard it, with just a second to spare, as he jumped from the rock behind her. She managed to skid out of the way, turn and dodge a punch. She landed one of her own right in the throat. When he leaned forward gasping for air, she tried to knee him, but he moved out of the way so her knee hit his thigh without doing much damage.

She struck again, but he got a hand up to block the blow. This time, when he punched, the blow hit her right above her gunshot wound and it nearly took her down.

But no, she wasn't going to get beaten by one of his *men*. She was going to take Frankie down, face-to-face.

He wants that too, she reminded herself. For one of Frankie's men to kill her wouldn't be revenge enough. He could have done that before she knew he was alive.

So, she fought. She ignored the pain and punched and kicked. Even as he managed to get her into a tight hold, she wriggled and *fought*.

"Where's Macmillan?"

She didn't let the question surprise her. The focus was getting out of this. But she filed it away for when she had the wherewithal to deal with the fact they knew *so* dang much.

For now, her only goal was meeting Frankie on her own terms.

"Macmillan is dead. Just like you're about to be." She managed to get her shoulder mobile enough to twist, then she bent, swiveled and used the full force of her weight to rear her head back and bash it into his nose.

He went down like a pile of bricks. Screaming bricks, but bricks nonetheless. Blood poured out of his nose. Shay swung her pack off one shoulder and quickly unzipped the pocket that would offer her an array of restraints.

When she approached him, he tried to fight again, but he was too distracted by his broken nose. She easily got his hands and feet zip-tied. "Hope someone finds you before you freeze to death," she offered.

Shay swung the pack back onto both shoulders and immediately began to move once again. She took a quick look through their camp to make sure there had been just the two of them.

It appeared to be, but even if Vianni thought they'd

be injured in the crash, her gut told her this wouldn't be the end of it. It'd get harder, the closer she got. More men. More resistance. This was likely a test.

She looked around. No one had come running, but they would have heard the gunshots and broken-nose guy's screams. They would have sent off some kind of alarm. She needed to keep moving, because intercepting the next round of Vianni men would be necessary to keep them from getting to Granger.

Shay grabbed one of the untouched mugs of coffee, drank it and then scooped some snow to douse the fire.

Then she went back to her long hike.

GRANGER FOUND IN many ways it was easy to slip back into the role of leader. After all, he'd been heading up North Star for more years than he hadn't. He knew how to throw together a tactical plan quickly, how to assess the people looking to him for leadership in the blink of an eye. He was naturally good at this and had the experience to back it up.

But there were things that didn't settle on his shoulders as easily as they once had. The heavy weight of the ticking clock that the more time they sat here and planned, the more danger Shay got herself into. And even though he hated it, he understood, to a small extent, what she was trying to do.

None of these people were inextricably linked to Vianni. They were simply linked to Shay, here for Shay.

And that was the last piece he didn't know how to reconcile with his former self. He wasn't doing this for the greater good. Or even for revenge. Somewhere along the way he'd accepted Anna's death and that need for revenge had slowly dried up into something else. Regret maybe. Some self-blame, sure. But not the fury that had once driven him.

He was here, assembling this team, figuring this out for Shay and Shay alone. No matter how little he wanted to admit that to himself. And that made his nerves coil tighter than ever.

"You're not on either of these teams," Cody said as Granger handed out assignments.

"No. They know I'm out here, Even if she tells them I'm dead, they know I'm out here, and Shay may not believe it, but they want me as much as they want her. I'll follow after her as if I'm on my own."

Wyatt looked at his brothers, exchanging some look that communicated more than words. "I don't think—"

"He's right," Elsie said. She looked at everyone who frowned at her. "Surprise is our best weapon. If they don't know Shay and Granger have backup, why let them know?"

"Because it leaves one of our men defenseless," Cody said, arms crossed over his chest. "*That's* against North Star policy."

"You're not North Star anymore, Wyatt," Granger returned coolly.

"Last time I checked, neither were you."

Granger smiled, or scowled. He wasn't sure. "So we don't have to follow the rules, then." He looked at the people standing around him. They didn't have much more time. Even if Shay found Vianni men and convinced them he was dead, they were going to need confirmation. They would come to the crash site and they would run into this group first.

They needed to get to work.

"I'll follow. Alone. That's nonnegotiable. We have to

use surprise and our numbers against them. They're not stupid. They won't be as clumsy as they were two years ago." Granger looked pointedly at Cody and Tucker, who'd been a part of that disaster.

"Clumsy? Didn't they shoot you and blow you up?" Tucker asked.

"I was a bit clumsy myself," he returned, trying to keep himself emotionally detached. And failing. "Which means both sides have had the time to fix the mistakes they made last time. Holden, you're in charge of the front group, and Reece, you're in charge of the back. Elsie, I want you somewhere safe to run computers."

Elsie nodded. "I'm headed to where Betty set up a clinic once we disperse. I've got cameras on everyone but you."

"We can't risk having one on me. No cameras. No comm units."

Elsie shook her head and opened her mouth to argue, but Granger held up a hand. "I want you all to move out first so you have a chance to surround their compound before Shay or I get there. Any questions?"

There were shakes of the head and then the soft murmuring of chatter as the groups packed up and began to move out. Granger trusted them all to accomplish their tasks. More backup and setup than an all-out assault on Vianni.

He hoped he and Shay could handle that part themselves. He glanced at Elsie. There was one horse left for her. Granger didn't like it.

Which, he assumed was written all over his face.

"I'll ride down to where we've got a vehicle stashed, then drive to Betty. I'll be fine," she said reassuringly.

"You shouldn't be alone."

"I can handle myself. Promise." She pulled a flashlight out of her pack. "And you can have a comm unit. Looks like a flashlight, even lights up." She clicked it on and then off. "But I'll be able to hear everything going on. And if you push the red button you can talk to me. I won't be able to communicate back so there's no chance they'll overhear anything. But this gives me ears on you."

"Elsie—"

She pressed it into his gloved hand, forced his fingers around it. "You're pretty badly injured, Granger. You're walking into the lion's den. Even if they have a great tech person on staff, they're not going to search your flashlight or care that much about it. Plus, it's got some heft and doubles as a weapon."

Granger took it and shoved it into his pocket. "Satisfied?"

Elsie didn't answer right away. She studied his face as if looking for something specific. "Granger, why do they want Shay? I know you say they want you too, because of this past of yours, but why is Shay so insistent it's her?"

"I think you know the answer to that, Els. Or you wouldn't know what questions to ask."

She frowned a little. "She was married to one of them?"

Granger nodded. It couldn't be a betrayal when he knew Elsie had already found that information out. But he wondered just how much she'd unearthed. "So was I." Elsie's expression didn't register any surprise and Granger sighed. "Those things are supposed to be eradicated from any record."

Elsie shrugged. "If people know where to look, they

can find just about anything. And if you recall, you never trusted me with that information, which meant I couldn't wipe it for you."

"I had someone just as skilled wipe it for us."

"Debatable," she replied, her confidence almost making him smile.

But the worry lingered instead. "So, you found out the pasts Shay and I were supposed to have wiped. What can Vianni find on us? All of us?"

Elsie took a deep breath. "Not a lot. I am a genius, after all. But enough, probably, if they know where to start. I've been working on something. I just…don't know if it's the right something."

Granger put his hand on her shoulder. "I'm going to trust you, Els. To figure it out. Okay?"

She nodded. "Okay. Go get her, boss."

Boss. No, that didn't feel right anymore. But he wasn't sure what did.

Except finding Shay.

Chapter Eight

The next group she ran across was larger, but no harder to take down. A campsite of four men, who took turns leaving their weapons behind to go relieve themselves. *Morons.*

She picked them off, one by one.

These weren't men from the Vianni compound who would have security clearance, Shay was beginning to realize. These were the kind of paid muscle that Vianni could always find with enough money. Thugs who didn't care what the job was as long as they got paid, or even sometimes men who owed Vianni a favor or two.

Certainly not the kind of men Frankie *actually* surrounded himself with. Eventually, she'd run into the real muscle. The dangerous kind with brains. If Shay had to guess, Frankie was trying to give her a false sense of confidence.

What he forgot, or she hoped he'd forgotten, was that she'd been around when he'd made certain plans. He hadn't given her credit for being smart enough to pay attention.

But she had. And she knew how he worked, especially now that she had some tactical experience of her own.

Her one worry was that men were spread wider and

might move around and get to Granger. She knew she was Frankie's primary target. He wasn't a man who let a wife just run away. He'd likely planned this for *years*.

So, she was the main target and she wanted to keep Granger as far out of it as she could.

Maybe Frankie had some unfinished business with Granger. She couldn't pretend to know all of her ex's twisted vendettas, but he'd been so proud of himself for helping to put Anna in a situation where she'd be murdered. To get back at Granger for some raid or another.

His own sister.

Even Frankie had to consider that revenge enough. In Shay's estimation, he had. God knew she'd regretted all of her choices at that point, enough to see Frankie for who he really was, but she hadn't known how to get out of it.

When he'd told someone about his plans to let Anna die in front of Granger, Shay had realized that somehow she had to get out.

Had to.

And in the way the world worked sometimes, it was Granger Macmillan who'd extended that helping hand. When his men had moved in on Frankie, he'd offered her a way out. When everyone had believed Frankie and his men were dead, Granger hadn't disappeared. He'd offered her the means to serve her penance.

He'd saved her, so even if Frankie was still after Granger, it was Shay's turn to do the saving.

She considered drawing attention to herself. Having all of Frankie's little factions descend on her so they would forget or leave Granger behind. More than once she'd stopped in a clearing, looked around, and considered her options.

Flare? Gunshot? Big bonfire? Or the simple, old-fashioned yell. *Come and get me, Frankie.*

But inevitably she kept walking.

Because, despite everything, she didn't have a death wish. She knew everyone thought these forays into handling this on her own was just that. It wasn't even self-sacrifice as far as Shay was concerned. It was just the way things were.

Frankie was *her* mistake. Now she had to pay for it. Ideally, she'd live through it. And Frankie would be taken care of once and for all.

But if she had to die to take care of Frankie once and for all, then she'd be okay with that. She'd accept that there was a certain poetic justice in it.

She thought of Granger. A tangled, complicated history. They'd never be any more than that.

And if you put this to rest? Survive?

She paused and looked at the dizzying peaks around her. The snow. The cold. The vast world she hadn't even known had existed when she'd decided to marry Frankie Vianni because it sounded *exciting*.

She'd certainly gotten her "excitement's" worth out of her adult life. So if she managed to survive, maybe she'd seek out something different for once. Something all the people she cared about seemed to be finding. Home. Family. A life.

Shay almost laughed out loud. She wouldn't know the first thing about any of that.

So, maybe it was time. Time to lay the trap. Maybe thirty men surrounded her and she'd be toast, but they'd take her to Frankie first. She would be allowed that final showdown. And she had to believe, no matter how much

Frankie had been able to dig up about her life the past ten years, he'd underestimate her skills.

He would underestimate *her*, and she would make him pay.

One way or another.

Shay set her pack in the snow and studied the area around her. But she took her time. She wanted the best chance at survival, and to take out as many Vianni men as she could before they managed to get her.

She worked as the sun shone high above, doing nothing to take the icy bite out of the air. But the sky was blue and the air was clear and the mountains were here. All around her. Strong. Stalwart. Impenetrable.

Frankie might have had a compound in Idaho the past two years, but she bet he didn't understand this place. The land. The sky. He didn't understand the power that came from the world around them because he was a man who thought he'd created the world.

That would be her advantage too.

Shay had her weapons loaded, a good vantage point with rocks as a decent shield from behind. She'd set off the flare and wait and see if anyone moved on her. If not, she'd come up with a new plan.

Before she could pull her flare out of her pack, she heard the faint *thump thump thump* of rocks tumbling down an incline. Someone was coming.

She moved quickly, making almost no noise at all, as she slid between the two jagged boulders that she'd planned as her cover. Then she listened. And waited.

She'd take this new group down and then find some way to attract the rest. If this was another small group of men, and she got them tied up well enough to suit her, she could search their things. Maybe find a comm unit and force one of them to call for backup.

She watched the gun, something strange prickling at the back of her beck. Because this wasn't right. This wasn't the way Vianni worked and...

And she recognized that glove. The stealthy way that shadow moved. "Damn it, Granger."

He stepped out from behind the tree, lowering the gun and smiling at her. Much like he had back at the airfield. Was she ever going to be able to outsmart him?

"Normally I'd offer to let you punch me again, but my head isn't up for it."

THE SHOCK AND anger that went through Shay's expression was at least somewhat satisfying, Granger decided as he watched her try and decide what to do.

He'd surprised her, and that was something.

"I left you behind for a reason," she said, and he could tell there was an attempt at calm in those words. Too bad her delivery was all barely leashed fury. "You should have stayed behind."

He'd promised himself not to lead with anger. From the very beginning, he wasn't going to be the man he'd been toward the end of his North Star days. Angry and bitter and desperate for a revenge that would somehow fix everything.

Now he understood, all the *emotions* stayed. Even when you got exactly what you wanted.

But Shay had always pushed his buttons, no matter what promises he'd made to himself. "You didn't honestly think I'd just let you...run away?" He couldn't think of a better word for it even though he knew that would put her back up.

"Of course not, but I thought North Star would arrive and—"

"Stop me?"

She scowled. "Yes."

"You thought your friends would find me and stop me from coming to find you? *Help* you?" He wanted it to come out soft, with just a hint of accusation. A reminder she had an army of people who cared about her.

But he was afraid that attempt at softness only sounded like hurt.

She didn't react. Instead, she looked around the woods, clearly watching for signs of other agents.

He shook his head. "They're not here."

"What do you mean they're not here?"

He could lie. Tell her that he'd convinced them to disperse. That it was just the two of them. It was a tempting lie, because it would potentially keep her safe if she had the stupid idea to go off on her own again.

It would probably be smart, actually, to keep her out of the loop. Tactical even.

Always gotta be the puppet master pulling the strings. She'd said that to him once. Years ago. He'd been surprised by her bitterness, and undeterred by whatever argument she'd put forth. He couldn't even remember now, but he recalled the words and the look on her face.

The expectation he should be better.

"Where are they, Granger?" Shay demanded, arms crossed over her chest, still standing inside the little crevice the rocks made.

"I've split everyone into two teams. Their orders are to stay back, but carefully surround the compound. We'll try to engage with as many of Vianni's men as possible before we bring them in, so the element of surprise can be used as effectively as possible in order to stop him."

Shay's scowl turned into something softer. Like confusion. "Two teams. How many people are here?"

"Take a look for yourself?" He moved forward, but not close enough for her to be able to reach his outstretched phone. He wanted her out from those rocks, so it felt less like he was the bad guy she was hiding from.

She huffed out a breath and slid out of the crevice and took a few steps toward him. "Someone fixed up your head."

Granger shrugged. "They cleaned me up a bit."

She kept her distance, only stepping as close as she needed to take the phone out of his hand. Then she looked down at the screen, her expression going from vague disapproval to some emotion he couldn't read.

"Mission Break Free," she said. "What is this?" She began to shake her head. "This isn't North Star. This isn't right. Cody and Jamison Wyatt have families. Reece has a family. He retired and promised his wife he wouldn't come back to—"

"As I heard it, Lianna was insistent he come help," Granger interrupted. "If it was to help you."

Shay shook her head. Maybe a little desperately. "No, I don't believe that."

He shrugged. "Doesn't matter if you believe it. He's here. Well, *out there.*"

"I don't understand this," she said, her voice tight, and when she handed the phone back to him and quickly turned away he caught the tiniest sight of something that had him stopping cold.

Tears. His heart twisted into a painful knot.

She cleared her throat, keeping her back to him. Then

fisted her hands on her hips, clearly working to appear strong and in control. "You have to get into contact with them and send them home."

Even now, she didn't get it. He wondered if she ever would, even if he spelled it out. She was so damn stubborn when she wanted to be. Insular and hardheaded.

Sound familiar?

"Even if I ordered them to go home, they wouldn't. They didn't come because I asked. You keep saying this isn't about me, well here you're finally right. These people came here for *you*. They love you, Shay. That's why they're here. They want to help because you're their family. You mean something to them. I could tell them to go, but they won't. You're going to have to accept that."

She shook her head, the blond braid waving at the motion.

"Why would that upset you?" he asked, wracking his brain for a way to understand this so he could get through to her and they could focus on the task at hand instead of her ridiculous need to handle this alone.

She mumbled something and he didn't catch it.

He moved around to the front of her. "What?"

She lifted her face, and there were tears there. Just a few, dotting her cheeks. "I don't deserve it," she said, enunciating each word like he was dimwitted.

But that didn't make any more sense regardless of how clearly she spoke the words. "Why the hell not? You've fought side by side with all of them." He wrapped his hand around her forearm. "You saved, protected, helped. Why shouldn't they do the same for you?"

She flung her arms into the air, out of his grasp, as she took a few steps back. "You don't get it," she said, too loud for the situation they were in, but maybe they were both a little beyond the situation they were in. "You always fought Vianni. From the beginning, you've been the good guy, Granger. It's like in your DNA." She pointed at him, then thumped her fist to her heart. "I married one of them. I knew he wasn't a good guy, and I married him. On purpose. Because I thought my life was boring and I wanted a little excitement."

She had never really talked about what prompted her to marry Vianni. He'd never asked. Granger supposed he'd assumed she'd been young and vulnerable and taken advantage of. He'd held out a hand to save her that night, because she'd looked terrified. Because she'd had a black eye. Because he knew Anna would have wanted him to.

He knew that victims blamed themselves. He'd seen that firsthand, but he didn't get the feeling Shay was recreating history to make things feel more survivable.

She meant it. Years ago, she'd chosen Vianni. He didn't know what that had to do with the here and now, but she couldn't go on laboring under the assumption they were somehow different.

"I haven't always been the good guy, Shay."

Chapter Nine

Why were they having this conversation? Shay wanted to scrub her hands over her face or maybe dunk her head in snow so she could *focus* instead of get caught up in whatever Granger was trying to do.

He had his own priorities and schemes. This would be another one of them. He knew how to manipulate people. Confuse them. Always for the greater good, but she wasn't interested in being his greater good.

She'd once had the kind of confidence to believe she saw through all that. The past two years had confused some things.

She looked at him, standing in the middle of all this natural beauty, a strong mountain of a man who had always done the right thing, even when he'd lost his way a little bit, trying to tell her he hadn't always been the good guy.

What utter nonsense. She rolled her eyes. "Yeah, you went a little off course a few years ago. That's hardly choosing the wrong side. You let revenge blind you. I didn't say you were perfect. You're human. But you're the good kind. Bone deep. And it's why you loved Anna so much, because she was too. The perfect pair."

"Anna wasn't perfect. I loved her. God, I loved her, but she wasn't some paragon of virtue."

"You forget that I knew her, Granger. You can't lie to me about her."

"No, you forget *why* you knew her. Do you honestly think a woman who spent time with her *mob* family and married a DEA agent didn't have some complicated feelings about right and wrong?"

A knot of dread wiggled around in the pit of her stomach. But that was silly. "Anna was a good person. I know that, Granger. And now really isn't the time to debate your late wife's—"

"How do you think Vianni knew how to avoid some raids, but not others? Why was Frankie always miraculously saved when we'd take down a section of Viannis?"

Shay blinked. She didn't have a good response to that. She'd never really thought about…

"You were married to Frankie. You had to know how many close calls he had. Him and no one else. How do you think that was? They didn't have the dirty cops on their side anymore. It was just them. So how did Frankie slither out from every attempt to arrest him?"

Shay tried to find words, but she was at a loss. Anna Vianni-Macmillan had been an angel. Sweet to everyone. Good and bright and *loved*.

By both sides.

But no one could be loved by both sides of right and wrong, could they? Not without being a little of both.

"Anna loved her family. She had a soft spot for Gio and Frankie, and they both used it against her. I never understood if she knew she was being used, or if she was naive enough to think they cared about her, but she wasn't immune to their brand of pressure. But she loved me too, so she wouldn't break off the relationship with me *or* her family."

"What are you saying?" Shay demanded.

"I'm saying, Anna slipped them information. Sometimes, if she'd overhear something about a raid or I mentioned where I was going, she'd tell her father." He looked up at her, and there was something there she'd never really seen in his hazel eyes. Not the pain of loss and regret, not that fire of desperate revenge. Just a certain kind of acceptance that the past was what it was. "And I pretended like I didn't know."

She opened her mouth to ask him *why* he'd do that, but she knew. It was all over his face. It had always been all over him.

He'd loved Anna.

Shay could only stare at him. Granger Macmillan had *known* his wife was leaking information to her family—the family he was tasked with bringing down. And he'd loved her anyway. Acted like he didn't know, even though he did.

The noble man so bent on revenge in those years after Anna's murder and he'd…

"Like you said, no one's perfect, Shay. No one's all good, and maybe no one's all bad," he said. "Anna wasn't totally virtuous and upstanding. I certainly haven't been. I tried to be. Good and perfect and always so righteous. God, I tried to be as some kind of penance, but I wasn't. I'm *not.* There's a lot of relief in finally accepting that. None of those people out there helping you think you are perfect. Maybe a little bit superhuman, but not infallible. They just want to be a part of keeping you safe, because it matters to them. You matter to them."

She wouldn't let emotions win again. It was stupid

and a weakness she couldn't afford. She'd blame those stray tears on exhaustion and hunger and move right on pretending Granger had never seen them. "Why is it so hard for everyone to understand that they matter to me so I don't want them in the middle of a mess I created myself?"

Granger seemed to take the time to really think that over, and a glimmer of hope went through her. He'd see it her way. He'd understand.

Then his jaw firmed, and he stood there so *sure* about everything. "Because it's insulting, Shay."

"It isn't—"

He grabbed her arm again, harder this time so she would have had to fight him off to escape.

Something she could have done. Easily. But didn't.

"You matter to me, Shay. To not use my skills, my abilities to help you *is* insulting. To not use all that you have at your disposal to help you—not just survive but to take down someone who deserves taking down, the whole damn point of North Star by the way, it's like spitting on everyone who cares about you."

Everyone, but it was his *you matter to me* that struck the hardest. Even now. "Granger…" She wished she had the words to end this. To *stop* this. He couldn't bulldoze her. Not now when it was so important. When half those people out there had families and loved ones and Frankie would kill them without a second thought.

And you too, Granger. Even with all those skills he was talking about. The men Frankie had would have a similar set of skills. They were dangerous, smart and certainly more ruthless than this first wave of men she had already beaten easily.

But wasn't North Star better? Wasn't that the *point*?

"We are by your side," he gritted out. "Now are you going to keep fighting that? Or do we get this done together?"

VERONICA SHAY HAD been in Granger's orbit for over a decade now. First as Frankie Vianni's wife, and thus both his wife's sister-in-law and someone he'd kept an eye on while being part of the agency that had been tasked with taking the elder Vianni down.

Then he'd known her as the young woman he'd saved during the raid that had allegedly killed her husband. Because she'd looked scared and defenseless.

She hadn't been, defenseless anyway. And Anna had been dead and he'd needed men. So, he'd trained her, and maybe she'd been focused enough not to see that he'd groomed her to take over North Star if he ever lost command.

He'd known her through all these transitions, assured himself he understood her, but he hadn't understood the depths of *this*. Some kind of martyr complex mixed with…not survivor's guilt. It was something more like victim blaming, with herself as the victim. Not that she'd ever call herself a victim. She thought she'd chosen the wrong path, and there was no making up for it.

Maybe she'd chosen to marry Frankie, but he doubted an eighteen-year-old girl from a fairly normal family by all accounts had known what she was getting into. There was no way she'd chosen a man she'd thought would abuse her, use her as a pawn and then track her down for some kind of revenge even though he was supposed to be dead.

"I feel *old*, Granger," she said after the silence had

stretched on too long. "Old and tired." Which didn't answer his original question, but he knew the feeling.

"Join the club, and consider that I've got another ten years on you."

She slid a look at him, as if studying him for the evidence of that ten years. It was there. He saw it every time he looked in the mirror. What he'd built was a young man's game, and it wasn't so much that he *couldn't* keep fighting, it was more that he'd lost the driving fire within him to do so.

Granger wanted to rest. He wanted to enjoy the ranch he'd settled himself on. Bring it back to life, rather than spend his days worrying about Vianni.

"You want to put the past to rest. So do I," he said, holding that gaze.

She nodded, so faintly he almost didn't see it.

"We started this together, Shay. When you took my hand outside the Vianni house. Let's end it together. Once and for all."

Again, she gave another small, imperceptible nod. "Do you think we can take care of things and keep North Star on the periphery? I couldn't live with myself if any of them were hurt in this."

"We can try."

She nodded, a little firmer this time. "Okay." She swallowed, clearly trying to recalibrate to a new plan. To having backup.

"We'll just do it together," she muttered, looking around the area they were in. "I've got everything set up to fight off as many as I can, but the end result is to be taken to Frankie. I'm not looking to *win*, just to put the odds better in my favor."

Granger nodded. "So a flare?"

"Yeah, and then sit back in this crevice, pick off as many as I can until they surround me. Then surrender."

"Will we both fit in there?"

"Barely, but it's doable."

"All right. Let's do it then. Before dark preferably." He glanced at the sky. The sun was already beginning its descent, but it was worth a try.

When he looked back at her she was frowning at him. "Aren't you going to pick it apart? Tell me all the holes? Take charge and do it *your* way."

"I have learned a lesson or two."

She arched a brow. "You hadn't when I asked for your help on Holden's case."

"You asked for my help on Holden's case less because you needed it and more because you were worried about me."

She looked startled for a moment, but he could tell from the expression in her eyes that he'd hit the nail on the head.

Something turned over in his stomach. An old feeling he barely recognized because his life was so different now.

Nerves. A distinct discomfort with not knowing what to do. When he'd had any indecision trained out of him long ago.

He thought of the raid on the little farmhouse in Nebraska for Holden's last mission. Shay had been shot. Not like last month, just a nick in the arm. It had affected him, in a way he knew meant he didn't have the objectivity he'd once had.

"It's a solid plan, and I don't have a better one," he said firmly. "I'm used to being the leader, yeah. It's a hard habit to break, but I always trained you to be my number two, Shay. I can train myself to treat you like a partner."

She seemed a little dubious, but she didn't argue anymore. A moment later, she got out the flare and set it in the middle of the clearing. "They might know it's a trap, but I figure if that's the case they'll just send more men," she said, pointing the flare gun in the air.

"Which works in our favor."

She nodded, then set it off. The *bang* wasn't exceptionally loud, but the bright light that emanated from it should be seen by anyone within a twenty-five-mile radius. Luckily the mountains they were in were isolated enough Vianni's men should be the only ones.

"North Star won't come running, will they?"

Granger patted the flashlight attached to his vest. "Elsie's listening right here."

Shay inhaled. Apparently she still wasn't *okay* with North Star being a part of this, but she was trying. Eventually she nodded, then pointed to the crevice. "I'll go in first, then we'll see if we can fit you too. Then we wait."

She slid into the crevice and he followed. Granger knew they had to find a way to both fit in the small space, but also still have at least the dexterity to shoot someone if they appeared. They had to move around to get situated, bodies brushing up against each other, her hair sliding across his cheek, the stubble of his beard scraping against the tip of her nose.

Once they were finally settled, they were face-to-face. They each had a back to the cold rock encasing them. Luckily, he was left-handed, so it worked that they both had their shooting hands free.

But that was where the luck ended, because the crevice was small and their backs pressed to the rock meant their fronts were pressed rather closely to each other. He could feel the rise and fall of her breath. See the patterns of different shades of blue in her eyes. He could feel every twitch, fidget and tensing of her body.

Which meant she'd feel his and *that* could spell bad news soon enough.

He should look away from her. Stare at the sky. At the world around them. Dimly, he was aware of all he *should* do, but all he could seem to do was stare at all that mesmerizing blue.

Her gaze held his and his heart thundered in his chest.

He should suggest he find another vantage point, another damn crevice. Because this was just the kind of thing he avoided, close quarters. Which meant he should look away, at least, because that was the point of this. Sit here and wait and *watch*. Not her. The world around them.

Her gaze dipped, to his mouth. He expected her to immediately look away, turn her head so they weren't even facing the same direction. They'd been here before, once or twice, a tense moment one of them immediately broke.

But she didn't.

And neither did he.

Chapter Ten

There were a million voices in Shay's head telling her to stop this. *Look away! Don't lean forward! Get out of here!*

There was a tenseness in his body that in any other circumstance she might have read as a reluctance. A refusal. She might have *convinced* herself of that, in any other circumstance.

But that was not what she saw in his hazel eyes, and instead of purposefully getting out of his orbit, she was stuck in this small space, staring right into his eyes. Where a softer version of something familiar she'd seen there before lurked. A version of that *thing* she'd avoided at all costs before.

But it had never looked or felt quite like this.

She knew people could change because of the great, vast changes she'd been through, but she'd never expected Granger to change. At least, not in this healing kind of way. Not when he'd been so bent on revenge. So consumed by grief. She hadn't expected him to become more…*human*. Like some regular guy who might have a life outside of North Star that wasn't the little hermitage he'd built for himself.

But it seemed like maybe he was ahead of her on that score.

She didn't know what to do with that knowledge and still she didn't look away, no matter how much she told herself she should. For ten years she'd avoided *this*. For a wide variety of reasons. She tried to remind herself of *any of them* as his body heat seeped into her. Cocooning her in warmth. *His* warmth.

She was so tired of fighting, wasn't she? And what was this but another fight? Why *not* be done with it? What did it *matter*? If she finally did the thing her body wanted so desperately to do.

So, she put her lips on his. An old daydream that had always embarrassed her, but never gone fully away. Because he was *Granger*, and despite his mistakes he was her paragon of everything she wanted in a man.

The feeling that jolted at the touch of his mouth to hers was so unexpected, so…*big*…she would have bolted away if she'd had room, but she had none. She was stuck here, and maybe she could have turned her head and mouth away, but his hand came up and held her cheek.

Keeping her in place, kissing her back in a far more *adult* way than she'd ever envisioned.

Her stomach seemed to jump on a roller coaster and take off, and she forgot about the cold stone at her back, the men who should be coming for them. She forgot everything. Because no matter that she'd occasionally let herself imagine what it might be like to kiss Granger Macmillan, she had never known how to imagine…*this*.

Because it wasn't superficial or casual like any other relationship she'd had in her life. This was a simple kiss, but it dug deeper than anything she'd ever experienced before. Burrowing beneath her defenses, ones she'd spent a decade building and perfecting.

He pulled away, and it took her precious seconds to realize her eyes had fallen shut and she needed to open them. When she did, she was met with all that hazel, and a small smile on his face she couldn't decipher.

Maybe didn't want to.

What on *earth* had she done? Years of self-restraint and common sense and she'd kissed him in the middle of all this? She really was losing her edge. "That…must have been my head wound."

His mouth curled, just a little at the corner, in a way that had her stomach swooping all over again.

"I think I'm the one with the head wound," he said, his voice low and rough.

She was so dizzy she thought for sure it must be her, but she couldn't analyze any of this. "Granger…"

"We'll put the past to rest. We both need that, but it doesn't have to be the whole past. There were good parts in there, and for me, they were mostly with you."

She was speechless. Utterly.

"But for now, we've got company." He pointed outside. She didn't see anyone, but when she forced herself to *focus*, she could hear the faint sounds of men on the move.

"Els, we're going to take out as many as we can, but the plan is to let them take us. Keep everyone back until we give the signal."

Shay stared at the flashlight he was talking into. He'd said… Oh God, he'd *told* her that Elsie was listening. And she'd…she'd…

"She can't communicate with me, she can only see and hear," Granger reminded her.

But…

"So, she heard and…saw all that before?"

His eyes stayed on the men carefully moving in as his mouth quirked again at one side. Amusement. "Imagine so."

Shay closed her eyes and felt an odd heat climbing up her cheeks. When was the last time she'd *blushed*? And over something so…

"Worry about living through the embarrassment once we've lived through this, huh?" He moved a little, edging toward the front of the crevice. "I'm going to go put up a fight. A dumb one. I'll take one or two down first, but once they've got me and insist you come out, do it. Don't lay it on too thick. Pretend like you don't care about me. Give them what they expect."

Give them what they expect. That was basically the gist of her plan, though she hadn't thought of it in precisely those words. They were on the same page.

Not leader to subordinate. He wasn't saving her.

They were in this…together. Fully. Maybe she'd been afraid that was impossible, when he'd always been the person she looked up to, but now she understood this all for what it was.

Working together. The team he'd made. Because it mattered. Not just ending Vianni, but her herself mattered. To him.

"Granger."

He looked back at her. She would have said he was all business, but there was something about the way his eyes tracked over her face, like he was soaking it all in.

She wished she could give him any of the words he'd given her. Something that would mean…anything. But all she could think to say was utterly stupid. "Don't die."

But he grinned at her. "Same goes, Veronica."

When she scowled at the use of her first name, he chuckled, and stepped out into the fray.

HE KEPT LOW and quiet, even as the men crested the hill.

A hell of a lot of men.

Well, Shay's plan had worked. He'd worried they'd wait them out. Or just send a small, ineffectual group like the ones before. But these guys were bigger, decked out in tactical gear. It seemed each wave was just a little better.

But the question he had was whether this was the last of them. Or did they have bigger men with bigger weapons waiting for them? He wanted to get through as many waves as possible before they surrendered.

No doubt there'd be another set at the compound once they allowed themselves to be taken, so the more they could take out here the better.

Granger ignored the twist of disquiet in his gut. It was dangerous business, letting themselves get captured by a group of well-trained henchmen who wanted to hurt them—not just kill them, but *hurt* them. A lot could go wrong.

But a lot could go right. Even as he braced himself for the first blow from a big man who's guns were still strapped to his side, his mouth curved. So far, things had been going all right, the destruction of his plane aside.

Shay had kissed him.

He might have laughed at the wonder of it, but instead he dodged a meaty fist and dealt an elbow to the gut. Kick, twist, uppercut. He wanted to fight as many of them as possible before he introduced his gun, because even with vests on, and the belief Frankie didn't want them dead before he could torture them a little bit, he and Shay could catch a stray bullet in the fray.

Best to keep the guns holstered for as long as they could.

A man grabbed him from behind and the guy he'd been effectively fighting landed a gut punch that hurt like the devil, but Granger twisted, kicked and had the man who'd attacked from behind howling in pain.

He fought off a few as the rest of the men searched the clearing, presumably for Shay. None of them found her hiding place or even seemed to consider that crevices could hide people.

Still not the cream of the crop, then.

"Where is she?"

Granger shrugged, and used the movement to feign a kick. When the man moved to block it, Granger swung his elbow into his opponent's nose.

Blood spurted along with a scream of pain.

Granger still refused to use his gun, which meant that as many men as he fought off, he was still getting a bit of a beating himself. Enough that he started to slow. One man grabbed his arm and before he could get a punch off, another grabbed his other, wrenching it behind his back. He still had his legs under him and he might have fought them off, but his vision was getting a little blurry. Granger blinked the moisture away, wondering if it was a new injury or his old one bleeding into his eyes. Either way, it severely limited his ability to make tactical choices.

"Where is she?"

"You guys are bad at your jobs," Granger replied.

Which earned him another hard punch in the stomach from the man in front of him. He bent over, but the other men still held him as he struggled to breathe from the nasty blow.

"All right, that's enough," Shay's voice said.

Granger would have laughed at the shocked looks on the conscious men's faces if he'd had the breath. They looked around, still clueless as to the location of her voice.

Shay stepped out of the crevice, looking like the warrior that she was. Her blond hair shone gold in the riotous sunset, and her chin jutted out in stubborn disdain.

She didn't point her gun at the sky, or keep it holstered. Instead, she aimed it at the man pointing a gun at her. He was the only one who had his gun out, further giving credence to Granger's belief they wouldn't kill anybody.

Yet.

"Put it down," the gunman yelled, and though most of the other men appeared to be completely calm, this guy seemed a little nervous.

Not a good combo.

Shay took a step forward and the guy's gun went off. Granger jerked against the men who held him, but they were strong and firm and Shay didn't go down, though her whole body jolted.

She glanced down at her vest, where Granger could only assume the bullet had hit. "You're going to regret that," Shay said, looking at the man who'd shot at her.

Granger knew that it must have hurt. Her tactical gear might have stopped the bullet, but the impact was still a hell of a blow. But she acted like it hadn't hurt at all as she charged the shooter.

"Guns down," someone shouted. "Guns down! Those aren't the orders."

Granger used the bolt of panic to his advantage. He wrenched one arm free, used his body weight to pull the other man to the ground and began to wrestle him into submission. He didn't expect to win, more wanted another distraction and everyone to report to Frankie that they had fought with everything they had rather than give Frankie any reason to believe they'd been captured on purpose.

So maybe it was time to pull out his gun and do some real damage. He reached for it, but because his peripheral vision was compromised, one of the assailants caught his arm before he could wrap his fingers around the handle of the gun.

He heard another gun go off, but two men were holding him down now and he couldn't see well enough to figure out if it was Shay or the nervous gunman. He kicked out, managed to dislodge one of the men holding on to him. This time he did get a hand on his gun and managed to shoot the man trying to get back up.

He whirled on the other man who'd held him, but was met with the barrel of a gun pretty much right between the eyes.

"There weren't any orders about you," the man said, his mouth curving into a dead-eyed smile.

Those words sent a cold bolt of fear through Granger, but he wasn't about to go down without a fight. He moved into a quick crouch, but before he could sweep out a leg to take the man's feet from under him, another gunshot went off and the man in front of him went down like a sack of bricks.

He looked behind him to see Shay holding the gun. She'd taken out all the men around her. He looked down at the man who'd almost put a bullet through him, then back at her. "Thanks."

"Don't mention it," she said with a smile, but it faded. "You're bleeding again."

"So are you," he said, pointing to a gash on her arm. She looked down at it as if surprised to find it there, then shrugged.

Without having to say anything, they moved back-to-back as another wave of men moved forward. These guys had even higher-powered weapons, more tactical gear and a size and bulk the previous men didn't.

"I think it might be time to surrender," Granger whispered, eyeing the men and then returning his gaze to Shay. If Frankie had this many men at his disposal wherever they took them, the odds might not be as heavily in their favor as he'd hoped. But he counted, and there were only five of these guys.

If the eight with security clearance was true, that left only a few back at the compound with Frankie.

She looked over her shoulder at him then offered a grin, reminding him of those early days in North Star, when she'd relished the fight. When she hadn't been afraid of anything or felt responsible for anyone. "I hope you're ready for this."

He'd put her in charge and she'd lost that bravado. Because the weight of leadership didn't sit so comfortably on good people, people who cared deeply. Sending people into danger weighed different when you were *invested*.

When they got to the other end of this, he would find a way to remove that weight he'd inadvertently put on her shoulders for the past two years.

He nodded and then slowly lifted his weapon as she lifted hers—in surrender this time.

Together.

Chapter Eleven

Shay stood, still back-to-back with Granger, breathing heavily and trying not to catalogue all the aches and pains she now had after that fight.

It had been a *good* fight. Men so often underestimated her ability to fight—either they treated her like a man because she was tall and built, or they thought they could outmuscle her simply because she was a woman. But she had a grace and flexibility difficult for most men who'd spent time building muscle and strength, and also that strength that so many guys didn't think to acknowledge.

It had felt like old times almost. To let loose like that. To fight simply to fight. With Granger. In the field. Not in charge of anyone or responsible for what happened to them.

Just a fight.

There was a freedom in that, but it was short-lived because she knew that her team, the people who'd become her friends and then her family, were out there, ready to swoop in and save her and Granger. He was mixed up in this because of her, and the fact that the man had been willing to shoot him proved in Shay's mind that Vianni wasn't here for him.

All they wanted was her.

But as they held up their weapons, and this new group of attackers moved forward, Shay had to fight back the fear they'd simply take Granger over to the side and shoot him. If the other man had been willing to—

She was grabbed roughly, and she fought it off instinctually. But the men took her gun and there were three on her, wrenching her arms behind her back and cuffing her. She still wriggled and refused to make it easy on them.

It wasn't just acting so Frankie believed they'd been caught against their will. She had too much pride to subject herself to this *easily*.

Shay managed to crane her neck to see Granger. They were doing the same to him. So no plans to kill him. Yet.

"Take one last look," one of the men holding her said, and then something was being pulled over her head, plunging her into even more darkness than the world around them.

"Isn't this a bit overkill?" she asked, though no one answered. They were out in the middle of nowhere, and night was falling, so what did blindfolding her do?

What did it *hide*?

That question roused an iciness that had nothing to do with the cold settling in her chest. But she wasn't alone. She had Granger, and an entire team of people out there watching and listening.

All ready to move. To act.

She couldn't let fear guide her. Not anymore. She'd been struggling with that for two years now. And while she still wasn't sure she was *comfortable* with all this help when she'd brought this problem on herself by marrying Frankie in the first place, she knew she had to find a way to come to terms with it once and for all.

She was pushed forward, and fought to stay sure-footed in the slippery snow and rocky terrain. Vianni's men wouldn't care if she fell and hurt herself. They would relish it, she had a feeling.

They couldn't kill her, but she doubted she had to be in pristine condition when they brought her to Frankie.

She tried not to think about what he would do, because there were too many terrible outcomes. Number one, killing Granger in front of her if her ex thought she had any emotional attachment to Granger.

And if Frankie knew what she'd been doing for the past decade, he also knew she had *some* kind of connection to Granger.

She swallowed down the wave of fear and horror that she might be walking Granger straight to his death.

But no. No, if that man back there had license to kill him, Granger didn't matter to Frankie. Even as a means of revenge.

Shay held on to that as she was pushed and pulled forward, trying desperately not to stumble as she walked blindly, too fast, in an uneven landscape.

They wanted her to fall, she could feel it.

Give them what they expect.

She frowned at Granger's voice in her head, but he was right. They'd expected her to fight, so she'd fought. And they'd expected to win, so in the end, they'd let Vianni's men win. Now, they wanted her to fall, and giving them what they wanted was going to help her in the long run.

Besides, planning her fall was going to be a little better than it happening accidentally. So, she slowed her pace until the guy behind her gave her a shove. Then she purposefully fell forward, and a little to the side—both in an attempt to brace herself for the fall and to keep her injured side from hurting more.

Of course, the rocky ground made even the attempt at a purposeful, graceful fall extraordinarily painful. Her shoulder hit a sharp rock, her hip and elbow knocking against hard rocks as well.

She didn't have to feign the cursing as pain shot through her. Her only saving grace was she had managed to land on her less injured side.

"Get up," one of the men ordered, pretending to be inconvenienced, but she could hear the laughter around her. They were all quite happy with themselves for "making" her fall.

She would *enjoy* taking them down. She allowed herself to imagine that as she struggled to get back to her feet. Her side ached where she was hurt, but to make sure they didn't see *that*, she adopted a fake limp so they'd think she hurt her leg on the opposite side.

The men snickered, even more pleased with themselves for having inflicted some harm.

She'd tried to keep track of how long they walked, but it was so dark in the hood, there was no good way. Shay didn't let herself fall again, no matter how much they pushed and laughed, because she couldn't risk severely injuring herself when she was already weakened from last month's injury.

They didn't seem to know about that. Surely Frankie did. He was the one who'd sent the men to hurt her in the first place. And he hadn't given his men that piece of information that might help them make her miserable and in more pain.

She didn't know what to think of that, and didn't have

time to figure it out as she was being roughly shoved into something…the back seat of a vehicle.

There was faint rumbling from the men who had to heft her a little bit to get her up into the seat, but no clear indication of what was going on.

She held her breath, anxiety filling her as she wondered if she'd be separated from Granger. What would they do then?

Someone bumped into her shoulder, and she immediately knew it was Granger. Similarly tied up and shoved into the back of a car.

It was a small, fleeting relief, but relief all the same.

"West," Granger muttered, likely to Elsie listening in from wherever she was. Would North Star be able to track the vehicle if they didn't have one of their own?

It didn't matter. They all knew where they were going. Out of Wyoming and into Idaho.

Straight to Frankie's compound.

GRANGER KEPT HIS shoulder pressed to Shay's, just a simple reminder or reassurance they were in this together. It centered him in a way he couldn't identify, and didn't have time to.

He had to concentrate. North Star was far enough out that muttering the direction they were going in so Elsie could verify they were being taken to Frankie's compound would be necessary. They wouldn't be able to follow without getting too close or they'd be marked.

Granger was pretty certain Shay would be dropped off at Frankie's compound. He wasn't so sure about himself. The man back there during the fight had been willing to kill him.

They hadn't done it, but they could have. Easily, when he and Shay surrendered.

Granger didn't know what to make of it. He just knew he had to keep his mind open to all the possibilities.

And one of the major possibilities he saw was that he and Shay would not be taken *to* the compound they knew about, even if they were taken *to* Frankie. At least at first. At least while he waited to see what North Star would do.

Because as much as this was about Shay, Granger couldn't get over the fact that when she had been shot, there had been an effort to make the people of North Star pay and suffer. Frankie wouldn't honestly think Shay had handled this alone, even if she'd tried to.

Granger hadn't verbalized that to her, in part because he just wasn't certain. It was just a possibility. And also in part because that was exactly what she was worried about and he didn't want to add credence to her worry that the people she cared about might be hurt in all this.

Was he lumped in with all that? Or was he separate? Did that kiss mean…

There was no room for error, for worrying about a *kiss* for God's sake. This was about life and death. Not their *feelings*.

He grunted irritably. At himself…and the situation as every jolt and bump of the car caused another ache in his bruised body.

"South," he muttered. He wished he could hear Elsie talk back. It would be a risk, but at least he'd be able to know what information she had.

He could even be wrong about those directions, about what he felt. It had been a long time since he'd been in this kind of high-pressure tactical situation.

Shay said nothing. She sat next to him silent, keeping her shoulder pressed to his.

Granger felt the car gently turn again, then muttered a new direction toward the flashlight. There were doubts, but at the moment he only had himself to depend on.

The vehicle began to slow and Granger tried not to let the dread creep in. He needed to be alert and ready for whatever was thrown at them.

"Coming to a stop soon," he murmured to Elsie.

"I was just thinking," Shay said, her voice low as the car completely stopped and the men got out. It would only be a matter of seconds before the back doors were opened and they were no longer alone. "Frankie has to know we know where the compound is. Which means…"

"We're not at the compound."

The back doors opened and they were pulled out. There was no opportunity to say anything more or exchange theories about where they *were* if not Frankie's compound.

They were moved roughly for a while still outside, but then Granger heard the distinct squeak of a door and he would have almost tripped over a step if not for the hard, unrelenting hand that grabbed his arm and pulled him up rather than let him fall.

"You're all heart," he said to whoever had him.

There was a grunt but no other response as he was shoved forward—this time without anyone grabbing him or pushing him. He was standing still, and he heard feet shuffle around him—including the hard thumps of what he assumed was Shay being shoved and managing to stumble but balance enough to keep herself upright.

After a moment or two, his hood was pulled off. Even if Shay hadn't come to the conclusion beforehand, he would have immediately known they weren't at the compound Shay had found and been searching for.

The space was too small. Not heavily guarded. This wasn't the kind of space Frankie would spend any time in. It was dirty and rustic, and not meant to bring anyone any kind of comfort.

But this was where they'd been brought. This was where their hoods had been taken off. He didn't dare look at Shay as he studied the room around them. He had to focus on facts, not feelings.

At best this was some kind of holding cell, and at worst... Well, there were a lot of *at worsts* depending on where North Star was.

And what Frankie was planning to do.

ELSIE ROGERS STARED at the map. She'd been able to follow the directions Granger had given her through the mic, but they didn't make sense.

Either he was wrong, or her map was. She had a bad feeling it was the map, and that it was very purposeful. Someone working against her.

She swallowed at the fear of that. How could she be working off a false map? And how could someone have the kind of access necessary to make that happen?

But now wasn't the time for the who or how, it was the time for how did she fight against what someone was trying to do to stop her.

She looked back at the information Granger had given her. She'd written down every direction, and she knew where they'd started. Maybe her map was wrong, but she still had the right directions.

"They didn't go where we thought they'd go."

Elsie blinked at the speaker and then scrubbed at

her eyes. She had to *think*. "No, they didn't," she said to Cody.

"That means we're in the wrong position. We need to move."

"Yeah."

"Elsie, where are they?" he asked.

Panic threatened to spurt up inside of her, but she knew that Shay wouldn't panic. Bad things happened, unexpected obstacles cropped up. A person had to stay calm and in control, no matter how worried they were about the people who might be in the crossfire.

"I don't know where they are. My computer's been tampered with." She had to fight back the wave of fear and failure. Both wanted to win. She was a computer genius and now she couldn't trust her computers.

But as long as Granger and Shay were alive she had the chance to bring them back home. She just had to figure out how to use do it.

She turned off her mic to Cody. "Betty?"

Betty Wagner, resident North Star doctor for the time being, poked her head into the room Elsie had commandeered for her computers. Useless computers at this point.

"We need a map of the area. *Not* your phone or a computer. A paper map."

Betty frowned. "The gas station might have one, I guess." She studied Elsie and then nodded. "I'll go get one."

"You have to be careful."

Betty nodded. "I've learned a thing or two about stealth. Stay here. Listen to the team. I'll be back as soon as I can."

It was Elsie's turn to nod. Once Betty left she allowed

herself one shaky breath and then swallowed. She straightened her shoulders and put her mic to Cody back on. "Okay, listen closely. This is what we're going to do…"

Chapter Twelve

Shay knew better than to be thrown by a change of plans. When you were an operative, you had to roll with any possibility. Plans were thwarted, danger mounted and you kept your head. No matter what.

But finding herself in a grungy little cabin with Frankie nowhere to be seen was a surprise she hadn't seen coming.

She'd expected to be taken right to that compound, but it was Granger's words that had been causing her to rethink that there in the back of that car.

Give them what they expect.

Frankie had known what they would expect, and he'd done the opposite. It made her blood run cold. If he knew enough to surprise them…

She couldn't finish that thought. She looked at the men in the room with them. Three inside. Likely the others remained on guard outside. All armed with tactical gear, big guns and nasty sneers on their faces.

She glanced at Granger without moving her head. Like her, he was studying the surroundings. But he didn't look at her, not even in his peripheral vision.

She studied his head wound. He'd bled through the bandage and his face and beard were caked with dried blood. How much longer would he be able to push through that? How much longer—

Get it together, Shay.

She had wanted to come on this mission alone because she didn't want anyone she cared about hurt, and because she truly did believe this was *her* deal. Her penance.

But beyond those very real, complex feelings of guilt and blame, there was this. She didn't know how to maintain her old brick wall. When she hadn't cared overly much if she or anyone else lived or died. She'd been an operative, and each mission had been about the end goal. Not about life and death.

But she'd lost that. Somewhere between the day of the explosion at the old headquarters and the day Granger had told her he was entrusting North Star to her.

And she'd known, last month when Vianni's men had been closing in, that she couldn't access that old part of herself. It was gone. Dissolved somehow.

Maybe it had been an insult to Granger and the rest of North Star to not use their skills, but she didn't know how to be the kind of leader Granger had always been.

And *this* was why. She was thinking about him and Elsie and everyone else rather than what they needed to do to get out of this predicament.

Unfortunately, there was no escaping this cabin. Maybe she and Granger could fight off the men, knowing the men wouldn't shoot to kill, but then what? It didn't get them what they wanted: an end to this.

And Frankie knew. He had to know that was their ultimate goal.

So, what was his?

Not her dead. He could have done that long before

she'd known he was still alive. Or at least, his end goal wasn't her dead without playing some games first. Frankie loved his games. He wanted her to pay for deceiving him, leaving him behind to die.

So, he'd want her to be afraid. Terrified. Hurt and devastated. But not dead. Not yet.

Would he understand what she was most afraid of? Would he have any concept of the woman she'd become? How could he? And if he still thought of her as that shallow, confused girl who'd wanted excitement, but not quite the getting knocked around and told what to do kind, what did he think she was afraid of?

She took a deep breath in an effort to calm her circling thoughts. They were good questions, but she needed to take it one step at a time. Not get overwhelmed by all the possibilities.

If she could get into the same room as Frankie, see him face-to-face, listen to what he had to say—no matter how many lies or fake stories he offered—she might be able to figure it out. What he wanted. What he expected.

And if she could do that, she could make this work in her favor. She had no other choice. Everyone she loved was on the line.

She looked at the three men inside. One of them had to be a leader or commander of some kind—the direct communicator to Frankie. She studied the one by the door. He mostly looked straight ahead, holding the gun close to his body. He didn't aim it, but he was ready to shoot if he needed to.

But not her. He wasn't supposed to shoot her.

This time, she didn't let herself look at Granger. She looked at the other two men. They both stood at windows on opposite sides of the cabin, standing in the exact same position the guy by the door was.

Door guy wouldn't be the commander she was looking for. If something happened, he'd need to go out. He'd need to be the first one to act. So, it would be one of the window guys.

Shay watched them for a while, waiting for *something* to distinguish one of them. She wasn't sure how long she waited. The frustration of standing there silently waiting for *something* made time stand still. But, when one glanced at the watch on his wrist, and she looked over at the other who didn't have a watch, she figured she'd found her man.

She looked right at him, waiting till his gaze swept around the room and landed on her staring at him. He didn't measure any surprise that she'd zeroed in on him, just held her gaze. Blankly.

"So, when do I get to have a tearful reunion with my supposedly dead husband?"

The man stared back at her. He didn't sneer or snicker like the men who'd led her there did. Maybe he hadn't been one of them, or maybe she just hadn't noticed one being quiet.

But that made her sure she'd targeted the right man.

"We just gonna stand around in silence? Let me tell you, as torture goes that's not quite the method I'd use."

Still, he didn't move or say anything.

Shay had to bite her tongue to keep herself from demanding something—anything. Standing there still and silent *was* a kind of torture.

She clenched her hands into fists and bit her tongue and waited. The silence was oppressive. The standing painful after so many injuries along the way. She wanted to fight. She wanted to yell. She wanted to—

Then she heard the faint slam of a car door. Watched as all the guards exchanged looks and the man at the door nodded and then slipped out.

The head guy looked at her and finally showed some semblance of being something other than a robot. He smiled. "Might want to pretty yourself up, sweetheart. Here comes the husband."

Shay didn't turn and look at the door. She didn't register surprise or fear or anything else. Instead, she kept her breathing even and imagined that she was encased in some kind of ice chamber. Still, frozen in place and utterly uninterested in anything around her.

She couldn't give *anything* away to Frankie, because likely *anything* could get someone she cared about dead.

GRANGER WATCHED SHAY still herself. She'd already been standing still, but relaxed. Everything in her tensed until she was like a statue. Not rigid or tense. Simply impenetrable.

Impressive. Granger tried to mimic it. But he hadn't expected Frankie to come *here*. He'd expected a long wait and some mind games before they were taken to the main compound. The *nice* compound, with all the trappings of wealth Frankie Vianni liked to surround himself with to feel important.

Granger didn't like how the man kept surprising them.

He heard the door behind him open, but he didn't turn to look and see if it was the guard returning or the devil himself. He stared straight ahead in an at-ease position reminding himself he'd dealt with worse than Frankie.

Ace Wyatt who'd once run the Sons of the Badlands, who'd been responsible for Anna's death in a more *actual* way than Frankie, had been bigger, slicker, meaner than Frankie.

Of course, he'd also been insane and fancied himself some kind of god.

Frankie didn't have that. He was just vicious, and smart enough to make the people around him pay if they didn't fall in line.

"Well, well, well." His voice hadn't changed, but Granger didn't turn his head. A surreptitious look to Shay showed him the same. She looked straight ahead, expression blank and military-esque.

Frankie took his time. He didn't appear in front of them for a while, as if waiting them out. Trying to get them to turn their heads to look at him.

He finally gave up the wait and came to stand in front of them. And it was definitely not the Frankie Vianni Granger remembered.

He'd bulked up, for starters. No longer tall and wiry in an elegant suit. He was a tall, muscular man who sported a dark beard now, looking more the Idaho wilderness survivor man than suave Chicago gangster.

A wiggle of dread tried to break through Granger's composure, but he didn't let it. He'd done a little survivor man-ing himself.

Frankie studied them with shrewd eyes. His father had been a sledgehammer. Too heavy-handed, too certain in his power. Where the original Vianni family had wreaked havoc as dirty law enforcement, the next generation had made the kind of mistakes that had gotten the original generation put behind bars, their control over the police department evaporating all because of Gio Vianni's blunders.

But Gio had managed to stay out of prison. He'd managed to make his family look on the up-and-up, while Frankie had taken after grandpa and built a brand new empire.

Granger knew the family dynamics. Anna had explained them to him in no uncertain terms. Gio might have been the figurehead of the Vianni family, but Frankie had been the brains behind their resurrection.

Frankie Vianni was smart. Cruel and vicious, sure, but clever. He'd always made a point of separating himself from the family business so the law couldn't touch him. While pulling all the strings.

And when he'd finally failed at that, he'd faked his own death.

That one still stuck in Granger's craw. Anna was dead and this weasel had managed to live. Over and over again, no matter how many people wanted him dead.

Granger himself included.

But he had learned something since he'd been shot and burned. Revenge was sweet, sure, but it also blinded. It warped what his mission should always be: stop a monster like Frankie from hurting more innocent people.

So, he couldn't think about Anna or what Frankie deserved. He had to cool off the red-hot anger deep inside of him. Had to remain calm and collected thinking about getting Shay out of this mess.

She might have married this man willingly, but she'd been a young girl who hadn't known what she'd been getting herself into. If there was any blame, no doubt ten years as a North Star operative was penance enough.

"An interesting duo," Frankie was saying, studying

them both. "My wife. My brother-in-law. A little piece of Chicago, right here in the Idaho wilderness."

"Oh, is that where we are?" Shay asked, pretending like he'd given something away even though Granger was well aware they all knew they were in Idaho.

Frankie only smiled. "You've gotten more clever, Veronica. I'll admit, I've been surprised at your development. I always figured you were the kind of stupid even a man like me couldn't fix."

Shay didn't take the bait. She shrugged negligently.

"And it seems you've worked out not just your mind, but your body," he said silkily, moving closer to her.

Granger had to curl his hands into fists to remind himself to stay where he was. Even as Frankie came to stand right in front of Shay, giving her a slow, disgusting once-over.

She stood her ground, appearing to all unaffected by the blatant perusal.

Frankie reached out and tapped her cheek with his index finger and Granger had to breathe through the red haze of *violence* that swept through him. It wasn't an overtly sexual or threatening gesture, and somehow that made it worse.

"You'll do quite well, wife," Frankie said. Then his gaze slid to Granger.

Frankie studied him critically, and Granger kept his face perfectly placid. Even as primal fury tried to wage war inside of him.

"I'll admit, I've never been able to completely figure this out." He gestured from Shay to him and back again. "Guilt? Revenge? Why'd you help her? When you had to know she was involved in all sorts of dastardly plans of mine."

Granger didn't say anything, and neither did Shay. They were definitely on the same page. Don't give Frankie anything he could use against them—words, emotions, reactions.

"Of course, that's a silly question isn't it?" Frankie said with a little laugh, his gaze fully on Granger now. "You knew Anna was involved in things and you looked the other way."

It was a shock that Frankie knew that, but maybe because he'd just admitted the same to Shay, it didn't hit like the blow it was meant to be. Granger was able to keep his reaction under the surface. Giving Frankie nothing.

"Admirable restraint, Agent Macmillan. *Admirable.*" He tilted his head to one side, studying Granger with a patient, searching gaze that didn't bode well. Then he smiled. "But we'll break you yet."

SABRINA KILLIAN DID not do *almost-died* recovery well. She pushed herself too hard. She snapped at anyone who dared tell her so. Including her boyfriend, who somehow still put up with her. Still managed to love her, no matter how much of a jerk she was.

Connor Lindstrom *might* be superhuman, not that she'd ever admit that to him. Especially when he was off helping Shay face her past and she was stuck here with Froggy, his S&R dog, while everyone else got to be out there in the fray.

"I'm not *that* injured anymore," she muttered to the dog, who had her head resting on Sabrina's lap, sleeping on the couch…where Sabrina wasn't supposed to let her sleep, but had been whenever Connor was out on a mission.

So *maybe* she had a soft spot for dogs. Sue her.

Her phone vibrated in her pocket and she answered it in a rush, hoping Connor had good news to impart. "Hey, how's it going?"

There was a pause. Not a long one, but enough of one.

She swallowed, trying to keep the fear out of her voice. "That bad?"

"We've lost track of them," Connor said matter-of-factly. "But Elsie's working on it."

"Lost track. Connor, that's not just bad that's a dis…" She trailed off as the dog half in her lap snuffled in her sleep. "Froggy can track them," she said.

"Yes, Froggy can track them. We don't want to lose our numbers here when everything is so up in the air, so…"

Sabrina practically jumped to her feet, waking up Froggy in the process. "I'll bring her."

"Yes, but you listen to me, Killian," he said sternly. "You are still on the injured list, you understand that? You're *just* bringing Froggy. That's *it*."

"You're adorable."

"Sabrina."

His voice was grave, and because she knew him she could tell he was tired and worried, and adding worry about her wasn't going to make him feel any better.

But he had to understand… "It's Shay."

"I know." He let out a long sigh. "Bring Froggy. Her gear and… Hell, bring yours too, but you're the *last* resort, Sabrina. Promise me you understand that."

"Yeah, yeah, yeah. I'll be there soon."

"Be careful. I love you."

He always said it with such *conviction*, even all these months later it hit her a little hard.

"Love you too," she muttered, which made him laugh. She'd never understand why, or maybe it was simply because he understood her and how that was still a strange, humbling thing for her to admit out loud to anyone, least of all routinely.

But she hung up the phone and looked at the dog. "Well, Froggy, we've got a mission. This one is important. You're going to find Shay for us."

And Sabrina was going to help bring her home.

Chapter Thirteen

Revulsion pooled in Shay's stomach. Once upon a time, she'd fancied herself in love with the man in front of her. Because he'd made her nervous, and all her friends had always giggled about boys who gave them butterflies. Because he'd paid attention to her and bought her presents when all her friends had complained their boyfriends wouldn't even take them to McDonald's and pay.

She knew she'd been young and sheltered and Frankie had targeted her because she was pretty and he fancied her dumb and weak enough to be the kind of woman who'd fit well on his arm. There were excuses she could make herself feel better with, sure.

But faced with the reality of the situation, she could only feel sick to her stomach over how stupid she'd been.

Still, that didn't change her current situation.

And Frankie was right. She'd changed. Gotten smarter and stronger, and she could feel ill over that young woman making bad choices, but *this* woman wasn't going to repeat those mistakes.

This woman had learned how to fight, thanks to the man standing next to her, and that's what she was going to do.

She had to be careful about what she said and how

she said it, but she couldn't stand Frankie's attention on Granger. So, she broke her silence.

"So, Frank," she said, knowing he'd hated that because it had been his grandfather's name, and he blamed his grandfather for all the work he'd had to do to rebuild the Vianni name.

Even though it had been his father who'd made the mistakes that had gotten Frank thrown in jail, where he'd died.

"I know I was a great catch and all, but this seems like an awful lot of work to get back a wife who clearly didn't want you."

Like she'd hoped, his attention turned back to her. He smiled, that cruel smile that had her stomach cramping, and a muscle memory wanting her to flinch and brace herself for a blow.

She managed to fight back the flinch, but it was a near thing.

"Oh, it wasn't so clear, was it, Veronica? You wanted me well enough."

Another roll of nausea went through her, but she held his dark gaze. "I think you have me confused with one of your prostitutes."

He let out a little tinkle of a laugh as though she had a delightful sense of humor. "You always could make me laugh, Veronica. It was a shame you were so stupid. We could have done great things together."

The sad thing was, when she'd been eighteen, she'd believed him. That she was stupid. That everything that went wrong was her fault. Luckily, she wasn't eighteen anymore.

"So," he said conversationally, walking away from her and Granger and toward the door. She didn't let her gaze follow him. She went back to looking forward at the wall.

"When do you think your friends will be arriving?"

Terror gripped her in a new way. *Your friends.* He meant North Star. And if he was bringing it up...

That meant he'd set a trap for North Star. Even though he had her, he wanted to hurt them too. She kept her breathing even, but it was a fight. No matter what Frankie's plans were, she couldn't panic, though God, she felt it pulsing through her.

Frankie couldn't see it. So, she forced herself to just breathe.

Granger cleared his throat, almost inaudibly. She looked at him. He didn't say anything, but she understood his expression well enough. It was like when he'd told her it was an insult not to use their skills to help her.

Those people out there who wanted to help her weren't weak and helpless. She didn't think they were, but something about fear made them all too mortal. And this situation was so fully hers, it would always be a blame on her own shoulders if someone got hurt.

She knew, she *knew* she couldn't think about all the people out there who could die, what it would mean to their families. She *knew* that and yet the panic wound through her tighter and tighter.

When this was *her* mess, and she didn't have anyone waiting for her. She didn't have a family anymore. No one to need her. No one to love her.

Except all those people out there.

Shay felt like crying. Partly because it was Granger's voice in her head, reminding her that just as she loved the people who'd become like her surrogate family, they loved her in return. If she could get past her own hang-ups, put herself in their shoes, she'd be doing the same damn thing.

"This isn't where they thought we'd be," Granger said under his breath. As if that was new information. Even though it wasn't, it broke her out of the circular panic whirl of her thoughts.

She frowned at him, but didn't have time to work through him saying aloud what they both already knew.

"What was that?" Frankie asked. Since they'd refused to look back at him, he'd returned to stand before them. He studied Granger's face. "What did you just try to whisper to her?"

Granger shrugged and offered Frankie a bland smile. "You must be hearing things, Frank."

Quick as a snake, Frankie reached out and punched Granger in the face. Granger's head jerked to the side with the force of the blow, but he immediately turned it back so he could look at Frankie. Other than the head move, he reacted not at all. Not a grunt, not a flinch, not even a bunching of muscles like he was preparing to fight back.

"I can make it hurt," Frankie seethed.

"I'm sure you can. Have your men hold me down, point their guns at me. You can inflict all kinds of damage, big man that you are. Kicking a man who can't fight back."

Frankie's expression went mutinous, but he held himself still. He'd curled his hands into fists as he sneered at Granger, breathing just a little bit too heavily.

Granger was trying to goad him into acting, into making a mistake, but after tense, silent minutes Frankie carefully got himself back under control. He didn't throw another punch, didn't order his men away.

He smiled at Granger. "I don't underestimate you, Macmillan. You're good at what you do." He stepped closer, so they were toe to toe, eye to eye. "But I'm better."

Granger shrugged negligently. "Guess we'll find out."

"We certainly will." He nodded to someone behind them. Then Granger was grabbed roughly from behind.

Shay couldn't prevent herself from reaching out. An instinct to stop everything. Granger shook his head and let the man drag him to the door.

But separating them was awful. What would they do to Granger?

And it was too soon. North Star would need some time to follow them. To figure out where they were. They needed more time. This was terrible.

Meant to be terrible. She looked at Frankie and he was grinning at her.

"Say goodbye, Veronica. It might be your last chance."

GRANGER LET HIMSELF be dragged. His heart beat a little too hard in his chest because likely more pain was coming. Possibly worse than that.

He'd fight it, but if Frankie ordered one of his men to shoot him in the head, that was pretty much it. North Star might be able to find them eventually, but even they would need more time.

If his time was up, his time was up. He could accept that. Maybe not from Frankie or one of his goons, but you put yourself in danger enough times you got a little fatalistic about death.

But what really bugged him was that Shay would spend the rest of her life blaming herself if he ended up dead right now. So, he had to think.

The guard pushed him outside where he was grabbed by another one. The original guard went back in, but Frankie soon emerged from the ramshackle cabin.

He didn't speak to his guard, and the guard didn't ask any questions. Whatever this was had been planned in advance.

Granger tried to predict what it might be. Some kind of torture—physical or emotional—as revenge for raiding his family, taking them down…or at least forcing the Viannis to fake their own deaths and go into hiding?

It just didn't gel. The problem was, nothing really did.

The guard gave him a shove and Granger narrowly missed plowing into a tree since his hands were bound behind him, but he somehow managed to keep his balance and merely bounce into the rough bark.

The guard roughly whirled him around, so now his back was to the tree and he was facing Frankie, who stood in front of him dressed all in black, hands clasped behind his back. He wore no weapons. Wasn't in a fighting stance. Instead, he simply stood and watched.

Waiting.

But for *what*?

"It's been fascinating watching you work the past few years," Frankie said casually. Then smirked. "Or not work, as the case may be in those early days of your recovery. I hope you've got those dogs and horses somewhere safe."

Granger had dealt with enough men who wanted to terrify him to know how to keep his game face, but the fact Frankie knew about his ranch and his animals was a shock. He didn't let it show, but he knew he didn't have quite the pithy response that would have shown the bastard just how unaffected he was.

Because he *was* affected. Even knowing his animals were in good hands. He'd moved the dogs to the Bluebird Inn and his horses to a neighboring ranch. Vianni men could burn down his place—it wouldn't make a difference. They wouldn't get what they were after.

And Granger doubted very much he was meant to live past this interaction with Frankie Vianni, so what did threatening him with things he'd never see again matter?

Even if it did make him sick to his stomach, Frankie had clearly kept tabs on him. When they'd been so careful. When they'd managed to be a secret for so long.

Something had happened in the past few months. Somehow, the Viannis had gotten through. Granger didn't know how. Elsie would have been able to see a security breech in their tech. And they didn't take on very many new people, certainly not without thorough background checks, especially after what had happened two years ago.

Two years ago…

Frankie had said for the past *years*.

Granger's mind whirled with the possibility that Frankie had been planning something for *two* years while North Star worked, fully ending the Sons and taking down corrupt military officials and weapons dealers.

Thinking that the Vianni threat had been eradicated completely. Because they hadn't known there were still some Viannis out there. Lying in wait.

"My Veronica did an admirable job running your little vigilante group, didn't she? I mean, she didn't take down any gangs like the great Granger Macmillan, but she held her own. Impressive. Surprising, really. I didn't think she had it in her."

Granger laughed. "You don't know her at all." At

least, he was going to do everything in his power to make Frankie think he didn't. Because it was better for Vianni to keep underestimating her.

"It appears I didn't, but deep down, Veronica is the same girl I knew. I was married to her. We shared a bed, Macmillan." Frankie smirked. "I know her well enough. And I know that the only reason she managed anything in the decade since you took her away is that she had a strong male lead to follow. To admire. To look up to, among other things."

Granger had to weigh his words. Be careful to make it sound like he was speaking out of spite or anger, rather than the truth. So Frankie believed he would let this all slip because Frankie had gotten the better of him. Because his side innuendos had effected him.

And maybe they had enough that his words would sound truthful when it wasn't the truth at all. "You remember a young woman you knocked around and manipulated, but I saved her from that. I taught her how to be a leader. How to separate her emotions from the task at hand. And then I left her in the lurch. We might work together well enough, but I'm no hero to her anymore."

Frankie made a considering noise. "Well, I'll give you one thing, she doesn't have much loyalty. She took her sister-in-law's husband at the drop of the hat, didn't she?"

Granger wanted to deny it—defend both Anna's memory and give Shay more credit, but it didn't matter what Frankie thought. The truth didn't matter here.

"You're no hero to her, but I'm betting the people who work for her are *something* to her. Why else would she try to keep them out of this? It was kind of you to bring them in. Much easier on me."

Granger didn't say anything. Agreements or denials

would both hurt here. So, he simply did what he'd done in the cabin. Kept his mouth shut and looked straight ahead, carefully devoid of any emotion.

Frankie looked back at the cabin. "You know, I always thought you and I weren't so different. It was why Anna played both sides. You and your DEA cronies trying to take me down, the Vianni family trying to do the same right back."

Granger tried to look horrified, since that was what Frankie so clearly wanted. "It isn't the same," he said, adding some rasp to his voice.

"Isn't it? Weren't you just me with the law behind you?"

It hurt, even though he knew it wasn't true. He also knew there was *some* truth to it. Because he'd bent laws, and done things he shouldn't have in the pursuit of justice. Or vengeance. Depending on the day.

"You let that one sink in for a while. Because lucky for you, I don't want you dead just yet."

And *that* was terrifying.

HOLDEN PARKER STOOD in a snowbank next to Connor Lindstrom. What had once been a suspicious and perhaps edgy distrust of one another had grown into something more of a friendship, if only because Sabrina insisted…and Connor was a sap over the woman Holden had always seen as a sister.

But that was why Holden was currently rather irritated with his friend. "I don't like it."

Connor shrugged, eyeing the white horizon. "You think I do?"

"She's not going to go back to headquarters once she's here."

"No, she isn't," Connor agreed.

Which was irritating. The guy never did want to *fight* or *bicker*, unlike Sabrina, who was always up for a good fight. And shouldn't be coming into this one. "Someone else couldn't have brought your dog?"

"Not as quickly since she was with my dog."

"I don't get why we need the dog anyway. Why Elsie is cutting off actual tech that will get us what we want." Of course, Holden did know. He just didn't like the reason. Because if their computer genius was telling them not to use their computers and comm units, that meant someone else was.

Connor didn't say anything to that. Holden supposed Connor knew he was complaining to pass the time not because he was that stupid.

"You think she'd marry me?" Connor asked. Completely and utterly out of the blue.

Holden didn't think much could surprise him anymore, but this sure did… "Huh?"

"You know her better than anyone. Or understand her better than anyone. She's not traditional. She's not…anything. So I'm asking, do you think she'd get to the point where she'd do something as traditional as marry me?"

Holden blinked and studied the man next to him. Connor kept his gaze on the horizon, his expression placid, but there was a tenseness inside of him that belied his calm demeanor.

And since Connor was anxious enough over his answer no matter how little he wanted to show it, Holden considered the question.

He did understand Sabrina better than most. They'd had similar views on life, though they often expressed them in different ways. His marriage to Willa had changed his outlook, and he figured that for Sabrina, those old views could change too. Now that she'd found Connor.

"The thing about Sabrina is… She grew up tough. She never really had anyone who loved her, not the way parents and family are supposed to anyway. Sabrina gave everything to the SEALs and then she's too injured to see that through. She's had tough break after tough break, but *she* didn't break."

"I know all that."

"I know you do, but my point here is that… It's not about being traditional or not. It's about not knowing what to do with it. Love and family and all that. North Star and you, it helps, but she's not going to know what to do with a marriage proposal. She might not even say yes, but deep down, Sabrina wants what everyone wants. A place to belong, people to love her. People she loves back. Traditional or not, marriage is the promise of that. It might freak her out at first, but yeah, I think she'd eventually say yes. Because though you do a better job of hiding it, you're as stubborn and obnoxious as she is."

Connor let out a little huff of a laugh. "Why does that sound like a compliment coming from you?"

"Because it is." Holden gave Connor's shoulder a little shove. "You're all right, Lindstrom."

"Yeah, you too," Connor muttered. He pointed toward the west. "They're coming."

Holden had been an operative for a long time, but Connor's ex-SEAL and S&R training never failed to impress him. Because in another minute, Sabrina and Connor's dog appeared at the crest of the hill.

She sauntered down the hill toward them, though

Holden wasn't fooled. That saunter was meant to hide her limp.

"Don't you two make quite a pair," she said as she approached with one of her trademark devil-may-care grins. But it didn't hide the tense set of her jaw, likely against the pain she had to be in.

"Aren't you supposed to still be using a cane?" Holden asked, smiling right back though it was a desperate attempt not to shake some sense into her.

"Betty cleared me to walk on my own last week, thank you very much."

"So, you thought you'd hike cross-country?"

Her gaze moved from Holden to Connor. "What have you got to say?"

He leaned in and gave her a quick kiss. "I'm glad to see you."

She blinked, and Holden realized Connor really was perfect for her because he could put aside all the concerns and fears he had about her health, and play her like a fiddle.

She scowled at her boyfriend, then at Holden. "Listen, I know my limitations. But it's Shay. It's Granger. I'm not going to get myself killed doing something stupid, but I'm damn well going to be out here doing what I can to bring them home."

Connor slid his arm over her shoulders and they both looked at Holden, the dog happily wagging its tail between them.

She gave Holden a smirk. "See, I can be reasonable."

He didn't bother to respond. "So, what's the plan?"

"Connor and Froggy will do their best to get a lead on Shay or Granger. Hopefully they're together, but if we get one, Elsie and her paper map can work on the other, hopefully. Holden and I will stay here and man the analog radio. If Connor needs backup, you'll go after him. Elsie's got a whole radio compound set up."

"Did she say what's wrong with the computer and comm systems from this century?" Holden asked.

Sabrina frowned and shook her head. "No. She was a little preoccupied trying to get everything set up without it."

Fair enough.

"When you find them, or even get a good, reliable idea of what direction they went in, you hold. You don't act. From everything we can tell we've got time, so we need to do this right. You radio your location and we go from there."

Connor nodded. "Promise me you're going to stay put and man the radios?" Before Sabrina could say *anything*, Connor fixed her with a steely glare. "Promise."

To Holden's surprise, she winkled her nose. "Fine," she muttered. "I promise unless there are extraordinary circumstances."

Connor rolled his eyes, but he apparently wasn't going to argue with her. "All right. Well, while you do that, why don't you think about marrying me?" He leaned in, kissed her soundly on the mouth, then began to walk away while Sabrina watched him go, her expression one of pure and utter shock.

Holden had to grin. He'd never seen her so taken aback, and he'd known her a long time.

"He's not serious," she muttered, but she didn't move. And she didn't stop staring at Connor's quickly disappearing form.

"Seems to be," Holden replied.

Sabrina whipped her head around and glared at him. "But…why?"

Holden reached out, gave her shoulder a little squeeze. "Bad news. I think he loves you, Sabrina."

She scowled at him and whacked his hand away. "Well, I know that."

"Love does funny things to people. Has them thinking about normalcy and not carrying around high-profile weapons through the mountains and woods trying to take down the bad guys."

"Sounds terrible." But she didn't sound so convinced. "How normal are you feeling these days?"

Holden rocked back on his heels. He scanned the area around them as he'd been doing since he and Connor had decided this was a good meeting spot. No sign of Vianni's men or the other North Star groups patrolling the area. They were far enough out no one should stumble upon them, but he kept a lookout.

And he decided he might as well be honest with Sabrina. If only to help her toward seeing marriage wasn't quite so crazy a thought. "Willa and I are thinking about having a kid."

"You're…*what*?"

"Not quite there yet, but getting there. Lianna walking around with that tiny baby is really doing a number on my wife."

"Your wife."

"Yeah, still weird."

"You love it."

"I do. I love her. And you know, I'm kinda growing to love the farm stuff too. There's something about living without feeling like there's a target on your back or someone to take down that just…sits okay. I could maybe live my life with a little less animal waste, but all in all, Willa makes up for it."

Sabrina's eyebrows were furrowed, and she still watched where Connor and his dog had disappeared. She held the radio in her hand.

Holden figured she wasn't going to say anything else, so he fiddled with the old-fashioned radio walkie Elsie had managed to get distributed to everyone. It would be tougher to communicate cross groups, and wasn't nearly as stealthy, but at least they'd be able to talk to Elsie.

"Search and rescue isn't so bad," Sabrina said into the silence after a while.

Holden looked down at her. She was staring straight ahead, to where Connor had disappeared. She had a line between her eyes like she was frowning even though her expression was placid.

"No, I don't suppose it is," he agreed.

"Connor's an okay pilot, and I'm an excellent tracker. Of course, we'd have to hire on some help if we wanted to start an S&R group. Obviously only if the North Star work ever dried up."

"Obviously. What kind of help?"

Sabrina shrugged. "More trackers. Some admin staff. That sort of thing." She finally looked up at him. "It's helping people without the target on your back."

And he realized that in the months since he'd "semi-retired" from North Star, that's exactly what he'd been looking for. A way to do good without putting his life on the line, time and time again. Because he wanted to go home to his wife and, yeah, start a family.

Leave it to Sabrina to find a way to offer them that. He cleared his throat, looked away from her and to the white world around them. Like old times. Old missions.

But maybe, *hopefully*, the last one. "But first, we help Shay and Granger."

"Yeah, just like they helped us once upon a time."

Shay and Granger—

Chapter Fourteen

When Frankie returned, Shay refused to demand where Granger was, though that's what she most wanted to do. But he wanted that desperation from her. He wanted her to fall into a blubbering mess at his feet. Frankie wanted her scared and desperate.

She thought about it. After all, weren't they a little bit giving him what he wanted? Playing into the way he thought they should act so they could take him off guard?

Shay looked at him, opened her mouth to say something deferential or pleading, but no words came out. She ordered herself to swallow her pride, though every part of her fought against it.

Then she thought back to what she'd been allowed to observe as her position as Frankie's wife. Nothing too important, but she'd once seen a man beg for his life. Frankie had gotten a lot of enjoyment out of that.

But he'd still killed the guy. Not in *front* of Shay, and maybe not even by his own hand, but she'd known— he'd made sure she knew—the man had wound up dead the very next day.

Had she ever seen anyone change Frankie's point of view? Anyone alter his plans? Not that she could remember, but sometimes he would act impulsively. And when he did that, he'd usually make a mistake.

It wasn't easy to get to that impulsive side of Frankie. He knew his own weaknesses and he ruthlessly tried to eradicate them. Likely, he'd gotten even better at it in the decade since she'd been married to him.

But didn't it make sense in the present to do all she could to enflame his temper? To try to get to that point where he made a mistake. Maybe he expected her to fall apart and beg, but wouldn't it fluster him more if she didn't?

Sure, it was risky. He could impulsively *kill* her or Granger, and then where would she be?

But maybe, if she poked the right places, it could end up showing a crack in his armor. Maybe she could get *somewhere* that would help them escape this if she made him really, *really* mad.

In Shay's estimation, it was worth the effort. But before she could try, to her surprise, one of the guards pulled Granger back inside the cabin. He was shoved roughly inside, but not left to stand next to Shay like before. They jerked his arms in separate directions and cuffed him to two hooks in the wall.

She searched his face for signs of new injury, but the blood seemed to be old from his head wound from the crash, and he didn't look any worse for the wear.

What *was* this?

"We'll play a little game," Frankie said, almost cheerfully.

Shay had to look away from Granger, had to ignore her own fear and remember her new objective. She sighed heavily. "A game? Really? Can't you just get this over with? Hurt us if you want. Kill us if you're going to. Why the drama?"

Frankie's eyes narrowed, but his smile didn't dim. "We've all got to find our own fun somewhere."

"Leave it to you for your 'somewhere' to be cliché villain in a sitcom." She blew out a long, bored breath. "All right. What's this dastardly game you want to play?"

Frankie's jaw set, but he wasn't falling for the bait. "We have a little discussion. You tell the truth and all is well," he said, but she could hear the tension in his voice. "You don't, then your hero here breaks a bone." He wasn't getting the enjoyment of messing with her when she acted unimpressed. When she poked at his pride and his ego.

So, she poked harder.

"Must feel real good having to chain him to a wall to have to hurt him. *Woo* boy, what a tough guy."

Frankie whirled on her. He didn't strike and he didn't say anything, but his breath came in short puffs and she knew she was getting to him. Fifty-fifty chance it was a mistake, but it was a really *gratifying* mistake.

Granger even laughed, and that *really* set Frankie off.

"Would you prefer I hurt you?" he asked, and she remembered that silky, dangerous tone of voice so well a part of her recoiled. That old, scared part of herself wanted to drop his gaze.

But she wasn't Veronica any longer. She'd built herself into Shay. A woman who wasn't afraid. Who led missions. Who risked her life to save others. "Are you going to leave me cuffed? Because that's not a fair fight."

Frankie burst out laughing. "You think if I took off your cuffs, you could *take* me?"

"No," she replied gravely. "I *know* I could."

"Shay," Granger muttered, a warning. Maybe for show. Maybe not. Shay found she didn't care in the moment. She didn't care about much besides getting the chance to punch Frankie in the face.

She didn't look at Granger. She held Frankie's furious gaze. Chin lifted. Challenge between them.

"You're strong. A fighter now?" Frankie said, his voice low and lethal before he let out another little laugh. This one sharp and mean. "Sending your minions off to do your dirty work for you?"

"Is that what I do?" Shay replied, and she wasn't sure how much the smugness she imbued in her voice and expression was an act and how much was just *there*, because no matter how many insecurities she had about herself as a leader, sending off her minions wasn't one of them. "Must have learned from you."

Frankie's eyes narrowed, but his voice remained that silky threat. "How many of your operatives have been hurt in the past few months? It seems like an awful lot. And yet here you are, unscathed."

She tried not to let her frown show. Frankie said *unscathed* like he didn't know about her gunshot wound, but it had been inflicted by one of his men. He was aware of all the injuries her team had suffered elsewhere. How could her own injury have escaped his unnerving breadth of knowledge about everything that had gone on with North Star the past few months?

But she watched him, not saying anything, and his gaze dipped for a momentary, almost unnoticeable second to the place where she'd been shot.

Could it be that he was *pretending* not to know?

"Well, let's see what you got." He shrugged out of his jacket like he was going to…fight her.

She looked at the men on either side of her. Then at Frankie, standing there as if ready for a boxing match. "You can't be serious."

He nodded at his guards. "Take her cuffs off."

She watched as the guards exchanged confused looks. "Uh, boss…"

They said it in the same uncertain, warning kind of way that Granger growled her name from his spot chained to the wall.

"Take them off," Frankie ordered, the three words sounding more like a snap of temper than a man in control.

Shay didn't really think she was going to get a chance to fight Frankie. Surely…this was some kind of trick. But with the cuffs off, she got into a fighting stance. "It's hard to believe you're going to let this be a fair fight, Frank."

"You think I'm afraid of you?" he demanded. "They'll stay back. I'll even give you a free sh—"

She hit him before he got the word out of his mouth. It was probably stupid, but she also knew he didn't actually expect her to do it. To be able to hurt him.

And God, she wanted to hurt him. She landed a sharp elbow into his gut and swung it upward to his his nose. He pitched backward on a yelp of pain so she kicked out, a hard rap meant to *really* hurt.

When his guards didn't immediately jump to pull her off Frankie, she *really* let it fly. Shay wanted him on the ground so she could pound into him, so she focused on that end result. She kicked, swept out her legs, punched when she thought he was dodging her other blows too well.

He managed to get in a few of his own. Decent

punches, strong and with that follow-through that had
sent her sprawling once upon a time.

But she hadn't known how to block or fight back then.
Now, she did. And she realized he'd allowed this fight to
happen because he knew about her injury. He kept aim-
ing for it. Trying to land a blow where she'd been shot.

She didn't let him. She angled her body, protected
her bad side, and landed blow after blow that he only
minimally dodged.

Get him on his back. Get him on his back… It was
the chant in her head, but no matter how many punches
and kicks she got in, he just wouldn't go down. He got
one good shot, and it hurt no doubt, but luckily landed
far enough above her wound that it didn't send her to
her knees.

"Enough!" Frankie yelled. He didn't run away or anything. He didn't stop trying to hit her, but pretty soon
she was grabbed roughly by the two guards. She would
have whirled on them too, but she still wanted Frankie
on the ground under her. So she kept going after him.

Her own mistake.

The guards pulled her off and roughly cuffed her
again. Frankie grabbed his jacket off the floor with his
back to her. He was breathing heavily and he put the gar-
ment back on with sharp, frustrated movements. When
he turned to face her, he straightened his jacket, sneer-
ing at her and seething with rage. Blood dribbled from
his nose and mouth. His eye was puffy and he looked
to be putting more weight on one leg.

Shay grinned at him. "How's it feel? Trying to pick
on someone who can fight right back this go around?"

He wiped the blood from his mouth with the back of

his hand. He was vibrating with a rage he couldn't control. "You'll pay for that."

She had no doubt she would.

But it had been worth it.

"YOU KICKED HIS ASS," Granger said in utter surprise. He didn't bother to hush his voice or try to play it cool. He'd kept mostly silent during Shay's fight because…well, he hadn't believed Frankie would let it happen.

But he had. And Granger had only been able to stand there, chained to the wall, in silent awe as Shay had gotten in blow after blow.

Giving Shay the opportunity to do damage had been a mistake on Frankie's part. And he figured she'd known it. She'd poked at his temper until he'd made that mistake.

"Oh, yeah I did," Shay said, with relish.

"Enjoy your childish snickering," Frankie said coolly. His temper strained at the edges. Even Granger could see he was struggling to win the battle against it.

But he was pulling it together. Or trying to. Granger had been a little leery of Shay poking the angry bear, but he'd kept his mouth mostly shut and let her give it a shot. She knew Frankie the best, after all.

And she'd proven herself correct. Proven that she was definitely on the right track.

Shay had hurt Frankie. *Really* laid into him. And that would stick with Frankie, a thorn in his side, for the rest of his life. It made him more dangerous, but it also made him more prone to a stupid mistake like the one he'd just made.

"I can't imagine letting a woman get the better of me," Granger said, and shrugged when Shay glared at him. He was trying to piss Frankie off, not tell the truth. "Especially one I was married to."

"Can you imagine your wife begging for her life? I can. Oh wait, it isn't my imagination, it's a memory. The Sons might have killed Anna, but I was there."

Granger understood this was a "two can play your game" situation. Frankie trying to infuriate him so he'd do something stupid. Granger knew he shouldn't react, shouldn't say anything. But... "She was your sister, man. What the hell is broken inside of you?"

"She was, at best, a liability."

"It doesn't matter," Shay said. "That's the past, and this is today. Frankie, you want to play some more or are you just going to get this over with and kill us? Move on with your life. Because this? This is boring and a waste of your time."

"You're so worried about my time?" he sneered.

"I'm worried about spending my last seconds on earth pretending like I care about anything you have to say."

"Oh, you'll care what I have to say. Because you aren't dying today. In fact, I plan on letting you live a very long time, Veronica. But you will watch everyone you love die."

"Everyone I love can do what I just did to you, Frank."

But Frankie laughed, and he zeroed in on Shay. "Soon enough, your team will find you. They'll track you down. Of course they will. And they will fall into every single trap I've left for them." He tilted his head. "You're not laughing so hard now, Veronica."

"I don't know what would give you the impression you could trick our team," Granger said, having a deep-seated need to keep Frankie's focus off Shay and on him. "Our team took down the Sons. We took down the old guard of Vianni who tried to silence a loose thread. We've always won. Why would now be different?"

Frankie eyed him, and smiled. Not in anger, and that had Granger's heart turning to ice.

"I've been watching you for two years, Macmillan. *Two years.* Since I nearly blew you up." He looked at Shay again. "I have had eyes and ears into every mission you've put together and fought. I know your team, maybe better than you do. And I know exactly what it will take to have them all exactly where I want them."

Granger couldn't help but slide a look at Shay. Her expression was grim, but she wasn't showing that she was afraid, even though Granger knew she was. *He* was.

He'd asked Shay to trust in their skills—his and North Star and everyone who wanted to help her. Now, he had to trust them too. It was hard. Especially if Frankie had been watching them for *two* years.

But the one thing Frankie couldn't know was that Elsie was listening. And Granger had to believe, hope, *pray*, that it would be the ace in the hole that kept them all from falling into Frankie's trap.

REECE MONTGOMERY HAD been enjoying his retirement, much to the surprise of everyone around him—even his wife, Lianna's, who still every once in a while asked him if he didn't miss it.

He didn't. Maybe it was age. Maybe it was maturity. But mostly it was just finally finding what he'd always wanted. Home. A family.

He didn't relish leaving both behind. Lianna had a lot on her hands with eight-year-old Henry and baby Lark, plus the bed-and-breakfast. She'd hired some help, but that didn't mean Reece relished being away from his family. Even if he was getting more sleep on a mission than he did with a fussy newborn.

Reece looked around at the deep, dark night around him. Frigid cold. No, he didn't miss this.

The other team had gotten Connor's search dog and were tracking Shay and Granger that way, but Reece's team had been given instructions from Elsie that she'd relayed from Granger. They weren't totally clear, so they'd split up to decide which path was best, with Reece standing back as lookout and communications.

Elsie had told him that Frankie Vianni was setting a trap for them. One Vianni expected them to fall into. Presumably so that he could torture Shay by hurting those who'd come to save her.

Reece had no way to get word to his team to be wary of traps. He could only stand here and wait for them to hopefully come back. But, while he waited, he thought about the problem at hand, and he worked up a plan.

One he desperately hoped he wouldn't have to suggest.

The first to return was Cody Wyatt, and though they'd all gone in different directions, Wyatt's brothers weren't far behind. They stood together in silence, waiting for the last member of their team to return. Reece wasn't ready to sound the alarm, but he was watching his clock. He'd give Gabriel Saunders, a North Star operative Reece had worked with quite a bit, another thirty minutes, and then they'd have to act.

The Wyatt brothers on the other hand, he didn't really know. His and Cody's time with North Star had only barely overlapped and they'd been in separate sectors. He'd been on the case when Shay had gone rogue with Tucker, but again, not much contact. He'd never met

Jamison Wyatt, and had learned from Elsie he'd only come because Shay had been part of a team that had saved him from an almost deadly run-in with his gang leader of a father.

The same gang Reece's parents had belonged to.

The world was small enough, he supposed, when you dealt in different kinds of revenge.

"Any word on the dog?" Cody asked, coming to stand next to Reece as he rubbed his gloved hands together. They didn't dare risk a fire, but Reece sure wished they could.

He was getting soft, all things considered.

Reece shook his head in response to Cody's question. "Not yet. These analogue communications really slow things down."

"Yeah, hard to track at night too, for everyone. I couldn't see any sign of movement in my quadrant."

"Me neither," Tucker Wyatt added. "But we're talking about a pretty big group of people. Even as dark as it is, they'd have trouble covering up their movements."

"Unless they had someone specifically designated to clean up their movements," Reece replied grimly. He'd worked a few cases like that.

"As long as we're being this timid and this careful, we're always going to be two steps behind, bad communications or not," Jamison Wyatt said.

Reece wished he didn't agree. But sometimes you had to take some risks to have a better chance of coming out on the other end with what you wanted. What would they risk to save Shay and Granger?

"The problem is, Elsie overheard this Vianni guy tell Granger that he's laid some traps for us. And he expects North Star to fall into all of them." Reece looked at the three men around him, shrouded in dark. Though Cody and Tucker had both worked with North Star in some capacity, they were outliers. Either their time with North Star had been brief or a long time ago.

He could only hope that meant they'd tell him that the idea he'd been formulating sucked, and they could continue being careful. Not taking risks.

But how long could they do that before Shay and Granger wound up dead?

"I have an idea, but I'm not so sure it's a great one," Reece said. "It's risky. Possibly riskier than we need it to be. But Shay and Granger allowed themselves to get caught on purpose. While I realize they both knew they were putting themselves in the line of fire to keep others out of it, I also don't think they went in there sure they would die. They had hope they could get themselves out."

"I agree," Cody said grimly. "Shay might have played martyr, but she's too good of an agent just to accept defeat even in sacrifice."

"So, maybe it's not a bad way to go. If this Vianni guy is laying traps for us, why not fall into one?" Reece offered.

There was a careful silence, a *considering* silence, and Reece half wished he'd kept his mouth shut. But he knew...deep down, this was the risk they needed to take. No matter how much he didn't want to take it.

"All of us?" Jamison asked, his voice calm and devoid of emotion.

Reece shook his head. "Not all. I think it's safe to say Vianni doesn't know about you three. Vera Parker is another outlier. If we send only who he thinks is in North Star, we might be able to fool him."

"You're an outlier too, technically," Cody said, nodding at Reece. "You've been out for a while, right?"

"But not that long."

"Long enough. I know you want to go in. We all do. But if we send in a team to be caught with Shay and Granger, we need a big enough team on the outside to extract. We only send in the people we *know* they'd expect. Who would that be?"

Reece bristled. If people were going in on his orders, he should be one of the people going in. "It depends on what they know."

"Okay, let's assume they know most of what we know," Cody continued. "Who is on the North Star roster right now that he'd expect to come save Shay?"

Reece hesitated, but honesty was the way to go. He had to remember what it had been like to be an agent and an operative. Emotions couldn't cloud decision-making. "Saunders, Trevino, Lindstrom and Daniels for certain. Parker is iffy. He's been semiretired, but known to show up when the mission is dire."

"That's five with Parker, which leaves us six out here. I say we go for it," Cody said.

"Lindstrom will have to get back with the dog," Tucker pointed out.

"Yeah, let's get a message to Elsie of our plan. Once Saunders is back, we'll move to reconvene with the other team and go forward."

Reece wanted to argue, but he kept his mouth shut. Sometimes a plan wasn't great, but it was the only chance you had.

And he'd take whatever chances he needed to get Shay and Granger safe. He owed them both that much.

Chapter Fifteen

Shay was tired of being taken off guard, but Frankie had done another one-eighty. While he'd left Granger chained to the wall, he hadn't ended up playing his "game." He'd left the cabin.

Likely to nurse his wounds. That at least made her smile.

She was cuffed, but could walk the room freely. Of course, the armed dude at the door meant she couldn't walk right out, but she could go stand next to where Granger was chained to the wall.

She understood that this in it of itself was a game. *Wait. Wait. Wait.* She was supposed to worry Frankie was off taking down the North Star operatives after her. It was why she'd wanted to do this alone and yet now that the threat was here…

Something about fighting Frankie had recalibrated her mind. Or maybe something about not being in charge. She trusted her team. Yes, it was possible they'd get hurt, but Frankie clearly underestimated them.

Even if he's been watching you for two years?

She couldn't let her mind dwell on *that* question, so she focused on the here and now. "Why is he leaving us together? Practically unguarded?" she muttered to Granger.

"On the inside. I'm sure we're guarded quite well on the outside."

Shay eyed the one guard inside. He was one of the guards who'd let her beat up Frankie. "They didn't exactly jump in to protect their boss, did they?" She spoke quietly, in the hopes the guard wouldn't hear, but the room wasn't all *that* big, so it was possible he heard everything.

Still, he only stood by the door and stared ahead. But Shay had to wonder, if she could get through to one of Frankie's guards…

"I feel like we're missing a piece of something. He wants us to wait around so he can kill our friends in front of us, okay. But then what? How satisfying is *that*?" Shay murmured.

"And what if our friends don't fall into his trap?"

Shay thought of the flashlight. Elsie was supposed to be able to hear everything. Including Frankie's little admission. Would it be enough to keep everyone safe?

She eyed the guard again. What if she could get him on her side? What might they be able to accomplish? She knew Frankie ruled with fear over loyalty.

She glanced at Granger. He too was staring at the guard. When he moved his gaze to hers, he shrugged in what limited capacity he had. "Worth a shot," he offered, apparently his thoughts going in the same direction hers were.

Maybe one guard couldn't get them out of here, but one guard might help them get out of here once things went down. Whenever that was going to be.

"Hey, buddy? When do you think your boss is coming back?" Shay asked, shouting across the room so it couldn't be mistaken that she was talking to him.

The guard shrugged and he didn't look at her. He'd been in here the whole time, but Frankie had left him behind. Was it because he trusted the man inside so much, or the men outside more?

Still, she thought back to when she'd been pounding on Frankie. It had to be clear to anyone with experience that she was way better than Frankie. And still they'd let her pound on him until Frankie had given the order to stop.

"I bet you enjoyed the show," Shay continued. She thought about walking toward him, trying to create a more conspiratorial atmosphere, but she wanted to wait for an in. A sign she might be able to get to this guy. "You've probably wanted to pop him a few times."

The guard's eyes flicked to her briefly. He said nothing and went back to looking at the wall.

But that look was an opening. Shay pushed off the wall and began moving toward him. Slowly, casually. "I've seen the way the guy treats what he calls 'the help.' I wouldn't blame you for not liking him. After all, you're not getting paid to *like* your boss."

She was halfway between Granger and the guard. The guard didn't say anything, but he was watching her now. So, she turned back to Granger. "You know who knew how to treat his men? Frank senior."

"Yeah?" Granger offered with some interest. "I never knew him."

Shay had never met Frankie's grandfather either. He'd been in jail the whole time she'd been with Frankie, but people had talked about Frank Vianni in hushed, awed tones. Not the way they talked about Gio or Frankie. "That guy? He knew how to earn some loyalty."

"Frank was all right, my dad always said," the guard said. He shifted when Shay turned back to face him. He adjusted his gun and he frowned, but he didn't tell her to stop talking.

"Yeah, that older generation, man. They knew how to do it."

This guard was youngish. In his thirties, maybe. Likely this was a family affair for him too. His dad had worked for Frank, maybe Gio. Maybe even Frankie.

"That's what my dad always said," the guard said, nodding slightly. "Didn't like the way the new guard was handling things."

"Who could blame him? Times change, sure. But that doesn't mean you start treating people differently."

The man slid a worried look to the door behind him. "*You* were *really* with Vianni?" he asked with some interest.

Shay shrugged casually, moving a little closer. "Was, yeah."

He looked at the door again, then to Granger on the wall, then her. "You learn to fight like that there?"

Shay laughed. "Frankie prefers everyone around him to be weaker than him. Even his muscle." She pointed at the gun the guard held. "That can do some damage, sure, but he could afford better for you guys. And that gear you've got." Shay made a dismissive sound. "I'd never equip my team with such a sad excuse for protection."

It was a bit of a reach. The gear the guard wore was perfectly acceptable, if a little bulky and old. But it'd get the job done.

But now the guy looked down at it with some concern, pulling a bit at the bottom of the vest like he was worried it wasn't big enough to protect him in a shootout.

He looked at the door again, then took a step toward Shay. The guard leaned his head in, kept his voice low. He still held the gun pointed at her, but she wasn't worried. She didn't want to wrestle it from him or take him out—there were too many like him on the outside—but if she could get him on *her* side, it might come in handy.

"How'd you get out?" he asked, his voice little more than a whisper.

Shay's excitement leaped, but she had to tamp it down. Get too eager, offer too much, and she'd ruin everything. She had to be calm and careful.

But if she could get this guard on her side… The possibilities were endless.

GRANGER DIDN'T MIND watching Shay work. She had an easy way about her that had often allowed her to do just this. Engage, probe without seeming to and convince. It had made her an excellent operative, the way she could blend in and out of a situation. Regardless of the situation.

It helped that she was a beautiful woman, and something about her looks made men a little less leery of her than they should be. Even if they'd just watched what she could do.

The guard was clearly intrigued by the idea she'd been a part of the Vianni family and then gotten out. Likely he was of the belief that if this *woman* could do it, surely he could too.

It was interesting a man this close to Frankie would be entertaining thoughts of getting out. A man whose

family had been working for the Vianni family for at
least a generation or two.

But that was the problem when you didn't reward
loyalty. When you fancied yourselves above the men
who'd come before.

Fear did wonders, but if a little awe or loyalty wasn't
mixed in, fear didn't win in the end. The earlier genera-
tions had been hard to shut down because their men had
been afraid *and* loyal.

But Gio and Frankie had done a lot to erode that.
Which was why, Granger supposed, Frankie had decided
to fake his death and hang out in the wilds of Idaho. If it
was possible, he'd be home in Chicago pulling the same
old strings, but it wasn't. And not just because he was
wanted for all his crimes.

Frankie didn't have the influence there. He needed
isolation to build up this team and keep them loyal to
him if only because there wasn't much else to do out
here.

If they could turn his team against him…

Well, it was something.

Shay stood close to the guard now. Granger could
hear their conversation. She offered some complaints
about the way Frankie used to treat his men. It took some
time, patience, but she eventually got him to share that
he'd been overlooked for a lucrative job that he felt he
should have gotten. When he'd told Frankie that he'd
spent his whole life in service to the Viannis, Frankie
had been dismissive of both him *and* his father.

Clearly this man had a lot of resentment for the way
his dad had been treated at Frankie's hands, but he felt
a generations-old duty to the Viannis. Could Shay get
past that?

"Loyalty. Look, I'm no mobster, but I'm no cop either. Sometimes you gotta bend the law, sometimes you get *paid* to do that, but if the guy paying you isn't going to bail you out, then what's it all for?"

"My dad owed a lot to the Viannis."

"The Viannis or Frank? Because Frank ain't here."

The guard nodded almost imperceptibly. He still leaned toward Shay in a confessional sort of way, but he hadn't loosened the grip on his gun. Clearly, he wasn't dumb muscle. He was being careful.

Still, he could be a formidable ally if they could get him to take that step. If *Shay* could get him to take that step.

After a few minutes of silent thinking, the man straightened, shaking his head somewhat regretfully. "Look, Frankie's paying me. More than you could possibly dream."

Shay sighed, but she didn't have anything to fight that with.

But Granger did. "How much do you think I can dream?" he asked.

Both Shay and the guard looked over at him. The guy's face went blank, almost as if he'd forgotten Granger was there and that he was with Shay alone.

"What are you offering?" the guard said shrewdly.

"You help us get out of here? More than Frankie is paying you. I guarantee you that."

The man studied him carefully. "How are you going to prove that you've got the money and will give it to me if I help you?"

"Good question. I'd need your help to prove I've got it, being as that I'm chained up and all. As for getting it after you help us escape, I figure you're a smart enough guy to track me down if I try to flake."

The guard shook his head. "I can't unchain you. I can't...help you guys. I'm just one person. Frankie's got a whole team. I'd love to take the money and run, but it isn't possible."

Granger attempted a shrug. "All I'm saying is, I've got the money. I'd certainly be willing to pay someone who saved my life. Take it or leave it, but the offer is on the table from now until I'm safe and sound." He maintained eye contact with the man. "You don't have to take it now to take it."

The guard didn't respond. Instead, he took a few steps backward to stand right in front of the door again.

Shay smiled a little and walked back to Granger. She arranged herself casually against the wall, then leaned toward him. "I can't tell if you're underestimating how much money Frankie pays, or if you're playing this guy," she whispered.

Granger stared at her. She really didn't know? "I don't think I'm doing either."

She scoffed. "You don't have that kind of money."

"Who says I don't?"

She gaped at him, but the door was opening and there wasn't time to explain to her that he'd always had more than enough money. *Money* was never the issue.

Frankie moved inside, and Granger knew immediately it was bad news for him and Shay. Because Frankie was *beyond* pleased with himself.

"We've got a few of your friends." Frankie smiled broadly. "Now the fun can really begin."

CODY WYATT HAD never once expected to return to the fold of North Star. Doing a few computer things here and there was one thing, but actually going into the field leaving his wife and daughters at home…

He didn't like it. They were his life and he'd left behind all the danger and uncertainty. Happily. Because his wife and girls filled all those holes he'd carried around before them.

And yet he'd come here because he owed his life to Shay a few times over. *And* because his wife had insisted. His wife who had somehow wound up knowing more about Shay than he did. "Veronica," he muttered. "She tells my wife and not me."

"I'd tell your wife a lot of things before I'd tell your hard head," Tucker offered good-naturedly.

Cody scowled at his brother. Though Tucker hadn't worked with Shay as long as Cody had, they'd worked a mission together. A mission in which Shay had purposefully defied Granger Macmillan to help save the woman who would become Tucker's wife.

Tucker had also left behind his wife to help save Shay. Because he owed her too.

They *all* owed her.

Cody eyed Jamison. His stern older brother hadn't asked questions when Cody had explained the situation. Cody had only had to mention Shay, and Jamison had volunteered. He hadn't needed his wife to urge him to do it, but then Jamison and Liza were always on the same page it seemed.

Jamison and Shay hadn't ever worked together, but Shay had been Cody's partner when Cody had stepped in to save Jamison from being killed by their father. Shay had been integral to getting Jamison and Liza and all the girls they'd saved from the Sons of the Badlands to safety.

Two of the girls who Liza and Jamison had then adopted. So, Cody supposed that's why Jamison hadn't needed urging. Shay had helped save the women who would become his family.

The three brothers were standing in the cold, the sun a tiny hint on the horizon. It would be better if they could continue to work with the cover of night, but that wouldn't last too much longer. Still, they had to wait. It would be a few more steps before the Wyatt boys got to wade into the fray.

Reece Montgomery, former North Star operative and de facto leader of their little group tonight, stepped into the clearing where the Wyatts waited.

"Step one is complete," Reece said flatly.

Which meant Vianni men had taken the agents named Zeke Daniels and Mallory Trevino. Connor Lindstrom and Gabriel Saunders would follow in step two.

"I'd feel better with video," Cody said into the silence.

"Wouldn't we all? We can't risk it. Elsie is adamant about that."

Reece was keeping in contact with their head tech, practically a full-time job with the old analogue radios they were using. Cody wished he had access to a computer. He could set up some kind of secure server, and it would enable him to do a lot of things that might give them better eyes and ears on what was going on inside wherever Granger and Shay were.

But it would take time. Elsie was using that time to keep everyone on the same page, and he was using that time to lay a trap with his brothers.

Cody heard the faint tapping, a North Star sign. A few minutes later, another North Star operative appeared. He came to stand next to Reece.

"I laid the explosives," Holden Parker said. "Good for me to go?"

Reece nodded. He looked grim and remote, but when he spoke there was something softer in his voice. "If that's what you want to do."

"I'd rather fight *with* Shay than wring my hands out here," he said, grinning at Reece with an ease that spoke of years working together.

"Be careful," Reece said, both a warning and an evidence that these men had a close relationship.

Because this new North Star under Shay's leadership wasn't like the well-oiled machine Granger's had been. Cody had appreciated Granger's ruthless efficiency, but he thought Shay's building a family might have done a lot more *good*, not just stopping the *bad*.

Cody glanced back at his brothers as Holden Parker disappeared into the trees once more. It would be up to the Wyatts now. Them and Reece. To fight from the outside, while the purposefully trapped operatives worked from the inside.

But it would only work if they could figure out exactly where Shay and Granger were.

And that was proving to be more difficult.

Chapter Sixteen

Shay had to work hard to keep her bravado in the face of Frankie's utter glee. "Sure you did, Frank. I bet all my operatives are right outside." She put all the disdain she could manage in her voice, hoping like hell the fear didn't shine through.

"Oh, don't be silly, Veronica. I'm not going to put you all in the same space so you can outsmart my guards. But I understand your suspicion. After all, you like to lie when it suits you. Why shouldn't I?"

"*I* like to lie?" She shouldn't be offended by a mobster's opinion of her truth telling, but it rankled. *He* was the liar.

"Still, I don't expect you to just believe me. You've always been a suspicious harpy."

"Harpy," she echoed, trying to fight back the wave of anger. Whatever names he called her didn't matter. Why was she letting it matter?

Frankie moved across the room. On the wall directly across from where Granger was chained, there was a drop cloth covering something. Shay had assumed it was furniture, but when Frankie pulled it off, it revealed some monitors.

Her dread increased, but she kept the bored look on

her face. Didn't even watch while Frankie fiddled with plugging some things into the wall. Instead, she looked at her boots, at the chains that held Granger to the wall, at the guard who wouldn't meet her gaze.

Eventually, Frankie crossed to her. She held his gaze to prove she wasn't afraid of him, even though it made her stomach roil with the lowering memory that she'd married him. On *purpose*.

"Have a look, Veronica, sweetheart." He reached out and trailed a finger down her cheek, like he used to. She did everything she could to suppress the shudder of revulsion that moved through her. He'd use that against her, and in their current circumstances, she couldn't afford to fight him off.

Luckily, he seemed too proud of himself over this monitor thing. He grabbed her chin. "Don't be difficult, darling." His grip on her face tightened, and he wrenched her head in the direction of the monitors. "I would never lie to *you*," he crooned into her ear, even as his fingers dug into her face.

She rolled her eyes at him and sighed with exaggerated impatience. But she did as he asked and looked at the monitor, ready to pretend to be unmoved. There were a couple black squares on the screen. Only one wasn't black. It showed some kind of room. Not like the one she and Granger were in. This appeared to be more like a basement. She wondered if it was in the compound she'd originally tracked.

But why would Frankie hold her and Granger out in this cabin *away* from that, and keep *her* operatives in his compound? Assuming he actually had them.

Frankie released her abruptly, swearing under his breath and stalking back to the monitors.

Shay moved closer to study the screen. She saw two people standing off to the side. Frankie muttered something into what she assumed was a comm unit and then the angle of the monitor changed. Suddenly she could see four people. Two of Frankie's men holding guns pointed at two of *her* people.

Zeke and Mallory. Mallory Trevino had been on board for two years. They'd picked her up on one of their last raids on the Sons. A fantastic fighter, great with weapons and a tenacity that put most of the other operatives to shame. She was married to another one of her operatives, but they'd both stayed on with North Star.

Shay studied her on the monitor. She didn't look any worse for the wear. No bleeding or bruising. Mallory didn't favor a leg or hold her arm. Granted, she might be pretending to be fine out of pride, but…

What if she wasn't hurt? That would be strange, because even if she'd somehow been taken off guard, Mallory would have fought. Tooth and nail. It would have taken more than one man to take her down, and she would have had to have suffered some injuries in the process. Even a gun to the head wouldn't have stopped her from trying to fight.

Shay turned her attention to Zeke. He was their newest recruit. A cousin of Mallory's who'd proven himself willing to play rookie and do whatever was asked of him without complaint.

He too appeared completely unharmed.

Maybe there were circumstances where Frankie's men could have been clever enough to capture Mallory and Zeke without giving them an opportunity to put up a fight, but Shay couldn't imagine one.

She *could* imagine why her operatives would have been caught without putting up a fight though.

Her mind racing, she looked back at Granger. He was staring at the screen with a pensive look. Did he see what she saw, too?

"Now, the first part of this game is simple," Frankie said cheerfully. "I'm taking my guards with me. You try to escape, your friends die. And I'll make sure you both watch it from here. They try to escape, you two die, and *they* watch. Fun, right?"

He walked over to her again and brought his hands up to her cheeks, framing her face gently.

She thought about head butting him. It would be enjoyable, and she knew the guard wouldn't step in *right* away. But there was something about the look in Frankie's eyes. Different than earlier. Not angry but not reckless either.

No, everything he'd planned was falling into place just the way he wanted. Her blood ran cold.

Something was off. Whatever he wanted... Too many things didn't add up. "Why the games, Frank? Just tell us what you're after. You've got us. Why wouldn't we give it to you?"

Frankie laughed. And laughed. His hands dropped from her face and he laughed all the way to the door.

He turned, his hand on the knob. He clucked his tongue. "I'm almost impressed. You've *finally* realized that *you* are not my end goal. Congratulations." He grinned at her then, a full-on challenge. "But if I told you what my end goal was, you might be able to stop me. And we can't have that, can we, my darling wife?" He chuckled to himself and left.

The guard gave them both an enigmatic look, then

he departed too. Apparently part of Frankie's game *was* giving them a means to escape.

Which meant, he didn't want them at all.

Shay stared at the now-closed door, a new wave of dread closing over her. If he didn't want her, or Granger, and they didn't know *what* he was truly after, how were they going to get out of this?

GRANGER'S WORST SUSPICIONS were confirmed by Frankie's exit. The way none of this added up had been weighing on him, and now he fully understood why.

If Frankie really wanted Shay, he would have hurt them more by now. Maybe killed them. The games were all well and good, but he wasn't really doing *anything* to them.

"What's Frankie playing at?" he asked, hoping Shay had some magical insight. Some theory that could move them forward.

"Psychological warfare?" she suggested, but he could tell by her expression she didn't believe it.

"Maybe, but…" He shook his head. "He could be actually torturing us. Or them. There are so many things he *could* be doing. But he's waiting around. Collecting us. Letting us stick together in pairs. That isn't the smartest move."

"He underestimates us." She said it as though she was trying to convince herself.

"He does, but this is more than that." Granger frowned at the screen. He looked at the two North Star operatives who didn't even look mussed. "They got caught on purpose."

Shay turned her gaze to the screen as well and let out a breath. "Yeah, I think so too. They'd be hurt if they'd fought back. And Mallory's hardly afraid of a gun to her head. She would have fought. Probably would have won too. But even if she'd have somehow lost, she would have the marks of a fight."

Granger nodded, glad Shay backed up his hypothesis.

Her gaze moved to him and she shook her head. "Well, we might not be able to escape just yet, or figure out what Frankie is after, but we can at least get you out of those."

"How?"

She looked around the cabin, then rooted around in corners and cabinets. A few moments later, she returned with a tiny screwdriver and a fork.

Granger raised his eyebrows. "Really?"

"You have no idea what I can do with a screwdriver and a fork," she replied, smiling at him. Clearly wanting him to laugh.

He couldn't quite manage it. Too much was at stake. He'd thought he'd understood what Frankie was after, but it was clearly something else.

Frankie had been watching them for two years. Why had he acted *now*? He was happy to mess with all of them, but wasn't intent on actually harming them. Even when he'd dragged Granger outside, all he'd done was say a few things to try and hurt him.

Frankie enjoyed casual cruelties like some people ordered a milkshake. He'd take the chance when he had it, but it clearly wasn't his goal. Their misery.

So what was?

When the first chain fell, a relief he hadn't expected coursed through him mixed with the surprise Shay had managed to get it off the wall. It was uncomfortable to be tethered to a wall, but also left him with a demoralizing feeling of being utterly helpless while everyone around him wasn't.

She silently moved over to the next one. The chain was still on his wrist—she'd only managed to get the whole chain out of the wall, not off his wrists, but he didn't care if he had to spend the next few weeks with the shackles hanging off his wrists. At least he could *move* and wasn't chained to a wall.

When the second one fell, his center of gravity went a little wonky. Like his arms suddenly weighed twice as much as his body. His back to the wall, he slid to the ground, his butt hitting the hard floor with a thud. "I'm fine," he said automatically. "Just felt like sitting."

She snorted, looking down at him from where she stood. "Yeah right. Dizzy?"

"I'm fine."

"Your head is not fine," she said, eyeing the wound on his head. "It's not *actively* bleeding, but no doubt you need stitches, food, water, rest." She touched his hair, just above the wound, tentatively. But it felt like a caress.

And that was something he couldn't think too much on. Especially since it brought to mind the kiss they'd shared and that was…well, hardly the point right now. "I'll get them eventually. How's your side?"

"Fine enough."

"Which is why you're bleeding through your shirt."

She looked down at her shirt and wrinkled her nose. "Might have popped a few stitches kicking his butt."

Granger finally managed a laugh. "On a scale of one to ten, how satisfying was it?"

"A million," she replied emphatically, which made him chuckle again.

It hurt his head, but there was something freeing

about being able to laugh, no matter how dire a situation they were in. "On the plus side, those two didn't get caught on purpose just for fun. There's a plan in place."

Shay nodded. "We probably shouldn't say too much." She nodded to the monitors. "Who knows who's listening." She lowered herself next to him, so they sat hip to hip. Her body heat seeping into him and hopefully vice versa. She was tired from digging him out. Tired from all of this.

"Rest," he ordered.

She eyed him. "And what are you going to do?"

"Play human pillow until you wake up or someone comes back."

"We can't just wait around."

"I think we have to for right now. Until we figure out what he's after. He's cocky. He'll slip up eventually." He kept his voice low. It was possible Frankie had the whole cabin bugged, but also possible no one was listening. They needed to communicate. If they did it in whispers, the risk had to be worth it.

Shay seemed to think over Frankie's inevitable slip, but as she did she gingerly rested her head on his shoulder.

Granger moved his arm around her shoulders, gratified when she leaned into him. Something eased inside of him when she did. Not just grateful that she'd lean, but comforted by the contact.

"He wants them to come after us. So he can kill them in front of us. In front of *me*. That's what he said."

"But when you asked him what he wanted just now, he said he wouldn't tell because we *could* stop him. You couldn't stop him if he wanted to kill Mallory. He could just go in and shoot her. Or have one of his men do it."

Shay's eyebrows drew together and she slowly lifted her head off his shoulder. Something like loss moved through him.

"I guess that's...true," she agreed carefully.

"And he didn't say he'd kill them in front of anyone exactly. What were his exact words?" Granger tried to remember precisely the way Frankie had said it.

"He said, 'you will watch everyone you love die,'" Shay said flatly.

His arm held her a little tighter, brought her a little closer. Now that they were in this position he couldn't stop himself from offering her comfort. Too close. Too many things to think about.

"Watch everyone you love die. That's a lot of people. If he wants us all to die in front of you, why are we separate? Why not toss us in the same place and blow us up?"

She pulled away from him just a hair, staring at him with something like horror crossing her features. His arm was still around her, but she'd leaned away a little.

Granger realized that he'd sort of suggested *she* loved *him* in some way. He cleared his throat, suddenly uncomfortable, and shifted on the hard, cold floor. Then he started to pull his arm away, but stopped himself.

He hadn't meant *love* love, and she knew that. Or should.

Unless...she *did* have those feelings for him.

Chapter Seventeen

Shay desperately wanted to stand, to get away from all...
this. They didn't have time for it, and she realized—too
late, clearly—when he'd said *loved* he just meant in the
same way she loved all of her North Star family.

Not that he surmised she'd been in love with him for
far too long. Her secret shame.

But he was smart and quick and she had the terrible
sinking feeling that he was probably putting it together
as they sat there.

Granger moved his arm, like he was about to pull it
away, and then he seemed to think better of it. He leaned
closer to her slightly turning his body so he could look
her right in the eye. From the expression on his face, she
knew he'd compartmentalized it all away.

Once again he was thinking of the mission.

Just like old times, she thought with some bitterness,
even though she knew it was the right thing to do in the
moment.

"He's luring everyone here," Granger said, excitement
making his whispers just a shade louder. "To kill them in
front of you. Okay, sure, it's revenge, but Frankie would
need something to be in it for *him*. He could have gotten
revenge on you anytime in the past two years it seems.

What's in it for him on top of the personal satisfaction of watching you suffer?"

Shay looked away from him. To concentrate, she had to. She stared at the wall and willed the embarrassment heating her cheeks away. "I can't begin to imagine. If I could…" She frowned a little as she trailed off. *Luring everyone here.* She knew North Star would follow, but she thought they'd send a team. She looked back at Granger. "Everyone. Is *everyone* here?"

"No, not everyone. I think there were some concerns about information leaking. Elsie pulled together the team members she trusted implicitly."

"Everyone important to me." She leaned closer to him again, keeping her voice a quiet whisper in the short distance between their faces. A theory began to form, one that made her heart beat hard, and oddly enough, hope spring warmly in the pit of her stomach. "Everyone we can trust. Here. Which means no one we trust is back at headquarters, at least in Elsie's estimation right now. We know Frankie knows the location of headquarters, and if we have every senior North Star member here, headquarters is easily infiltrated."

Shock slammed through his expression. "He could be after some kind of information. If he was working with Ross Industries, or any of the other groups we've taken down in the past few months, he could want the information in Elsie's computers. He's been watching for two years and still hasn't been able to get what he wanted or needed."

Shay didn't argue at his use of the word *we*. They didn't have time for her to point out she'd had to drag him into missions kicking and screaming before this one. She'd remind him of that later. "And if he wants that information, we're superfluous. *This* is a game. A distraction."

"And he can kill us all when it's over, but for now, he just needs the chance to get in and get that intel. And he might need one of us to get it. Or he wants to use what he finds against us. If he wanted us dead, we would be dead. So, this isn't about us. Not now. Not yet." He leaned his head toward the flashlight. "Elsie, do you hear me? We need people at headquarters. Not here. Headquarters."

Elsie couldn't respond to tell them she'd heard them. Or communicate that she understood. They just had to hope she was listening. And that she didn't send anyone else to be captured by Frankie.

Because apparently that was *exactly* what Frankie wanted, even if they fought their way back out again.

"She'll get it communicated to everyone," Granger said, and she wanted to be reassured by his certainty. It *exuded* from him. His tone of voice, the way he held himself.

And she realized, in a way she hadn't before, that it was an act. He wasn't sure. He wasn't certain at all. How could he be?

When you were a leader, you pretended. He was faking, so they could move forward with the mission regardless of any uncertainty. He'd *always* been pretending. Every mission. Every order. And...

"You never told me," she said hoarsely, feeling unaccountably emotional. "You threw me into the deep end and you never told me it was all an act."

He had the audacity to frown as if confused. "What was an act?"

"The bravado. The knowing everything." She moved away from him, out of the comforting weight of his arm.

More than anything, she wished she could look at him without the pain in her eyes, but she knew he'd see it. She couldn't *hide* that. "I thought something was wrong with me that I didn't always know the right thing to do, or if a decision I made would work out. You made me think I *had* to have absolute certainty, and I always felt less because I didn't."

Shay got to her feet because she knew this wasn't the time to hash this out. Hell, what they *should* be doing was trying to escape. Trying to get to headquarters themselves. They were *operatives*. They had done riskier things, fought off bigger threats.

So what in the world were they doing sitting here talking about the past? About her *feelings*? Why was she even bringing it up?

"I'm sorry," he said. And he sounded like he meant it, which somehow infuriated her even more.

"You're *sorry*?"

"You're right. I didn't...tutor you in the way I could have. I didn't plan to..." He got up himself, and she had to bite her tongue to keep from telling him to be careful. She had to curl her hands into fists to stop from reaching out to make sure he was okay.

Because no matter how angry she was, how many old hurts were swimming to the surface, she didn't want to see him in pain. Weakened. *Again.*

She'd been afraid, despite all her efforts to pull him out of that burning building, he was going to die. And he hadn't. But a part of him had. He'd been in a wheelchair. Had sequestered himself away. He'd cut them all off for a time and...

"I'll admit, I didn't handle passing the baton very well," he said gravely. "I never planned to pass anything.

North Star was mine. It wasn't really, but I needed to think it was. Back then, it was my revenge and I guarded it ferociously. I didn't see it that way at the time, but the past two years..." He let out a sigh. A heavy sigh born of loss and change and understanding.

Shay found suddenly she wanted none of it. Fear threatened to swallow her whole. She didn't want Granger's truth or his honesty. "This isn't what's important," she said, trying desperately to convince herself.

"Maybe not, but I have a feeling we'll never talk about if we don't have it out now. We're alone, Shay. Maybe someone's listening, but what does it matter if Frankie hears our issues?"

"What does it matter if we never talk about it?"

A muscle ticked in his jaw. "Maybe you plan on dying here, but I don't," he said, and where he'd sounded tired before, he only sounded angry now. Angry and still so certain.

It's an act. It's an act. But it was hard to believe that when his gaze held hers so fierce and determined.

"Neither of us are dying here," he said, an order that brooked no argument. "I plan on walking out of this and having a future, and I want you in it."

GRANGER HADN'T PRECISELY meant to say that. It was a truth he'd been turning over in his head for a while now, but he also understood that he couldn't crash into Shay's life with his own epiphanies. He'd kept his distance for a reason, and allowing her to make her own choices was one of them.

Or at least, he'd convinced himself it was one of them. Maybe it was his own cowardice.

But now she'd opened that door, and he could have let

her shut it. Like they'd both done in the past. But that's not what he wanted. Not anymore. They'd played this game for too long, and it was time to put an end to it.

"Hold a gaze too long then look away. Pretend it isn't there. We've done plenty of that. For a while it was necessary, but it isn't anymore."

"Pretend *what* isn't there?" she asked, but her voice was hoarse and her eyes were wide with something he so rarely saw on her. Fear. He should have some sympathy, some patience, but he didn't. Not with his head throbbing and his emotions churning.

"Do you really want to play dumb, Shay? It doesn't suit you."

"And I suppose you know what would?" She crossed her arms over her chest with a mocking look. "Tell me, Great Granger Macmillan, what would suit me?"

"You think I don't understand you? That I don't see through you picking a fight so you don't have to deal with the actual *emotion* here."

She looked away, pretending to scoff, but the fact that she'd broken eye contact told him everything he needed to know. Because no matter how little she *wanted* to deal with her emotions, they were all at the surface.

Shay felt betrayed by him. By the way he'd left her in charge. And he'd realized he'd done it badly, but he hadn't realized she'd struggled so much. Internally, clearly, because no one who followed her, him included, had guessed.

He stepped toward her, and she eyed him warily. He could tell she wanted to step away, but her pride wouldn't let her. She lifted her chin.

"So, I am sorry. You're right. I didn't do the things I should have done. I didn't know how, and I was so wrapped up in my own failures I didn't think... I only knew you could handle it. And you have. No matter how you've felt, you have run North Star as well, if not better, than I did. You know that. The team you've built, the fact some of them have left to build actual *lives*, it's a testament to the leader you are, no matter *how* you feel about it."

Her jaw worked, her eyes suspiciously shiny, but she didn't lower her crossed arms and she didn't acknowledge any of those words.

"I wish I could have done things differently, but in the moment, I didn't know how."

"You almost died," she said, her voice barely more than a whisper. It wasn't absolution exactly, but it was close.

Except... "You made sure that didn't happen." He reached out and touched her face. Which had him thinking about that kiss back between the rocks. She'd initiated that, and before that moment he'd convinced himself that whatever Shay felt for him was a little residual hero worship. He'd saved her once, under far better circumstances than she'd saved him from not so long ago.

But she'd kissed him like they were equals. She'd kissed him in the *moment*, and he hadn't thought about the past. He'd only thought about her and now, and he had to believe she was in the same boat.

Or she would have been disappointed. Unaffected. She was neither. Then. Now. He bent his mouth to hers, but she pulled back.

She stepped away from him, something very young and vulnerable on her face for only a second before she schooled it away. "You're attracted to me. Sure. You want us to be honest about that? Fine. There's attraction on both sides."

He laughed, and maybe it shouldn't be quite *that* bitter, but he knew what it was to…go down this road. It was hard and it required a raw, soul-deep honesty he truthfully hadn't been quite ready for when he'd married Anna.

But he had to remind himself that Shay had never loved and lost, she might have built a family with North Star, but her first experience with a romantic relationship was the childish choice she'd made with Frankie, and ever since then her only relationships had been within North Star. They might have shaped her, helped her gain confidence and strength, but even old hurts could make smart, strong women unsure.

So he tried to keep his voice gentle. "If it was about attraction, and only that, it wouldn't be so damn fraught, would it? It wouldn't require this dance we've been doing for *years*."

At the word *years*, her gaze jerked back to his. She swallowed unsteadily. "You loved your wife."

"I did. But she isn't here. And that took some time to…accept. To work through and figure out what that meant. I love a lot of people, Shay. When they die that love doesn't die with them, and love sure as hell isn't finite. I don't only have a cup of it to dole out. It might be easier if I did, but that's not the way the world works."

Every time he said the word *love*, she took another step back. As if carefully retreating from an angry bear. "Why are we talking about this?" she asked, and she looked at him with such *hope* that he'd sweep it under the rug. That he'd close the door they always closed.

But he didn't want to anymore. He took all those steps

she'd retreated. He wanted to reach out and touch her, but he thought maybe she'd listen better if he delivered it like an order. Like a mission.

It was *his* mission.

"I am in love with you, Veronica. Shay. Whatever you want to be called. Whatever you want to do. Fight. Hide. Lead. Follow. It doesn't matter, it hasn't *mattered*, because I am in love with the person you are. And yes, I needed time away from you and North Star to figure it out, but it was *inexorable*. This feeling."

She looked *horrified*, and he wanted to laugh, honestly. Leave it to him to fall in love with a woman who'd be horrified by a confession as honest as that.

He held her gaze, unafraid of his own vulnerable feelings. He'd loved and lost before. It was nothing he wanted to experience again, but as long as she stayed alive… Well, the rest didn't matter so much.

She looked away, and said nothing. She held herself so still like she believed if she was still and quiet enough he'd forget. Pretend it never happened.

But whatever she was staring at made her eyebrows furrow, and then her eyes widen. She pointed at the monitors on the opposite wall behind him. "A second room just appeared on the screen."

Chapter Eighteen

Shay's arm shook. It was inexcusable, because no matter what Granger had said that might have pierced her very soul, a second box on the monitor had clicked on and she had a bad feeling that meant another North Star member had been apprehended by Frankie's team.

On purpose or not?

I am in love with you.

It couldn't be. *He* couldn't be.

She lurched forward when Holden came on the screen. "No."

Granger turned around to see what she saw, and followed as she crossed the room. She wanted to punch the screen. Three of her operatives, in separate cellar-like rooms. She was shaking her head without understanding. "Why did you do this, Granger? They'd all be safe if you hadn't done this." She knew it wasn't fair to blame him, but fear from this and fear from everything Granger had said to her was making her irrational.

"He's unhurt. Look at him," Granger said in her ear before he gave her a little shake with one hand. "He meant to get caught."

"Idiot. That stupid, moronic, idiotic *fool*." She swore a few times to make herself feel better. "He's supposed to be retired. He's supposed to be in Nebraska on that little farm with Willa and raising cows or some stupid thing."

But she said *stupid thing* and a longing she didn't understand welled up in her. She found Reece's choices baffling. A bed-and-breakfast? With people coming and going? A ready-made kid—no matter how cute Henry was, Shay didn't know how he dealt with the emotional minefield *that* had to be.

But Holden's life… Well, there was something about his wife's little farm that had seemed charming. Downright…homey. No matter that Shay knew nothing about farms or animals, she'd been a little jealous.

And hadn't understood that any more than she understood Granger being in love with her.

I am in love with you.

He'd said it with such conviction, like it was his one and only truth.

"You know a ranch isn't all that different from a farm," Granger said. "Mine's still small, but I have plans to expand. I always wanted to be a cowboy when I was a kid."

She turned to stare at him. Had he read her thoughts? Was he…offering something?

He shrugged, looking back at the screen. "If you like that sort of thing."

She could not make sense of him. Of this. They were *prisoners* of a man who, technically, might still be her husband, since they'd both only faked their deaths. And that man was likely trying to get some kind of sensitive information from North Star headquarters and Granger was talking love and ranches.

"We have to survive this," she said, meaning to sound

like a scolding schoolteacher, but it just came out kind of breathless.

Granger nodded. "Yes, we do. So, why not have something a little extra to survive for?"

She blinked, unable to fully take it on board. Any of it. "That head wound has done a number on you, Macmillan," she muttered and turned her gaze back to Holden on the screen.

He looked as brazen as ever. Lazily leaning against a wall, grinning at someone out of sight with that sharp-eyed glint she knew meant he was trying to rile them up.

"Why are they getting caught on purpose?" Shay muttered, studying the screens as if they could tell her. Mallory and Zeke sat in a corner of the room they were in. They looked relaxed and unbothered.

Granger took her by the arm, and God help her the way her heart leaped at his big hand curling around her arm was a *problem*.

But she shoved the feeling away as he pulled her over to the cabin corner farthest from the monitors.

He took her hand, gentle. *I am in love with you.* It echoed in her head, over and over, in that same calm, serious tone. Like he knew exactly what he was saying. Like he had no doubts.

He gave her palm three quick taps. And she realized he wasn't holding her hand to hold her hand. This was no offer of comfort or support or *love*. He was going to communicate with her through taps like they did in the field sometimes.

She nodded, signaling she was ready for him to start, and she forced herself to focus on the taps of his thumb against her palm and what they signified instead of the feel of his other fingers holding the top of her hand in place.

They have three. Still nine out there, plus Betty and Elsie. Divide and conquer.

It made sense. Get more operatives on the inside, keep some on the outside, then you have two distinct fronts. Except those on the inside were locked up and without any access to weapons. They'd have to rely on some kind of diversion.

Diversion. Her head whipped back to Holden on the screen. She pressed Granger's thumb out of the way with her own, a sign it was her turn to tap. Then she gave him one simple word. *Explosives.*

Granger considered, then nodded.

Holden was an explosives expert. He would have, hopefully, known where to lay some before he got caught. If he had some kind of detonator to set them off, he would and it would be diversion enough to fight their way out.

Then what?

She inhaled deeply and slowly let it out. Granger had gotten her all…out of sorts. She couldn't think clearly and it was all his fault.

Shay looked down. He was still holding her hand. Their fingers intertwined. Gently. Carefully. Perfectly.

Shay felt like she had in the moment she'd stood in front of all of North Star while Granger explained he wouldn't be back and that she would take over. He was reordering her world and she wasn't *ready.*

But she didn't pull her hand away.

GRANGER REALIZED HE was actually holding his breath. Everything felt so tenuous, Shay's hand in his most of all.

So he didn't breathe and he didn't move. He just let his mind turn over all the information they had. Be-

cause though he'd learned a thing about how dangerous it could be to compartmentalize, sometimes it was
necessary. Sometimes it was life or death.

Holden had clearly gotten himself caught before Elsie
had been able to relay his message about headquarters
being the real target. He *had* to believe Elsie was listening. That she *could* get the information to everyone.

But what if she'd missed it? He released his breath and
leaned his mouth to his flashlight. All the while keeping
Shay's hand in his. "Elsie, if you're listening, it's imperative to get everyone off this site and get them to headquarters. Stop whatever is going on at headquarters," he
repeated in a low tone. "Vianni might have heard this,
so make sure everyone is watching their backs."

Shay blew out a breath, shaking her head. "We should
do something."

He understood she felt useless and frustrated, sitting
here, playing prisoner. He felt it too, but he also knew
that sometimes a plan took patience. "Like what?"

She held his gaze, as if searching his eyes for something very specific. Her fingers twitched in his, but he
didn't let her go. "If we try to escape, we could stop
anyone else from getting captured," she said. But it was
with a note of hopefulness, because she already knew
the pointlessness of that plan.

"And leave Zeke, Mallory and Holden behind?" He
used the tapping to communicate again, not wanting to
risk anyone knowing who was still out there. *Still eight
out there. Give Holden time.*

She shook her head again, not in disagreement but in
annoyance. Because she knew the answers. She knew
what they needed to do—she just didn't *like* it. But this

was Shay, and for her, hope sprang eternal. She never fully gave up.

It was one of the many things that had added up to make him fall in love with her, when he wasn't looking, when he was desperately trying not to. All that trying not to seemed so silly now.

He used his free hand to cup her cheek. His thumb brushed across her cheekbone. She was pale. They likely both were. They'd been beat up pretty good with minimal food and water and sleep between leaving and now. She was still recovering.

But they'd survived physical wounds time and time again. It was the emotional ones that seemed so hard.

However, she held his gaze, and she didn't pull her face or hand away. It was like the moment in the rocks, when she'd kissed him, except there was a lot more wariness on her face now. He had a feeling the word *love* had put it there.

Color had crept into her cheeks, and her breathing was far more shallow than it had been. He didn't doubt she had *some* feelings for him, even if she didn't express them. But he wasn't sure what she felt was…the same.

And he knew, he'd never have the opportunity to get through to her like this. In real life, she'd disappear, throw herself into a mission, bar him.

No you won't let her do that. That was a bone-deep conviction. He wouldn't let her disappear, but he also knew how to seize a moment when it was presented to him, no matter how ill-timed.

"I know you're attracted to me, and I know you care about me." She jerked under both hands, but he held her still. Trapped—unless she wanted to fight him off, which God knew she could. "I know there are some tangled past feelings mixed up between us. But I know what I feel for you in the here and now *isn't* about the past. The man I am now is not the man I was then and—"

"Yes, you are. You're the same *man*, Granger," she said softly, gently, as if it wasn't a slap. "You simply started understanding yourself now."

He opened his mouth to deny it, but no sound came out. "I made...mistakes. *You* pointed out many of them. I lost myself and—"

"I understood what you were doing. It's why I called you out. Not because you were irredeemable, but because I knew it was a road you'd regret going down. Because you weren't that guy, no matter how hard you tried to be. I've always seen *you*. Even when you didn't see yourself."

It was some kind of absolution he hadn't known he was still looking for. Relief and comfort. Even if he wasn't sure he believed it.

"We've both changed, sure," Shay continued, looking fierce and certain. "We grew up. We dealt with our losses and our blows. People...grow. But you're not a different man and I'm not a different woman."

"So what are you saying then?"

"Just that..." She looked down at their joined hands, her eyebrows drawn together. He'd seen her fight off gangs of men and take bullets and stab wounds with equal aplomb. She wasn't afraid of anything.

Except this.

She exhaled, her breath fluttering across his cheek.

Blue eyes. Intelligent and scared. He let his thumb drag against her cheek again and her breath caught. She shook her head, vaguely, not a refusal so much as a rebuttal to some inner thought she was having.

But then she leaned forward and pressed her mouth to his. Again. It was gentle, and careful, and he let it stay that way. Let her set the tone, the pace. Let her make the choice.

He wanted *her* to make the choice that would make *her* happy. She pulled away, but not fully. Just her mouth from his mouth, and she exhaled unsteadily. Then she leaned her forehead to his chest, almost like surrender. "I've loved you for far too long, even when I desperately, definitively, didn't want to. Including this moment."

He slid his hand over her messy braid. If that was supposed to hurt his feelings, she misjudged how much he wanted her to love him. "I'll take it."

She let out a huff of breath, something very *close* to a laugh, but before he could say anything or she could, the door flew open with a loud bang.

They both jumped, not coming apart in guilt as much as surprise and an innate readiness when a threat dawned. Though both now stood in a crouch, ready to fight off an invasion.

Operatives to the last.

Frankie stood frozen in the doorway, studying them. As if he'd seen it all. Or heard it all. But no, he looked faintly confused, so Granger didn't think he'd heard or seen anything. Nothing specific.

But he certainly…suspected something. His eyes were too narrow, his gaze too discerning.

"We have another one of your friends," he said, suspicion still all over his face. "This one was a bit of a surprise, I have to say. I didn't think you'd have *old* operatives coming to your rescue. But maybe the new set aren't quite so loyal." He closed the door and strode over to the monitors and tapped the one that showed Holden.

The kiss and emotion finally drained away enough that Granger got it though to his brain he should stand or sit, no longer crouch ridiculously waiting for an attack that wouldn't come.

Yet.

Shay straightened at the same time he did, like they'd recovered and come to the same conclusion simultaneously. Frankie looked back at them, still that odd puzzlement on his face. Almost a…detachment.

Oh, he obviously wanted to mess with them, but this wasn't *about* them. It became clearer with every interaction.

Granger looked at the screen where Holden still stood, casually and cheerfully. If Holden had laid explosives. If he was waiting for the right time to set them off and create that diversion—

The door opened again and the guard Shay had talked to earlier stepped in. "Boss?"

"This better be important," Frankie barked, not bothering to look away from the monitors.

The guard looked at Granger and Shay, an inscrutable look on his face. He walked over to Frankie. "Peretti found this on the prisoner." He held out a tiny black box. "Some kind of detonator."

Granger's hope congealed, turning to acid as the detonator was passed to Frankie.

There would be no diversion.

Chapter Nineteen

The disappointment was like a knife to the heart, when Shay's heart was way too exposed as it was.

Holden's plan wasn't going to work. No diversion. The plan was shot.

She should be working toward a plan B. They all should be, but her brain was scrambled.

Why did she keep *kissing* Granger? And why had she admitted she *loved* him? But the shock on his face when she'd said he was the same man he'd always been had undone her.

He always did. So why was she fighting it when he wasn't?

She looked at Frankie warily, to find him examining her. He was a cunning man, and a strangely insightful one when he wanted to be. When he wasn't busy obsessing over himself. He could, on occasion, read people when he wanted to manipulate them.

He wanted to manipulate her, both related and unrelated to what he wanted. Revenge. His goal. There was something at headquarters he wanted. It explained the siege a while back. He'd found out their location, found a way to get them all out of the way, but then the men he'd sent had bungled it all.

Or *had* they? Frankie had been watching them for two years he said, somehow having done something back after the explosion. But he hadn't moved until *now*. Something had changed. He'd accessed *something* when she'd been shot.

He looked away from her and back at the monitor, and she surmised he understood that she too could read him, even when he could read her. Even ground.

"Your friend was going to try to blow us up," Frankie said as if working through the information. "Clever," he admitted with a nod toward the monitor. "Except the part where he kept the detonator on his person. I don't think someone planning on getting caught would do that." He turned to her again, all easy smiles. "Do you?"

Shay didn't let her reaction show. He was making it clear Holden hadn't gotten caught on purpose, but...

She refrained from looking at the monitor while Frankie was studying her, but she thought about what she'd seen. Holden's causal demeanor. He was an excellent actor and could charm just about anyone.

But some of his skills had dimmed after *falling in love*. When he'd suddenly had someone to live for and come home to.

Wasn't that why she was so deathly afraid of her own feelings? Reece had left. Cold turkey. And it was like he *had* become a different man, though she understood fundamentally he hadn't. He'd just kept his real self better hidden than anyone she'd ever known.

She didn't want that kind of transformation. It terrified her.

Holden hadn't cut everything off as Reece had, but he wasn't quite as good at his job anymore.

She was going to lose Elsie and Betty all because

they'd found men to *love*, all because they'd found something outside of North Star to set their sights on.

They had all *changed*, not who they were but what they wanted and what they valued and Shay couldn't bear to go through that again. She'd done the whole metamorphosis once. It was hard. It was painful. It led to confusion and loss and she didn't *want* it.

Of course, if she lost today to Frankie, she was going to lose North Star altogether. Possibly her life and those she loved. *That* was a little scarier than change.

Not the losing North Star so much. *That* didn't terrify her the way it should have. The way it once had. It almost…almost felt like a relief.

She snuck a glance at Granger. It wouldn't feel that way for him. Or some of her younger operatives. What would Sabrina do? *She* hadn't changed for love. She'd been severely slowed down by almost dying and all, but she hadn't…

Okay, she had changed. Not in any obvious ways. Not in any *big* ways. It was more in her awareness. Like Holden. She was more careful. Kinder.

She had someone to come home to. She had been given a softness and an understanding she didn't quite know what to do with, but it had become enough of her that she returned it in a way she hadn't before.

Shay had watched love make some of the people she cared for above all else in this world *better* people.

And none of that would matter if they all didn't find a way out of this without anyone getting hurt.

Shay knew that meant she had to act. Not because she was frustrated and tired and strung far too tight, but because it was time. North Star had men on the inside, men on the outside. Likely Elsie knew headquarters was the target since Granger had relayed that information twice now.

It was time for all hell to break loose for Frankie.

So, she moved toward him. She gave Granger a look. *Stay exactly where you are*, she willed him. He watched her, and she could see the careful wheels in his head turn. He gave her an imperceptible nod.

He understood what she was going to do. And, thankfully, he approved.

Shay couldn't let out a breath of relief though. She had to keep herself calm and casual. So she kept her eyes on Frankie, not the detonator in his hand. If he turned to look at her, study her, she would stop and stare at Holden and allow herself to worry.

Because that's what Frankie wanted from her, and for now she'd give it to him. If she could get to the detonator.

She didn't look back at the guard. She'd trust Granger to give her some kind of sign if he started paying too close of attention.

She inched across the room. Frankie noticed but didn't tell her to stop. She pretended to be horrified and unable to look away from the monitors. Moving close like she could save them through the screens.

When she was close enough Frankie was in reach, she gave one brief look back at Granger. He'd moved, but closer to the door. He was chatting casually with the guard. Keeping the guard's focus split so he could fight him off if something occurred.

She'd take Frankie. He'd take the guard.

Perfect.

Shay was *this* close to reaching out and getting her hands on that device. She considered grabbing it and running. But Frankie had a gun on Granger, one hand curled around the handle, because he sensed her being perhaps a little too close.

If she *was* just a diversion, he might kill her in a fit of pique before she could both push the detonator *and* stop him. So she stopped where she was.

Frankie held the detonator cupped in his hand. All she had to do was reach out and slap the button on the detonator. All she had to do was be faster than him and use the chaos that ensued to make her move.

He glanced at her, and she quickly moved her gaze to the monitor. Holden was standing there, looking like he didn't have a care in the world. He looked like he might actually be *whistling*. She wanted to laugh, but instead closed her eyes and let out a sigh like she was in pain.

Then, quick as lightning, she reached out and slapped the detonator. She couldn't tell if she'd managed to press the button because she had clearly taken Frankie off guard. The small black box clattered to the ground.

Shay quickly, *carefully* put her boot on it, depressing the button for sure this time, without crushing the device.

Nothing happened.

They all looked at each other in shock. No booms. No shaking of the ground. Absolutely no indication any explosives had gone off anywhere near them.

Frankie said something into what she assumed was his comm unit. His scowl deepened. He shoved Shay out of the way and picked up the detonator, then studied it, fury crawling into his features. He threw the detonator at the guard. "Have Peretti check this out. Is it a decoy?"

The guard nodded and immediately disappeared.

Frankie's hand was still curled around the handle of

his gun and Shay watched, mind scrambling, as he decided what to do.

He *wanted* to kill her. She could tell that. But he didn't.

"That was very stupid, Veronica," he said, his voice sharp and razor-thin. A man on a tightrope.

Shay shrugged. "It was worth a shot."

Frankie pulled in a slow, measured breath. He looked at the monitors, then, slowly enough to have Shay's stomach curdling, his gaze turned to Granger.

"You'll come with me, Macmillan," Frankie said, sounding overly formal.

Shay nearly reached out to keep Granger right where he was. It would have been a grave mistake and she just narrowly kept her arms at her sides.

Frankie smiled at her like he knew exactly what she'd been thinking. "I think Veronica needs to learn her lesson." He took Granger by the arm and opened the door. He yelled at one of the guards outside to come in. "Make sure monitor three is on," he said to the guard when he stepped inside, and then roughly jerked Granger out of the cabin.

GRANGER'S MIND WHIRLED trying to make out what had just happened. He wasn't so worried about Frankie. Not yet. He was keeping them alive for a reason.

Frankie had clearly *wanted* to kill Shay right there. His hand had twitched on that gun with a fury that even Granger had to admit was ruthlessly pounded back.

Why hadn't Holden's explosives worked. Had it just been a threat? A trick? If so, for what purpose?

Frankie's hand was like a vice. Granger thought about

fighting it off, but the man wasn't stupid. They were only alone for a moment or two before three guards appeared.

He transferred Granger to the guards, one on either side with a firm grip on either arm and one behind pushing a gun into his back.

Granger wasn't concerned for himself just yet. He'd survived worse. As they propelled him forward, he took the time to notice the world around him. He'd lost track of time inside the little cabin. The way the sun slanted through the trees he could only guess it was getting toward afternoon. He didn't study the surroundings for too long, too afraid he might see a North Star operative and give them away.

Granger considered his chances of fighting the three guards off. The head wound held him back a little bit, that and not having any weapons. Still, he'd fought off more men on his own before. What was his record? Five or six?

Three, well four, wouldn't be impossible, but Frankie hanging back made it risky. The mobster would have backup, or his own gun to shoot Granger with if he felt like it.

Maybe he'd get more information and insight from Frankie if he went along with whatever this was. More intel to pass along to Elsie to prevent whatever was going on at headquarters. *If* she was still listening.

So, he was lead by all these guards on a long march. It must have taken an hour at least. The sun had moved that far. Granger had to admit he was feeling a little woozy. Head wound. Lack of food, water and sleep. The piercing, bitter cold.

Once upon a time he'd been trained for this, but the last two years had been more about recovering from his injuries and enjoying ranch work, not so much building himself back into a man who could withstand this kind of torture.

He thought of Shay, holding herself back when Frankie had grabbed him.

For her sake, he'd withstand a lot no matter the circumstances, even if it took sheer force of will.

They began to approach some buildings, and Granger had to wonder if this could be the compound they'd originally mapped. Was this where Holden, Mallory and Zeke were? Maybe he'd have a chance to rendezvous with all of them.

Was Frankie that stupid?

Granger eyed him as the guards pushed him into a doorway. Inside was a cold cement room that looked an awful lot like the ones on the monitor back in the cabin.

Frankie followed him inside, but the guards stayed outside. One hovering in the doorway, but the other two quickly dispersing.

Granger had to smile. He could definitely take two of them.

"These are your new accommodations, Macmillan. Don't worry, you won't be staying here long."

"You marched me all this way just to kill me? Sounds like a lot of extra work for nothing."

"Except here they'll never be able to find your body and pin it on me," Frankie said with a smile that had Granger's nerves beginning to hum.

He might be able to take Frankie and his guard but they *were* well armed.

Granger studied Frankie standing there, looking smug and superior. He just needed to get under his skin. Like Shay had.

"Why don't we settle this just the two of us, Vianni. Man to man," he said, nodding at Frankie's gun. "Show your team here you aren't a coward."

Frankie's nostrils flared and his hands curled into fists, but Granger couldn't quite get him going the way Shay could.

When Frankie spoke, his voice was cold and controlled. "I let Shay do that. I'm not stupid. I suppose you've done an admirable job improving the muscles of your little operatives, but I much prefer to use my brain."

"Whatever you gotta tell yourself after your ex-wife beats you up."

"She's *still* my wife, Granger. You might do well to remember that."

Granger snorted. "Sure, I'm really worried about it. Your marriage and your *brain* that got you so far in life. What with hiding away in a cabin in Idaho rather than living the high life in Chicago."

Frankie's hands uncurled from fists. The sparking anger seemed to cool. "I'll get my life back," he said. Calmly.

Granger laughed, trying to make it caustic enough to reignite the other man's anger so he made a mistake. "Yeah, sure."

But Frankie simply shrugged out of his jacket, and then pulled his gun out to examine it. "I would have done this in front of her, but she'd get in the way. Probably try to save you. Foolish girl that she is. So, this will have to do. Her watching from afar." He pointed at a camera bolted to the wall above. Then he used the gun to point at Granger. "Take off the vest," he ordered.

And that's when Granger realized that Frankie might

still want Shay alive for some reason, but him on the other hand?

Not so much.

Chapter Twenty

Shay watched the monitors, nerves strung so tight she could barely breathe. She knew she should be searching for a way to escape, trying to get some kind of message to North Star or *something*.

But she kept watching to see if Granger's face would appear on the screen.

"It's going to be a while."

She whirled around. Released a breath. She hadn't noticed the guards had switched because she'd been too absorbed with willing Granger's face to appear. The man from before was back. The friendlier guard.

She marched over to him. The only thing that kept her from grabbing him by the vest and shaking him, demanding help, was the way his grip tightened around his gun.

She stayed where she was, just a little beyond arm's reach from him, and narrowly resisted clasping her hands together and getting on her knees to beg. Plead. At this point, she'd do whatever it took to get to Granger.

Because there was something about the way Frankie had led him away that gave her the horrible feeling she'd never seen Granger again.

"Help us," she implored. She looked at the guard, let-

ting every emotion show on her face even knowing it
was unlikely he'd be moved by an emotional plea. He'd
probably killed men. He worked for a mobster for heav-
en's sake, but she'd do anything. *Anything.*

"Look, lady, there isn't anything I can do." He almost
sounded apologetic. Or she was just that desperate to
believe she had a chance.

But Shay decided to grab on to that faint apology
for dear life. "Granger said he can pay you more than
Frankie is." She inched a little forward.

"Yeah, but everyone would have to get out alive for
that to happen." The guard shrugged. "Chances of that
aren't great for your guy. Look, I feel for ya and all, but
I'm not risking my neck."

Another inch, a careful inch, as her heart pounded
so hard in her ears she could scarcely hear. She held the
guard's gaze. *Look at my face. Look at my face.* "Just
let me go," she cajoled. "That's all you have to do. Not
save me. Not help me. Just let me walk out that door."

He scoffed.

Keep your eyes on my eyes.

"Come on," he said. "I'd just wind up dead."

"Okay, let me go, and you run too." She did everything she could to make it sound conspiratorial instead
of desperate. "We both just run. If Frankie's preoccupied
with Macmillan he won't know for a while."

"You can't pay me. *He* was the one with the money,"
the guard said, jerking his chin toward the door Granger
had been pulled out of only ten minutes or so ago.

Shay swallowed at the bile that wanted to rise in her
throat. She didn't have time for fear, and she certainly
had to entertain every possibility, if only to get out of

here. "If Macmillan is dead, I'll get his money. You can count on it."

There was a pause. She moved another inch and then another. He glanced down at her feet and Shay froze, holding in her last inhale.

"You'll probably just kill me instead of pay me," the man said skeptically. He adjusted his gun, not quite pointing at her, but closer. So he'd only have to lift it an inch or so to do some damage.

"We aren't Frankie," Shay said, with bone-deep conviction as she kept looking at his face, willing him to look up at her. "We aren't the Viannis."

He was frowning at her feet, noticing how close she was. How close she'd moved. She hoped to God he chalked it up to her pleas and not to what she was about to do.

"Please," Shay said, letting her voice shake, letting all the fear she felt make that word tremble like the desperate begging it wasn't.

He looked up at her again. "I ca—"

She'd gotten close enough she could finally act. She elbowed him in the throat first, and then immediately grabbed his gun. He had more than one on him, so a struggle ensued. She had to get them all. She had to run.

She had to get to Granger.

Shay didn't want to hurt the guy. He'd at least *entertained* kindness, even if he hadn't been able to follow through.

But this was Granger's life on the line, and that made her a lot less empathetic.

She kicked one gun away, but he managed to get an arm around her neck. Clearly she'd blown any chance of getting him on her side. She lifted a leg and got a good kick into a vulnerable place. He didn't go down but his arm loosened enough she could whirl and punch.

Gut, chin, throat.

The guard gasped for a breath, but he still didn't go down. He reached for the gun holstered on his leg so Shay lunged for it too.

She swept out a kick meant to take him down, but he swiveled enough for it to do the damage.

He was a *much* better fighter than Frankie, or any of the other men she'd come across on her way here. No wonder he was guarding her.

Still, none of that mattered. She had to get to Granger. She'd do anything, use any skills she'd honed, to make that happen.

He landed a knee that made her legs buckle, but she fought tooth and nail to remain upright. She feinted a kick and then instead spun around with an elbow. It landed with a sickening crack against his nose.

The guard let out a grunt of pain as blood spurted and Shay used the momentary surprise to knock him over. He landed with an *oof* on his stomach and she jumped on top, using a knee in his back to keep him down while she quickly divested him of all his weapons and tossed them to the far end of the room.

She was still wearing her vest so she pulled some zip ties she always kept in one of the pockets and began to restrain him.

"You really think you're going to get away?" he asked, sounding bitter and resigned.

"I'm going to try." She gave him a friendly pat on the shoulder as she studied her handiwork. He was still on his stomach, hands tied behind his back, ankles tied together. He might be able to get upright or crawl out to the other guards.

But she'd be long gone by then.

She stood, breathing heavily. She felt a bit woozy and her gunshot wound pulsed with pain, but she couldn't hold on to any of those feelings because her brain just kept thinking: *Granger, Granger, Granger.*

The other guards could be coming for her. She should be more surreptitious, more careful. *Don't do something stupid or you can't get to Granger.*

She took a deep breath and slowly, carefully edged the door open. Looked around. She saw white. Trees. No one else.

Shay slid outside. In the distance, standing in a small circle were a group of guards. It almost looked like they were standing around a campfire, and it was directly where the footsteps—Frankie's and Granger's—led.

She moved around the back of the cabin. In front of her was nothing but trees, and she didn't spot anyone. There *was* a camera pointed at the place she would need to go, but unless that camera came with a gun, she wasn't worried.

She'd move into these trees, then with enough distance, head east. As long as the footprints led in that direction the whole way, she'd be able to pick up the trail a ways out.

If not, Granger had the flashlight radio to Elsie. He wasn't totally alone. If she couldn't get to him, someone would.

Someone *had* to.

She made a run for the woods, zigzagging through trees just in case, and trying to keep as quiet as possible.

When someone silently stepped out from behind the

tree she was just about to dart around, she barely swallowed back a scream. *Gabriel.*

He grabbed her arm and Connor also appeared, Froggy at his side.

"Luckily Froggy led us to you just in time, huh?" Connor said, already moving forward, in the same direction Shay had been going.

Gabriel was pulling her along.

She wanted to crumple in relief and exhaustion, but there was no time. "Granger?"

"Wyatts and Reece are on him," Gabriel said as they quickly moved through the trees.

There wasn't a group she trusted more. But she trusted herself the most. "Can you get us there?"

Gabriel shared a look with Connor. Connor nodded.

"We can get you there. We've got a Jeep a ways out. They walked, so it'll be worth the time added. If we run."

"What about—" Shay gestured at the guards who were starting to realize something was amiss. One spotted them and pointed and yelled.

Gabriel held up a little device, that looked suspiciously like the one Frankie'd had earlier. "This'll keep them busy. Other one was a decoy."

Shay let out a breath. The danger wasn't over, but something inside of her loosened. She could fight for Granger's life. For her own. "Then let's go," Shay said, already moving into a full-on run.

The explosion sounded behind them before the first gunshot.

GRANGER STEELED HIMSELF for the gunshot, so the burst of static had him flinching. But it was no gunshot.

It was Frankie's comm unit. There was a frantic murmur of voices. Frankie put the earpiece in his ear, and his frown turned into a thunderous scowl.

Granger couldn't hear any of the words. But Frankie's were clear. "She what? How long? An *hour*?" Frankie whirled away from Granger and stalked away. He kept his voice low, but Granger caught little snatches of words. Sentences.

"Don't say another word until you've got her in custody. If you have to kill her, so damn be it."

She'd escaped. Maybe that guard had helped her or maybe she'd just managed all on her own. Granger laughed, big and booming no matter how it hurt his head. How could he *not* laugh?

Shaking his head in awe, he supposed this was part of why he loved her. She'd always managed to make what seemed impossible *possible*. Here she was, doing it again. "She got away," he said, more to himself than Frankie.

Frankie lifted the gun again. "All the more reason to kill *you*."

"Yeah, I guess." Granger shook his head, but it didn't matter. Shay had escaped, and that was all she'd needed. Frankie's men wouldn't capture her now. Not with North Star out there lying in wait.

"Why are you smiling?" Frankie demanded. His finger hovered over the trigger and Granger *knew* there wasn't much chance he got out of this alive. Frankie would kill him out of spite if nothing else. Right now the man was shaking with rage, but he was clearly trying to get his temper under control.

It would probably be best if Granger let him without

poking at him. It might prolong his life. Give North Star agents a chance to get here.

But he couldn't stop himself. It just struck him as all too funny. "You're going to kill me and then what?"

"None of your business."

"What do you get out of it? Satisfaction? For what? A few minutes? An hour? It doesn't last. So what's the point?"

"There is no point in killing you. You're right. You mean nothing, and I am killing you as nothing more than a momentary pleasure—a mix of revenge, hurting Veronica and hating your guts. But it would be *beneath* me if that's all I was after. You built your beautiful North Star for good, but now it will be mine and it will do terrible things and make me very, very rich."

It shocked Granger, and maybe Frankie as well. The cold self-satisfaction melted off his face as he seemed to realize he'd explained his plan to Granger.

His sneer widened and he shoved the gun into Granger's chest.

Granger couldn't be sure Elsie would have heard all that. So, he repeated it as succinctly as possible. "You don't even want information. You want to impersonate us."

"No, I will use all your processes, contacts and resources and the good name you've built to destroy. Not just the thing you built, but anything that suits me." He was scrambling to justify telling Granger his plan, trying to make it sound like it was something he was doing *to* Granger.

But in the end, all Frankie really wanted was North Star, and maybe it was age or time or just knowing that life was unpredictable and dealt blows you didn't expect, but it didn't hurt the way it might have once upon a time.

"Thank you for telling me that, Frank. Really." He knew that he'd likely die. No one was coming to save him, but even with the vest off, the flashlight was right there and Elsie had to have heard that.

So she could stop Frankie. She could stop North Star from being used for its opposite purpose.

He had some regret over dying, over not getting that shot with Shay. Regret it had taken him this long to take the chance.

But at least he wasn't going out without having stopped something.

"I'm going to kill you," Frankie said, making a point of shoving that gun barrel into his chest even harder. "North Star will be mine. I'll ruin everything you were, and I will stop Shay. She will be my prisoner for the rest of her miserable life. I want you to know that before you die. Just because I can, I will ruin everything you are and were."

Granger shook his head, looked Frankie right in the eye. If he was going to die, he was damn well going to do it with his head held high. "No, Frankie, you won't."

But the last word was drowned out by the loud echoing sound of a gunshot.

Chapter Twenty-One

They ran and as far as Shay could tell, no one followed. The explosion had worked at keeping the guards busy or injured or unable to get through the blast's aftereffects to follow.

"What about Holden, Mallory and Zeke?" Shay asked breathlessly.

"They're being held closer to where Granger is. Before Holden allowed himself to get caught, he set some explosives strategically where it would allow them to get out. It was all connected to the same detonator, so they should be escaping their rooms right now and meeting up with the Wyatts and Reece," Gabriel explained.

He pointed up ahead where a Jeep came into view. They didn't slow their speed, simply jumped in. Gabriel took off with a speed that should have scared her, what with the fact they had to dodge trees and boulders.

But she couldn't entertain fear. She was too busy mouthing prayers to keep Granger safe. To keep her *family* safe.

Gabriel drove like a bat out of hell, God bless him, and when he skidded to a halt, they were all jumping out simultaneously with the jerk of the car being thrown into Park.

Connor and Gabriel began to run, so Shay followed. A strange calm had come over her. She was with her operatives. They were going to save Granger. Things were going to be okay.

Because she willed it. Because she would do whatever it took.

They wouldn't come this far only to lose Granger. She simply wouldn't allow it.

But she came up short in surprise when she saw Sabrina standing next to Reece. "What on God's green earth are you doing here?"

Sabrina grinned. "Good to see you too, boss. Had to bring out the dog," she said, jutting her chin at Connor and Froggy behind her. "Don't worry, I've kept away from the fighting fields."

She didn't have time to scold Sabrina, so she'd make sure to remember to do it later. Shay turned her attention to Reece who stood with his arms crossed surveying Cody who was laid out with a large rifle, balanced on a rock. He had his eye on a scope and his fingers around the trigger.

"Holden is out, he's helping Mal and Zeke take down the rest of the guards, so I sent the other Wyatts and Nate to make sure they're all good. Which works, because it took the guard who was stationed out here away," Reece explained, as if not at all surprised to see them.

Still when she got close enough, he clapped her on the shoulder. A quiet *glad you're okay*. She swallowed at the lump of fear and emotion in her throat and gave Reece a faint nod.

Shay looked out over where the gun was pointed. They were high up on a ridge, below a small valley with a collection of buildings spread out.

"Mal and Zeke are in that far one," Reece said, pointing out to a squat building far off in the distance. She could just barely see specks of people. She had no doubt her team would take down Frankie's guards.

"Granger's in this one," Reece said pointing to the small one closest to the ridge. *This* was the compound she'd discovered in the beginning, but Frankie must have known that. That's why he'd used the other cabin, to try and cause confusion. To be able to separate them, not just in these small buildings, but by location.

And it didn't work, you little bastard, did it?

But it wasn't done yet.

"Once the guard was gone, we could see this little window," Reece continued to explain. "More of a slot really, likely to pass things through or let some natural light in."

"I've got Frankie," Cody said, his eyes on the sight. "You're not supposed to be able to see through the window, it's some special glass or plastic, but I've got a special sight that sees through it. I can take him out with one shot."

Take him out. It would be over. Frankie would be dead. She looked at Cody's finger curled around the trigger.

No. "You can shoot, but don't kill him," Shay said.

Cody looked up from the sight. "Isn't that a risk?"

Shay shook her head and then gave Cody a nudge so he moved out of the way. She took over. Laid out like he'd been, looking through the sight.

"He's not going to die a noble death," Shay said, adjusting the gun and her finger around the trigger. "He's not going to be some gangster myth. I trust Granger to do what needs to be done once we immobilize Frankie.

That bastard is going to waste away in prison just like his father. And *that* will eat him alive." She watched through the sight, as Frankie shoved the gun into Granger's chest.

Then took her shot without qualm.

GRANGER KEPT WAITING for the pain to slam through him. He could hear the gunshot. The echo of it. But nothing hurt. He was still on his feet, didn't fall, and there was no sudden blow of pain after the shock wore off.

He was standing. He was fine.

Frankie wasn't. He was writhing on the ground, holding his right wrist. Blood pooled underneath it. The gun had fallen out of his hand and lay on the floor, forgotten.

As if in slow motion, Granger looked around the room. There was a small rectangular window on the door, giving off light. There had been plastic or glass there, but it was broken now.

He'd been saved.

He didn't know how they'd managed, but they had. His knees nearly gave out as he looked down at Frankie, the shot still echoing in his head.

Frankie was moving. Not writhing in pain anymore. No, with his left hand he was reaching for the gun that had been shot out of his hand.

Granger quickly stepped on Frankie's left wrist to stop his attempt to grasp the gun. He exerted a crushing pressure that had Frankie's grip on the gun loosening and caused a blood-curdling scream to emanate from his mouth.

The door burst open and Shay and Cody ran in. Cody immediately went for the gun on the floor, while keeping his gun trained on Frankie.

Shay launched herself at him and he narrowly caught

her without falling over. "It had to be the two of you," he muttered, holding on to Shay for dear life.

"Your best operatives of all time? Of course," Cody offered with a grin. "But Shay took the shot."

He clearly said that for Frankie's benefit. And that had her grip on him easing as she turned to look at the man sprawled on the ground looking downright apoplectic.

But he didn't have any recourse now. Reece and Gabriel entered and between the three of the men, they grabbed Frankie by the arms and got him to his feet.

"Betty's nearby. We'll bring her down to start checking everyone out. She'll bandage him up before the feds get here."

Shay took a step away from him, to stand in front of Frankie.

"Any last words before you're thrown in jail, just like Daddy dearest?"

He tried to spit on her but she dodged it with a grin. "Mature, Frank. Real mature."

"We'll take him out," Reece said. He nodded at Cody and Gabriel, a clear sign they should all clear out and leave Shay and Granger alone.

In the room, absent of any noise, and Frankie's blood on the floor between them, they surveyed each other. He supposed she was doing the same to him as he was doing to her: studying for any sign of new injury, any chance this was a dream.

"So, you saved my life. Again."

"Bad habit," she said, her voice hoarse. "Granger..." She trailed off, like she didn't know what to say.

He didn't either. What words were there? He'd been determined to live, but the last half hour or so he hadn't been so sure *he'd* make it. And now he had. Because of her.

Maybe it should humble him, but he could only count himself lucky he'd offered a hand that long ago night back in Chicago.

So, no, there weren't words. There was only moving toward her, kissing her and holding on for dear life.

Because now that's what they had.

She held on just as tight, kissed him back just as fiercely. Until someone clearing their throat interrupted.

Slowly, hating to do it, he pulled away. And glared at the interruption.

A grinning Betty, with a bag likely full of all sorts of torture tools to clean and stitch them up.

"Hate to break this up and all," Betty said, biting back a grin. "Like *really* hate to, because if you're kissing, I've just won a very old bet with Elsie she likely doesn't remember, but the two of you need some serious medical attention."

Betty moved in briskly, instructing them both to sit down. She checked out Shay first, clucking over her gunshot wound not yet healed, and the bumps and bruises. She let Shay go, shooing her out of the room, then turned to him.

Betty swore and muttered to him about stitches and staples and concussion protocol. He only listened with half an ear so he could occasionally say yes ma'am at the appropriate moment. Otherwise he stared at that small window, broken, as sunset filtered through.

He was alive. Shay was alive.

They'd won.

People came in and out to update him while Betty stitched him up. The federal agencies that had responded had cleared out. The Wyatts had gone home, though not before Shay and Granger had both thanked them both.

When he was finally released from Betty's evil clutches, his head hurt worse than before. Though she'd given him a pain pill that *should* start kicking in.

He looked at her. She'd stitched him up more than once, also had a hand in saving his life a few times. "Thanks, Bet. I sure hope that's the last time we meet like this."

She grinned at him. "Me too," she agreed.

They stepped outside into a quickly cooling night. Someone had started a little campfire, and almost everyone was standing or sitting around it. Shay was seated, flanked by Reece and Holden. Connor and Sabrina were standing, Froggy lying in between them. Elsie was pacing slightly outside of the circle under the watchful eye of her boyfriend.

His family. Who'd all come together. To help each other, save each other. Do right when there was wrong. Something expanded in his chest, an overwhelming pride and awe—a humbling one.

He hadn't set out to build this. They'd made his revenge into something beautiful. Meaningful. But he'd at least kind of set it into motion.

With Betty, he joined the group of people.

"Well, now that we're all here," Elsie muttered, coming to stand in the middle of the circle. She wrung her hands together, her eyes darting from person to person until they landed on Granger himself. "Um, I have to tell you all something."

"Sounds like bad news, Els. I think we've had enough of that," Holden said teasingly, smiling gently at her.

She didn't smile back. "I know. I'm sorry, but… It

has to be done." She bit her lip, looking around at all their faces again. But when she began to speak, she once more looked at Granger directly. "I did something when I heard what Frankie was planning." Nate Averly had come to stand behind her and rubbed his hand up and down her back and she smiled gratefully at him.

Love, clear as day. Granger let out a breath. When he'd started North Star, the goal had been what had happened here today. Putting an end to the evil that had hurt his wife.

But what he hadn't counted on, planned on, what he still wasn't sure how it had happened, was all this *love*.

"When we started figuring out Frankie infiltrated our stuff somehow, that his target was more North Star than any one person, I started…putting together a…a…well, I guess you'd call it a doomsday device."

Granger blinked, suddenly not thinking so much about love. "Doomsday," he echoed.

"It erased…everything. Any trace of us…ever." Elsie swallowed. "I wanted to wait for your okay, but he was going to kill you and…" She took a deep, shaky breath. "None of you exist anymore, unless you had identities not tied to North Star like I did. I—I even got rid of North Star's money."

Granger's jaw dropped at that. "How?"

"Charities. Foster organizations. Women's shelters. Anywhere that might have taken in a victim of Vianni or the Sons." She moved forward, looking at him specifically with a pleading in her eyes. "If Frankie could do it—infiltrate us, figure us out—someone else could too. It was only a matter of time. And someone else would have had the same idea. I couldn't stand the thought of

North Star being used for bad when everything we did was for *good*."

Granger didn't fully know how to absorb this information, but the trepidation on Elsie's face told him...

Well, it told him everything he needed to know. He walked over to her and took her by the shoulders, looked into her shiny eyes. "Elsie, you did it exactly right. You saved us. Not just North Star, but all of us." He gave her a fatherly hug, because God she made him feel old.

Then he turned to face them all. The family he'd collected. The family Shay had made from that. "All of you had a part in this."

"There's one last step." Elsie held up a small detonator like the one Holden had made a decoy of. "Blow up headquarters. Any last chance people figure us out. Holden said the blast will burn everything down, and it can be done without causing damage to anyone or any other properties. I just have to push this button."

There were nods around the fire. Encouraging. Understanding.

"People won't have a place to live if I set this off," Elsie said, looking apologetically at Sabrina, Connor and Froggy and then Mallory and Gabriel.

"We've got plenty of room at the B and B," Reece replied. "We'll take in whoever needs it until people find a place."

"We've got room at the farm," Holden agreed. "Same goes."

"And I've got room at my ranch. Long term," Granger said.

They all nodded. Firm agreement, even if not *happy* agreement. Because this was change, and leaping into the unknown. Back to that real world they'd all escaped, but he searched all their faces and knew they were all on the same page.

This was the right thing to do.

Elsie handed him the device and he stared at it. This would put an end to North Star. To everything he'd built.

But the man who'd built North Star had...changed. Maybe he wasn't a different man like Shay had said, but he had *changed*. Matured. Begun to understand himself.

He pushed the button, and they all said their good-byes to North Star. Quietly, they sat around the fire. In couples. In groups. Leaning on each other. Watching the fire and ruminating.

Because North Star had brought them all together, and now it was gone.

Shay slid her hand into his and he looked over at her and smiled. It was strange. Sad, even, but good too. He squeezed her hand, a silent *I'm okay.*

Because he was. They all were.

Sabrina cleared her throat. "Con and I have talked about... You know, someday when we were too old for North Star or whatever, starting a search and rescue operation." She shrugged restlessly. "We'd need more than just the two of us to do it."

Connor took Sabrina's hand in his. "Pilots. Trackers. People willing to train the dogs. Money's going to be a bit of an issue but—"

"I wouldn't count on money being an issue," Granger interrupted.

"He's loaded apparently," Shay offered.

"North Star S&R?" Sabrina said with the quirk of her mouth.

"No. It'd need a new name," Granger insisted.

"Why?" Elsie asked. "North Star was a good one."

"I named North Star that because it was going to be my…center. My everything. S&R or any job won't be my guiding light anymore. It shouldn't be any of yours. It'll be a job, and a good one. Maybe even a legacy, but not your guiding principle."

Shay leaned her head on his shoulder. Everyone looked at each other.

"It should be something simple," Betty suggested.

Shay lifted her head up off his shoulder. "Well, we just blew ourselves up to start over, so why not Phoenix?"

The heads around the fire nodded, and it seemed just right. A rising from the ashes. A new start without losing each other. A new venture, using their skills to help people.

Just like they'd always done.

After a while, they finally began to disperse, some people going with Reece to the Bluebird Inn. Others headed with Holden to his farm. A few people, Shay included, heading to his ranch.

He got everyone settled at his rather ramshackle house. Likely they could work together to make the accommodations a little nicer. But Shay wasn't in his room where he'd left her. He had to search the house, then step into the dead of night to find her sitting on the stairs of his porch, each of his dogs on either side of her.

He scooted Ripken out of the way, though the dog wiggled into his lap with a happy tail-thumping glee.

"You going to sleep? Betty says it's rather important and blah, blah, blah."

"We'll sleep soon enough," she returned.

He looked up at the brilliant blanket of stars above. He liked the *we*.

"I just kept thinking over what you said around the fire. You said it wouldn't be your guiding light."

He was looking at it even now, that bright, guiding light. The star he'd looked to too many times to count. Since he was a boy. But it had come to mean something else.

Just like the woman beside him.

"So what will be?" she asked.

He thought that over, still staring at the North Star above. "This ranch," he said. "My own sense of right and wrong." He turned his gaze from the stars above to her sitting next to him. "You."

He held out his hand and she looked at it for a moment. She knew what he was offering. Not just a place to stay, but from here on out, love.

And a lifetime together.

She let out a breath and slid her hand into his. "I guess that works."

"You guess?" He scoffed. "You've been in love with me for *years*."

She chuckled and leaned her head onto his shoulder. "I do love you."

"I love you too," he murmured, and kissed the top of her head, and they watched the stars for a while.

And spent the rest of their lives together.

* * * * *

LET'S TALK

Romance

For exclusive extracts, competitions
and special offers, find us online:

f facebook.com/millsandboon

🐦 @MillsandBoon

📷 @MillsandBoonUK

Get in touch on 01413 063232

For all the latest titles coming soon, visit

millsandboon.co.uk/nextmonth

JOIN US ON SOCIAL MEDIA!

Stay up to date with our latest releases, author news and gossip, special offers and discounts, and all the behind-the-scenes action from Mills & Boon...

 millsandboon

 millsandboonuk

 millsandboon

It might just be true love...

MILLS & BOON
Desire

Indulge in secrets and scandal, intense drama and plenty of sizzling hot action with powerful and passionate heroes who have it all: wealth, status, good looks…everything but the right woman.

MILLS & BOON
MEDICAL
Pulse-Racing Passion

Set your pulse racing with dedicated, delectable doctors in the high-pressure world of medicine, where emotions run high and passion, comfort and love are the best medicine.